By the same author

Dark Lantern
A Very Civil War
The Widow
The House on the Hill
Three Sisters

Out of the Shadows

CAROLINE ELKINGTON

Copyright © 2020 Caroline Elkington
All rights reserved
www.carolineelkington.net

For Marina with much love and thanks for all the high-pitched, high-speed reading.

You can come out from under the desk now.

One

The noise was a physical assault. A cacophony of sound which left you reeling, your head throbbing and your skin vibrating. A tidal wave of human voices both deep and sharp, soft and loud, reaching up into the dark of the night sky, sweeping everything aside; it had no edges, no beginning and no end. Trumpets blared and drums pounded. Women shrieked in voices so shrill they could shatter glass. Animals roared and bellowed and grunted their misery into the warm, compassionless night air. Discordant musical bands competed for attention and barkers promoted their wares with convoluted exaggerations through makeshift megaphones. The fizz and crackle, whistles and ear-splitting explosions of fireworks which filled the sky with cascading stars, battered the senses and lit up the awed faces that turned to watch them.

The howl of a hungry wolf.

The smells of the exotic wild animals, imprisoned in their cramped cages, the scent of their fear; humans and their odours and the unsuccessful masking perfumes, the stench of excrement of every kind, all mingled with the aromas of food and alcohol and smoke from flaming torches and lamps and braziers making the air into a heavy soup which you had to fight your way through.

The violent crush of the crowd, the sharp elbows and nudging shoulders, the pushing and shoving, the unacceptable closeness of humanity.

Along the edges of the main thoroughfare, stages and booths, balconies on the point of collapse, weighed down with inebriated onlookers, dancing girls and fire-eaters, giants and dwarves and a learned pig. A fat lady, a bearded lady, a wirewalker and puppet-shows. Tumblers, conjurors, acrobats, puppeteers and clowns. Performing tigers and elephants. Bearbaiting and cockfighting. All the cruelties of man and beast in one place and for just a few shillings.

"I *swear* Theo, it's just down this avenue! You'll be glad you came. I couldn't believe my eyes. And Babyngton was *beside* himself. He stared and stared. Eyes like saucers! Not far now."

Sir Anthony Calver led the way, clearing a path through the throng of people with his usual youthful enthusiasm, not bothering to apologise or excuse, just elbowing the bystanders to one side so that his friends could make some progress. Elegant ladies held scented handkerchiefs to their delicate noses and tip-toed through the mixture of straw and sawdust and mire. Peacocking gentlemen fought off swarms of pickpocketing urchins with their beribboned ebony canes as though duelling.

They finally reached a large rickety booth, adjoining a tavern, the entrance covered with a painted cloth depicting a ship against a turbulent ocean coming to grief on some jagged rocks. Sir Anthony waited until his little group had caught up and then, with an excited grin, pushed the canvas aside and entered the booth.

An ugly brute of a fellow was standing in his way.

"Two shillings," he growled at them, "Each!"

"Good god, I had forgot!" exclaimed Sir Anthony. "Well, it's worth every penny, I tell you!" and he thrust a hand into his breeches pockets and pulled out a handful of coins and passed them to the surly doorkeeper.

The entrance was illuminated with a motley array of lamps and candles and hung with blue silken cloth. The five gentlemen gathered together to await their turn and four of them exchanged long-suffering glances. They'd all had a fair amount to drink before setting forth on this adventure and were still feeling mildly good-natured about the whole thing. They had learned many a year ago that Sir Anthony could be hard to restrain once he had the bit between his teeth and a few brandies inside him. There had been that famous incident with the flock of sheep for which his father, a stickler for propriety, had never forgiven him. It was still brought up every time he put a foot wrong, which was frequently. The problem with being so extremely wealthy was that the ordinary could be so very dull — life needed to be enlivened at every opportunity. His redoubtable mother refused to allow him to purchase a commission in the Lifeguards in case he was maimed or killed; having lost his older brother in a riding accident two years previously, his family were, he felt, all unreasonably vigilant where the only son and heir was concerned. As the only son, with two married older sisters, he was now under constant close scrutiny and consequently felt like a menagerie exhibit which, unfortunately for his loyal friends, compelled him to seek increasingly outrageous entertainment to keep tedium at bay. It was his good luck that his chosen band of merry men were, with just the one exception, willing to follow him into any kind of mad caper, however dangerous or ridiculous it might be. They viewed him as a boisterous puppy, who needed a good deal of exercise and affection in order to prevent him becoming involved in something really perilous; keeping him on a tight rein was their main mission.

The one exception was eyeing him with considerable misgiving and Sir Anthony was looking a little hot under his vastly over-starched and high collar points.

"You'll thank me when you see! I know it doesn't look like much but it's beyond anything! Babyngton, you'll back me! You thought it outstanding, did you not?"

Mr Tom Babyngton had the grace to look somewhat discomfited when asked to face up to his ineffably incomparable hero, "I — I most certainly thought it to be an *exceptional* exhibit, Theo! I feel sure that you'll agree, once you've witnessed it for yourself. It's like nothing I have ever seen before. Quite the thing, y'know."

Theo Rokewode raised an eyebrow and favoured his friend with a slight smile, "I am all anticipation, my dear."

"Try not to be — " began Sir Anthony, "Too — *you!* You'll enjoy it more!"

The smile widened, creasing Rokewode's lean face and lightening his habitually saturnine expression, "I'll make a valiant attempt to be less — me. *Lay on, Macduff*." He nodded toward the doorkeeper, who had popped his large head out to call them into the mysterious inner sanctum.

Sir Anthony beamed at his friends and led the way, followed by Mr Tom Babyngton, Sir Leander Gage, Lord Frederick Knoyll and lastly a reluctant Theodore Rokewode, who was wondering why he had ever agreed to this particular escapade as it had sounded doomed from the very start. He had very little faith in his friend's choice of neckcloth, let alone his discovery of a spectacular freak show at Bartholomew Fair. He sighed and ducked his head under the canvas curtain and straightened up in what appeared to be a dark and dank cave which smelt faintly of stagnant water.

"Remind me never to pay attention to Tony or any of you when you're in your cups," he murmured to Freddie Knoyll who was trying ineffectually to stifle slightly hysterical schoolboy giggles.

"As Tony is always in his cups that will prove exceedin' difficult. Oh, by Jupiter! What *is* this, Theo?"

By the light of a single lamp, they were shown to some hard benches arranged along the back edge of the booth and were commanded to sit by the brutish doorkeeper.

The sound of Freddie Knoyll's barely muffled snorting continued until a brusque word from his friend curtailed his mirth.

Someone coughed and then there was faint music, a flute played a low and melancholy tune and after a moment a voice began to sing a wordless and haunting refrain. The voice was such that it raised the hairs on your arms. It was hard to discern if it was animal or human, it sounded like a searching wind in the uppermost branches of winter trees or the distant cry of a child lost in the wilderness or the song of some strange and wonderful bird singing high above the clouds. They had never heard anything like it, and it silenced them.

The sound washed over them, dazing them and made them think of things they hadn't considered in decades. Sir Anthony couldn't help but think of the day his brother had been killed; Leander Gage remembered his first stolen kiss with his childhood friend, Matilda; Freddie Knoyll recalled the day his father left the family, never to return; Tom Babyngton thought of his dear old dog, Caesar, and Theo Rokewode was taken back to his first encounter with his present mistress, twice widowed and renowned beauty, Margaret Sheraton.

Then, the coloured lanterns and candles were lit, and the cave began to glow, the light gilding the draped silk and cleverly wrought rock walls; as the lights moved, they could see in, what seemed to be the distance, a dais upon which there was a dark, eerily lit pool of water and perched on the edge of it, with her tail in the water, a mermaid.

There was an audible intake of breath from several of the gentlemen and still nobody said anything as the music and the song continued.

The mermaid was combing her long white-blonde hair. She was wearing nothing but the sparkling silver tail and her hair, which wrapped around her like curls of gilded smoke; nothing was left to the imagination and what was on display was beautiful beyond description. She had the face of an angel, a goddess, *Venus!* The English language did not have adequate words to conjure her beauty. Five male hearts were thudding in five chests.

As she sang, her tail glinted sparks in the half-light and the comb flashed brightly.

Her audience was mesmerised into submission and then it was over. The candles and lanterns dimmed and went out and the voice gradually faded away and they were left in the dark.

It took them a moment to shake themselves out of their reverie and get to their feet.

They were ushered to a door at the side of the booth and suddenly they were out on the main walk and feeling a little bewildered.

Sir Anthony Calver looked at them all with wide expectant eyes, "What did I tell you? Was that not the most extraordinary thing you have ever heard? That voice! Her beauty! I have never seen her like. She's utterly enchanting! I plan on meeting her. I'm going to wait until the end of her show and introduce myself!"

"You utter dolt! What makes you think that a creature like that would wish to make the acquaintance of a paltry schoolboy like you!" exclaimed Leander Gage rudely.

"I don't care! I simply *must* meet her."

"Damnation, Tony! I expect she'll have armed guards! You won't be able to get anywhere near her. What would you say to her anyway?"

Sir Anthony tossed his rather long dark blonde curls and grinned sheepishly, "Goodness, I don't know! What *does* one say to a mermaid?"

"Sometimes, I wonder why I ever became friends with you, Calver! It beggars belief the schemes you come up with, but this takes the cake. Talking to a mermaid, indeed! Fool!" huffed Leander Gage, "You must have taken leave of the very few senses you possess!"

"I shall wait for her, nonetheless. But don't let me keep you. You can all go on ahead to St James's Square for supper and I'll meet you there."

His friends argued amongst themselves and after a few moments of futilely trying to persuade him to give up his Quixotic quest, they wandered off onto the main thoroughfare and made their tortuous way back from whence they came, looking forward to a glass of decent wine and some supper. Sir Anthony watched them go with the slightest of shrugs and then realised that he was not alone. Theodore Rokewode was still leaning, in the most languid fashion, against the side of the booth.

"Theo! Do you not go with them?"

His friend let out the faintest chuckle, "And leave you here to be beaten to a pulp by our fair mermaid's guardians? I think not! Your mother consigned you to my care and I must honour her wishes. I will stay, if only to have the dubious pleasure of watching you make a complete cake of yourself."

"And it's nothing to do with you wanting to have a closer look at the mermaid?"

He received a pained look, "My dear fellow! What would Margaret say? I doubt she would be particularly happy to hear that I'd been frequenting freakish side-shows at the fair!"

"Much you care for what Mrs Sheraton thinks! She pretends to be disinterested in you, but we all know that if you offered, she'd accept, just like *that!*" and he snapped his fingers sharply.

"Well, I hope she isn't setting too much store by my doing so because I'm afraid she will be deeply disappointed."

"Gad! You're a cold fish, Theo. Oh, look! Here come the last customers. Now the booth will close for the night. Let us wait over here by the exit."

The last few stragglers left the booth by the side door and the doorkeeper fastened the front entrance.

A few minutes passed and Sir Anthony began to pace impatiently.

Then suddenly there was a shout from inside the structure. A high-pitched scream and within seconds smoke and flames were billowing out from under the painted canvas screen.

"Good god, Theo! What the deuce — !" shouted Sir Anthony dashing towards the front entrance.

"Wait! Tony! Don't be a fool! The side entrance!" snapped Theo Rokewode as he ran swiftly to the exit door.

There was a loud crashing from inside and another piercing cry. Sir Anthony swore roundly and began to beat on the door with his fists. Rokewode pushed him to one side and threw his shoulder against the panelling. It gave way after two attempts and they were in the booth, in the dark and breathing in thick, choking smoke.

Rokewode quickly took off his neckcloth and tied it around his face and gestured at Sir Anthony to do the same, he then cautiously approached the inner curtain and pulled it aside.

The cave was aflame. The silk hangings on the walls and whatever combustible material the fake rock was constructed from was providing ample fuel for the fire, which was spreading fast. The heat was tremendous and for a moment forced him back a step with its ferocity. He felt Sir Anthony at his side, and they pushed forward into the room. Outside they could hear people in the crowd screaming as it dawned upon them that the fire was serious.

"I can't see a damn thing!" shouted Sir Anthony over the noise of the fire and collapsing structures. "Where is the mermaid? Has she escaped?"

Rokewode's eyes were streaming and he was finding it hard to breathe. He knew the fake rock pool was over to his left and started to edge his way in that direction when something small and ferocious hurled itself at him out of the darkness, hitting him in the midriff and knocking the wind out of him. He snatched at it and grabbed a handful of hair and held it fast. He peered down at it and saw it was a girl, her face black with soot and her eyes wide with terror. She was tearing at his coat with small, frantic hands.

"Go with my friend, he'll show you the way out!" he shouted at her, but she kept pulling at him and shaking her head.

"You must get out of here — the whole place will collapse in a minute! Tony! Take her out and I'll see if I can find the others."

He tried to hand the girl over to his companion, but she would have none of it and tugged at his arm with both hands, her eyes pleading.

"All right! Show me!" and he allowed her to lead him further into the wall of dense smoke. The flames lit the way, and he could just make out the edges of the pool and then realised that the ceiling had partially collapsed onto it.

From beneath the smouldering and flaming debris he could see the sparkling tail of the mermaid.

"Tony! Over here!"

Together they quickly cleared away the beams and pieces of ceiling and on seeing the state the mermaid was in, Sir Anthony tore off his coat and covered her nakedness with it, as his friend, by far the stronger of the two men, picked her up in his arms and bore her out of the collapsing building.

They burst out into the open and gulped in lungfuls of cleaner air, coughing and choking, their eyes sore and streaming. Theo lay the mermaid down a safe distance from the now out-of-control flames and looked around for the wild girl. She was nowhere to be seen. He told Sir Anthony to stand guard over the mermaid and ignoring his friend's shouts of dismay, he ran back into the booth.

He could see nothing but black swirling smoke and taking a few tentative steps, felt the toe of his boot touch something on the floor. He bent and unceremoniously dragged the body up and fled the booth just as the whole ceiling caved in and the building collapsed in an eruption of flame and flying missiles of wood and metal and glass.

He was thrown to the ground by the force of the blast and landed on top of the girl, who didn't stir. He waited until it had stopped raining wreckage, shielding her from the worst of it with his body.

Eventually he was able to sit up and take stock. Sir Anthony was sitting with a limp, half-naked mermaid in his arms and the girl beside him seemed to be unconscious. They were surrounded by a throng of curious people goggling at them and officials were arriving with pails of water and shovels. The crowd was gradually pushed back, and room was made for some passing soldiers to help organise putting out the fire and begin clearing up. Someone asked Sir Anthony if he wanted help, but he just shook his head, seeming perfectly content to sit in the mud, smiling down at the exquisite but oblivious creature in his lap.

After about ten minutes a small posse of men arrived, including a local doctor and demanded to know how the fire had started. Rokewode was able to hazard a guess and told them he suspected that he thought it must have been the candles in the entrance setting the silken drapery alight. The doctor made a rather perfunctory examination of the two victims and pronounced the girl miraculously unhurt and the mermaid suffering from some minor abrasions and the inhalation of smoke. He assured everyone that given a little time and some brandy, that they would soon be as right as rain. The officials then asked where the others were and on Rokewode asking *what* others, they replied that although the doorkeeper and a young flute-player had managed to escape, the mermaid's father and another male assistant had not yet appeared.

Rokewode asked about the father and found he was the owner of the side-show booth and the two men were hired help.

"What about this lady? Who is she?" asked Theo Rokewode, nodding to the girl beside him, now covered in his coat and with her head resting upon his knee.

The man peered at her, "Ah, yes, I believe she assists Miss Biddy."

"Miss Biddy?"

"Biddy Pippin. The mermaid. Her father, Henry Pippin, I fear has perished in the fire along with the second hired man. A sad business, I must say. What will you do with the ladies, sir?"

"What will *I* do with them?" said Rokewode raising his eyebrows in mild surprise.

"Well, we can't take them. They'll need medical help I should think."

"And you expect *me* to organise that?"

"I can provide you with a hackney coach."

"Oh, damn you!"

"I beg your pardon, sir!"

"Get the hackney," snapped Rokewode explosively.

The man then bridled, "Well, that's all very well but how do I know that you're a fit person to take these poor unfortunate ladies with you?"

Rokewode ground his teeth and reached into a pocket in his coat to retrieve his card which he handed to the official.

The man turned it to the light and his face relaxed into an ingratiating smile, "Ah, Lord Rokewode! I beg your pardon — I had no idea. You are quite smeared with soot and do not look much like an Earl at the moment! Of course, you may take the ladies, I have no doubt that your credentials are in fine order."

"Well, then you're an idiot. Get the damn hackney!"

Two

The hackney jolted along, bumping its, by now, rapidly sobering passengers as though they were on a rutted country lane rather than a decently surfaced road in London.

"Good Lord, man! What are you about?" bellowed Sir Anthony, banging on the ceiling of the cab with his cane, "I can barely stay on the seat!"

His friend smiled ruefully at him, "It's late, he wants to be in his bed not transporting a suspicious group of revellers across the city. One can hardly blame him."

Sir Anthony was forced to laugh, "We do make a bit of a spectacle, do we not! But, I say, Theo! What an adventure! What a splendid wheeze! The others are going to be mortified that they left before all the fun started!"

"They're sure to be heartbroken," said Rokewode, straight-faced.

"I say, but where are we going to take them? Do you have a plan? We can't just carry them around with us like this, it really won't do!"

"*Now* you begin to see our dilemma! A little late, if you don't mind me saying! We're on our way to Grosvenor Square."

"Are you *mad*?! Your mother? She'll be in her bed b'now! Gad, Theo! She'll have your guts for garters!"

"I know. However, we're not left with much choice. Ah, I think yours is coming round, Tony. We're nearly there now, you'd better calm her; it wouldn't do to be seen carrying an hysterical female into my mother's residence. That really would give her something to complain about."

"But what shall I say?"

"Whatever you decide, you'd better decide quickly!"

The mermaid stirred and coughed, just as the coach drew up outside a grand newly built mansion in Grosvenor Square. With some difficulty and a fair amount of swearing the two men managed to manoeuvre their burdens out and pay the coachman, who cast them a disgusted look before driving off into the night at great speed.

They mounted the steps to the house and pulled the bell.

Moments later the door opened, and they were greeted not by a footman but a small lady of later years, a white lace cap covering her grey hair and tied under her chin and an expression of alarm upon her intelligent face. It took but a second for the alarm to turn to pleasure.

"Oh, well, bless you, my lord! What an absolute delight! And at such a sociable hour too! Do come in for I am sure that Lady Rokewode will be just thrilled to see you — and your — guests." She said all of this with a decided twinkle and stood aside for them to enter the hall.

"Thank you, my dear Miss Edie, I knew you wouldn't be put out of countenance by our arrival, although I wasn't expecting you to answer the front door. What good fortune brought you downstairs at this hour?"

"I was making some hot milk for your mother — it helps her sleep. She's in the habit of going to bed at an early hour if she has no guests staying." The elderly lady showed them into the withdrawing room and efficiently flew around the room, lighting candles.

Each gentleman laid his burden down on a sofa and Rokewode went immediately to the bell pull and gave it a good tug.

Miss Bell approached Sir Anthony, "Ah, a mermaid. Of *course*. A fishing expedition, perhaps?" She found a shawl draped across a nearby chair and carefully arranged it over the mermaid's upper half and then removed Sir Anthony's coat and returned it to him. She then took off her own shawl and covered the other girl with it.

He laughed, "Not at all, Miss Edie, I'm afraid it was an ill-advised venture to Bartholomew Fair. There was an accident — a fire."

"Oh, my goodness! That would explain your sooty faces and make a little more sense of this beautiful mermaid here. I shall go at once and fetch clean cloths and some water. Perhaps a little brandy, my lord?" and as Sir Anthony's eyes lit up, she tut-tutted, "Not for *you* sir, for the ladies, to help them come round!"

"Oh, of course! Splendid notion."

As Miss Bell left the room, a footman arrived at the door and looked expectantly at Rokewode, who silently admired the man's ability to take not the slightest bit of interest in the two maidens, one a mermaid, sprawled upon the sofas.

"Lord Rokewode?"

"Paston, just the man! Would you please send for Doctor Emerson urgently?"

"At once, my lord," said the footman, backing from the room.

At this point the girl let out a quiet sigh and moved her head a little on the cushion. Rokewode immediately went to her side and squatted on his haunches beside her. He took her hand and gently chafed it, "Miss? You can wake up now, all is well. You are safe. Tony, brandy!"

Sir Anthony poured out two tumblers of brandy and handed one to his friend.

Rokewode put his arm under the girl's shoulders and helped her raise her head and carefully tipped some brandy into her mouth. She choked and turned her head away. "Just a little more, Miss. You will find it beneficial." She took another couple of sips and then shook her head. "There's a good girl," he said in soothing tones. Her eyes flashed up at him and he wondered what he had said to offend her.

"I say, Theo, the mermaid awakes!" announced Sir Anthony exultantly. "Hallo there! Miss Pippin? I am Anthony

Calver, and this is my friend, Theo Rokewode. We were fortunate enough to be able to come to your assistance when your booth caught fire."

The mermaid, Miss Biddy Pippin, opened her enormous doe-like eyes and was gazing up at the fair Adonis leaning over her, with astonishment.

"The fire!" she whispered in such affected accents that her rescuer took her hand in his. She coughed delicately and gently removed her hand. She tried to sit up, but her tail rather hampered her efforts and her eyes opened even wider, "My father! Is he — ?"

"Miss Pippin, I am afraid to have to tell you that your father — he — I am so sorry — " faltered Sir Anthony, lamely.

For a moment he thought she hadn't understood, that he hadn't explained himself clearly enough, but then she seemed to relax and fell back against the cushions, and he was certain she had mistook his meaning. He thought perhaps the smoke and the shock had had an effect upon her understanding.

"That is to say, your father is — *dead*," he said, rather too bluntly.

She looked up at him and smiled a smile of such heavenly beauty that his heart very nearly just stopped.

"Yes, indeed, sir, I understood what you said and could not be more grateful for the news."

"Grateful? I'm not sure that I — " said Sir Anthony, in some confusion. He had noticed that not only was her accent perhaps a trifle — affected but her reaction to his announcement was not at all what he had been expecting. He thought there would be a fit of strong hysterics, or perhaps, at the very least, a need for smelling salts to be administered. He was just wondering how to proceed when Miss Bell returned.

She was delighted to see that the ladies were beginning to recover and busied herself attempting to clean up Miss Pippin's face and hands and keeping up a comforting soliloquy the whole while. Sir Anthony introduced his friend's nanny to the mermaid with no sign of discomfiture at all.

On the other sofa, Rokewode was questioning the girl, "I'm afraid we don't know your name yet, Miss — ? Could you tell us what happened in the booth — how the fire started?"

Miss Pippin sat up very suddenly and called out, "Oh, no! Please sir! Do not try to make her speak! You will only distress her!" She struggled to sit up properly and swing her tail over the edge of the sofa, "Oh, devil take this tail! I must take it off!" She turned to Miss Bell, who was still trying to clean her up and protesting *sotto voce* about her wriggling so, "Dear Miss Bell, do you have some clothes I might change into — I am finding my costume very hampering. I really must go to my friend before she is put all about." She smiled so sweetly that Miss Bell agreed at once and said she would get the maid to prepare two bedrooms for them and find some suitable attire for her to change into and she left the room again.

"Oh, I thank you so much! How kind. My friend's name is Persephone, and she cannot speak, so please do not make her try!"

"Persephone? A stage name?" asked Rokewode.

"No, most certainly not. Sephie was never on the stage!"

"Miss Persephone — ?"

Miss Pippin giggled, "Oh, sir, it's just Persephone. That's all it has ever been. Ever since I have known her. But everyone calls her Sephie because Persephone is a monstrous big name for such a tiny creature! It makes one wonder what her parents were thinking when they saddled her with such a ridiculous *soo-bree-kay*!"

Sir Anthony's eyes met Rokewode's over her head and a look passed between them.

"Persephone. That is certainly an unusual name. What does she do at the fair?"

"Why, she — helps me, of course. I need assistance getting in and out of my costume."

"And your father — ?"

The beautiful face froze, "It was his idea — the booth — the show. He arranged everything and I — I was given no choice in the matter. If it hadn't been for Sephie — I think I might have taken poison," she declared with defiance.

"Oh, no!" cried Sir Anthony, much moved.

Persephone coughed and was patted absent-mindedly on the back by Rokewode who was watching his friend's face as he, in turn, gazed foolishly at Miss Pippin.

"I think I have a headache coming on," said that lady rather faintly.

"I shouldn't wonder, after all you have been through," said Sir Anthony sympathetically. "Miss Bell will be back in a moment and then you may retire to your room and have a little peace and quiet for I'm sure you must be quite done in. What an adventure!"

Rokewode looked down at Persephone and saw that she was watching this exchange with interest.

"Are you all right, Miss Persephone, if I may call you that?"

She nodded and a slight smile curled the corners of her mouth. Her countenance looked most odd with her face almost entirely covered in a thick layer of soot.

"Tomorrow, you will have to meet my mother and I'm afraid there is no way to coat this in sugar — she is an absolute termagant. Lady Rokewode is intolerant of most ordinary things so I've no idea how she will receive the news that she has two complete strangers staying in her house. I feel sure though that she will rise to the occasion. Ah, here is Miss Edie back again. I expect you have already surmised that she was once my nanny and even though I'm past thirty now, thinks that I'm still in long-coats. Is all under your command now, Miss Edie?"

She smiled indulgently at him, "I believe so, my lord. Their bedrooms are being attended to as we speak and I have arranged for some suitable clothes which your dear sister left here on her last visit, to be put in this lady's room." She gestured to Miss Pippin, "I'm afraid that there is nothing that will fit Miss — ?"

"Miss Persephone," supplied Rokewode, "And Miss Biddy Pippin. Miss Pippin's father was lost in the accident, Miss Edie, and she is suffering from some degree of shock, I think. Tony and I will make ourselves scarce while you prepare Miss Pippin for the removal of her — er — tail and then she will be able to climb the stairs without having to be manhandled again."

Miss Bell agreed, and the two men made their excuses and left the withdrawing room, passing a lady's maid on their way out. Miss Bell had asked the maid to assist in the delicate procedure of transferring the two young ladies up to their allotted rooms without them being seen by too many of the staff. The maid, who had seen many a strange sight whilst working for this household, allowed her eyes to only slightly widen on seeing the sparkly tail draped over the edge of the sofa.

* * *

Theo Rokewode and Sir Anthony Calver removed themselves to the library where a fire had been lit for them. Miss Edie, thought Rokewode, with a warm smile.

"Devil take it, Theo! What a night!" declared Sir Anthony, helping himself to a large brandy from the tray on the sideboard and throwing himself into a chair by the fire.

Rokewode stood before the fireplace and contemplated his friend with a jaundiced eye, "It's mostly brandy that is to blame for this calamitous evening in the first place. Do you really think you should be imbibing more at this hour?"

"Ah, one little sip will hardly hurt! After the fine adventure we've had! I told you that you'd thank me. Would you have missed this for the world? I certainly wouldn't! Miss Pippin!" he said on an enthusiastic sigh, "What a beauty! What a voice! And so brave, she barely turned a hair when she found herself in a strange house and heard of the death of her father."

"I think she was downright glad to be rid of him," murmured Rokewode.

"Well, yes, I must say she seemed not very keen on him. But she has clearly been forced into this terrible occupation. Who would do such a thing to their own daughter? A villain, that is for sure. To tell the truth, Theo, I find myself quite shocked. The life she must have led, how she must have suffered, it's beyond our comprehension. You will own though that she has beauty beyond compare!"

"That I will admit. Miss Pippin is indeed a very beautiful girl. And her voice is quite magical. However, by the sounds of it, it's most fortunate that she had Miss Persephone to help her through what must have been a very trying time."

"Trying! She has had to suffer oafs and fools ogling — "

"Like us, you mean?"

Sir Anthony laughed reluctantly and went a little pink, "I was not *ogling*! I was there to appreciate her talent — "

His friend shook his head, "Deluded, my dear. Her talents were all too obvious!"

"Theo! She is but an innocent in this. Surely you can see?"

"I see very clearly."

"Well, I see that you're too jaded to appreciate a living, breathing goddess in our midst. It must be your close acquaintance with Mrs Sheraton. She's ruined you, my friend. And what about that odd little creature, Miss Persephone? What a peculiar guardian to have!"

Rokewode frowned, "A small but truly fierce guardian, I would say. She saved Miss Pippin's life at the risk of her own. Odd, yes but loyal and courageous. She reminded me of a terrier I once had as a boy, a game little beast but always getting stuck down rabbit holes."

"A short-legged terrier?" asked Sir Anthony with a snort.

"Tony. Behaviour not befitting a gentleman. I think you've had enough brandy now. It's strange, I can't quite recall what the dog looked like now."

Sir Anthony laughed, "I can't recall what Miss Persephone looks like! She was so covered in soot and was so small and plain. What a misnomer she's been saddled with!"

Rokewode was about to reprimand his young friend for his less than chivalrous comment when he realised that he couldn't remember the girl's features at all either.

"Ah, now, I remember," he said, "A little white terrier, called Blossom."

"How do you think she lost her voice?"

Rokewode considered this for a moment, "Perhaps she never had one. Perhaps she was born mute and was put upon the parish, which might, in turn, explain her lack of a surname."

Sir Anthony tossed back the last of his brandy, "You think she may have been a foundling?"

Rokewode shrugged, "Possibly. I wonder how they met and why she decided to work for Mr Pippin and his talented daughter?"

"It's a damned mystery. It's like one of those drolls at the fair. The Diabolical Mr Henry Pippin, the Sea Siren and the Mute."

"Anthony!"

Sir Anthony was saved from further reprimand by the fortuitous arrival of Miss Bell, who had just come to say goodnight, and tell them the news and retire gratefully to her bed.

"My lord, Sir Anthony, the girls are soon to be safely tucked up in bed and the mermaid's tail will be hidden away in the linen press in the Yellow Room where nobody will ever sleep because it is such a bilious colour! Miss Pippin was already nearly asleep as she stood, she is understandably suffering from the headache. I intercepted Doctor Emerson as he arrived and took him straight to the girls. He says that miraculously Miss Pippin's injuries are minor — some abrasions and bruising which he has treated with vinegar water — and he says she was extremely lucky to be so little damaged by the fire or the falling debris. He does say that it will take a while for their chests to clear completely and recommends walks in the fresh air and plenty of liquids. I will admit, I am rather shocked by poor Miss Persephone's injuries!"

Rokewode glanced up in surprise, "Miss Persephone was injured?"

"Yes, indeed, Doctor Emerson found her hands to be seriously burnt. Badly blistered and with open wounds on the palms. He has cleaned them and put ointment on them and bound them in clean linen bandages. She wasn't keen at all to be treated and tried to stop him, but I told her firmly that if she didn't obey, she may very well end up with infected wounds, and then where would we be?"

"Good god! I held her hand and chafed it to try to wake her up! I didn't even notice. She must have been in agony and she — damnation! I was about to say she didn't say a word!" Rokewode took a breath, "Of course, nobody asked her if she was injured. We were all so concerned with Miss Pippin, and Miss Persephone is so quiet and unassuming — that is, when she wasn't attacking me! I thought for a moment I was being clawed by a wild animal escaped from The Menagerie! A very small tigress intent on rescuing her cub."

Sir Anthony looked quite put out, "Well she might have indicated that she'd been hurt. I feel mortified that we took no notice of her."

"You took no notice because you were otherwise engaged." Rokewode shook his head, "She must have tried to remove the fallen beams and debris by herself. With her bare hands. No wonder she flew at me, she must have been terrified that Miss Pippin would be burnt too."

Miss Bell watched her beloved Theodore turn things over in his mind and smiled to herself. He had always been a clever boy, too clever by half sometimes and always so impatient with other people's frailties. Sometimes he astonished her with how slow he could be, over the simplest things. How he couldn't see how his poor mother was terrified of being old and alone and losing her once-famed looks and it made her inclined to find fault and test his patience to the limit. He couldn't see how his younger sister, Kitty, could be so flighty and thoughtless, when all she really wanted was a little praise and attention from him; she was like a small child crying "Look at me!" He had never understood his father, choosing to believe the Earl only needed a son to carry on the name and title, when his lordship had clearly adored him but was too hide-bound to be able to say anything. He was, for an intelligent being, rather short-sighted and inclined always to believe the worst of people. She was also of the opinion that being such a very striking looking young man had done him no favours. Those who were blessed with good looks were too easily forgiven, she found. He'd been allowed to get away with some extremely wayward behaviour as a boy and was often excused the worst excesses because his smile was so engaging and his manners could be, when he so chose, quite charming. She had seen him at his worst and his best and loved him regardless. He had always treated her with warmth and respect, and nothing was ever too much trouble for him, where she was concerned. The Dowager Countess was another matter altogether, he had seldom had time to spare for her, especially since the unexpected death of his father, from a heart attack three years ago. He had done all that was proper on inheriting the title and estates, but his heart was obviously not in it. He'd made all the right noises and had taken his seat in the House of Lords but anyone who knew him could see there was no fire in his fine hazel eyes and worried about the lack of connection between him and anyone but his close acquaintants. He had erected impenetrable barricades and even his dearest friends had occasionally come to grief upon them. And once his mother had heard about his liaison with That Awful Woman (as she habitually referred to her) matters had seriously deteriorated and relations between mother and son had become decidedly frosty. Miss Bell had heard tell of Mrs Sheraton and couldn't help but wonder if the unfortunate choice of mistress was deliberate, in order to discomfit his mother. This new development, with the mermaid and the odd little mute girl was bound to prove diverting. There was no denying that life in Grosvenor Square was about to get a good deal more entertaining, thought Miss Bell with a decided sparkle in her eye.

"Miss Edith, I shall accompany Sir Anthony home in a moment but will be back promptly at eleven in the morning so that I can help deflect any wrath away from our guests. Then we must establish some kind of scheme to keep everyone happy, and make sure that Mama does not fall into convulsions when she realises she has fairground folk residing with her. I can rely upon you to make sure that they are both suitably attired for their first interview with Lady Rokewode?"

Miss Bell inclined her head, "Of course, my lord, I will do my utmost to make them presentable. I must say that once the fish-tail had been removed, I felt we had more chance of success on that score! I have asked for someone to be at Catesby and Nash Mantua Makers as soon as they open in the morning. They sell ready-made gowns, you understand?"

Rokewode smiled at her, "So I am led to believe! I might have known that all would be in hand with you at the helm!"

"I must admit to being a trifle anxious about finding any ready-made gowns in a small enough size for Miss Persephone, but I feel with a tuck here and a pleat there, I believe we shall come about."

"I have implicit faith in you, Miss Edith. You have never let me down."

"My lord, if I may be so bold? What is to become of the ladies once they have been suitably attired and introduced to Lady Rokewode?"

"Ah, there you have me at a disadvantage! I have absolutely no idea at the moment. It's certainly a dilemma. Perhaps our dear friend here might have some thoughts on the matter?" and he eyed Sir Anthony ruefully.

That gentleman opened one sleepy eye, "It's no use looking at me! You're the brains in this concern, not I! I am but an insignificant supporting player."

"In that case, the play is doomed to be cancelled before it has finished its run!"

Three

It was the quality of the light on her eyelids that woke her. An unusual noise had initially disturbed her sleep and brought her to consciousness, but she was finding it difficult to put a name to the sound; so she opened her eyes, curiosity getting the better of her desire to remain so cosily tucked up and comfortable.

The first thing she noticed was her hands. They were very painful and heavily bandaged. Then, she observed that she was in a canopied bed and not a bony truckle bed. This made her sit up quite suddenly.

She immediately realised the unfamiliar noise had been a maid opening the curtains because the same maid was hovering beside the bed, looking at her hopefully.

She smiled at Sephie.

"Morning, Miss Persephone. I'm Ann Weston. Miss Bell has sent me to assist you in your toilette. She says to tell you that as yet, there are no gowns for you to wear but there will be some coming from the Mantua Makers before the morning is out. So, shall we get you ready?"

Sephie nodded with a mixture of caution and joy. She was like a child in a pudding shop and gladly gave herself up to the luxury of these new and exciting, if transitory, circumstances she found herself in. Ann helped her to bathe, although was unable to persuade Sephie to remove her chemise. Ann quickly realised that her new mistress was unused to having a maid and probably somewhat shy about allowing anyone to see her in her natural state. She was confident that she'd eventually become used to it.

About an hour later and Sephie was still feeling very much the same and, until the knock on the door, could not conceive that she could become any more buoyant.

And then another maid arrived bearing several boxes of gowns.

The next hour and a half was spent in a state of euphoria as she tried on the beautiful clothes and had her hair dressed by the lady's maid. When they had finished, she twisted and turned, admiring herself in the looking glass. The effect of the new yellow silk gown was slightly spoiled by the bandages; Ann had tried to squeeze them into some pretty lace mittens but had been defeated by the size of them.

The maid had found some delicate silk flowers to tuck into her mousey brown hair and a gauzy fichu to wrap around her shoulders.

Timid tapping on the door announced the arrival of her friend, Miss Biddy Pippin, and as she entered the room, all of Sephie's optimism disappeared in a small puff of disappointment, to be immediately replaced by heartfelt admiration for Biddy's modish new look. A tiny voice in the back of her head told her that she shouldn't be so ridiculous; a church mouse would always remain a church mouse no matter how cleverly it was disguised with bright gewgaws.

Biddy Pippin was no longer a mermaid — she was a goddess fallen straight from heaven itself.

Her borrowed morning gown was pale sea-green silk, embroidered with tiny pink roses, with a full skirt worn over a white petticoat, her tiny waist emphasised by a tightly tied pink sash and a cloud-like gathering of white silk decorously covered her shoulders and décolletage. Her hair was so blonde it was almost white, each curl seeming to glow in the morning light; her cheeks were pink with excitement and her pretty little rosebud mouth was all smiles. She looked quite entrancing. Sephie clapped her hands with delight and kissed her friend on her rosy cheek.

"I know, Sephie! Am I not second to none! Observe, if you will, the feathers in my hair! Have you seen the like? I look like a parrot! It's so amusing. And my shoes! They are a little too tight but so deliciously pretty; I shall wear them even if my feet bleed!" She watched her friend's expressive face and saw that she too shared her rapture and was gratified. Then, remembering that she should be reciprocal in giving compliments she admired Persephone's new round gown, "Why, my dear, you look like a proper lady! Turn around and let me see the back. Oh, a darling little train! And such a becoming shade of yellow, it suits you perfectly. You look like a spring flower."

Sephie's smile curled at the corners and lit up her ordinary face and Biddy thought that she looked almost passable for a moment. But then, she caught sight of herself in the looking glass and forgot all about her friend.

* * *

"I *beg* your pardon! Did you say *fairground?*" fulminated the Dowager Countess in ominous tones.

Her only son sighed and prepared to do battle, "Yes, Mama, I did. Bartholomew Fair. It has always been a great draw for crowds of the very finest people — *The Ton*, even Royalty have been seen attending. Anthony and I, along with Tom Babyngton, Leander Gage and Freddie Knoyll, were all there to see the plays, and Tony is particularly fond of — puppet shows. They amuse him."

"*Puppets?!*" was all Lady Rokewode could manage, her face a picture of shock and disapproval.

"Well, you know what he's like and I made a solemn promise to his mother that I would keep an eye on him because of his tendency to fall into scrapes. I could not allow him to stay at the fair alone, so I remained with him and was fortunately there when the stage caught fire. Miss Pippin and Miss — Fane," he quickly improvised, "were both standing nearby watching a play and were injured in the aftermath. Miss Fane bravely attempted to put out the flames and her hands were burnt. They were separated from their companions and nobody would help them, so Tony and I brought them here in a hackney cab. This seemed to be the safest place for them. We knew you wouldn't turn away two young ladies in such desperate need."

"*Ladies!* They cannot be ladies! Ladies do not frequent fairgrounds! I want them out of my house this instant. And I most certainly do not want to have to fraternise with them. What an appalling notion! I have never been so outraged in my life. Insulted in my own home! What on earth were you thinking, Theodore? Have you lost your mind?"

"No, indeed Mama, I have not. I'm afraid brandy is in a small part to blame for the adventure. Tony was three sheets to the wind when the idea came to him and there was no stopping him once the thought had entered his stupid head. It was just unfortunate that it should have ended in such a dramatic fashion. I beg you, just give the ladies a chance! They're most unexceptional."

There was a knock on the door and Rokewode rose to his feet as Miss Bell showed the two ladies into the morning room.

"Well," enunciated Lady Rokewode, fuming, "*Unexceptional!* You are clearly in urgent need of spectacles."

Ignoring this clearly audible aside, Rokewode greeted the ladies with some astonishment. They looked very different to how he'd last seen them. He cast a grateful look at his old nanny and received a satisfied smile in return. She had supervised the transformation in the blink of an eye and with great success. He was transfixed by the apparition before him and had to shake himself out of the foolish reverie so that he could make the necessary introductions.

Lady Rokewode held out her hand rather ungraciously and Miss Pippin touched her fingers lightly and sank into a deeply respectful curtsy. Then, Miss Persephone came forward and shyly greeted her reluctant hostess.

Lady Rokewode inclined her head so slightly it was barely perceptible and gestured to the sofa. The two girls did as they were bid and sat.

There was a moment while they all just observed each other. Lady Rokewode now only too aware of the reasons behind her son's imprudent escapade, gazed with manifest suspicion upon the exquisite vision before her.

"I have to tell you that sadly Mr Henry Pippin, Miss Pippin's father, was lost in the fire, Mama."

"I am sorry to hear that. He was at the fair with you?"

Sensing that the conversation could be veering in the wrong direction, Rokewode intervened, "Miss Pippin is unwilling to talk of it at the moment, it is too fresh in her mind."

"Of course, I understand. You will, of course have to go into mourning as soon as possible, Miss Pippin. And Miss Fane, I observe that your hands are bandaged. They must be very painful."

Sephie cast a furtive glance at Rokewode and swiftly assuming that she was now Miss Fane she smiled in response and nodded at the Dowager Countess and made a small shrug as though to say her hands did not hurt that much.

Theo Rokewode noted that it was fortunate that she had such an expressive face, even though it was decidedly unmemorable otherwise, she seemed able to convey with only the slightest effort exactly how she felt. He thought that the pale-yellow gown she was wearing this morning was a good deal better than the plain black she had been wearing the night before but realised that anyone seen in the vicinity of Miss Pippin would pale in comparison. She showed no signs of being aware of the comparisons being made and sat serenely with her damaged hands resting in her lap.

Finding it entirely unsatisfactory talking to a mute girl, Lady Rokewode turned her still stormy gaze upon Miss Pippin.

"Am I to understand that you are residing in London, Miss Pippin?"

"We are, my lady. Miss — Fane and I came from Hampshire with my father and hired lodgings for a few days especially so that we could — visit Bartholomew Fair and see the sights. It was to be a particular treat for us because we live in such seclusion as a rule. Of course, now — without support — we shall find it difficult to return to our old life in Whitchurch. If it hadn't been for Lord Rokewode and Sir Anthony coming to our rescue, I cannot conceive what might have happened to us. They were so very courageous, fighting their way through the smoke and flames, risking their lives heroically for two complete strangers! We cannot thank them enough for their daring or you my lady for taking us in when our situation looked so bleak!"

Lady Rokewode's face had frozen into a polite mask. Her good breeding forbade her from remarking upon Miss Pippin's somewhat over-refined accents, but she marked it and made a mental note to talk to her son about it later. Things were going from bad to worse. She was beginning to imagine having to introduce her close circle of friends to these peculiar creatures and finding herself talked about in derogatory terms. It could not be born! It was horribly obvious to her that her son was attracted to the Blonde Goddess and although she had, at one point, thought that *anything* would be an improvement upon That Awful Woman, she was now having second thoughts. There was no way on earth that she could welcome Miss Pippin into her ancient and highly esteemed family and dishonour the name. Her husband would turn in his grave. In fact, the whole family would be spinning like tops in the family crypt!

Rokewode was watching his mother's face and holding out very little hope for a positive outcome to the meeting. He had seen that look before and knew it bode ill for all concerned.

Miss Bell, who had been sitting quietly observing all of this from her place on the perimeter of the circle thought it was time to intervene, "My lady, if I may say so, I was thinking perhaps that you could invite Lady Kitty to stay, to keep your guests company? I feel sure she would be more than happy for an excuse to visit and would find chaperoning Miss Pippin and Miss Fane around to see the sights a welcome change from being at Royston Manor, which we all know she finds somewhat tedious."

Four pairs of eyes turned to her. She returned their gaze with equanimity. She was not a lady who was easily abashed; a long career as nanny to the Rokewode family had ensured that she was inured to any kind of embarrassment. She had realised quite quickly that it didn't do to show one's discomfiture in front of one's employers.

Rokewode waited for his mother to reply. He had learnt not to be seen obviously forcing her hand.

She was clearly mulling the idea over, a tiny frown creasing her forehead.

"I think that it might be just the answer, Miss Edie. I will write immediately and beg her to come to our aid. I think she will find it — entertaining." And, she thought, it will hopefully keep Theodore out of the clutches of That Awful Woman, for a while at least! Yes, it was the perfect solution. She glanced around at the company and saw that Miss Fane was peeping at her from under her eyelashes with a look of such clear comprehension that she actually blushed. She'd no idea why she coloured up because the little creature could have no clue to her thoughts, but she felt she'd been *read like a book!* It was unnerving. She responded by sticking her chin in the air and looking down her fine straight nose and was even more put out when The Oddity had the temerity to smile at her. It was only the very slightest smile where the corners of her mouth curled upwards, but it was so very *speaking* — which, of course, was strange as Miss Fane could not utter a word. Fane, she mused — she had once known some Fanes from Oxfordshire and wondered if there was any connection. But, oh, it would be wonderful to see Kitty! They hadn't seen her in an age, and she missed her high spirits about the house. Theodore was far too like his father to be good company and always exuded an air of wishing to be somewhere else when he was with her.

"Well, that's settled then," said Rokewode. "Kitty is to be the answer. Will you ask poor Ambrose to stay as well?"

"Must you always call him *poor* Ambrose? I'm sure he is blissfully happy being married to your sister."

"The man is a veritable saint."

"Theodore! They are extremely well suited."

"Like a marriage between a parakeet and a sheep."

Miss Bell stifled a snort of laughter and turned it quickly into a cough. She really would have to have a word with his lordship and remind him to mind his manners. She could not help but admit that his description had hit the nail uncomfortably right on the head though.

"Ambrose is a steadying influence on Kitty."

"Yes, Mama," said Rokewode studiously avoiding Miss Bell's eye.

The sound of the front doorbell peeling through the house made them pause.

"Well, who on earth could be calling at this time of day!" asked Lady Rokewode testily.

A few minutes later, the door opened and Paston appeared, "My lady, there are two constables from Bow Street in the hall. They are desirous of seeing Lord Rokewode immediately."

Miss Bell glanced quickly at Rokewode and sent a warning look towards Miss Pippin who had turned pale and put a hand to her mouth, in an undeniably guilty fashion. Miss Fane raised her eyebrows slightly but otherwise showed no emotion and Lord Rokewode rose to his feet, saying he would come at once.

He left the room without a backward glance and the door closed behind him.

Silence fell.

Miss Bell cleared her throat. Miss Pippin fidgeted with her fichu. Miss Fane sat very still and watched Lady Rokewode who reached for her vinaigrette with a shaking hand. She struggled with the stopper for a moment and then found it was being removed from her grasp by Miss Fane, who, despite her bandages, deftly twisted the top off and handed it back to her. She took a reviving sniff and sank back against the cushions, murmuring her thanks for the assistance because although she was thoroughly put out by the morning's events, she was, above everything, very well-mannered.

Sephie, returning to the sofa, shared a sparkling glance with Miss Bell.

* * *

"My lord, my colleague and I are here to investigate the incident at Bartholomew Fair last night at around ten thirty. As we understand it, there was a fire in a booth — a booth owned and managed by a Mr Henry Pippin. Would you know anything about this?"

Rokewode leaned against the edge of his desk and fixed his inquisitor with a steely glare, usually enough to quell any upstart who dared to challenge him. However, this upstart did not seem in the least bit troubled by it and continued to look at him with placid but keen interest.

"Yes, I would Constable Thursby. As you probably already know I was there with my friends and although three of them had left by that time, Sir Anthony Calver and I were still looking around the fair at the — puppet shows. Sir Anthony has a particular fascination with puppets. The fire started in the booth not long after our friends had left and was out of control within minutes. We went to see if we could help and thankfully were able to be of assistance to Miss Pippin and Miss Fane. Unfortunately, we could not rescue Mr Henry Pippin or his other doorkeeper. I am afraid they must have been overcome by the smoke which was dense and choking and the rear of the booth backed up against the wall of the adjacent inn, so there was no other way out."

"Thank you, my lord. May I ask if you knew any of the victims?"

"No, I most certainly did not."

"Or had you previously — had knowledge of either of the ladies involved?"

Rokewode's eyes narrowed dangerously, "If you are implying — "

Constable Thursby held up a hand, "No, my lord, I am not implying anything! I just need to know if you had any connection with those involved in this. We have to rule out foul play and make sure that there is some justice for the dead and the bereaved."

"Of course, I understand. You're only doing your job."

"Indeed. The ladies in question, have you ever seen them before?"

"I have not."

"As I understand it, they are at present residing here, with your mother, Lady Rokewode. Would it be possible to have a word with them?"

Rokewode didn't flinch, "I am sure they would be happy to help in your inquiries. I will go and fetch them, if you would care to wait here?"

He left the room and crossed the hall to the morning room. He walked in on a farcical scene of four females sitting in complete and utter silence. Miss Bell had taken up her sewing, his mother was staring into mid-air, deep in thought and Miss Pippin was pleating her skirt as though her life depended upon it. He glanced at Miss Persephone and met such a look of amused pleading that he very nearly laughed out loud.

"Miss Pippin, Miss Fane, the constables from Bow Street would very much like to ask you about the fire. If you would come with me?"

Sephie jumped up with evident relief and turned immediately to help her friend up. As she passed him at the door, she peeped up at him and gave him a heart-felt look of gratitude.

He raised his eyebrows in mild surprise and followed them out.

The interview with the two constables did not begin well. The ladies seated themselves and looked expectantly at the officials. Constable Thursby was for a moment unable to speak, he seemed to have a frog in his throat, he had to cough loudly to get rid of it. Miss Pippin, who was used to this kind of reaction to her breathtaking beauty, couldn't help smirking just a little.

The constable tried to avoid looking at her and addressed Miss Persephone instead, "Miss Fane, could I ask you if you remember anything about the incident last night?"

Miss Pippin giggled, "You can *ask* her, but she won't be able to answer because she is mute! I'm surprised you haven't already discovered that in your investigating! *Really!* Poor Miss Fane, to be treated so! How could you be so callous, officer?"

The constable looked decidedly uncomfortable, "Sorry, Miss, we had no idea. I apologise for troubling you. In that case, perhaps you could answer the question?"

"Oh, of course! Happily! I really do not remember much at all, I'm afraid. I had just finished my last performance and Sephie had come to help me get out of the pool, when we realised that the booth was on fire. It spread so quickly — we really had no time to think. There was no sign of either of the doorkeepers. Sephie went immediately to find my father to get him to help but either she couldn't find him, or he was drunk again, or he didn't understand what she was trying to tell him. I suspect he was drunk. He was addicted to rum, you see? It made him rather difficult at times. I think I may have screamed because the fire had reached the roof above me and then Sephie came running just as the ceiling collapsed. I remember no more until I woke up here. Will that suffice, Constable Thursby?"

The officer gulped, "A very concise and helpful account, Miss Pippin! Going from what bystanders have said and other performers and the organisers, your father had been drunk and spoiling for a fight a little earlier in the evening and witnesses have said he was frequently worse for wear. So, it seems he did perish in the fire due to his own carelessness. Firstly, having naked flames so close to the silk hangings in the entrance and secondly being under the influence of rum when he should have been making sure his daughter and her friend were safe. It is lucky that Lord Rokewode and Sir Anthony were in the vicinity and were willing to risk their lives to help. Although, speaking of heroism, I think as we can see, Miss Fane has proved that a heroine can take any form."

The heroine could not help a wry smile at this backhanded compliment.

"Good God, man!" said Rokewode in stunned accents and cast Sephie an apologetic look but met her laughing eyes and said no more on the matter.

Four

Mrs Sheraton examined her perfect nails and for a brief moment contemplated throwing something precious and breakable across the room. Bad news travelled fast and, in her case, with friends like hers, it moved faster than a greyhound after a hare. Of course, it was entirely her own fault for choosing such flawed friends, but one didn't want one's inner circle to be too perfect because then one had nothing to hold over them when trusted allies were required. The problem with being a devious and manipulative woman was that there would always be times when one needed help to defeat one's enemies and needing help made one vulnerable. She did not like being vulnerable. So, her carefully selected coterie contained a variety of defective human beings all of whom were desperate for her approbation and had their own secret reasons for putting up with her vicious tongue and temper tantrums.

She managed them with great dexterity, the puppet-master and her obedient little puppets. But she always had to tread warily in case one of them decided to turn the situation to their own advantage. Her reputation could easily be permanently damaged before she could right matters; it could be exhausting always being on one's guard.

And now this tiresome news! Her exquisitely sculpted mouth tightened into a hard thin line and her nostrils flared with the effort of keeping her extreme displeasure from showing. She allowed herself a small, irritated sigh. Mrs Alice Yelverton was watching her from oh, such innocent eyes and yet Mrs Sheraton knew they masked her delight. This is the sort of thing they lived for, the misery of others, except this time it was about one of *her* possessions and it was *her* misery!

Not that she was actually miserable, she was incandescent! How could anyone resist her sophisticated charms? She knew what men needed and was prepared to sacrifice herself on the altar of their basest desires if it got her what she wanted. At this precise moment what she wanted was to make someone suffer. What she had been angling for these past two years was vast wealth and a nice title to go with it. It had been hard work, but she had not once spared herself or anyone else in her quest to reach the top of the social ladder. Her chosen mate was without doubt the most attractive in many ways; his good looks were incomparable, and his riches were many, including impressive stables, several town houses, and two country houses, one of which was Rokewode Abbey for heaven's sake! There was also a hunting lodge and a very fine summer house on the coast. That would do for now at least. He had a seat in the House of Lords and was mostly well thought of in the highest social circles. His manners were excellent, and he never lost his temper; he was generous to a fault and had superb taste in clothes and jewellery, always knowing exactly what would suit her. He was a little too young for her, by twelve years, although thankfully he had no idea of the age difference because she made sure she always looked her best and told convincing lies about her past.

One thing that had been gnawing like a hungry mouse at the back of her astute mind was that he had never introduced her to any of his family, which rankled and made her even more determined to break through the barriers he had erected to keep her separate from his personal life. She had, over the two years they'd been together, met some of his friends but she felt that was because it was difficult to avoid them in the circles they frequented. She knew she was fortunate to still be thought acceptable in those circles but was becoming concerned about the amount of time it was taking to bring him around to her way of thinking. If her plans didn't move on fairly swiftly, she would have to find a way to expedite them. She disliked being hurried. Perfect planning needed clear thinking and that could not, *must* not be hurried.

Alice Yelverton smiled, "Margaret my love, there is surely no need to become agitated over this! It is merely a rumour. Edwina heard it from Lavinia who heard it from — "

"I am *not* agitated! I don't care about the architect of this malicious tale. It must be true because it is so easily refutable. One would only have to make a few discreet inquiries to discover if they were staying at Grosvenor Square. That would be simple enough. No, that part must be true. But, this girl, this Pippin creature — if she is as young and as beautiful as they say, then I will have to resort to more drastic methods to reel him in, and quickly. I cannot, *will* not lose him to an artless fairground virgin."

"But surely you cannot think he would marry such a low-born person?"

Mrs Sheraton curled her lip, "God, no! He would never sully his grand family name, but she might distract him long enough for him to forget all about me and I'm not going to allow that to happen. I have put a good deal of effort into this plan and will not be defeated by some freakish aberration. No, this just means I shall have to marshal my troops rather more urgently than I had initially expected. It is of no matter."

Mrs Yelverton thought otherwise, she had seen the sudden change in her friend's demeanour on hearing the unwelcome news and the hastily assumed mask of indifference. Although she would rather enjoy seeing Margaret get her just deserts, she also desperately wanted to be by her side when she ascended the throne. It would be extremely beneficial to have a wealthy and grateful countess as a close friend. She couldn't wait to tell the others, Lady Litton, Augusta, and Selwyn; they would be sent into transports of delight to hear the latest *on dit*. She practically rubbed her hands together in anticipation of the joys yet to come.

*   *   *

Two nights after the incident, Sir Anthony Calver arrived in Grosvenor Square looking particularly dashing in a dark blue evening coat, buff waistcoat and breeches and an artfully knotted Osbaldeston cravat. Theo Rokewode lifted one quizzical eyebrow at him as he entered the room and Sir Anthony grinned back at him, shamelessly. He had managed to get himself invited for dinner and had spent at least two hours getting ready, much to his valet's dismay. Always punctilious about his attire, this sudden escalation in his employer's devotion to his choice of neckcloth made the valet apprehensive that there may be some *female* on the horizon. A female meant that things might change and that meant that his job would become more difficult and he was, by nature, a rather shiftless sort of fellow and preferred to have more time to himself to sit in the kitchen and think of money-making schemes. Tying endless cravats was not his idea of a worthwhile occupation; he was considering handing in his notice but working for Sir Anthony had its hidden rewards— his employer was less than scrupulous about keeping a tally of household accounts and was in general an undemanding master — and he had no desire for that to change. He also had several other irons in the fire which meant any changes of career were out of the question.

Sir Anthony greeted Lady Rokewode with his usual ebullience, asking how she did and relaying polite messages from his mother. As he chatted to his hostess, he had one eye on the reason for his visit and the reason his valet was now sitting in the kitchen in a state of despondency. Miss Biddy Pippin, in a coral silk evening gown, and looking absolutely radiant, was talking animatedly with Rokewode, who was leaning forward to catch her every word. Next to Miss Pippin was Miss Persephone, who was listening attentively to the conversation, her bandaged hands resting in her lap. Miss Edith Bell was in her accustomed place, in a chair placed slightly behind and to the right of Lady Rokewode's chair. What he didn't know was that she always sat there because she knew Lady Rokewode was deaf in her left ear and would sometimes miss what people were saying to her, so Miss Bell would discreetly prompt from the wings to save her embarrassment.

Bishoptree, the ageing and infirm butler, came to call them to dinner and Sir Anthony jumped up so that he could slyly steal a march on his friend and host and lead Miss Pippin into dinner. Rokewode offered his elbow to his mother and Miss Persephone and Miss Bell walked to the dining room together in amiable silence.

Lady Rokewode sat at the shortened dining table, with Miss Bell on one side and Sir Anthony on the other. Rokewode was at the head of the table with Miss Pippin on his right and Miss Persephone on his left. Unfortunately, they were all separated from each other by an enormous bowl of flowers in the middle of the table, or fortunately.

Miss Bell saw it as her duty to keep Lady Rokewode adequately entertained so that she didn't dominate the conversation with her tedious complaints. She chatted away to her about all manner of subjects including the weather (unseasonably warm), the price of ostrich feathers (extortionate), the fashion for coral jewellery (pearls will never be beaten), the quality of the beef (very fine indeed) and the latest Ann Radcliffe novel (A Sicilian Romance, if you please!).

Sir Anthony was able to flirt discreetly with Miss Pippin, over the delicious repast, but was slightly disappointed when she did not respond in a like manner, but very firmly held him at arm's length. Miss Pippin thought it only proper in a lady wearing such a pretty coral silk gown and a jewelled comb in her hair. He could flash his pretty eyes all he liked but she was not going to be found wanting by her rescuer's regal mother. She was determined to show her that just because she had been discovered at a fair did not mean that she was below the salt and she was not going to fall into Sir Anthony's eager arms until she had taken a good look at his friends and *their* expectations. She had no intention of throwing herself away, at the first opportunity, on just anyone; she had been blessed with a beautiful face for a reason and she would make sure that it didn't go to waste. She had always had secret hopes and ambitions and now that she had been freed from her father's tyranny, she was finally at liberty to make the most of her attributes. She liked Sir Anthony — he would make an unexceptional and lenient husband — but she wanted more than just a handsome face. She wanted adventure! She'd been trapped in that hateful mermaid costume and all the while her very fine legs had just wanted to be free to run, to escape. She looked at Sephie and thought wherever she went, she would take the poor little thing with her. Sephie had been a good friend in her time of need, often standing between her and her drunken father to protect her and stopping the blows from raining down on her. And thankfully Sephie was no competition when it came to comparisons; her own beauty could only be enhanced by the contrast. She caught herself being less than generous and a tiny frown marred her perfectly smooth forehead. How unchristian! If she had any flaw, she mused, it was probably vanity. She must remember to try to curb any such defects in case they disfigured her face, an ugly thought might make a permanent and visible mark. Sir Anthony was eagerly describing a horse race he had recently attended, and she tried to focus on what he was saying but, having no interest in horses or sport in general, she was finding it difficult to concentrate and her attention wandered in order to eavesdrop upon what Lord Rokewode was saying to Sephie.

"…and of course, once she realised that the teasel must be cut out of her hair, she screamed the house down! I don't think she's ever forgiven me. Her maid had to adjust the style of her hair to accommodate the shorter tresses and for a few weeks neither would speak to me. I fear I was a very trying brother. I believe though, you will find her to be extremely — enlivening. She runs poor Ambrose ragged. He's a man of more — sedate character than my sister. And a keen ornithologist, much to Kitty's chagrin. Royston Manor is over-flowing with stuffed birds in glass cases. If you are at all fond of birds, you would find it deeply depressing!"

Sephie's eyes lit up and sparkled with laughter and he thought again how odd that such a plain little face could convey so much more emotion than Miss Pippin's, which, like the work of art it was, was inclined to be somewhat lifeless, although clearly Sir Anthony was not of the same opinion, if his besotted expression was anything to go by. Rokewode had seen his friend fall in and out of love so many times he'd lost count and at the moment had no real concern about this surge of misplaced ardour. All his other *amours* had faded away of their own accord after the initial giddy passion had worn off and Rokewode had no doubt that this unfortunate episode also would die of natural causes before too long. Sir Anthony's passions were quick to ignite and just as quick to be extinguished.

He suddenly realised that he had been gazing absent-mindedly at Miss Pippin for rather too long and turned back to Sephie to find her smiling up at him with a good deal of perspicacity. For a brief, inexplicable moment he wanted to defend himself but decided that it would just make him appear foolish, so he kept quiet.

"Theo!" called Sir Anthony, from behind the flower arrangement, "I was just saying to Miss Pippin that we could make up an expedition while the weather is fine; perhaps take a picnic to Hyde Park which is very close at hand and might prove diverting for the ladies? And Doctor Emerson *did* recommend fresh air for the ladies! Or we could take your fine carriages and parade around to see the fashionable at play. What do you say, Theo?"

"It sounds like an excellent proposition. I'm all for it unless the ladies have any objections?"

Miss Pippin beamed at them, "I think it might be a charming way to spend an afternoon, my lord. Lady Rokewode, you'll be accompanying us, will you not? I could not for a moment contemplate such an adventure without you being part of the company. It would quite spoil the enjoyment!"

Good god, thought Sir Anthony in some dismay, what on earth is she doing?

Lady Rokewode fixed the Blonde Goddess with a basilisk stare, but it was met with such wide-eyed innocence that her resolve faltered, "That's kind in you to say so Miss Pippin but

I must reluctantly decline. I am never at my best in the late afternoon and dislike being bumped along the roads in even the finest carriage. At my advanced age, it's best to stay within your own environs as much as possible."

"That's such a shame," said Miss Pippin, making a good show of being disappointed.

"But, of course, Miss Bell will be happy to go with you as chaperone, will you not, dear Miss Edith?" said Lady Rokewode, with something of a snap.

Oh, hell and damnation, thought Sir Anthony, that's torn it!

"Why, thank you!" replied Miss Bell, "I'd very much enjoy a little jaunt in the park, my lady — the fresh air would be most invigorating. And to have such dashing young companions! Why, it'll be just the thing to help the ladies recover from their terrible ordeal. What a splendid notion, Sir Anthony," and she met his fulminating gaze with perfect equanimity and not a little gentle mockery.

It occurred to Sephie, who was very much enjoying this exchange, that Miss Bell was nobody's fool. She may have been merely the children's nanny — a lowly position of great uncertainty for a dependent spinster — but she was fortunate enough to have been absorbed into the household as companion to Lady Rokewode, when the children no longer needed her. And yet, despite all of this, the elderly lady somehow managed to stay true to herself. There was a pugnacious light in her eyes and a very determined but humorous set to her mouth. She may be dressed all in the shadowy muted tones of someone wishing to blend into the background and arrange her hair in an old-fashioned manner but there was more to Miss Bell than met the eye. She could see that Lord Rokewode was very fond of her, treating her more like a maiden aunt than an employee, often asking her opinion and always making sure that she was comfortable and included. This, thought Sephie, spoke well of both of them. She was very worried though about her friend Biddy, who had that dangerous look in her eye — a look which told Sephie that there would be trouble ahead. She'd seen it many times before and knew she was plotting something. Sir Anthony seemed to be a nice sort of boy, harmless and amiable, if a little predictable in his *tendre* for Biddy. She didn't blame Biddy at all for her attitude to life — she had suffered enough for several lifetimes. Her father, Henry Pippin, had been a drunken bully, with no thought in his head but making enough money to drink himself insensible every night. She was glad he was dead. The world was a better place without him in it. Once Sephie had joined their company, not entirely of her own free will, she had seen that Biddy needed her help and although their life was not a happy one, she felt she couldn't abandon her friend. So, she had, for some while, been planning their escape but then Fate had unexpectedly stepped in and rescued them. She and Biddy would leave together and set up home somewhere safe and perhaps take in sewing to make an honest living. Biddy could continue in her theatricals if she wanted; she certainly had the face to become a famous *something* on the stage! Although, Sephie was reluctant to admit, even to herself, that Biddy had few actual talents that might be turned into a respectable living. And looks didn't last forever. This unforeseen interlude in their lives was very welcome but Sephie couldn't see it continuing, it wouldn't be long before they found out her history and realised that she was little more than a cipher and a fraud to boot. Her heart sank as she contemplated how their lives would soon change again, for the worse this time. Somehow it would be even harder to return to their previous existence having tasted the bitter-sweet delights of this unfamiliar world in Grosvenor Square.

Lord Rokewode, catching a glimpse of a fleeting expression crossing Sephie's face, wondered what had caused such trepidation.

"Well, that's settled, then," said Rokewode, "We shall sally forth in all our glory to Hyde Park the day after tomorrow. I'm sure the ladies will need some time to buy new hats for the occasion — hats are important. And you might as well enjoy yourselves before you enter formal mourning, Miss Pippin."

After dinner, the ladies retired to the drawing room, leaving the gentlemen to drink their wine and converse.

"Shall I warn the cook that a picnic might be required, my lady?" inquired Miss Bell.

Lady Rokewode readily agreed, and they discussed what might be suitable for a summer picnic in the park.

Sephie and Biddy sat together on the sofa and had a one-sided conversation about their day.

"I have to say I am very reluctant to put on black for Papa! He does not deserve my grief, even though I will have to pretend. I shall wear it, as I have no choice, of course, but shall feel very hard done by indeed! I look so washed out in dark colours! Have you noticed how attentive Sir Anthony is, Sephie? I can tell that he already likes me but I'm being cautious, I promise. I will not rush into anything. Anyway, although he's very sweet, I don't think he's the one for me."

Sephie raised her eyebrows.

Miss Pippin shook her head in amusement, "Oh, Sephie! I shall not fall for the first man who makes cow-eyes at me. I have bigger fish to fry. Look around you! The maid says that Lord Rokewode owns this house as well as many others, manors and all sorts! Sir Anthony will come into nothing but an insignificant park in Wiltshire and only has his townhouse until then. He is very amenable, but I fear his heart is not in it. I would be just another passing fancy. You see, their mistake is that they think that because I am beautiful, I am stupid!" She leant closer to her friend and whispered, "I cannot help but think that beneath my lord's austere (but very handsome) exterior there may beat a passionate heart and I intend to try to awaken it! Oh, do not look at me like that, dearest! I cannot help it. You know I can't! But, whatever happens, I will take you with me. We shall be together," and she patted Sephie's hand complacently.

Five

Mrs Sheraton tapped a finger against her perfect jawline. A picnic in the park? How irregular. How Arcadian. How *nauseating!*

The Hon. Selwyn Vauville flicked a speck of dust from his lapel and waited patiently for the axe to fall. The troops had been alerted and were awaiting orders. Margaret was like their very own Boudica or perhaps more like Cromwell, he mused, happily lost in his reverie. This was certainly going to be quite a campaign! She had always been extremely inventive when it came to meting out revenge, she was ruthless, and her victims never saw the end coming. One had only to think of poor Mr Bertram Littleby, who made the fatal mistake of gossiping about Mrs Sheraton to his cronies, when he was supposed to be her bosom-friend. Once she had spread the rumour that he was bedding the much beloved younger wife of an elderly and influential peer, his life was virtually on the rocks and he soon realised that she would never relinquish her hold on his scrawny neck until she was satisfied that he'd learnt his lesson. So, he shot himself. And that was that. Did she feel remorse? Not a bit. She'd laughed uproariously when she heard the news and declared that people were so gullible and would believe anything if it contained a little truth. When asked what she meant she'd explained that Bertram Littleby had other, much more interesting and damning predilections, which had made him so vulnerable to her machinations in the first place but would not have been readily believed. So, one only had to create a tale with its roots in a more believable reality. Bertram was often to be seen in the company of the peer's beloved wife because he was utterly besotted with her young and very handsome brother. But nobody would turn a hair at that! A mere commonplace! No, but just twist it a little and allow the insecure and elderly peer to do your work for you. So much more satisfying.

"So, Margaret, *mi amore* what is the plan?"

A slow, slow smile, like a crocodile, "Why, I think that we shall be needing some fresh air, don't you? I believe Hyde Park beckons. We had better confirm the details with our source and make sure we aren't chasing them up and down Rotten Row all afternoon! And then we shall make sure that any comparisons are in our favour, yes? I mean, this Pippin creature is a nobody — hardly any real competition. But we must be certain. First, we test the water and see if there's any reason we should be concerned and then we draw up the battle plans and go to war. But I am confident that there's no need to panic. I've made myself indispensable to Rokewode over the last two years and have confidence in my power over him."

Mr Vauville nodded affably and poured himself another glass of wine. Mrs Sheraton always had the very finest wine, paid for by Lord Rokewode, of course. He cast an admiring glance over his elegant hostess, who was looking particularly stunning today, in a gown of emerald green, her un-powdered black hair shining like a raven's wing, catching blue lights in the ringlets, which artfully caressed one snow-white shoulder. If he had any interest in older women, he would be at her feet, like every other gentleman of her acquaintance, but he was revolted by females over a certain age — they reminded him of his clingy, whining mother, whom he hated with a cold and deadly passion. He had a mortal fear of decay, of shrivelled skin and flesh falling away from the bone; the scent of death terrified him. He liked his paramours as young and fresh as possible and would do anything to acquire them. And this was the reason he stayed close to her, at her beck and call, because she knew far too much about him but was a very fine procuress. He had needs which must be satisfied and she was able to provide him with some of the finest delights there were to be obtained in this wonderful, dissolute city. Naturally, his weakness made him susceptible to attack and he had to weigh up the possible cost of his proclivities against the inestimable pleasure he reaped from them. In the end, the sybarite in him always won.

"A reconnoitre of the enemy, then? To see what we're up against? Perfect. You upon Satanas, in your new riding habit. Not even Aphrodite could compete!" He gave her an arch look, "I think when Rokewode discards the child I might step in and rescue her!"

Mrs Sheraton laughed, "Everyone wins!"

* * *

Miss Bell had just poured tea into four fine pearlware bowls when she heard the front doorbell peal. She looked up at the bracket clock on the mantlepiece.

"Well, I never," said Lady Rokewode, as ever, "Who could that be?"

Miss Bell didn't immediately respond as she always felt that asking who it could be just as the bell rang was a rather futile exercise. "I feel sure that someone will come and tell us before long, my lady," she said placidly as she handed the tea around to the guests.

"Yes, of course. But, still, I would like to know who would call at such a time."

"It is quite a normal hour for callers, my lady."

It wasn't until some half an hour later that Lady Rokewode finally had her curiosity satisfied.

Rokewode strode into the drawing room, his face thunderous.

"What on earth is the matter, Theodore?" asked his mother, watching him take a furious turn about the room and wishing he wouldn't behave so carelessly in front of strangers.

Miss Pippin, genteelly sipping her tea, wisely kept her own counsel but thought Lord Rokewode looked rather splendid in a temper.

He eventually came to a halt in front of the fireplace, "Of all the — ! You would not credit — !"

Lady Rokewode sighed, "Do you have to call off the picnic? Is it going to rain?"

"Rain! What has that to do with anything, Mama? I have just had another visit from the damn Bow Street constables." At this there was an audible intake of breath from Miss Pippin. "They have had time to investigate further and the officers have now examined the sight of the accident thoroughly. I'm very sorry ladies but I have some bad news to relay. Constable Thursby says they haven't been able to find any trace of your father's remains. They have found the body of the other doorkeeper but nothing else."

Miss Pippin's eyes were very wide, "But, my lord, what does this mean? I don't understand."

"It means that your father cannot officially be declared dead. Unless they find his body, they must assume that he's still alive."

Miss Pippin turned a little pale and Sephie grasped her hand tightly, "But there was no way out of the booth! He *must* have perished. They have not looked properly. They must have missed something."

"I fear not, Miss Pippin. They have dismantled the booth entirely and despite an exhaustive search, found only the body of the unlucky doorkeeper."

Miss Pippin covered her beautiful face with her hands and emitted a soft wailing sound. Sephie took her in her arms and rocked her gently.

Lady Rokewode looked on in some confusion, "Surely, this is a cause for *celebration?* Her father lives!"

Rokewode shrugged his broad shoulders, "Yes, it would normally be a moment of great joy Mama but unfortunately we forbore to tell you that Mr Henry Pippin was a tyrant who mistreated his poor daughter dreadfully. We felt that he had brought his early demise upon himself through his addiction to rum. However, it seems that the devil looks after his own."

"Well, I never," said Lady Rokewode just as the door was thrust open and a lady dressed from head to toe in sky blue silk, a huge straw hat bristling with a profusion of white egret feathers, a small white yapping dog tucked firmly under her arm, entered the room with some panache.

"This house is like a mausoleum! What are you all doing hiding away in here? Hallo, Mama! Look, I have a new little dog! Isn't he adorable? He does bark a good deal and is inclined to bite, but I feel sure he will stop all of that nonsense once he settles down. He's still very young, just a puppy really." She floated across to Lady Rokewode and dropped affectionate kisses on her cheek and then turning to Rokewode, proffered her flushed cheek for him to kiss. She then warmly embraced Miss Bell and told her she should try the new style of lace cap with dangling lappets because it would suit her very well.

"Kitty!" exclaimed her mother, "What on earth are you doing here so soon? I wasn't expecting you until at least next week!"

"Oh, falala to that! As soon as I received your letter, I was throwing clothes into a portmanteau! This has come as a lifesaver, I was — ah, at last! Here is dear Ambrose!" she cried as a stocky gentleman made his way slowly into the room, as though he had lost his way and was trying to find an escape route. "Now, who are these two delights sitting so quietly?" she continued, without drawing breath.

Rokewode had greeted his sister's bewildered husband with a handshake and a sympathetic slap on the back and quickly made the introductions.

Lady Kitty greeted Miss Biddy Pippin, "Why, you are the most exquisite thing I have seen in an age! You make me quite jealous. I was beautiful once, was I not Ambrose?"

"You still are, my dear, you still are," he murmured.

"And Miss Fane, your poor hands! Still bandaged, I see. I hear that you've been quite the heroine! I'm sure I could never have been so brave. I fear I would have run away. But to beat out the flames with your bare hands! So, courageous, my dear!"

Sephie gazed up at this elegant human butterfly with absolute wonder. So many words tumbling out of her pretty mouth and so many restless movements, it made one quite exhausted just watching her. She didn't seem to stop and think, just fluttered on from flower to flower, directionless, but lovely to behold. She had wide-apart chocolate brown eyes, under dark arched brows and the long family nose, a wide mouth and the whole was framed by her hair, in a fashionable hedgehog style, powdered grey, a cap with a pretty frill of muslin and then a straw hat on top of all that which commanded attention, bedecked with bunches of blue and white ribbons and trembling feathers. Sephie, for the first time in a very long while, wished she had a voice so that she could converse with this lovely soul. She suddenly felt quite envious of Biddy's chattiness and natural lack of diffidence. She wanted above anything to make this lovely whirlwind of activity her friend. She quickly schooled her too-eager face and looked away but caught the eagle eye of Lord Rokewode; he smiled and raised his eyebrows, making what could only be described as the long-suffering face of a much put-upon brother. She smiled back at him, her dimples making their first appearance.

Miss Bell, observing all, had a delicious attack of goosebumps, which prickled her all over and made the hair on the back of her neck stand on end. Well, she thought to herself, that could just be the answer. *God moves in a mysterious way his wonders to perform.* And anyway, her goosebumps never lied.

Lady Kitty threw herself down onto the sofa beside Sephie, in a cloud of cerulean silk and let out a dramatic sigh, "What a tedious journey, all bumping and bouncing and not a moment's respite! Poor Amadeus! He howled from Tunbridge Wells to Sevenoaks and then whined from Sevenoaks to Greenwich. He only gave up as we approached Hyde Park. It was as though he knew we were nearly home!"

"*Amadeus?* Good God, Kitty! Surely, you haven't named your dog after the great Mozart?"

"Of course! You have a big name to live up to, don't you my precious?" said Lady Kitty, kissing the puppy's nose and ruffling his feathery ears. He objected strongly to this sudden rough treatment and let out a high-pitched yap, for which he received a sharp tap on his head and then more noisy kissing. "So, Theo! A picnic? Whoever heard of such a thing? You going on a picnic? What on earth induced you to make such a reckless plan? It is so unlike you." She smiled at him innocently and pursed her lips, then let out a peal of laughter when he fixed her with a crushing glare. "I am so glad I am here to witness it. You have room for us do you not? Ambrose and I have talked about nothing else all the way here! Well, *I* have, anyway! Will you have to hire an extra landau? We could always go in our travelling coach but of course, then we wouldn't be able to see the people in all their finery perambulating like peacocks up and down Rotten Row!"

Sir Ambrose Roysten looked helplessly at his brother-in-law hoping for moral support, but Rokewode was suddenly overcome with mirth. "Sorry, Ambrose," he said, his shoulders shaking, "I'd rather ride a cow down Rotten Row! She's *your* wife!"

Lady Kitty stamped her foot, "Oh, I will not be talked about as though I'm a gabber and a chatterbox! If I left all the conversation to you and my darling husband, important matters would be neglected, life would grind to a halt. Nobody would say anything. Things would be deadly dull! Would they not, Mama? Papa was not much of a talker; he was content to sit in sepulchral silence through breakfast and supper, unless, of course, you wished to discuss hunting, racing or pugilism *ad nauseam,* as there was little else he would converse about!'

Her mother nodded in agreement, "Kitty is right, Theo! The men in the family are not much given to communicating. Nothing would be accomplished at all if it were left in the hands of the Rokewode or Roysten gentlemen."

Miss Pippin cast a concerned look at her friend after all this nonsense about silence and chatting but saw with some relief that Sephie's eyes were alight with amusement as she listened to the repartee going on around her; in fact, she had never seen her so animated, she was like a different person. Watching her, Miss Pippin wasn't sure she liked it. She had an uneasy feeling that given half a chance Sephie would be more than happy to be assimilated into this family just like Miss Bell. Miss Pippin found she was a trifle put out by the notion and then sensing that those unchristian sentiments were raising their ugly heads again she took Sephie's hand and gave it a quick squeeze. Sephie smiled at her and tried to convey to Biddy that she was just fine. In fact, she had seldom been happier, sitting observing a real family together, bickering and laughing and loving each other — it was a treat she'd never experienced before, and she never wanted it to end. She felt warmth and affection, and, despite the wry insults, she could feel the strong bond they had. They could mock each other, and nobody clenched their fists ready to wipe the smiles away with sudden and terrifying violence and nobody cowered in a dark corner hoping to avoid the inevitable blows. There was just laughter and Sephie was so very hungry for that, she could feel her spirits lifting, although in the back of her mind was the ever-present mean little voice reminding her that nothing lasts forever, and you only got what you deserved, and she knew in her heart that she didn't deserve any of this.

Rokewode cast his eyes up, "Mother, if Ambrose and I don't chatter away all day long it's only because we are unable to get a word in!"

"Theo! You're abominably rude! It's no wonder you're not married — no sensible woman in her right mind would have you!" said Lady Kitty, unpinning her hat and throwing it carelessly upon a nearby chair. "Oh, that's better! That monstrosity weighs as much as a baby elephant! It quite makes my headache. I could barely get it into the coach. And when I first put it on it made Amadeus bark frantically, just as though he thought I were being attacked by a large bird of prey!"

"It seems that everything makes that dog bark. What a singularly pointless beast it appears to be," remarked her brother.

"Now, now, children!" said Lady Rokewode in a cajoling tone, "There's no need for all this absurdity, we have guests, and they must be wondering what kind of people they have fallen in with! Do please mind your manners."

Lady Kitty taking not the slightest bit of notice of her mother's admonishment leant forward and addressed Miss Pippin, "I have just the hat for you, my dear! For the picnic. It will be far more becoming on you than me. I couldn't resist it, but I'll readily admit it makes me look a little sallow and *squashed* but you'd look absolutely entrancing in it. And Miss Fane, I have the prettiest pink shawl which I think will go well with your colouring."

Sephie, who had become accustomed to standing in the shadows, was overcome by this generosity and could only beam at Lady Kitty, her eyes gleaming.

"Brother? Who is to accompany us on our jaunt about the park? Are we to form a lengthy cavalcade?"

Rokewode shrugged, "The procession is certainly getting longer by the minute. We are now at least three carriages, including the carriage for the staff and Tony, Leander, Babyngton and Freddie will be joining us, but I believe they'll be on horseback because they show off to great advantage when prancing about on horses! We meet up at Hyde Park corner and the servants will then proceed to the very pastoral area beside the Cake-House to set up the picnic. We shall, meanwhile, take a ride along Rotten Row and view the exotic life to be seen there and show off your extravagant hats and then we shall adjourn to take a look at the famous Ring, where they were used to parade in Cromwell's time and show off *their* hats although it's not what it was in days of yore and afterwards on to the woods beside the Cake-House for the picnic and syllabubs."

"It sounds an absolute delight! Ladies, we shall coordinate our outfits so that we are not outdone by anyone. I've brought enough gowns with me to furnish a Christmas Ball! Although, I'm afraid I have nothing that will fit Miss Fane. One of my enormous hats would snap her neck, she's so tiny!"

"Miss Persephone has some more gowns coming this afternoon and the milliner is bringing an array of suitable hats to try on. It is all in order," declared Miss Bell quite decidedly.

"Ah, of course, it is, darling Miss Edie! I should have known. Persephone? Now, that is a name to conjure with! Such a big name for such a little person! How came you by it? Oh, of course — !"

"My dear friend had a *very* literary father," answered Miss Pippin, airily, "She was most fortunate she didn't end up being called Polyhymnia or some such thing!"

"Persephone is a beautiful name," agreed Lady Kitty, "Let us hope she doesn't get carried off by Hades!"

Six

The day of the picnic dawned, and the weather was favourable, not unbearably hot or windy, and no rain on the horizon, which meant, said Lady Kitty, that feathers were the order of the day!

Sephie was slightly surprised to find Lady Kitty, still in her night attire, a satin negligee and lacy robe, begging admittance to her bedroom at an unfashionably early hour, demanding to see the gowns that Catesby and Nash had delivered the day before. She swiftly assessed them and with a calculating glance at Sephie, who was perched uneasily on the edge of the bed in only her petticoat and chemise, she shook out a redingote in a grey striped silk with a pale pink underskirt, "This one, I think! It's not too fussy and won't swamp you with miles of flounces and too many bows. I must always be careful not to wear pastel colours, they make me look insipid although I can wear the largest hat ever created because I am tall like Theo. I daresay you are very used to allowing Miss Pippin to command all the attention and I'm sure if I were in your place, I would be reluctant to push myself forward too, but I've already perceived in you a delightfully strong-willed streak. Oh, yes, indeed, when Miss Pippin speaks *for* you! Your eyes flash and it's quite clear that you don't like it. I don't blame you either! Have you tried writing down what you want to say? No, too slow? Yes, I can quite see that. Well, we will find some sort of solution. I understand from Miss Bell that there is a book, written by a Frenchman, explaining the use of a kind of language spoken with your hands? Perhaps it might be useful?"

Sephie had never heard of it and gave a slight shrug.

"Would you be interested, if I could find someone who knows about it?"

Sephie nodded, eagerly.

"Oh, bless you my dear! What a life you must have led, I cannot even begin to imagine! Theo has told me a little about what you have endured. But you are with us now and we shall find a way to make things easier for you. I'm quite determined. And as both Ambrose and Theo will tell you, I can be dreadfully stubborn when I want to be. So, today, we shall have some grand amusement and we won't allow Miss Pippin to steal all the admiring glances away from us! I've had the splendid notion of arranging the carriages just so. You shall see! I couldn't sleep last night for making plans. I like to organise people, you see. It is a deplorable failing for which I am often criticised, but I notice whenever there are important plans to be made, they always call upon me! So, I know they appreciate my talents."

Sephie was captivated by Lady Kitty, and watched her from wide, shining eyes as a child might watch a puppet show. She had never in her life been with anyone so warm and friendly and perspicacious. She just seemed to know what she was thinking and never made Sephie feel awkward. When Biddy kindly provided her words for her, she always felt that they became a little twisted in translation and often it was more about what Biddy wanted to say rather than her own thoughts, but she was grateful to have someone who cared enough to be a go-between at all. Sephie's life, before Henry Pippin had found her, had been a living nightmare. It hadn't been much better afterwards but at least she'd had Biddy to cling to when times were hard. In her old life she'd been all alone and had no choice but to fend for herself. Being alone, she found, was enough to drive one to the river's edge to contemplate its muddy eddies with longing.

As these thoughts chased each other across Sephie's face, Lady Kitty swore to herself that whatever else she did with her empty but extremely comfortable life, she would make sure that this odd little creature before her was never hurt again.

Kitty thought there was something mysterious about Miss Persephone Fane — she appeared to be hiding something and couldn't tell anyone or *wouldn't* tell anyone.

Lady Kitty was, and always had been, a rebel, driving her parents to despair and her brother to tear his hair out at her hoydenish antics. Theo had urged their parents not to push her into marriage with Sir Ambrose Roysten, who had proved to be her most ardent and reliable suitor, but the Earl was adamant that his daughter needed a calming influence, and he was convinced that poor Ambrose could provide that. Theo could see that when his sister had nothing to occupy her, she merely found some trouble to stir up for entertainment and even when Ambrose had, on his father-in-law's stern advice, removed his young bride to the wilds of Kent and the gloomy Roysten Manor, he could not keep Kitty out of mischief. The Earl had bellowed that what she needed was half a dozen brats hanging on her skirts and she had wept noisily and said that she hated children with their dirty hands and runny noses and would rather die than have any.

What I need, she said to herself, is a splendid mission to take my mind off the tedium of being a responsible adult and encroaching middle-age. She looked at Sephie's eager face and tried to imagine herself in her position. She couldn't.

"And these are the hats? This one with the roses is adorable. Oh, but I think this one will be ideal. I must say I think we shall cover everyone with envy! I shall tell Ann not to powder your hair, you're too young yet and I only powder because there are threads of grey appearing and I don't want Ambrose to think he has an old wife — he might run off with someone younger! No, no! I know I goad him, but honestly, he's everything to me. You see, when we first married, I may not have been so keen upon the idea, although I was delighted to be leaving home to begin my own household, my father being an intolerant sort of man to live with and I was desperate for some freedom and independence! In the beginning, he was utterly besotted with me, never said much at all but his puppy-dog eyes would follow me around the ballroom. It was tiresome at first and embarrassing; my friends laughed at him quite openly, but he took no notice. He steadfastly remained on the perimeters of my life, but made no effort to engage my attention, it was exceedingly odd. He seemed happy to just observe from afar. I had many other beaux and *numerous* offers of marriage, but I was too busy skylarking to settle down and besides, none of my admirers really took my fancy. They were either too rackety or extremely dull and several were far too like my father for comfort. Very critical and strict. The last thing I needed was to find myself married to such a man when that was what I was trying to escape! Oh, I had such fun, Sephie! You don't mind if I call you Sephie? It suits you! I think I must have known that summer was my last spree before marriage, and I was determined to make the most of it. Then, I looked up one day and he wasn't there. I must say that it gave me the strangest sensation. At first, I merely shrugged, and my friends and I laughed unkindly; they said he'd become bored with waiting for me or he'd found someone else, someone more amenable and so we forgot him and carried on as though nothing had happened. Or, at least, *they* forgot him. Every so often I would find myself looking for him on the edge of the ballroom or in the park or the theatre and was always disappointed. Weeks passed. I decided that it was only natural to make some polite inquiries. I found out, to my consternation, that he'd been in a bad carriage accident. Really very serious injuries and not expected to recover! Well, I was thrown into a state of anxiety and confusion. I didn't know which way to turn. For some inexplicable reason, I approached my brother and he just looked at me as though I was the stupidest person on earth! He said, "Get your hat, you silly creature!" and he bundled me into his curricle, and we took off without any further ado to Roysten Manor. My heart was in my mouth, I had no idea what to expect — I thought Ambrose may be dead or dying! Well, when we got there — what a commotion! We were allowed to see him but only after we'd been given such a lecture by his mother and his aunt and his awful sister (who is not shy about saying what she thinks!). We were quite chastened and in great fear of what we might find! Indeed, he was lying back against the pillows and looked most unwell, his face thin and grey, his arm in a sling and his leg in a splint. I hesitated on the threshold, I have to admit that I was in two minds about whether to flee or not! He opened his eyes and saw me and, well, I must say his response was very gratifying; he smiled so bravely at me. I was quite overcome. I approached the bed and held his hand and he murmured, "So, this is what I have to do in order for you to take notice. In which case, I'm prepared to do it every day, for the rest of my life." I'm not proud, I'll tell you that I wept and told him roundly that he was a nincompoop for not sending for me at once! He just laughed (very weakly) and said he thought I wouldn't even notice he wasn't there. I told him that I'd grown used to him being there. "Like a familiar pet," he said wryly. So, I kissed him, in the most brazen fashion and demanded to know if *that* was not proof enough that I did not think of him as any kind of domesticated animal! He laughed again, which I decided was the most lovely sound and he kissed me back and then I accidentally hurt his broken arm by leaning on it too heavily and — that was that! It turned out that he was just shy! But I can tell you he's an absolute darling and *very* good at kissing!" and she laughed delightedly at Sephie's astonished face. "And, on top of all that, I have my brother to thank for my happiness! So very exasperating."

Sephie jumped up and on impulse, threw her arms about Lady Kitty, who after a moment's surprise, returned the embrace just as enthusiastically. Then she set Sephie at arm's length and looked at her intently, "My dear child, I want you to know that you have a friend in me, whatever may occur! D'you hear me? Whatever it is that troubles you, have no fear, I will stand by you. Theo would — "

Sephie pulled away from her and shook her head vehemently, holding up her bandaged hands and fighting sudden overwhelming emotion.

Lady Kitty was alarmed by the strength of Sephie's feelings, her predicament was obviously far more serious than she had initially thought. But she was not one to give up easily and she laid a calming hand on Sephie's arm, to try to soothe her agitation, "There, I have alarmed you and I swear I didn't mean to. I meant only to reassure you! I allowed my tongue to run away with me. I'll say nothing to Theo, if that's what you want. Although, despite the fact that I tease him, he is just the man for a crisis. He remains calm whereas I become too embroiled and cannot be logical. You would do well to remember that. He would never do anything to hurt you. Come, we shall forget this! Let us just think about hats and syllabubs!"

Sephie couldn't help a watery smile because Lady Kitty's mood changed like the weather in April, but her heart was pounding loudly in her chest at the thought of anyone, particularly Lady Kitty and Lord Rokewode, finding out about her past.

She would rather disappear forever before that happened.

* * *

Two black and green open carriages, with silver lamps and coronets, luxurious scarlet squabs and cushions, drew up in front of the house, making such a spectacle that curtains were twitching all around the square. The servants jumped into the big travelling coach which was stuffed to the roof with wicker hampers and rugs, ice buckets and champagne bottles, parasols and awnings and they set off before the family carriages in order make a start on setting up the picnic in the proper style. They'd had so many contradicting instructions from Lady Kitty and Lady Rokewode that they looked anxiously to each other for confirmation.

Lady Kitty directed Miss Pippin to the second landau and Paston handed her in, just as Sir Anthony Calver and Lord Frederick Knoyll arrived.

"Ho there!" shouted Sir Anthony, from some distance, "Fine style! All the goddesses gathered! What a glorious sight!" He and Freddie Knoyll waltzed up to them, arm-in-arm, both decked out in cutaway long-tailed coats: Sir Anthony in blue stripes and cocked hat, Freddie in scarlet and sporting a dashing wig and chapeau-bras. They wore Hessian boots, and snow-white cravats and looked absolutely splendid.

"Ah, just in time," said Lady Kitty, "How do you do, Anthony, Freddie! You're both in this carriage. Anthony, please do behave, no shouting at the ladies as you pass by! Miss Bell, you are chaperoning, I wish you the best of luck. Thank you, Freddie! Are you comfortable, Miss Edie? *Ambrose!* Where on earth have you been dilly-dallying? Come along, you're in the first carriage next to me. Now, where is my brother? No, Anthony, kindly do *not* rearrange the cushions like that, it looks most irregular. Ah, Theo, at last! Goodness, it's like a military campaign to get you all in order. Oh, dear where is Amadeus? Ah, thank you, Sephie, where did you find him? You're lucky he hasn't bitten you! Now, are we ready?"

Miss Pippin caught a glimpse of Lord Rokewode as he stepped into the other carriage in buff knee breeches, top boots, a cream waistcoat and a cutaway frock coat of dark blue with silver buttons and couldn't help being envious of Sephie sitting next to such an Adonis. Of course, she knew he would rather be in the other carriage with her. I mean, she thought, what will they *talk* about! And she had to suppress the slight smile which appeared on her pretty mouth in case it left an ugly mark.

A word to the groom and they were off. Sir Anthony let out a loud "Tally Ho!" but was immediately quelled by a look from Miss Bell, who, despite her ebullient charges, was very much looking forward to the day ahead.

Sephie noticed that Sir Ambrose reached for Lady Kitty's hand to give it a squeeze and exchanged a look of such understanding with his wife that it made Sephie's heart glow.

"Are you quite comfortable, Miss Fane?" asked Lord Rokewode, solicitously.

Sephie nodded and beamed up at him, her cheeks flushed a delicate pink. Oh, yes, she thought, I couldn't be any happier or more comfortable! Thank you for asking. How polite you are and what beautiful hazel eyes you have, they look golden in the sunlight, like a lion. And such a lovely lazy smile, oh, for goodness' sake, Sephie! Stop being ridiculous! The first charming and handsome man who speaks to you as though you're a human being and not a piece of cheap property and you behave like a schoolroom miss! She lowered her eyes and fixed her gaze upon Amadeus who was chewing the leather strap on the seat. She reached down and scooped him up into her arms and stroked his ears. He settled down contentedly, thinking what a peaceful place it was to be and rested his chin on her arm and went to sleep. Rokewode, observing this, thought that animals always seemed to know whom to trust.

Lady Kitty, resplendent in a round gown of jade green and a hat weighed down with bright pink roses, frowned at her disloyal dog and noted Sephie's pink cheeks and downcast eyes and hoped she wasn't setting too much store by Theo's innate good manners. He had always left droves of hopelessly charmed females in his wake and she felt desperately sorry for them because she could see that they thought his attention was personal.

The carriages were expensive and well-sprung and travelled along the town roads with very little disturbance to their passengers apart from the intrusive noise of the wheels and metal horseshoes striking the stones. They joined the orderly queues of coaches on Park Lane and entered the park by way of the turnpike.

"Oh my! Everyone and his dog have come! What a frightful crush," said Lady Kitty with girlish delight. They squeezed through the area by Apsley House and made their way towards Rotten Row and, after a bit of jostling, cleared the melee of gigs and carriages and horses that collected near the entrance and eased their way along the popular bridleway until they found themselves with some space to breathe as the traffic thinned out a little.

Their carriages moved forward at a steady walking pace so that the passengers could admire the extraordinary array of humanity on display, all gathered in this one place with one common purpose — to show off their wealth and good taste to anyone who cared to observe them. And hats. So many beautiful hats and bonnets, thought Sephie.

She craned her neck to see a particularly extraordinary couple in a smart gig, the lady all decked out in a frightening shade of purple and a hat crowded with birds of paradise and the gentleman in such a towering wig that he could barely keep his head upright, a garish striped, pink coat and more makeup than his lady-friend. Sephie was astonished and enraptured and hung out over the edge of the carriage in her eagerness not to miss any of the astounding sights. On seeing an extremely corpulent lady in puce satin with practically a whole ostrich balanced upon her head, Sephie leant out a little too far and a firm hand on her arm held her steady. He didn't pull her back into the carriage, just held her so she wouldn't fall out and get trampled to death under the horse's hooves. She peeped back at him and smiled. He raised a quizzical eyebrow. Her dimples appeared. Then, another hat caught her attention and she pointed excitedly. Rokewode laughed.

Lady Kitty shook her head, "Sephie, you will have a seizure if you don't calm down! Try to at least *appear* as though this is all beneath you! Your eyes are practically out on stalks. I cannot believe Amadeus is sleeping through all of this, I thought he'd bark at everything."

"And yet you still brought him?" said her brother scathingly, eyeing the comatose dog with ill-feeling.

"He was cooped up most of yesterday, he deserves a treat. Although I must say I'm deeply disappointed in the depth of his loyalty!"

"A creature with some common sense at least."

"Very amusing. Oh, Ambrose, look isn't that the Chetwoods? I do believe it is! Wave at them! Oh, there, it *is* them. How silly she looks in so many girlish frills. Mutton dressed as lamb. What *was* she thinking?"

"Friends of yours?"

"Oh, *very* dear friends. I've known them forever."

"Pity your enemies then."

"Well, Fidelia never had much taste. I mean, just take a look at her husband. What a vision. A case of April and December. But, rich as Croesus, apparently. Seven children. All girls and every single one sadly made in his likeness! Money can't buy you everything."

At this point Sephie jumped to her feet in order to get a clearer view of another absurd fashion spectacle and Rokewode grabbed the back of her skirts and discreetly steered her back into her seat. She bit her lip and turned pink. After that she tried very hard to contain her excitement and behave much as Lady Kitty, as though she didn't care a jot for all the exotic passers-by. She pretended she was a lady of distinction and kept her face quite expressionless. Rokewode was sorry to have spoiled her childlike enjoyment and cursed himself for being so strait-laced about public opinion.

The Row was teeming with vehicles of every sort, containing some of the city's most prominent people, dukes and duchesses, earls and countesses, a foreign prince or two, some notable actresses and an opera singer who was causing a sensation amongst her followers. There was a good deal of jostling in order to get close to her, young men threw flowers and their calling cards into her barouche and Sephie thought she was the most frivolous thing she had ever seen, a vision in white and silver.

Rokewode leant close to murmur in her ear, "A duel was fought over her just last week between two noblemen who should have known better and one of the combatants sadly died of his wounds. The other has fled the country to escape inevitable arrest and ignominy. You'd never guess it now, would you? Look at her, how she waves and smiles, without a care in the world. *La belle dame sans mercy.* How foolish men are."

Sephie still thought she looked like something fallen from heaven but made no sign of her dissent. She did wonder at his embittered tone though.

Lady Kitty was relieved to see Theo treating their guest as the child she was, it certainly put her growing concerns to rest.

At the same time, she hoped he was not developing an interest in Miss Pippin, who despite her extraordinary beauty, was not at all suitable in any way. She glanced over her brother's shoulder to the carriage behind and could see Sir Anthony Calver waving his hat at a group of ladies standing under the trees by the Serpentine, chatting to some soldiers in their scarlet uniforms. Miss Bell was poking him disapprovingly with the point of her parasol. Freddie Knoyll was laughing his head off and Miss Pippin was looking a little as though she'd dropped a guinea and found a penny.

They drove the whole length of The Row and then back again, just to make sure they hadn't missed seeing anyone. Lady Kitty began to complain about the dust being stirred up by the horses' hooves and covered her nose with a lace handkerchief.

"I think it's time to sound the retreat," said Lord Rokewode, "Have you seen enough, Miss Fane?"

Miss Fane, who would have happily stayed there all day ogling the wonders on display, reluctantly nodded in reply. But it was with a heavy heart that she was torn away from the sights and sounds of the *beau monde* at play although she also had to admit that the dust was becoming a little too thick and choking. She very nearly forgot herself again, as they made their way towards The Ring when she gleefully spied herds of deer and flocks of sheep grazing beneath the ancient trees. But at the last moment recalled Rokewode's displeasure and pressed her lips together and tried to look demure and obedient but it required quite an effort to restrain herself. Several times she turned around to peer back at the second landau and assumed that Biddy was having a wonderful time as she didn't once look in her direction.

As they approached the area where The Ring had once reigned supreme as *the* place to show off, Rokewode provided Sephie with a little history. It was no more than some fields and a handful of decrepit old elm trees now but apparently it had once been the place to emulate your heroes, their horsemanship, the prowess of the whipsters driving their carriages around the oval track, their smart clothes and adoring *belles* sitting beside them. She could picture it all in her mind's eye and thought how romantic it must have been, the Royalists with their long hair and feathered hats and the ladies in billowing clouds of silk, fluttering like butterflies — she grew quite wistful as she imagined the scene.

"Someone tried to assassinate Cromwell here too," said Rokewode with a faint smile.

Sephie looked at him curiously, eyebrows lifted in uncertainty.

"*Twice.* It's true. Obviously, they weren't successful, and it ended badly for them but at least they tried." He gave her a considering look, "Of course, I have no idea what your politics may be, Miss Fane, perhaps you're a Roundhead in disguise?"

She grinned at him and shook her head and then shrugged because she wasn't sure she'd ever considered her political views, she'd been too busy just trying to stay alive, which had seriously distracted her from becoming any kind of a Bluestocking.

Their carriages had just bounced around the track near where the ghost of The Ring was purported to be and were heading off towards the picturesque meadow where The Cake House, a timber and plaster building from which you could buy cheesecake and syllabubs, nestled amongst the trees next to a lake. Sephie spotted the picnic area under the shade of the trees, the awnings and parasols standing out against the sea of green.

It was at this point that they were approached by a phaeton in smart yellow and black livery, drawn by two perfectly matched white horses and with two riders flanking it.

Sephie heard Lord Rokewode curse roundly under his breath.

She looked around him to see what had caused his displeasure.

Seven

Lady Kitty's horrified gasp was audible for everyone to hear. Sephie looked around at her companions and noticed they all wore the same expression, one of profound dismay. Lord Rokewode was blocking her view, so she inched forward on her seat to see what they were all staring at so frigidly.

The driver of the magnificent phaeton was a gentleman, a diamond of the first water, a paragon of fashion and style. Dressed in citrus green satin with black trimmings and buttons, pink waistcoat, a much curled and powdered wig with a small black tricorne perched on it and an enormous nosegay of pink rosebuds pinned to his lapel. He brought the phaeton to an elegant stop beside their landau. The riders came into view. Sephie could see a bay horse bearing a gentleman in smart but conservative riding dress and then a glossy, black horse pranced into her vision, its perfect coat shuddering with energy and life, its neck arched, its ebony mane rippling almost down to its knees. Seeing this beast, Sephie drew back a little. On its back, riding side-saddle, a female in a bright scarlet habit, modelled on military uniform, with frogging and rows of black buttons and a black stock; shiny black ringlets curling about her face, a large black hat with black feathers, a nonsense of a veil obscuring the top half of her face. A ravishing face, all cheekbones and jawline, aquiline nose and eyebrows like the wings of a swift, a mouth that was in perfect proportion and the ideal shade of red. Sephie found she couldn't catch her breath. This woman emanated danger and sensuality.

She urged the horse nearer to their landau, controlling its skittish behaviour with ease, "Theo! What an unexpected surprise. And Lady Kitty too. Well, I *am* glad that I decided to venture out today, I so very nearly didn't. What a treat to see you all. Sir Ambrose, how do you do? We so rarely see you in town these days." Her eyes slid from one passenger to the next and alighted briefly upon Sephie, who recognised immediately that she'd been dismissed as not worthy of serious consideration.

Finally recollecting himself, Lord Rokewode said, "Miss Persephone Fane, Mrs Margaret Sheraton. This is Mr Selwyn Vauville, and Sir Leonard Tiploft."

Sephie could do no more than incline her head and smile very slightly. Mrs Sheraton's gaze barely rested on her for a second before returning to Lord Rokewode. Sephie noticed his fists were clenched, the knuckles white. His face was set like granite, his mouth a grim, thin line and his eyes narrowed and smouldering. Whoever this Mrs Sheraton was, nobody seemed terribly pleased to see her.

"And is that Sir Anthony and Freddie Knoyll I spy in the next carriage? That must be your dear old nanny I believe and the other pretty lady I have not been introduced to yet."

"Indeed, my mother's companion, Miss Bell and that is Miss Fane's friend, Miss Biddy Pippin," said Rokewode, "We're on our way to have a picnic and as you can plainly see the servants are waiting, we mustn't keep them. I bid you good day, Mrs Sheraton, Vauville, Sir Leonard," and he tipped his hat and ordered the coachman to continue. However, Mrs Sheraton was not giving up so easily, she allowed her mount to sidle and side-step, as the carriage moved forward and kept pace with them.

Lady Kitty was clearly outraged and was about to say something pithy when the sound of hooves thundering across the turf caught their attention and they watched as Mr Thomas Babyngton and Sir Leander Gage cantered towards them, their faces wreathed in smiles.

"Hallo! Apologies for being late, Babyngton couldn't find the nose on his face even if it were pointed out to him; he got lost coming from his house to mine! We made all haste, but the crowds were a damn nuisance, milling about with no direction — it took an age to get through the gates but we're here now!" declared Sir Leander Gage.

"Ho! Mrs Sheraton! Is that the famous Satanas? What a very fine beast! Are you picnicking with us?" enquired Tom Babyngton not even slightly aware of the awkwardness of the situation.

"Why, Mr Babyngton, what a delightful idea! How kind! Have you enough provisions for us?"

"Oh," said Babyngton turning a dark shade of pink, "I see. I — well, you see — not my place of course to — *Theo?*"

The vision in the phaeton piped up, "An Arcadian idyll beneath the ancient elms, how can we resist? The ghosts of Cavaliers and their ladies may dine with us and perhaps even some of the victims of the duels fought here. What a charming notion."

Lady Kitty, staring hard at Rokewode, was fuming but she saw him suddenly come to a decision.

"I'm sure there is ample champagne. We would be overjoyed to have you join us. The more the merrier." There was a note in his voice that his sister recognised, and it sent a chill down her spine. She decided to stay silent and let him take the lead, he never did anything without very good reasons. She just had to trust him. However, she was damned if she was going to be polite to That Awful Woman! How *dare* she? And if she thinks that Theo is going to be forgiving, then she is sorely mistaken in his character; he was not one to forget such a gross imposition and he was and always had been, stubbornly unforgiving.

Miss Bell, watching the drama unfolding ahead of them, was hugely interested to finally see what all the fuss was about. So, this was the notorious Mrs Sheraton! She could certainly now understand why she had managed to hold sway over so many impressionable young and old men, but she was finding it difficult to fathom why Lord Rokewode was so intrigued by her. To Miss Bell's intuitive eye, she could see that the lady was not as young as she would like to be and was desperately keen to disguise this fact. She could also see that despite her studied air of sophistication, she was just a seething mass of jealousy and greed. And she knew this would mean there was trouble coming. She had no doubt, however, that her dear Theodore would be able to deal capably with anything untoward. He was not a gentleman to be trifled with despite his customary impassive demeanour; he had hidden depths and fire which he had, since his father's death, learnt to master but she felt that given the right or *wrong* circumstances that that control would be severely tested and then she wouldn't want to be in the firing line.

After a moment of indecision, the carriages and riders made their way to the picnic area beneath the trees. The awnings were erected, and the rugs laid out on the grass, champagne was chilling in the ice buckets and the servants were putting the final touches to the picnic. There were cushions for the ladies and a small chair for Miss Bell's comfort, which Rokewode guided her to and made sure she was settled before instructing an under-footman to bring her champagne and something to eat. Just as he turned away, she reached out and put her hand on his arm, "My lord? May I offer a word of caution?"

"Of course, dear Miss Edie, I am all ears."

"This — situation we find ourselves in — it requires a cool head to steer us through the turbulent waters. We don't want to capsize!"

He smiled, "Have no fear, I'm not planning to do anything rash. I just felt that it was probably best not to make a huge scene, which would only have exacerbated the problem and allowed the gossipmongers to gain even more power." He gave her hand a reassuring squeeze, "I promise, I shall not disgrace you."

Miss Pippin was slightly taken aback to find she was expected to sit upon the ground; she had had grand visions of a long dining table and chairs but apparently the whole idea was to behave like workers in the fields and eat with one's fingers! Well, she had done that before! She had no desire to return to her earlier life, she wanted to forge ahead into a better future and leave her old life behind. This was not her notion of how the *beau monde* should behave. And, to top it all, this Mrs Sheraton had descended upon them and seemed set on disrupting everything! She was just a little too strikingly beautiful for Miss Pippin's comfort and commanded the attention of all around her with an ease which made Miss Pippin somewhat tight-lipped. Even with the flattering attention she was receiving from Sir Anthony and his friends, she felt that it wasn't quite as whole-hearted as it had been. Like children seeing a new toy, they'd very quickly lost interest in the old one. She also knew that her artless appeal could never compete on the same level with Mrs Sheraton, who seemed to vibrate with a sultry allure a mere girl of nineteen could never hope to achieve. But she had youth on her side, and she knew that gentlemen were, on the whole, easily led and mostly rather shallow; she believed when faced with a lady of great beauty but later years, they may be tempted to taste her rather conspicuous wares but when it finally came to giving themselves up to marriage, they would be looking for someone young and healthy to give them an heir. Mrs Sheraton may have more knowledge in the bedchamber and be able to entertain a gentleman with a greater degree of sophistication, but youth would always win in the end.

Sir Anthony arranged some cushions and helped Miss Pippin to make herself comfortable and found her a glass of champagne. She took a sip and wrinkled her delightful little nose and he thought how sweet she was, how innocent.

"Is that to your taste, Miss Pippin?" he enquired.

"Thank you, Sir Anthony, it's very — nice. It could do with several lumps of sugar in it though!"

He laughed and went to find her some at once. Lord Frederick Knoyll hovered, and she smiled warmly at him, "Lord Frederick, won't you please be seated?"

"Oh — Miss Pippin — thank you but I was wondering if I might fetch you something to eat? Perhaps, a little roast beef or a boiled egg?"

She giggled, "Why, that would be perfectly delightful. I'll be happy with whatever you choose. Except, I feel obliged to tell you that I don't like fish very much."

He grinned at her, "No lobster for you then! You don't know what you're missing!" and he dashed off to do her bidding. She carefully arranged her blue muslin skirts about her, to show a little more of her pretty ankles than she ought and adjusted the ribbons of her straw hat.

The most recent additions to the party stood a little to one side surveying the scene. Mr Selwyn Vauville regarded Mrs Sheraton with a good deal of rancour, "I cannot help but blame you for our present predicament. I feel like the spectre at the feast. I shall not forget this in a hurry. Oh, dear God, here comes Babyngton!"

Mr Tom Babyngton stepped up to their awkward party with undisguised embarrassment; he only knew them by sight and unfortunately, reputation, but realised that, having so carelessly put his foot in his mouth, he had to somehow make up for his mistake, so he had taken it upon himself to shepherd them into the midst of the gathering so that they didn't just lurk on the periphery making everyone feel damned uncomfortable.

"Mrs Sheraton, if you and Sir Leonard and Mr Vauville would care to come and sit down, I will see that you are brought some champagne and food," and with an extravagant flourish he gestured towards one of the rugs set out on the grass. Mrs Sheraton and Sir Leonard exchanged a meaningful glance and reluctantly followed him.

"This is entirely your fault!" hissed Sir Leonard, "I cannot sit on the ground in this coat! It's made of the very finest French satin for heaven's sake!"

Mrs Sheraton laughed unkindly and lowered herself onto the cushions with great aplomb. Sir Leonard was poised for flight, his face turning an unattractive shade of purple.

"Oh, just sit down! You're making a spectacle of yourself, Leonard. I need you to help reel in that rather taking little thing. I can see she's not very happy with her lot, which will make her all the riper for picking. I can see that Selwyn has his eye on her already. A coupling made in heaven!"

"She has a certain air about her," mused Selwyn Vauville, "Plebeian through and through and yet desperately yearning to be one of us. How far would she go to be accepted into the upper circles I wonder?" He was watching the girl's greedy eyes and letting his imagination run away with him. He had so many plans for her future.

"Selwyn! Your degeneracy is showing. You need champagne. Leonard, *sit!*" snapped Mrs Sheraton.

He sat as though propelled by an invisible hand, but every line of his outraged body spoke of his feelings of strong revulsion.

Sephie sat down beside Miss Bell, because that's where she felt safest. Lady Kitty was still in a fearful temper and was likely to explode at any moment if anything should dare go awry. She had no desire to be anywhere near That Awful Woman and her cohorts in case they turned their vitriolic tongues upon her, a thought which made her go quite cold with fear. Sir Anthony was very sweet, but he and Lord Frederick Knoyll were too busy competing for Biddy's attention and Mr Tom Babyngton was engaged in trying to make amends for his *faux pas*. She didn't know Sir Ambrose well enough to attach herself to him, although he did look very benign and humorous, if a little distracted. So, that left Miss Bell and Lord Rokewode, oh, and that nice Sir Leander Gage, who had a kind face and intelligent eyes. He was not above average height, wiry and agile, with light brown wavy hair, cut short and artfully arranged in the latest style and he had a ready smile which made Sephie think he was probably a very trustworthy gentleman.

Miss Bell leant forward and asked if she was all right. Sephie nodded and gave her a look which spoke volumes.

"Indeed, my dear, indeed! What a to-do! For a moment I truly thought that Lord Rokewode would blow his top, but he managed to regain his composure quite handsomely. It must have been very hard for him though. What a t*errible* woman. Can you believe her effrontery? Of course, she must have somehow found out he would be coming here today and arranged to "bump into" him. It is extremely unlikely that this was an accident; the Park is so enormous — it would take a small miracle to find anyone on the off chance. No, she must have an informer. Oh, my word, I just thought, you *do* know who she is, do you not?"

Sephie shook her head and shrugged.

"Goodness. Well, I suppose you ought to know. Forewarned is forearmed." She leant a little closer, "She is notorious in some circles — she has quite a chequered past flitting from one nobleman to the next, trying to find a rich enough taker. Finally, she seems to have settled — upon, I'm sorry to say, Lord Rokewode!"

Sephie put a hand to her mouth and her eyes opened wide.

"Yes, I *know!* It's hard to believe, is it not? I must say, having finally met her I am disappointed in him, I thought he had more sense. She's quite clearly, what I would call a fair Cyprian. She is utterly shameless and is angling for the highest title and the deepest pockets. Something seems to have upset her equilibrium and she's come to examine the lie of the land. I expect she heard about new guests arriving at Grosvenor Square and was alarmed by the descriptions of you both."

Sephie smiled and tapped Miss Bell on the back of her hand, shaking her head and wagging her finger very expressively. Miss Bell laughed, "You're certainly not a vain girl, I must say! Which makes a pleasant change. Vanity is the root of so many problems. You see Mrs Sheraton there, once a great beauty, the world at her feet — now she must always fight to remain so and as the years take their toll, she will become ever more desperate to cling onto her youth and therefore anyone who is younger and more beautiful is bound to come under close scrutiny. She sees Miss Pippin as competition for Lord Rokewode. And then, there is Miss Pippin herself, who will come to rely upon her pretty face to get her what she wants in life and she has the conceit of extreme youth and cannot believe that she will ever fall prey to ageing herself so has little sympathy for those who have. Without constant approbation she feels worthless and unloved. That makes her an unreliable friend, no, don't look like that! I'm sure she's been as kind as she can be to you, but you see, you're not any danger to her ambitions. I think she's genuinely fond of you, but I feel compelled to urge you to not rely upon her too much. Oh, dear, how I do go on! My father would say that I was a gab-monster! What I would say is that you need to choose your friends wisely. Now, where is your champagne?"

Miss Bell caught Rokewode's eye and he came immediately to see what she needed. With no compunction at all she sent him off to find champagne and a plate of food. Sephie thought she'd rather have lemonade but didn't care to try to make that understood. Sometimes making herself understood was just too difficult so she was inclined to accept whatever was offered without complaint. It could occasionally make things rather awkward. After a few minutes, Rokewode returned with a glass of champagne and a plate piled high with delicious things: beef and duck, eggs and cheese, cucumber and lettuce and tomatoes and tiny pastry pies. Sephie raised her eyebrows.

Rokewode laughed, "A man sized portion? I'm afraid that was inevitable. Eat what you can. It'll do you good. And there's cake and jelly and trifle to follow which I am certain will be very much to your liking!"

Everyone was tucking into their meal, some with gusto and some with an appearance of delicacy and good manners. Miss Pippin was feeling far more satisfied with matters; Sir Anthony had not left her side and Freddie Knoyll seemed determined to keep her amused. She had noted, with some dissatisfaction, that Sir Leander Gage was not yet a dedicated follower and had drifted over to where Sephie was sitting with that dull Miss Bell. Lord Rokewode was also there and pouring Sephie yet another glass of champagne! She wondered why Sir Leander

Gage was not one of her admirers; he just didn't seem interested in her and wasn't prepared to hang on her every word. This, naturally, made Miss Pippin very determined indeed to engage his interest just to prove a point. She didn't like to fail and although, at first, he had not been flamboyant or wealthy enough to attract her, she now saw him as something of a challenge — she would conquer both Sir Leander and Lord Rokewode!

Sir Leander Gage, at that very moment, was thinking what a cake Anthony was making of himself; never one to be shy of acting the fool, he was fawning over Miss Pippin with no thought of dignity or suitability. Sir Leander, had Miss Pippin but known it, was not only exceedingly wealthy but also very conventional. He came from a long and illustrious line of extremely dignified and strait-laced ancestors, who looked down upon him from their magnificent portraits with opprobrium. He had always felt he had a lot to live up to and consequently tended to be rather stiff-necked and had little time for those he considered irresponsible or immoral. He had never been impetuous in his entire life, it wasn't in his nature, he was cautious and thoughtful, and he found people with too much energy fatiguing. He liked Miss Fane because she was peaceful, but it wasn't just because she had no voice, it was that she had a gentle spirit. She reminded him of Matilda, he thought wistfully. Miss Matilda Fleete. He sighed. If only he *had* been more — impetuous. If only —

He saw that Miss Fane was observing him from her lively grey eyes. She cocked her head to one side like a sparrow and he knew it was a question.

"Ah, just reflecting on regrets," he said.

Her head cocked a little further.

"First love. Opportunities wasted. Love lost. You know the old story!"

She shook her head and patted the rug next to her. He obediently sat beside her, and she rearranged herself so that she was facing him and waited.

"Miss Matilda Fleete. She lives in the village near our family estate in Oxfordshire. Her father is the parson, an excellent man. As children we became friends with a shared love of books and wildlife. We would spend our days wandering in the woods looking for woodpeckers or squirrels and comparing notes on ornithology books. We were very similar in character. We were wild to a fault and often up to our ears in some mischief or another, but I was always steady and reliable and sensible. My mother used to say, "an old head on young shoulders". I'm fairly certain that she didn't mean it as a compliment! Anyway, inevitably we grew up and grew apart because I went to Eton and Oxford and then came here. She stayed in the parsonage. She wrote to me several times, but I didn't respond. I don't know, Miss Fane, I don't *know!* And now I hear from a mutual friend that she's engaged to be married. I thought at first that I was happy for her but as the weeks have passed, I've decided that I'm *not* happy at all. In fact, I am decidedly *unhappy*. Naturally, I realise that I have only myself to blame and that there's nothing to be done. I must just learn to live with the consequences of my inertia. It is a salutary lesson."

Sephie put a hand on his arm and then mimed writing.

"I fear it's too late, Miss Fane. She is betrothed to, of all people, Adam Gibbs. *Adam Gibbs!* A prosier, more stupefying, vacuous, irksome fellow you could ever wish to meet! I cannot see how she could ever have settled for him. It makes no sense."

It made sense to Sephie. She could see that Miss Fleete had waited for word from Sir Leander and when none came, she had patiently waited some more but eventually accepted the first proposal she received after she'd given up all hope of Sir Leander coming up to scratch.

"I wish you could tell me what you're thinking," murmured Sir Leander, watching her face, "I feel sure that it would be very comforting and wise."

She lowered her eyes, took a breath and then poked an accusing bandaged finger into his chest.

"Oh," he said with a wry smile, "Perhaps *not* so comforting! You think the fault is mine? Yes, sadly, I do too."

There was suddenly an explosion of raucous laughter from their uninvited guests and everyone turned to look at them. It shattered the tranquillity of the afternoon and woke everyone up from their pleasant trancelike states.

It stirred Mr Tom Babyngton to decide it was about time for a bit of a change and he stood up and coughed loudly to draw everyone's attention, "Um, ladies and gentlemen, I was wondering if a little entertainment might be on the cards. We recently had the privilege of hearing the most sensational singer and I was thinking that with a little gentle encouragement she might be persuaded to sing for us again this afternoon! Miss Biddy Pippin, what do you say?"

Sephie glanced quickly across at her friend, her heart in her mouth. Oh, no! *Biddy!* What could she do to avert this catastrophe?

Eight

Miss Bell saw the consternation this unexpected announcement caused and didn't panic, which is what had made her such a very good nanny in the first place. She observed Miss Pippin turn first pale and then flush scarlet and knew something was grievously amiss.

Miss Pippin swallowed nervously; her mouth had gone dry and every sensible thought had fled her mind.

"I — I would really rather not, thank you. I'm sure nobody wants to — " she faltered.

"Oh, *do* sing for us, Miss Pippin!"

"Yes, *do!* She sings like an angel!" declared Babyngton with unbridled enthusiasm. "You simply must hear her!"

Miss Pippin, sensing no cessation to the demands, stood up suddenly, her plate falling unheeded to the ground, she put out a hand as though to stop the clamouring and burst into tears.

At exactly this moment Miss Bell started to choke, as though she had something caught in her throat, she waved her hands frantically and people began to run around looking for a glass of water and a fan to cool her down. Lord Rokewode muttered to her under his breath, "Well done, you wily creature!" She winked at him and continued to cough theatrically.

Meanwhile, Sephie had leapt to her feet and dashed to her friend's side; she put her arms about her and led her away from all the commotion. She found a spot behind a tangle of elms and tried to calm Biddy down. She stroked her back and made *shushushing* sounds. Biddy's sobbing was loud to start with but after a while quietened to childish hiccupping. She was quivering with fright and every few seconds seemed to convulse with cold shivers.

"Oh, — *Seph* — ie! I — didn't know what to — *do!* They would have — found *out!*" she buried her face in her hands, "I cannot — *bear* it! I can't go back now! They — must think me — such — a fool!"

Sephie shook her head vehemently and gave Biddy a little shake.

"I cried in —*front*— of them! Oh, what if they — ?" Biddy whispered.

Sephie frowned at her and mimed closing her mouth and locking it with a key.

Biddy smiled wanly, "I know — you wouldn't tell. You can't! But what if they *made* me — sing? Then the truth would be — out." Tears began to fall again, "They'd discover — that I *can't* sing! I'm just a fraud! Oh, Sephie! They might guess it was — *you!*"

Sephie was anguished and didn't know what to do. She just kept shaking her head as though denial would stop the truth from coming out.

"They mustn't find out. They must *never* find out! I don't want to be just a pretty face. I want them to adore me for my talents! Wearing a fish tail is not a *talent*. Being pretty is not a talent. Oh, why is it *you* that has such a heavenly voice? It should be *me!* It's so *unfair. Why* can you sing so beautifully when you can't *speak?* It doesn't make any sense. Nobody would believe such a voice would come from you. Oh, sorry, Sephie, that sounded mean. I don't intend to be unkind, sometimes my tongue runs away with me. Please forgive me."

Sephie embraced her friend warmly and holding her face between her shaking hands, she kissed her cheek.

"You're too good Persephone — no-one would ever suspect you were a foundling. Oh, there I go again! Honestly, I could cut my tongue out sometimes!"

She peered out from behind the tree trunk towards their odd encampment and saw that most of the guests were standing and talking together earnestly. Miss Bell was being fanned by Lady Kitty and Lord Rokewode was helpfully patting her back.

"What shall we do now? Can we run away?"

Sephie shook her head and stuck her chin very firmly in the air and then with a flick of her finger she pushed Biddy's chin up too and nodded.

"We just pretend all is well?"

Sephie pointed to Biddy's throat and coughed in a deliberately pathetic fashion.

"We — tell them I've lost my — singing voice?" Her face lit up as Sephie wafted her hand to and fro in the air, "Oh, because of the *smoke?* That's brilliant! You're so clever! What would I do without you?"

Sephie smiled and they linked arms and together strolled in a carefree manner back to the picnic.

Having quickly regained her confidence, Miss Pippin, made a short speech in which she apologised for allowing her distress to overwhelm her, and then explained that due to inhaling the smoke from the fire at the fair, she had lost her singing voice. She added that she was hoping with time it would return. There was a little round of appreciative applause and then it was all forgotten.

By everyone apart from Miss Bell, who had been keenly observing their faces and knew that Miss Pippin and Sephie were lying.

A great show was made of the fancy desserts as it was clear a lot of trouble had gone into the intricate fashioning of them. Sephie was enchanted by the bright colours and decorations. Sir Leander Gage laughed at her blatant enjoyment and with the help of a footman, dished out a large helping of all the puddings. Having a very sweet tooth, she savoured every mouthful with her eyes blissfully closed. Lady Kitty nudged her brother in the ribs and pointed out Sephie's reaction and he smiled, thinking that it was sometimes as though Miss Persephone had very little experience of things others thought merely commonplace. As though she had not been in the world for long enough to become familiar with the perfectly ordinary. He frowned and wondered what her life had been like working for a disreputable drunkard in a fairground booth. It couldn't have been much fun. He would enquire into Mr Henry Pippin's whereabouts, he wanted to make sure that he was no longer a threat to the girls or anyone else. As soon as things had returned to normal, he would contact Constable Thursby again and see if there had been any further developments. He wasn't keen on the uncertainty. There must be a reason why the man had wanted to disappear so completely and going by what he had already gleaned, he was convinced that it would not be a good reason.

Mrs Sheraton was thoroughly enjoying herself. She had always taken great delight in other people's discomfort; the day was turning out to be even more entertaining than she'd hoped. It had been like attending the theatre to see a farce! Some of the actors had been outstanding in their roles and the plot was interestingly convoluted. She was tempted to throw bouquets at the stage! She could see that with a little tweak here or there that she could make things a good deal worse too, which was a satisfying notion. Miss Pippin was a perfect example of someone who was so desperate for acceptance that she would be open to any kind of suggestion however outrageous; one would only have to appeal to her worst nature in a subtle and convincing manner and she would be a useful weapon in her bid to become the next Countess of Rokewode. She knew that it was going to take a while and some vigorous cajoling to bring Rokewode about again, but she had complete faith in her powers to win anyone around given time. He had already shown that he was much enamoured of her, the jewellery, the gowns, that phaeton Leonard was driving! All gifts that showed the depths of his devotion. But she also understood that he liked things done a certain way; one must never give any hint of pride or avarice, and he could not abide deceit — that would always be the death blow. She had seen those who tried to dupe him or lied to him in order to profit from it; they had been cut loose and jettisoned without hesitation. She did not plan to be one of those unfortunate fools; she'd gradually learnt how to manipulate him almost without detection and had proved her worth in many ways. She just had to be very careful not to let her ambition and desires cloud her judgement. As a rule, her instincts were sound and even if, as they had today, they went a little astray, then she would just strive harder to right the ship.

She could see that things were about to deteriorate as Leonard was spoiling for a fight and Selwyn was plotting to storm Miss Pippin's citadel, although she was fairly sure that her citadel had already been stormed at some point. Miss Pippin did not have the look about her of a girl who was without experience; she may play at being the innocent, but Mrs Sheraton had seen the signs which told her a different story. Miss Pippin was a clever, controlling and devious girl and she thought they would deal very well together once she had won her over to her side.

But for now, she had had enough, and she gave a signal to Leonard and Selwyn and they said their farewells to their reluctant hosts. They shook hands and bowed and kissed reluctant cheeks and then left as quickly as they could. Being Machiavellian was exhilarating but being charming and well-behaved was exhausting — she needed to rest.

"Damn it, Margaret! Have you taken leave of your senses? He will never forgive you for that!" exclaimed Selwyn furiously.

She sneered, glad at last to be herself, and allowed him to assist her up onto Satanas, "Yes, he will, eventually. Oh, I know he'll be angry for a while but that will just make him think about me and he won't be able to think about me without wanting me! I know exactly what I'm doing."

"Well, you know I hate to be pedantic, but my coat is *ruined*, beyond repair," said Leonard mournfully, as he climbed into the phaeton and picked up his whip.

"Oh, a pox on your stupid green coat, Leonard! It makes you look like a frog anyway! I cannot believe you paid money for that hideous rag!" snapped Selwyn.

"I didn't. I owe my tailor hundreds of guineas but he don't mind because I'm such a good advertisement for his work."

Selwyn guffawed, "Seeing that coat I would be certain to shop — *elsewhere!*"

"You're hardly a recommendation for *your* tailor! Wrinkled breeches, puckered waistcoat and ill-fitting coat! Is your tailor a one-armed blind man?"

"Stop bickering! When I'm the Countess of Rokewode, I shall be able to buy you any number of slime-green coats! I'm without a feather to fly with and I'm sick of it. You must be patient. In the meantime, I have some of his jewellery we can pawn, and he'll never notice. He must never suspect that we're in desperate need of his fortune or else he might start to become suspicious. I've been pondering while you two have been fretting about your coat and lusting after virgins; I have a new plan. It may sound a bit drastic, but I think we need to cut away at his foundations, make him less secure and then he will need me even more."

"And your plan is — ?"

"It involves building on today's revelations."

"I didn't hear any revelations!" said Selwyn with a frown.

"Did you not? Well, you must pay more attention, my dear. We'll need all the ammunition we can lay our hands on. Lord Rokewode has weaknesses which make him vulnerable. He loves his family. That is a fatal mistake. He's loyal. That is a mistake. He despises liars and cheats. Oh, *dear!* And he would never dishonour his family name. And so, we have a veritable gold mine. Once we're married, I know how to keep him happy. I'm not stupid. My husbands didn't leave me, they *died!*"

Leonard sent her a sly sideways glance, "Yes, but *how* did they die, that is the question on everyone's lips!"

Mrs Sheraton looked affronted and then laughed, "Darling, at least they died with smiles on their faces!" And she dug her heels into Satanas's flanks and galloped away, her laughter floating out behind her like a pennant.

* * *

"Thank God! I thought they'd never leave," said Lady Kitty, flinging herself back down onto the ground and reaching for a fruit turnover, "What a fiasco! Thank you, Miss Edie! Your intervention was masterful. You actually managed to turn a terrifying shade of purple — it was a *tour-de-force!*"

Miss Bell waved away the praise, "No, no! It was nothing at all. I just held my breath for a while until I felt myself become a little faint."

"Our very own Sarah Siddons!" remarked Rokewode and patted her shoulder fondly.

"Oh, I hardly think so," she demurred, but rather gratified by all the praise.

Mr Tom Babyngton raised his glass to her, "Dear Miss Bell, we salute you! For saving the day! And, for my part, I wish to apologise for being so birdwitted. As you are all probably aware, I'm not blessed with the quickest brain but dash it, I really made a mull of things today."

"Do you know what, Tom? I wouldn't have had it any other way, it opened my eyes to a few things which needed closer scrutiny. It will be, in the end, rather beneficial, although you are an utter dolt sometimes!"

Babyngton mumbled another apology but Sir Anthony slapped him heartily on his back and told him to buck up!

"And thank you Miss Persephone, for watching over us all and offering support wherever you could," added Rokewode, raising his glass.

Sephie blushed and frowned at him, unhappy at being singled out for praise.

Miss Pippin wondered when someone would toast *her*. She thought it jolly unfair that the two dullest people there had been complimented for doing so very little.

For a while, in order to recover from the trials and tribulations, they wandered idly in the meadow and lolled on the rugs and chatted in a desultory manner about everyday things; they finished the champagne and nibbled on the leftovers. The evening was still warm, the sun just easing down the sky and casting a golden glow across the park. They could hear cowbells in the distance and the cowherds calling their cattle in and somewhere the last few moments of a cricket match before the light faded and Sir Anthony, Sir Leander and Freddie Knoyll volunteered to go to the Cake House and purchase a tray of their delicious syllabubs and cheesecakes. Sephie's eyes gleamed at the thought and she watched them stroll off across the meadow and cross the rustic little bridge to reach the well-known shop. Not long afterwards they returned triumphant, bearing trays loaded with puddings and frothy drinks. Sephie couldn't help herself — she leapt up and skipped across the grass to see what they'd brought.

Cheesecake! Sephie sank her teeth into the delicious concoction, sighed with happiness, licked her lips and then took a big gulp of the syllabub. Her eyes opened wide — it was extremely alcoholic. She choked and went bright pink.

Sir Leander patted her on the back, "Not you as well! Dear me! What a day. Are you all right? Too much wine in it?"

She nodded, trying to catch her breath.

Then, for some reason, perhaps because of the relief of everything returning to normal, after the awkward tension of the afternoon, they started to smile at each other for no particular reason and the smiles turned to laughter. Sephie looked around at them and grinned — the sound was so delightful, she wanted to remember it forever. Lady Kitty fell backwards onto the rug and giggled helplessly, while her adoring husband smiled down at her and Sir Anthony hooted and slapped his thigh merrily. Miss Pippin couldn't think what was happening and thought they'd all gone quite mad — she'd had a *terrible* day, and nobody seemed to care. Lord Rokewode shook his head, the laughter lines deepening around his eyes and Miss Bell chuckled quietly. Freddie Knoyll punched Tom Babyngton in the arm and told him he was a jingle-brained nincompoop which made Babyngton give a loud snort of laughter and it set everyone off again.

On the way home, Sephie sank back into the soft upholstery in the carriage and sighed with sheer contentment. It had been a day of contrasts, ups and downs and pleasure and pain. But it had been the best day of her life. Whatever happened in the future, she would always remember it. It would sustain her in the empty years to come after her deception had been discovered, after everyone found out that she was a liar and a fraud and shunned her.

"A penny for your thoughts, Miss Fane," said Lord Rokewode.

She glanced up at him, surprised out of her forlorn reverie and smiled a little wanly.

"Still thinking about the cheesecake?"

She nodded happily.

"It has been a most interesting and testing day. Thank you for your part in calming things down. No, don't glare! I mean it. You were indeed like a soothing balm. It's a rare gift to be able to see what people need. I don't think I've ever witnessed Leander open his heart to anyone before. He is generally a closed book. Renowned for his famous put-downs but mostly avoided in case one gets one's head bitten off for trying to meddle."

Sephie pointed to her heart and mimed something breaking in two with her still-bandaged hands.

Rokewode nodded thoughtfully, "I thought as much. Miss Matilda Fleete? Ah, poor Leander. One only realises what one has when it is lost. We shall have to help him come about. I wonder, are all his hopes for reuniting with Matilda truly crushed?"

Sephie stared into the distance for a moment and then her eyes lit up and she shook her head and held up a small, but knowledgeable finger.

Rokewode raised his eyebrows, "You have an idea? Yes. All right, I have an idea as well. In my mother's house, I will find a dip pen and some paper, and you can tell me all about *your* idea. Do you think that might work? Good. Then we shall see what we can do." He considered her for a moment, her face slightly turned away as she watched the world go by with a slightly faraway expression. Something was troubling her.

"Then, perhaps you could write some of your story down for me? I'd be most interested to see how you came to be at Bartholomew Fair. It seems an unspeakable place for a young girl to end up." She continued to contemplate the fashionable people parading along the street and the phaetons and gigs dashing to and fro as though in a daze. "You can trust me," he said softly, only just audible above the sound of the carriage wheels.

She peeped up at him, her lips compressed into a tight little line as though to keep any emotion at bay. She made a slight shrug. But, she thought, you can't trust *me*. One day you will find out and then you will want to have nothing more to do with me and that day will be the worst day of my life.

"Of course, you don't have to. I just thought you might like to explain the reasons you became embroiled with such a reprobate as Henry Pippin. I can see that Miss Pippin had no choice in the matter but you're not his daughter."

Ladies in enormous feathery confections, gentlemen in skin-tight pantaloons, fluttering fans and jostling city-folk, beggars and harlots, street-sellers carrying their wares and calling out in loud voices, stray dogs darting between the swishing skirts and buckled shoes — all passed Sephie by, she saw none of it. Her mind was elsewhere. No, I was *not* his daughter, he made that quite clear when he tried — no, I will not think about that! I must try and extricate us from this spider's web of deceit. Oh, what will he think when he finds out! They have all been so good to us. I cannot bear to deceive them. Perhaps if I told them the truth — ? No, they could never forgive me. They would throw me out and where would I go? Back to the fair? A tear slid down her cheek and she impatiently brushed it away.

"Good God! Sephie! I had no wish to upset you! I'm so sorry. You don't have to tell me anything if you don't want to. I just thought — "

Lady Kitty, seeing her brother floundering, decided it was time to step in.

"Nearly home! I cannot wait to climb into my bed. I am absolutely *exhausted*. Dead on my feet. All that fresh air, it's really not good for one. Sephie, you should have used a parasol, I fear your nose is dreadfully sunburnt! I hope it doesn't freckle! I have some very good lotion to get rid of freckles which I will lend you. It contains Buttermilk, Almond Oil and Lemon. It is very beneficial to the skin. Maria Wingfield swears by it."

"She's about a hundred and ten years old!" announced Rokewode in disgust, "Sephie doesn't need freckle remover, she has perfect skin. A few freckles won't spoil it."

"I'll have you know that Maria Wingfield is thirty-four!"

"Well, that just goes to show that beauty lotions don't work! Leave Sephie's face alone!"

Sephie, listening to this exchange, felt a traitorous glow somewhere inside her chest. She tried to squash it, but it just grew. On the one hand she knew she had to leave before the truth came out and on the other, *she had perfect skin!* And Lady Kitty was going to lend her some of her very own lotion! Just as though she were a member of her family. A daughter or a sister. It was like a dream. And Lord Rokewode had unwittingly called her Sephie instead of that rather stiff "Miss Fane", which wasn't her name anyway. Her given name sounded so pretty when he said it. But she would still have to leave. She and Biddy had to remember that they couldn't get used to living in Grosvenor Square. It was impossible. For Sephie, it was already too late. Her heart had found a home.

Nine

Sephie chewed the end of the pen and gazed out of the window onto the square. It was raining and there was a slight chill in the air. She'd wrapped the pink shawl Lady Kitty had given her around her shoulders and was sitting in the library at the desk, some daunting sheets of paper in front of her and the pen. Paston had lit the fire and the room was warming up a bit but Sephie still felt strangely cold.

The night before they had all retired to bed in such a state of exhaustion that nothing more had been said about the day's strange and wonderful events. Lord Rokewode had escorted Sir Anthony and Lord Knoyll back to their separate abodes and then continued on to his house in St James's Square and had not yet turned up at Grosvenor Square. Sephie had woken up early, filled with a sense of bubbling excitement which she was unable to understand. She'd dressed with special care and raced downstairs but everyone was still in bed recovering from the previous day's exertions so there was nobody to talk to. She'd read a book for a while but then was so cold, she'd had to go and find her new shawl and ask Paston to light the fire. She'd then decided to write down her ideas to help Sir Leander with his broken heart. But once faced with a pen and the blank sheets of paper, her mind had emptied. She'd been sitting chewing the pen for half an hour and nothing at all had come to her. All she could think of was how *someone* thought she had perfect skin and she kept picturing a certain pair of hazel eyes glinting gold in the sunlight.

She carefully wrote the date and the address on the top of the page in her painstakingly neat script.

Then she sat and stared for a while longer.

She got up and took a turn about the room. She put some more coal on the fire. She examined the books on the shelves. She looked out of the window and watched an elderly lady teeter past on her pattens, being dragged along by a large mastiff. She tried to see her reflection in the window. She was wearing a new silver-grey gown with a striped muslin petticoat and Ann had put a pretty pink bandeau in her hair and the shawl looked becoming with the whole. She thought she looked almost passable.

She returned to the desk and picked up the pen again. She tried to put herself in Miss Matilda Fleete's shoes. Matilda had been best friends with Sir Leander, and they'd spent their childhood in each other's pockets. They knew each other well, perhaps too well. If Sir Leander had ever thought about Miss Fleete, it would have been as a playmate, a sister almost and when they grew up there would have eventually come an awkwardness; as children they could do anything they liked but as adults they would have been expected to behave with propriety. It would have changed the ease with which they were able to engage with each other. Suddenly, they were no longer just friends they were potential lovers and there would have been talk of chaperones and plans for the future and Sir Leander would have become skittish and bolted before he had even thought the whole thing through. And then it was only when he heard Miss Fleete had chosen someone else that he'd remembered the easy amiability of their early years and realised, too late, that his feelings for her had gone deeper than just friendship. Sephie knew too that Miss Fleete had only finally taken umbrage when he had not answered her letters and in a fit of understandable pique had taken the first offer available. She didn't love the terrible Adam Gibbs. (Although she only had Sir Leander's word for it that he *was* terrible.) Miss Fleete probably didn't even like him, but she wanted revenge, she wanted to make Sir Leander sorry for appearing to forget her. Which was entirely understandable if a little drastic and self-destructive. And permanent, if she couldn't be prevented from taking such a rash step. Two, no *three* lives would be ruined.

Sephie chewed on the end of the pen again and watched the early morning traffic trundling past the window; milk carts and waggons loaded with hay for all the stables, a flock of shorn sheep and an angry man chasing a muscular and mean-looking dog with a large side of meat clamped firmly in its jaws. It was as though the whole world had to come through the square. They all had lives elsewhere, wives and children, husbands and reasons for getting up in the morning and someone to go to bed with at night.

In a clattering of hooves, a smart curricle drew up outside the house. Sephie stood up and watched, her heart thumping a little too enthusiastically in her chest.

A groom appeared from nowhere and dashed to the horse's heads and Lord Rokewode jumped down from the driving seat, with easy athleticism. Sephie flew back into her chair and arranged her skirts and patted her hair into place.

She heard the front door being answered by Paston and held her breath. Then, she heard his light tread going up the stairs and she slumped back into the chair, feeling foolishly deflated.

Lord Rokewode tapped on his mother's bedchamber door and let himself in on her command.

The Dowager Countess was lying in her bed still, wearing a very becoming lace nightcap, attended by her lady's maid (whom she immediately dismissed), and sipping hot chocolate while looking at some fashion plates spread out on the counterpane in front of her. She saw her son and her face lit up and then she recalled that she still was out of humour with him and she lowered her brows quickly.

"Oh, Mama! Must we fight? I need your advice," he said in cajoling tones.

She pursed her lips, "Advice? What advice could you possibly want from your poor unfortunate, much-neglected mother?"

He smiled tolerantly, "I will always need your advice. I cannot do without your sound good sense."

"Oh, now I *know* you are bamming me! Really, Theo, you are such a wheedler."

He sat down on the edge of the bed and helped himself to one of the bread rolls from her breakfast tray.

"I learnt it from the best!"

"I *never* wheedle!" she protested without much conviction. "What advice?"

He spread a little butter on his roll and stretched out his long legs, "I'm in a bit of a fix, Mama."

"Oh, please tell me it's not That Awful Woman!" demanded Lady Rokewode, wrinkling her nose with distaste.

"Mrs Sheraton? No, it's not. But, while we're on the subject, I don't want you to lose sleep over her — there's no need, I promise. No, it's partly the problem of Tony and the increasing violence of his passion for Miss Pippin and partly what to do with our unexpected houseguests. I'm afraid there's trouble coming when Miss Pippin's father is traced — he sounds to me to be an extremely shady character. And I get the distinct feeling that the girls are being rather economical with the truth. You probably haven't had the chance to observe her at close quarters yet but Sephie is not good at hiding her feelings; her face is far too expressive for her own good She gives a good deal away without knowing it. Miss Pippin, however, is quite adept at concealment. Something peculiar happened yesterday at the picnic which threw them both into a quandary, and I cannot help but think that they're supporting each other in some kind of deception. I don't know yet what it involves but I will find out before long. I was also wondering if you had any advice about Tony — you've known him since he was a small boy. I have no wish for him to become a victim of some designing female, if I can prevent it; he is too trusting and has always been far too easily duped."

His Mama was delighted to be trusted with this confidence and felt at last her beloved son was making some kind of headway. "It's probably not very helpful advice, I'm afraid, but my experience with all the young people I have ever known tells me that the moment you say they mustn't do something, they will yearn to do it all the more. My suggestion would be that you should push them together at every opportunity! There is then a chance that she will, in an unguarded moment, let her mask slip and he'll see who she really is. And he will eventually tire of her if she becomes a mere commonplace and the magic and the mystery are removed. Of course, you could always help that along by showing a discreet interest in her yourself — a tiny bit duplicitous but it might set the seal on the matter. I believe if given the choice between a Baronet and an Earl, she will more than likely show her true colours. Although it goes without saying that nothing can come of such an attachment. On the other matter, of what to do with them? I'm perfectly content for them to stay here; it's considerably enlivened the house and I rather like that quiet little creature and it's brought Kitty to our door, which is a blessing in disguise because we don't see nearly enough of her now that she's buried in some Kentish backwater."

"There, Mama, I knew you would have an answer. I'm pleased that Kitty can use this as a reason to descend upon you. However, please do make sure you send all accounts to me and I'll see that they're paid. The costs are not to come out of your pocket. This is entirely my doing; I should have tried harder to stop Tony dashing off on another of his ridiculous capers. I might have known it would end in disaster — they nearly always do! I cannot think what to do with our guests in the long run anyway; one cannot send them back to the fair or allow Henry Pippin to take charge of them again and the only other recourse would be some kind of workhouse, which, of course, I cannot countenance. No, I am very much afraid we are responsible for their welfare until we can find suitable positions for them."

Lady Clara Rokewode put her cup down and looked at her son in some astonishment, "Positions? You cannot expect them to become governesses or companions, surely? Miss Pippin? As a *governess?* Imagine the trouble she would cause! No respectable lady would employ her! Not if they had any sense. And who would employ a mute? Oh, I'm sorry, but we must face facts! Miss Fane could possibly become a seamstress? A cook? Some occupation where she is not required to speak. Theo, darling, it's going to be a gargantuan task to see these girls safely settled. I hope you know what you're taking on! So many complications and puzzles," she smiled at him, "It's really rather *entertaining!* I hadn't realised just how bored I'd become. Theo, you're putting crumbs all over my bed!"

Her son chuckled unrepentantly and leant over to kiss her cheek, "I have been very badly brought up!" Then he became serious, "But, Mama, do not fret about anything, I have it all in hand, I swear."

She patted his hand and brushed the crumbs from her counterpane, "I know dear. You are so very like your father."

"Oh, do not say so! I would much rather be like you. He was so — demanding and never satisfied no matter how hard you strove to please him. And intolerant. And *proud!*"

His mother said nothing but studiously sipped her chocolate.

"Dear God, Mama! You're not serious, surely!" he laughed but then suddenly stopped, "He was *impossible!*"

"Yes, dear, he was but I loved him despite that."

"Well, that's certainly an unexpected facer!" He lifted her hand to his lips and kissed it, "Thank you, I think! I will attempt to be a better son and brother and friend although I cannot promise any miracles!"

* * *

Sephie had just given up all hope and relaxed when the door opened to admit Lord Rokewode.

She couldn't help it; she blushed furiously and kept her head turned away hoping the telltale colour would abate before he saw it and thought it was because of him.

"Good morning, Sephie! You are up and about early. A most unusual occurrence in this household; in fact, unheard of! You're writing letters?"

She turned to greet him with a warm smile, knowing her colour was still a little high. She shook her head and gestured to the paper on the desk in front of her and shrugged.

He approached, "Ah, I see. Ideas? Can I see?" She nodded and handed him the sheet of paper.

How interesting, he thought, observing her carefully formed lettering; she writes like a child, no flourishes or ornamental loops, just plain and ordinary, as though she were still practising her letters with chalk on a slate. He wondered if it was the bandages hampering her movement.

He read what she'd written, "I see. And how do you propose to bring about this wondrous scheme?" he raised an eyebrow, "It's going to be hard to engineer. Although, I believe if we can somehow find a way, that you could be right; jealousy can certainly be life-altering."

To her dismay the colour crept back into her cheeks, but she had no choice but to ignore it and taking the paper back from him, she wrote again. He came and stood next to her and looked over her shoulder.

"An expedition? Indeed? Well, that would certainly shake things up. Where does — ? Leander's estate is in Oxfordshire. Which is about two days away, by post-chaise, depending upon the weather, of course. He has a very impressive place, bordering a good-sized river; Fairtree Manor, fifteenth century. Nice little village, church, good land. And you'll be very relieved to hear, a simply splendid ballroom. Does that make you happy? Yes, I thought it might. So, we escape London and make our own entertainment in the wilds of Oxfordshire? Highly irregular I must say but I'm starting to suspect that you are rather, shall we say, unconventional?" He watched her face change from interested to concerned. "I mean that as a compliment, Sephie! Ah, and there I go calling you by your nickname again, Miss Fane."

She wagged a disapproving finger at him, her brows knitted together.

"Sephie? All right. As long as you think of me as Theo. Is that fair?"

She nodded eagerly. It sounded like heaven to her.

"A Christmas Ball it is then. I suppose we really should warn Leander as it's his house — it may come as a bit of a shock! As you may have guessed, he's not much given to holding social gatherings. Half a dozen friends in a room is about his limit. Crowds make him as cross as a bear. Have you ever been to a Ball, Sephie?"

She shook her head and beamed at him.

"Well, you and Miss Pippin had better start planning your gowns and anything else you'll need for the adventure. I know how long that can take. You had better start thinking about feathers and such things. Ah, here is Miss Bell! Come to chaperone us, dear Miss Edie?"

Miss Bell practically flew into the room, her shawl fluttering and her face rather pink from the headlong dash downstairs.

"Oh, my lord, you are such a tease! I'm just come to make sure that all is well, having heard that you were here at such an early hour. I hope nothing is amiss?"

He cast a mischievous glance at Sephie, "Nothing at all, I can assure you. Sephie and I were just planning a Christmas Ball. In Oxfordshire."

"A Ball! Oxfordshire? This sounds *most* irregular!" she gasped.

"Well, that's exactly what I just told Sephie, but she refuses to listen and is *insisting* upon an unspeakably grand party at Fairtree Manor."

"Miss *Sephie*!" breathed Miss Bell, in astonished tones.

'I know! For someone so small, she's remarkably high-handed. You should be warned, Miss Edie, she'll probably make you come with us, to be bounced about in a post-chaise for two long days and to eat stewed mutton and sleep in a lumpy bed in some remote coaching inn."

Miss Bell clasped her hands together beneath her chin, "Oh, I would like that above anything! May I ask what this ball is to honour?"

"Sephie is going fishing. She's planning to catch a wife for Sir Leander. I have a feeling the whole thing is going to be vastly entertaining and will make Sir Leander wish he'd never decided to go and see a mermaid sing in the first place! I cannot wait to see his expression when I tell him."

Sephie pulled a nervous face and Lord Rokewode laughed, a sound which Miss Bell thought they didn't hear nearly enough these days.

"And poor Sir Leander is not yet aware that he's holding a ball at Fairtree?"

"No, indeed, he hasn't even the vaguest idea. We only just found out ourselves, did we not, Sephie? Is it to be a masked ball? Costumed? Themed? It must not be too out of the ordinary as it's a country ball and also Leander is a little straitlaced. His only living relative, his grandmother, makes his life pretty miserable. Responsibility has always been really high on his agenda, as you've probably noticed, but he is alternately nagged and suffocated by Baroness Gage. You have a good deal of work to do Sephie if we are to pull off this miracle! You must draw up a guest list; you can ask Kitty to help with all the names and I'm sure that Miss Bell will assist, — she has a very fine copperplate. Then, there are the entertainments to be considered, singers, musicians, jugglers? Perhaps, a small theatrical troupe? Decoration for the ballroom and the gardens. What will be on the menu? Cold or hot collation? Pineapple ice-cream? Oh, *now* your eyes light up! Finally, I have caught your interest. You are too easily bribed, Miss Fane! I must remember that in case it should become necessary at a later date."

"Theodore! Where are your manners?"

Lord Rokewode made a show of looking abashed but rolled his eyes at Sephie. She hid her grin behind her hand and turned away towards the window. A phaeton was just drawing up at their door. She pointed at the visitors with delight.

"Well, I'll be — !" muttered Rokewode under his breath.

Miss Bell craned her neck to see who had come, "Goodness! At *this* hour!"

They heard the front door open and loud voices.

The library door opened and Paston announced the visitors, "The Lord Frederick Knoyll and Sir Anthony Calver, my lord."

"Ho there!" cried Sir Anthony striding into the room, "Theo! Miss Bell, how d'you do? And Miss Fane, looking exceedin' pretty this morning! Come to see how you all do today!"

Rokewode narrowed his eyes, "Have you indeed? Would you like to go up and see my mother? I'm sure she'd be delighted to see you."

"Good God *no!* I mean — what a shocking idea! Are you *mad?* Your mother would eat me alive if I turned up in her bedchamber at this hour!" ejaculated Sir Anthony, his face expressing his full horror.

"Then what, precisely, are you both doing here at such an ungodly hour? I haven't seen either of you up and dressed before midday since — well, *ever!*"

Sir Anthony looked at Lord Knoyll helplessly, "We were just — passing."

"On your way *to* — ?"

"To a boxing match," supplied Lord Knoyll, obligingly. Sir Anthony casting his eyes up.

Rokewode raised his fine dark eyebrows, "A *boxing* match, you say? Before noon? I'd like to go with you. Whereabouts is this fictitious boxing match?"

Completely oblivious to the danger, Lord Frederick Knoyll slapped him on the arm, "Told Tony you'd want to come! Splendid, we'll make up a party!"

Sir Anthony shook his head and threw himself into a leather reading chair, "Been rumbled, old fellow! No point in further prevarication! Told you, smart as a whip. Any chance of some breakfast, I'm famished!"

Miss Bell dashed away at once, saying that she would organise something for everyone.

"A *boxing* match!" scoffed Sir Anthony, "Was that really the best you could come up with, Freddie?" he shook his head in despair, "Surrounded by utter dolts," he declared. "Miss Fane, have we interrupted your letter writing?"

She looked at Lord Rokewode for help and he smiled, "Sephie, as she would prefer to be called, is making endless lists."

"*Shopping* lists," uttered Sir Anthony, unimpressed.

"A guest list for our Christmas Ball."

Sir Anthony sat up, "Ball? What? This is the first I've heard of a Rokewode Christmas Ball! Dash it! Keeping it under wraps?"

"It's the first *any* of us have heard of it," said Rokewode, "And it's not to be a Rokewode affair, *per se* — it's going to be a gigantic headache for Leander, thankfully."

"Good God! *Leander?* Are you sure? Doesn't sound like him!"

"No, You're right. It's nothing to do with him. It's all down to Sephie, I'm afraid. Entirely her idea. She's doing a little scheming on Leander's behalf. I'm but an innocent bystander. With loose purse-strings!"

"Well, I've never heard the like," said Lord Frederick Knoyll. "Gage having a party! It's a wonder he don't fall into the megrims."

"Ah, yes, but, you see, at the moment he doesn't know he's having a Ball," said Rokewode with a wry smile.

"He — what? Doesn't *know!* No, you've slipped the leash now! No idea what you're talking about! How can he not know?"

"We haven't told him yet."

Sir Anthony and Lord Frederick Knoyll stared open-mouthed, their eyes goggling.

"No. Theo! Doing it too brown! What?"

"According to Sephie, it will be held at Fairtree."

"Speechless," pronounced Sir Anthony, "And the Beastly Baroness is *au fait* with these plans?"

"Cleverly, you've detected the other small snag in our scheme. The merest hindrance — it shall be dealt with directly. But first we have to break it to Leander that he is hosting a rather large event from his house. I doubt he'll mind, once he realises it's entirely for his benefit."

"In what way could a room packed full of people possibly be for Leander's benefit?" asked Sir Anthony, "He'll have a seizure. He can barely cope with a small card party in his own drawing room! It was all we could do to get him to Bartholomew Fair; we had to get him befuddled on huge quantities of punch! No, it won't do, Theo! *Can't* be for his sake!"

"It is, I assure you. Sephie and I are conspiring to sort out the devil of a tangle he's managed to get himself into. Miss Matilda Fleete and some wretched usurper, Adam Gibbs? Just announced their betrothal. Thrown him into a major fit of the sullens. Decided he actually quite likes Miss Fleete now, having previously spurned her tentative advances. I suspect he just panicked and fled, sensing dozens of parties and interminable socialising on the horizon and imagining himself being the centre of attention at large gatherings in his honour! It would be his worst — *is* going to be his worst nightmare. So, we have taken the bull by the horns and er — gone behind his back."

"Tellin' you, *seizure!* We'll need brandy and smelling salts on hand to revive him. Don't believe the Beastly Baroness will let this pass though — she'd be afraid she might lose her grandson to another woman and that would never do. Who would she bully and dote on? It'll be a miracle if you can pull this off, Theo. Although, I have a gut feeling that Miss — *Sephie*, might be a bit of a miracle worker! Abject apologies — shouldn't have said gut! There, said it *again!*"

Sephie twinkled at him and chuckled silently. He was such a delight! Words just tumbled out of him with such ease. It actually made her envious, the way he was able to express his feelings almost before he'd thought. Her feelings were trapped behind a wall, desperate to escape. But she swore to herself that she would do this one thing — resolve Leander Gage's romantic Gordian Knot — and then she'd be perfectly prepared to disappear before she was found out. Before she could see the disillusion in Lord Rokewode's eyes and know that he despised her. Yes, one last adventure and then she'd steal away, and nobody would miss her or be any the wiser.

Ten

"No," said Sir Leander Gage adamantly. "Absolutely not." He folded his arms across his chest and stood firm. The two pairs of eyes gazing at him were extremely appealing, but he was having none of it. His life was worth more to him. His grandmother would murder him. He had no wish to die. God, but Sophie's eyes were so irresistible! "No, I cannot countenance such a thing. You must be out of your minds. Completely deranged. Attics to let."

"Perhaps, you need time to consider it," said Rokewode with a shrewd smile.

"I don't need any time at all. The answer is emphatically no!"

Sophie rose to her feet and approached him. She put a small hand on his arm and looked up into his face pleadingly. He turned away. He could not be bought or bribed or otherwise persuaded that having an enormously expensive and disruptive social occasion in his house, where his grandmother resided, was a good idea at all. The very idea of having to explain such a thing to the Baroness made his stomach churn. And besides that, a *Ball!* In his house! So many awful people and they'd all expect him to talk to them. He gave a horrified shudder and looked back at Sophie to make final his rejection of their ridiculous notion. Oh, devil take it! She had tears in her eyes!

"No!" he said in failing tones.

"He's on the rocks, Sophie. You have him."

Sir Leander couldn't help a reluctant smile, "Damn you, Theo! To use such a pernicious weapon is below the belt. Unsporting. To be perfectly frank, I thought better of you. You're truly not the man I thought you were."

Rokewode's shoulders shook, "A perfectly aimed low blow, Sephie."

"*Treason doth never prosper,*" quoted Sir Leander despondently. He sat down on the nearest chair and put his head in his hands.

"It's not as bad as all that, Lee! All we have to do is win around your beloved grandmama and all will be well. Once you become accustomed to the idea, you'll begin to see that we — or rather, Sephie, only has your best interests at heart. She clearly has a deeply romantic streak because she's determined that Miss Fleete shall be made to see the error of her ways before she takes the final and disastrous step towards marriage with the apparently unspeakable Mr Gibbs. She has put a great deal of effort into the planning already. Guest lists, all written out. Invitations, gilt-edged, are being designed. Musicians and actors. And feathers. Copious amounts of feathers. Many ostriches will have to be sacrificed." He saw Sephie bite her lip and chuckled. He found it oddly satisfying, making her smile. She was such a strange little thing.

Sir Leander patted her hand, "All right, you win. *This* round. But if it all goes to pieces, I shall know who to blame!"

"Sephie, naturally."

"No, *you!* I can see that Sephie only means well but you are enjoying my discomfort, positively revelling in it! Besides, Sephie has very pretty grey eyes, so I'm naturally more inclined to forgive her!"

The pretty grey eyes turned towards Rokewode laughing and he had to agree with his friend; although not by any stretch of the imagination beautiful, they were so eloquent that one could be forgiven for thinking they were very fine eyes indeed.

'So, what happens now," asked Sir Leander in a resigned voice, "I feel as though I'm nearing the cliff edge and am about to be pushed off."

"We will all be there to hold your hand, won't we Sephie?"

She nodded fervently and squeezed Sir Leander's hand, which was still holding onto hers as though it might save him.

"But how can we be sure that Matilda will accept the invitation? She can be extremely mulish."

"We will, of course, be inviting Mr Adam Gibbs and her father as well. Nobody in the district will want to miss out on such a momentous event. For god's sake, the last Ball held at Fairtree was sometime in the last century to celebrate the beheading of poor King Charles! The Gages are not much given to dancing and making merry. They're a dour, Puritanical bunch."

"Thank you," said Sir Leander, "We can't all come from a long line of rakehells like you! My family are God-fearing and restrained."

"You mean as dull as ditch water? But, Leander, though I mock, I wouldn't have you any other way. You prevent me from reverting to my own rather dissolute beginnings. My ancestors would be bitterly disappointed to see what I have become — a mere milksop. I'm letting the ghosts of the Rokewodes down!"

Sir Leander let out a shout of laughter, "Milksop? I think not, my dear friend! You have any number of females chasing after you and I expect you allow a good few to catch you too! And, of course, there's the oh-so-charming twice-widowed Mrs Sheraton!" He caught a slight frown from Rokewode and a quick glance at Sephie told him he'd forgotten they had company. He quickly buttoned his lip. It was sometimes difficult to remember that Sephie was there with them, as she couldn't join in the conversations. But he saw, a little too late, the disheartened expression that she disguised by turning away from them. Damn, thought Sir Leander, damn and blast! So, that's the way the land lies! That won't do at all. He had no wish for poor Sephie to get her heart broken and if he was right, she was heading for a good deal of pain and anguish. He was very fond of the girl; she was an eccentric little thing, and he would not allow her rather original spirit to be squashed by his friend's legendary carelessness. He knew what that kind of heartbreak could do to one's life. She was too much the innocent to be allowed to fall into such a bear trap.

Sephie wished they'd all stop mentioning Mrs Sheraton. She didn't want to be constantly reminded of her existence. It was quite enough that she had met her face to face and had been forced to acknowledge just how irresistible she was. She wanted to forget all about her.

* * *

Miss Pippin was thrilled. Utterly beside herself with excitement and joy. The news of the Ball filled her with a desire to spin around the room, her skirts whirling. But it immediately struck her that there were several flaws in the plan.

"We can't dance. We've never been taught! It wasn't exactly a requirement at the fair! We'll have to sit by the wall like those flowers that grow by walls. Also, is Miss Fleete pretty? I really do hope not. And, I have heard of a shocking new dance, called a waltz — I wonder if we'll be allowed to do it? Oh, and if we are to have a Masquerade, I really don't want to wear a mask! I would be exceedingly foolish to disguise my best asset!"

Biddy had been rather relieved to find out that the reason Sir Leander Gage had not joined her growing legion of admirers was that he loved another. That made perfect sense. It wasn't because he had found her lacking in any way. She was still a little put out that the arrangements for the Christmas Ball were being made by Sephie, of all people! Sephie had never even been to a Ball, or to a formal dance of any kind. Biddy had to admit that neither had she, but that was beside the point. Why, on earth would Lord Rokewode ask Sephie to organise the whole affair? She wasn't going to be able to ask any of the suppliers or entertainers anything. She supposed Miss Bell would do that for her, as the old nanny seemed to have been asked to participate. It wasn't going to be a very select Ball if they were going to ask just *anyone!* Oh, she did hope that Miss Fleete looked like one of the freaks at the fair! She couldn't bear it if she was prettier than she was. She had no wish to see her admirers paying attention to anyone else. Still, she was sure things would turn out in her favour once she found the right gown; she was confident she could outshine any other female there.

Sephie wrote the answers to Biddy's considerations down on a spare scrap of paper that wasn't entirely covered in notes for the ball.

1. *Lady Kitty says we can have a dance master teach us.*
2. *Wallflowers!*
3. *I have no idea, but I expect so.*
4. *I doubt it, as it's to be a country ball.*
5. *You'd be the only one not wearing a mask. Wouldn't that look a little peculiar?*

Biddy frowned, then remembered that it would crease her forehead and stopped. "It's a pity we couldn't have the Ball here in town. So many more stylish and important people would be able to attend. In the country it'll just be boring vicars and ancient farmers and the local squire all clumping about in hobnail boots to the hornpipe dance."

Sephie wrote,
"You're being very mean-spirited, and it will show on your face!"

She knew that would stop her; all she ever had to do was suggest something might mar her beauty and Biddy would stop. It wasn't that she was a horrible person, it was just that having had such a deprived and loveless life, Biddy had become obsessed with the only thing which made her stand out from the crowd. A neglected child paraded before strangers because of her extraordinary looks; it was where she had earned her recognition and reward and it had been extremely damaging. Somewhere inside Biddy was a good person, a girl with a kind heart and a generous spirit but that side of her had been temporarily mislaid.

She wrote that she would need help deciding upon a gown and that Lady Kitty would be taking them shopping in a few days' time. She also suggested that Biddy begin to think about what she might need for the rest of their stay in the country as one didn't want to be caught without the appropriate walking dress or riding habit.

"Riding!" cried Biddy, "But we *can't* ride!" and she burst into tears.

* * *

Lady Kitty and Miss Bell escorted the girls all about town in a search for fabrics and furbelows, hats and bonnets, ribbons and fichus. They spent several exhilarating days traipsing about from shop to warehouse, from *modiste* to haberdasher, in order to find just the right items. Lady Kitty had a way about her which commanded attention and Biddy was envious that within seconds of walking into any emporium every employee in the building would be fawning over her, holding out lengths of materials, Italian gauzes and embroidered muslins, satins and silks; every conceivable type of fabric there was on earth passed by Lady Kitty's long straight nose and was either immediately discarded with a dismissive wave of her hand or allowed to be put on one side for her to peruse more closely.

Every time Sephie was offered an ostrich feather to examine, she had to smile, remembering Theo's light-hearted words.

The theme of the ball had been decided with half an eye to the sedate nature of most of the prospective guests. Miss Bell and Lady Kitty had talked Sephie round after quite a tussle. Sephie rather fancied the idea of being masked and costumed; she thought it sounded exotic and great fun to be unrecognisable, but Lady Kitty said that many of the Oxfordshire locals would be outraged at some of the possible characters the city dwellers might come dressed as. It didn't bear thinking about — a half-naked goddess flaunting herself in front of a country parson or Baroness Gage! But as she was so very disappointed, they decided that masks could be worn with normal ballgowns. Sephie clapped her hands with delight and quickly wrote it down in ink before they changed their minds.

They gave their mask designs to the milliner; she employed a very good seamstress who made such fripperies and she promised to have them made up exactly to the drawings. They left the establishment carrying a few small boxes containing headdresses and other such pretty delights and were making their way down the street towards their next destination when it suddenly began to rain.

"Oh, what a nuisance!" cried Lady Kitty and quickly looked around for a nearby hackney coach; seeing none, she put up her flimsy parasol to protect her hair. "We must find shelter until it passes. We could go back into the milliners or continue in the rain to the glove and fan shop in Bond Street?"

Miss Bell thought Bond Street would be nearest, so they dashed helter-skelter along the pavement, trying to avoid the other passers-by and the rapidly increasing puddles.

Sephie suddenly thought she spied a hackney and without much coherent thought apart from the fact that the hem of her gown was sodden and sticking to her legs and was in danger of getting spattered with mud, she stepped into the street and waved her hand at the coachman.

The next thing she knew she was lying on the ground and a crowd of people were staring down at her and rain was dripping into her eyes and running down her neck, despite the fact that several strangers were kindly trying to shield her with their umbrellas. She tried to sit up, but someone pushed her back onto the ground. She didn't want to be lying in the mud! Then she saw a face she recognised. Lady Kitty, thanks goodness. She'll explain what was happening. Her head hurt and her shoulder felt a little odd.

Lady Kitty was barking orders in a voice which would have scared away a wild bear. "I said, *stand back!* You're going to squash her! *You!* Give me your umbrella! Now, hail a hackney. *At once!* She can't lie here in the rain — she'll catch her death.

Thank you, sir, for your coat, most kind, I will pay for any damage, of course. Sephie, my love? How are you feeling? Are you hurt?"

Sephie managed to sit up with assistance but there was a sharp pain in her left shoulder, and she looked down at her bandages and saw they were muddy, and the ends were coming undone and trailing and her skirts were filthy. What a mess! She looked up at Lady Kitty with a question in her wide eyes.

"You were hit by a carriage as you stepped out into the street. It was going far too fast and must not have seen you."

Sephie remembered nothing.

A portly man edged forward. He was florid of complexion and wore a striped waistcoat in vivid pinks which strained around his balloon-like stomach, the fastenings looking as though they might burst open at any moment under the pressure.

He coughed in an apologetic manner, "My lady, I witnessed the collision and if you don't mind me saying, it didn't look like an accident to me! That driver went straight for her! And, I might add, those horses were under control, not runaway, I'd lay my life on it."

"Thank you, sir, but that cannot be! Why would anyone wish to run down my friend? It makes no sense."

The man pulled down the corners of his mouth and wagged his head, "Plain as day. Saw it with my own eyes. Headed straight for her and kept going once it'd hit her. Can't say more than what I saw but here's my card, just in case you need me to supply testimony. Major Walter Cobham at your service," and he handed Lady Kitty a rather damp business card.

She eyed it with some misgiving, "Attorney at Law. Interesting. Thank you." She tucked it into her reticule and went back to ordering everyone around. Sephie was by this time soaked to the skin and shivering.

Miss Bell held out her hand to her, "Come, Miss Sephie, we must get you up and into a hackney." Several gentlemen pushed forward and within seconds Sephie was being lifted up and set on her feet.

"What a spectacle," said a curious onlooker, "She looks like she's been dragged through a turnip field."

Then, suddenly the crowd parted and Sephie was peering up through the now driving rain into Lord Rokewode's furious face.

"I saw Miss Pippin standing on the pavement. What in God's name — !" He took one look at Sephie, whose legs had started to shake rather alarmingly, and he scooped her up and marched off with her through the astonished throng.

A minute later she was being carefully arranged in a hackney coach and the others were squeezing in around her. Lady Kitty was holding her hand and peering at her as though she might faint away. Lord Rokewode was instructing the driver and then he was sitting on the padded seat next to her and taking off his coat to wrap around her.

At his peremptory request, Lady Kitty tried to explain what had happened. At the end of the rather convoluted tale, she handed him Major Cobham's card.

Rokewode studied it and slipped it into his pocket. He then fixed Sephie with a frowning stare which so much discomposed her that she shut her eyes. This was partly to do with the terrible pain coming from her shoulder and partly because he looked so cross.

They arrived at Grosvenor Square and there was a bit of a commotion as everyone alighted from the hackney and the footman paid the driver. Then, once everyone had rushed inside, to get out of the rain, Rokewode was able to lift Sephie out and carry her into the house. He strode straight up the stairs to her bedchamber, where he laid her down on the bed, which caused her to audibly suck her breath in. He stood for a moment looking down at her and then gently sat on the edge of the bed, careful not to jolt her.

"May I just touch your shoulder, Sephie?"

She nodded but was gritting her teeth, her jaw quite rigid.

He felt the offending joint, "Thought so. Dislocated. And clearly extremely painful." He stood up and went to the door, "I'll be back in a few minutes. Don't move! Here comes Kitty, she'll make sure you're comfortable. She's dislocated her shoulder, Kit. She must be in a great deal of pain. I shall send for Emerson and fetch some brandy."

His sister nodded but he noted that she was looking quite pale and distressed, "She'll be all right, don't worry," and with that he left the room.

Lady Kitty realised that she wouldn't be able to get Sephie out of her gown without hurting her shoulder so she called Ann, who was hovering in the corridor, and much to Sephie's dismay, they managed to cut her out of her clothes, although she wouldn't let them remove her chemise. Once this difficult task had been achieved, they were able to get her into some dry clothes and cover her up with the counterpane. She looked like a bedraggled urchin but at least she was warm.

Miss Pippin came to see what was going on and was concerned to hear about the injury but privately felt that it had been very much Sephie's own fault for jumping out into the street in such a reckless manner. She asked if there was anything she could do and was relieved when Lady Kitty said everything was in hand, so she crept away to go and lie down on her bed for a while to recover.

Rokewode returned with a decanter of brandy and a glass. He was alarmed by the colour of Sephie's face which was nearly the same colour as the pillow. Her eyes were closed, and her mouth compressed. He poured some brandy and coaxed her to sip some, saying that it would help with the pain. She allowed him to lift her head but not without some discomfort and he tipped some of the liquid between her lips. She coughed and spluttered a bit, but he kept encouraging her, so she obeyed and drank some more.

Half an hour later Doctor Emerson arrived in a somewhat agitated state, having been dragged away from his home minutes after he'd just returned from attending a very long and difficult birth. He was tired and a little grumpy but seeing his patient's wan face, he immediately reverted to his professional style, took off his coat and rolled up his sleeves. Having ascertained how the injury happened and examined his patient, he asked Lord Rokewode if he'd mind assisting as he would have to pop the shoulder joint back into place. He warned that it would very likely be painful and suggested a good swig or two of brandy or a few drops of laudanum beforehand would help. Rokewode opted for the brandy as laudanum came with some side effects he would rather not be responsible for inflicting upon the patient. Sephie was past caring, she just wanted the pain to stop.

Under the doctor's careful instruction Rokewode climbed onto the bed and after apologising profusely for what was about to happen, he held her so that she was unable to move while the operation was performed. Sephie had a thought appear mistily through the pleasant haze of brandy fumes. She was in Theo's arms and for the brief moment before Doctor Emerson manipulated her shoulder joint back to where it should be, she felt a kind of delicious contentment but at the same time realised that it could never happen again.

The pain was excruciating and thankfully she fainted.

Eleven

For the second time that day Sephie woke up to find concerned faces staring down at her. Lady Kitty was perched beside her on the bed and chafing her hands, which felt different; she looked down at them and saw that the bandages had been removed.

"Doctor Emerson said it was time. Look, they are well healed. I am starting to suspect you must be terribly accident prone! I think we should wrap you in cotton wool to keep you safe from now on."

Sephie gave a rather feeble smile and her eyes slid to the others in the room. Doctor Emerson was looking pleased and pulling on his coat. She turned her head with only the slightest wince of discomfort and saw that still sitting on the bed was Lord Rokewode.

"The doctor has assured me that with a little care and rest your shoulder will be as good as new. You must wear a sling for a couple of weeks and then avoid any strenuous activity until it's properly healed. You're extremely fortunate that you were not more seriously injured. You cannot just go leaping out into the street in London. It is far too dangerous — the carriages will not stop for anyone. How are we to keep you from further harm, I wonder? You must promise to be more cautious in the future and think before you throw yourself into danger."

Sephie nodded obediently but had long ago recognised that she was cursed with reckless impulses she couldn't control. It had brought trouble upon her many times before, but she had learnt to live with the consequences.

Rokewode, reading the rebellious expressions flitting across her face, realised he might as well save his breath. He was relieved to see some colour coming back into her cheeks.

He'd been walking from his home in St James's Square towards his mother's house in Grosvenor Square when he'd first seen the crowd gathered around in the rain and a forlorn-looking Miss Pippin standing on the periphery of the onlookers; he hadn't known what to expect but then he caught sight of Miss Edie and Kitty and finally spotted Sephie's rain-soaked, muddy figure being lifted from the ground and for a panicked second had thought the worst. His relief when, as he fought his way through the circle of people, and saw her standing, albeit shakily, on her own two small feet, was palpable. He had been angry. Angry that she should have so stupidly risked her life, angry that someone had hurt her and angry that he had so nearly been goaded into losing his temper in front of strangers.

"You must do exactly what the doctor advises. And hopefully you will soon be fit enough to enjoy the rest of your stay here. The Christmas Ball is months away, so you'll certainly be well enough to put the finishing touches to all the preparations and luckily, it's your left arm. But if you want to come with us to Fairtree Manor for the Ball you will have to stay out of trouble. Now, if I were you, I'd finish this glass of brandy, it might help you sleep." He handed her the glass and she drained it, coughing a little as she swallowed it. Rokewode slid from the bed and he and Doctor Emerson left the room together, without, Sephie noted sadly, a backward glance.

Oh, dear, she thought, yet another expense for him! She must behave and do as she's told, or he'd throw her out before the Ball and she so desperately wanted to make sure that Sir Leander and Miss Fleete found happiness with each other again. It would be splendid if there could be this one happy ending. It would make everything worthwhile.

Lady Kitty stayed with her until she'd fallen asleep, which didn't take long because of the shock of the accident and a large quantity of brandy.

Once she was sure that the patient was sound asleep, she tiptoed out of the room and joined her brother downstairs in the drawing room.

He was sitting stretched out in an armchair beside the fire with a glass of brandy in his hand.

"Something for the shock?" she asked with a tired smile as she sat down in the opposite chair. She closed her eyes for a moment and heard him get up and go to the sideboard, a clinking sound and then a glass was pressed into her hand. She thanked him without opening her eyes.

"Is she asleep?"

"Finally. Poor child. That must have been agony but there were no tears. If that had been me, I'd have screamed the house down," replied Lady Kitty, taking a large unladylike gulp of her drink.

"You would indeed. Your scream could crack glass. Sephie was indomitable throughout. When Emerson put her shoulder back in, I'll admit that most men would have made a fuss, but she just closed her eyes, clenched her teeth and bore it bravely. Remarkable." He swirled his brandy in its glass, observing its progress from sleepy eyes, "It makes me wonder what she may have endured before we found her. I'm beginning to believe that in the past she's suffered a good deal more than we first thought and bears the scars. Of course, she cannot, *will* not speak of it. I asked her to write down some of her history for me, but she became quite skittish at the suggestion, so I have said no more on the subject."

"Very wise," said Kitty, stifling a yawn. "This accident though Theo — that gentleman, Major Cobham, he seemed to think — in fact was absolutely *convinced* that she was knocked down deliberately! It does seem strange that the carriage driver didn't stop to see if she was hurt. If anything, it sped up. The Major seemed to me to be an honest sort of fellow, hearty and sensible. I can't think why he would say that if it weren't true. He has nothing to gain by it."

Rokewode finished his brandy in one go and put his glass on the table, "Intuition tells me that you're right. Bond Street isn't a racetrack like some streets. Drivers take care, on the whole and there's also plenty of room to stop and it wasn't that crowded today because of the rain. No, I think the Major was, unfortunately, correct in his summation. Someone tried to hurt Sephie on purpose. I have my suspicions but of course, have no proof as yet."

Lady Kitty forced her tired eyes open, "Who would want to hurt such a dear girl? It's ludicrous."

"I agree. I think it may have been the infamous Mr Henry Pippin."

Lady Kitty sat up in her chair and rubbed her eyes, "Biddy's father? But, what on earth makes you say that?"

"Oh, I don't know. Something smoky about the man. First, he sells his daughter to the public and makes her perform half-naked and drinks away the profits. Then, and here I'm only speculating, he had Sephie working for him with no chaperone or guardian and probably no wage. Then he's dead but he's not dead. Disappears. No word to his daughter. Not the behaviour of an honest and upright gentleman, I'd say."

"Agreed," said Kitty. "So, what are we to do about it? We can't allow Sephie and Biddy to walk about London without someone keeping a constant watch over them now. Oh, this is too bad! Indeed, it's not at all what I expected when Mama invited me to visit!" She grinned at her brother, "But, I will say, that it certainly is unexpectedly exciting living with our mother and her bizarre, adopted children! Although, I think I'm about to fall asleep in my chair, I simply must go to bed. We'll talk more about this in the morning. Will you be here?"

"I will. First though I shall pay a visit to our Major Cobham and see what he has to say and then I'm looking forward to another friendly chat with Constable Thursby." He rose elegantly to his feet and escorted his sister to the bottom of the stairs, kissed her on the cheek and told her to keep an eye on the girls and then let himself out of the house.

* * *

Sephie was sitting up in bed listening to Biddy chatting; she was describing how awful the accident had been for her. She had, apparently, felt quite faint when she saw Sephie flying through the air and had looked around for somewhere to sit but there was nowhere. It had been extremely trying. And the rain! It had spoiled her bonnet which was meant for sunny days only. And nobody took a blind bit of notice of her as she stood on the pavement getting wet and rudely bumped by strangers trying to get a closer look at the aftermath of the accident.

Sephie was only half paying attention, Biddy's words and complaints flowed over her and she nodded every so often to show willing. But her mind was elsewhere. She tried not to dwell upon it, but she was finding it exceedingly difficult to put it from her mind. Firstly, the look on Theo's face when he saw her in the street, all covered in mud and soaked through. He had been fit to explode. Then, the way he'd swept her up and carried her off! And the way he'd held her in his arms while Doctor Emerson had mended her shoulder. She could still feel the warmth of his body next to hers. It made her breath catch in her throat and gave her goosebumps. She felt as though she'd woken from a beautiful dream and her only desire was to climb back into its warm embrace. She had to keep giving herself a shake to bring herself back to reality, she knew she was being stupidly unrealistic but some perverse little part of her was determined to hang onto the unfamiliar but delicious feelings she'd experienced. It was such an alien feeling for her to want to be close to someone.

"…and it's not as though you've ever organised anything before! It just seems odd. I think I'll wear the blue, what do you think? Sephie?"

Sephie stared at her friend and wondered what she'd missed. She nodded and smiled. It didn't really matter what colour Biddy wore; she'd look like an angel anyway.

* * *

Lord Rokewode was sitting in the offices of Major Walter Cobham, whom he found to be a convivial fellow with a good understanding. He had been pleasantly surprised. Having expected a rough-at-the-edges sort of country gentleman, he'd discovered a rather alert and downright astute lawyer who knew his business inside out and had a keen eye for detail and thankfully wasn't given to hyperbole. This suited him well for he wanted to get to the truth behind the accident with as little complication as possible. Cobham gave him a succinct description of what he'd seen and proved he had fine recall. The level of detail he was able to provide, in what must have been a matter of seconds of action, was astounding. He then handed Rokewode a sheet of paper where he had thoughtfully written his account of the event down and signed it.

"Anything else, and I am happily at your service, my lord. Not just for this business but anything else that you might need — er — advice upon," he cocked a grizzled eyebrow at the Earl and saw the faintest indication of something cross his face. "My lord? *Anything*, at all. Conveyancing. Managing landed properties," he gave Rokewode a calculating look, "Investigations."

Lord Rokewode pondered this for a moment, "Investigation? Is that so? There is a small matter I would like someone to look into — discreetly, it goes without saying, of course."

"I am nothing if not discreet. If you don't mind me asking, has it anything do with the "accident"? I will admit to wondering why anyone would wish to injure such a harmless looking girl. It had me intrigued from the outset, my lord."

"Yes, it would be to do with that, and the young lady involved in the incident. I believe the driver was her employer from Bartholomew Fair and the father of the other young lady who was at the scene in Bond Street, Miss Biddy Pippin."

Cobham picked up a quill, "May I make some notes?"

Rokewode nodded assent and continued, "Mr Henry Pippin, a drunk and a scoundrel and I don't yet know what else besides — but I suspect the worst — faked his own death in a fire in their entertainment booth Ah, you've heard news of it!

He disappeared that night, abandoning the two girls to their fate and leaving one doorman burned to death. Hardly trustworthy behaviour. Miss Fane badly burnt her hands trying to help her friend. The daughter had been callously used as an exhibit and Miss Fane, who is mute, was her assistant but, and here it is purely supposition — I suspect that something else may have been going on behind the scenes. I have no reason other than my intuition to make me think this. There is something about Miss Fane, Major Cobham, something doesn't ring true, I can sense some kind of mystery. To be more precise, Fane is an assumed name as she only seems to have been given one, Persephone. She can't or won't explain anything about her past and Miss Pippin is an accomplice in whatever this hoax may be. There are definite clues that Miss Fane may have been a foundling, which might explain the lack of a surname. There are large gaps in her knowledge; she is like a small child looking at the world for the first time. It's all fresh and new to her but at the same time her general understanding is sound. Wherever she has been during her early years, she's managed to retain her natural intelligence and, astonishingly, her sense of humour, despite what I have to believe has been a traumatic upbringing. I have to say that I am curious about the whole thing and would like to know the truth once and for all."

"I understand from Lady Roysten that the girls are residing with your mother in Grosvenor Square at the moment? Would this be a permanent situation for them?"

Rokewode clamped his lips together and shook his head, "At the moment, Major I have no real idea. My mother, Lady Rokewode and my sister seem to be content to have them there and I'm happy to fund the venture, for now. They will certainly be with us until Christmas as Miss Fane is planning a Ball and I wouldn't want to deprive her of that pleasure." A slight smile curved his mouth as he remembered her suppressed laughter over the ostrich feathers.

Cobham took a minute to make some more notes before looking up again at Lord Rokewode and contemplating him from under beetling brows, "Which brings me, my lord, to a rather delicate matter — whether or not any discovery that I might make would have a detrimental effect upon your family's relationship with these two girls."

"Blunt and to the point, Cobham! That is hard to answer but I cannot think that there could possibly be anything bad enough to make us throw them out into the snow. I will answer as honestly as I can in the circumstances, and state that it wouldn't have any effect."

More scratching from the lawyer, "That puts my mind at rest. I am unfortunately in the business of having to tell people news they may not wish to hear, and it makes my job even more difficult to accomplish and more distressing for the families involved. Is there anything else I should know?"

Rokewode shrugged his broad shoulders, "Not that comes immediately to mind. Will you take the job?"

Major Walter Cobham gave his new client a long hard look, "I will take it, with pleasure, my lord. With one caveat."

"Which is?"

"That if, by any chance, the findings of the investigation are not what you expected and Miss Fane is no longer welcome in your home because of this, that my wife and I should very much like to make her our ward and take her in ourselves."

Lord Theodore Rokewode had seldom been more confounded. He stared at the lawyer for a full minute before he regained the powers of speech, "You wish to *adopt* Sephie? But you didn't even talk to her!"

"My wife and I are sadly childless, and I saw something in that young girl's face and demeanour after the accident which made me absolutely certain that whatever else she may be, she is an innocent child in need of love and security. I would lay my life on it."

"I am absolutely staggered! Of all the things I expected you to say — !" Rokewode rubbed his hand across his eyes, "I fear you must be a little mad, sir, to even consider taking on such a burden without first getting to know her and finding out about her history."

Cobham gave a rich chuckle, "If there's one thing I have been blessed with, it's the gift of shrewd insight into the nature of people. I knew as soon as I saw you that you were a proud and intolerant man, Lord Rokewode, but underneath that hard veneer, you are honourable and compassionate. And I believe you took both girls in without asking for their credentials! Miss Fane, I could see straight away, was frightened and lost and yet as brave a creature as I have ever set eyes upon. A dislocated shoulder, you say? And no tears. And burning her hands in the fire? I would say she was an exceptional female! Her eyes tell the tale of her pain."

"That much is, without doubt, true. Those eyes — !"

"*Les yeux sont le miroir de l'âme.* So, we have an agreement, Lord Rokewode?"

Rokewode rose and put out his hand and Cobham clasped it firmly.

* * *

Lady Rokewode had decided, in her inimitable fashion, that they would start as soon as possible. "There's no time like the present," she said cheerfully. "I have engaged Monsieur Hercule Tijou. He will be here soon. This is also why Freddie and Tom are here — they are to be your dance partners. Although, I must say that I would have preferred someone other than Tom, as he has two, possibly three, left feet."

"Thank you, my lady!" said Tom Babyngton, "I am flattered to have been asked and am always happy to help."

"Well, we're about to find out just how much help you'll be!" she responded with some asperity. "Now, where on earth are the others? We can't dance a cotillion without the numbers!"

Lady Kitty was sitting on one of the chairs which had been pushed back against the wall to make room for the rehearsal in the drawing room. The carpet had been rolled back to reveal the wooden floor and the spinet had been moved from the parlour into the corner of the room and Miss Bell was going through the sheets of music which were kept under the padded lid of the rosewood duet stool.

"Are we not going to be short one female partner?" queried Lady Kitty idly. "It's lucky Ambrose is no dancer of any description or we would be in real trouble."

Her mother counted up those who had already arrived and those still expected with her fan, twice, "Oh," she uttered, "So we are, my arithmetic has never been very reliable."

"*You* could dance, Mama. You used to be a very graceful dancer."

"I most certainly will *not* be dancing! My lumbago would prevent me!"

"You don't have lumbago."

"I *do*, Doctor Emerson, diagnosed me and said I should try not to become agitated as it exacerbated my condition."

"That was when you decided to have headaches because you didn't want to go to the coast for the summer. You have never had lumbago."

Miss Bell, seeing that this discussion might spiral into an argument, created a welcome distraction by playing the opening bars of some suitable dance music she'd found.

"I think I hear them, at last!" said Lady Kitty, much relieved.

After a few moments the drawing room door opened and Sir Anthony sailed in, all smiles, followed by Lord Frederick Knoyll and more reluctantly by Sir Leander Gage.

"We're here," announced Sir Anthony unnecessarily.

"Thank heaven you alerted us to the fact — we could so easily have missed it," said Lady Kitty sardonically.

"There's no need to be moody, Kitty! Apologies for tardiness, Lady Rokewode!"

"You're *always* late," said Freddie, "And you *always* blame me!"

"Well, that's enough of that! I didn't know you were coming Leander! Where is Theo?" demanded Lady Rokewode.

Sephie had already noticed his absence and thought forlornly that perhaps he wouldn't come. She had finally had the sling taken off and was feeling a little more normal; it had proved to be quite an encumbrance and meant that they couldn't hold the dance classes until she was able to at least raise her arm without flinching.

"I was persuaded to come by Tony," complained Sir Leander, gloomily. "Not at all my thing, dancing. But as Tom is even worse, they thought I might be an asset."

"Gad, I like that! Worse, indeed! At least I can make conversation while dancing. Dancing with you must be like dancing with an Egyptian Mummy!"

"At least my dance partners don't get their toes regularly broken!"

"Are you two going to fight all afternoon?" complained Kitty.

"Probably," replied Rokewode as he entered the room.

Sir Leander happened to be watching Sephie at that moment and seeing the very speaking look on her face, quickly created a diversion.

"The ladies are outnumbered Theo! Would you care to join their side?"

Rokewode laughed, "I would not, thank you — far too tall! I vote that Freddie should be sacrificed for the sake of the Ball. He's not above your height and will make you an excellent partner."

Sir Leander didn't look amused by this plan and began to object but everyone was already standing and taking their places so with very little good grace, he stood opposite his friend Freddie who pretended to flirt with him.

"Why, Sir Leander, how charming of you to ask me to dance — I am quite overcome!"

"Oh, do pipe down, Frederick!" snapped Leander.

Biddy quickly manoeuvred herself to be Anthony's partner and Kitty was with her brother, while Sephie found herself lumbered with Babyngton.

"Now, whoever is dancing with Sephie, watch her left arm — do not wrench it! It is not healed properly yet," ordered Lady Rokewode.

Miss Bell struck a chord and so the dancing began and there was complete bedlam, as several of the dancers, including Tom and Leander, turned the wrong way and collided with their nearest neighbours.

"I think we should be circling in the middle?" said Kitty trying not to laugh — "*Le Grand Rond*, I believe!"

Paston opened the door and announced Monsieur Hercule Tijou, whose mannered and theatrical entrance made Kitty snort with delight. Introductions were rushed through and before long M. Tijou had his dance cane tapping on the floor in time to the music and he was shouting heavily accented and mostly unintelligible instructions to the dancers. Freddie was severely reprimanded for doing a most unnecessary pirouette and spoiling the line and then Babyngton trod heavily upon Sephie's toe and the dancing had to stop for him to apologise profusely.

"*Balance! Rigaudon! Attention!*" shouted M. Tijou impatiently. "*Maintenant, Le Grand Rond encore!*" And he pounded the floor with his cane.

Then Tom was supposed to grab Sephie's right hand but took her left rather too vigorously and she winced as her shoulder bore the brunt of the unintentional assault.

Rokewode who witnessed the flinching and the biting of her lip, brought the dancing to yet another halt, "We shall change partners, Tom! Come and inflict your worst on Kitty, she at least will be able to give as good as she gets. But I must warn you, she never fights fair." He moved across the room to stand in front of Sephie who fortunately was already rather flushed from the effort of trying to avoid Tom's large flying feet. She looked up gratefully at Rokewode and hoped he wouldn't be able to hear her heart thumping loudly over the sound of Miss Bell's very competent playing.

"Would you rather sit this one out? Does your shoulder hurt?" he enquired.

She shook her head and indicated that she was completely fine and, she thought, as happy as a spring lamb.

M. Tijou waved his cane and off they went again. But this time, under the guidance of their very particular instructor, the pairings seemed to work much more smoothly and after one or two minor mistakes, the dancers found their rhythm and almost completed a full sequence before Tom managed to kick Kitty in the shin, which had her hopping about the dance floor clutching her leg in agony.

Order was once more restored by the ruthless Frenchman and they began the dance yet again.

At one point Sir Ambrose poked his head around the door to see what all the thumping and laughing was about and seeing Freddie and Leander concentrating hard as they circled each other in the middle of the group, made him clap a hand over his mouth and swiftly retreat.

When it was necessary for Sephie to use her left arm, Rokewode told her not to raise it and they made a pretence of the movements on that side, so that she put no strain on her shoulder.

During one of the sequences, with M. Tijou shouting, "*Moulinet! Moulinet!*" at them very loudly, they crossed arms, their hands touched in the movement of the dance and their eyes met and for a moment they both forgot their next step and the dance collapsed into disarray around them.

"Theo! Dash it all! We'll have to start again now! We'll be here all night at this rate. Watch what you're *doing*," reprimanded Sir Anthony.

"So sorry! I've no idea what I was thinking. It was Sephie's fault," said Rokewode smiling roguishly at the innocent party. She glared at him, shaking her head despairingly but M. Tijou was already pushing them back into their places ready for the next attempt at getting through the entire dance without having to stop. They practiced for nearly four hours before Lady Rokewode called a halt to the proceedings declaring that she was thoroughly exhausted having done nothing but sit and watch and clap her hands.

Miss Bell had sore fingers from playing the spinet and everyone was rather fed up with being relentlessly shouted at in French as though they were naughty schoolchildren.

Monsieur Hercule Tijou, was politely thanked by everyone and after making appointments for further rehearsals, abruptly took his leave, but the moment they heard the front door close behind him, they all dissolved into helpless giggles.

"My feet are *killing* me!" grumbled Babyngton, taking his shoe off and massaging his stockinged foot.

"Don't know why *your* feet are hurting! You were treading on everyone *else's* toes!" exclaimed Sir Leander acidly.

Miss Pippin had had a wonderful afternoon dancing exclusively with Sir Anthony; he had been attentive and patient and surprisingly nimble in the dances. She was a little disappointed to discover that she wasn't the best dancer but, in the end, had managed quite creditably and improved as the afternoon wore on.

Kitty, slumped in a chair next to Rokewode, watched as Sephie went to Miss Bell to help her put away the musical sheets and tidy up. "Very graceful dancer. A natural," she murmured.

"Thank you," responded her brother, with a slight smile.

She flashed him an exasperated glance, "You know damn well what I mean! Danced effortlessly with you. Odd, as you're inconveniently tall and she's so ridiculously tiny."

"Indeed," said Rokewode, his eyes following Sephie as she found Miss Bell's shawl and arranged it around the elderly lady's shoulders and then flew to help Lady Rokewode to her feet and find her fan which she had somehow dropped down the side of her chair. He wondered what Cobham would find out about Sephie and the Pippins.

"What is it, Theo? I know that face! You're brooding!"

He frowned, "I was just considering whether I had made a serious mistake or not."

"Oh, indubitably!" she laughed.

Twelve

Sephie eyed the pony with considerable suspicion. It didn't look at all trustworthy despite what its owner was assuring her. It looked as though it had brutally sharp teeth and hooves that could bruise flesh and break bones. She shook her head vehemently and took a step back.

Sir Leander was surprised. This was the first time she'd shown any kind of hesitation or fear and it seemed out of character. He glanced at Theo who was clearly just as perplexed as he was. Sephie had gone a little pale and was clutching her gloves and the bunched up the train of her riding habit in tense fists.

Across the stable yard, Sir Anthony was having no difficulty at all getting Miss Pippin into the saddle of her chosen mount, a docile mare called Snowball. She was keen to be better than Sephie at *something*. And she knew her friend's weaknesses well and was not exactly *happy* to exploit them but wasn't going to miss a chance to shine on her own account. Horses, she remembered, were one of the things Sephie avoided; she would jump skittishly if one came too near and could only just bear to be in a carriage pulled by them because she knew they couldn't escape. The mere sound of one whinnying close by would make her flinch and shy away. Biddy had never managed to ascertain why they had this strange effect upon someone who was normally almost reckless and although she was loathe to admit it, courageous. She guessed it was just another memory from Sephie's dark and mysterious past which had left its mark.

Leander was holding the horse by its bridle and wondering what on earth could be done about this stalemate. "Perhaps if you just stroked — ?" he began, hesitantly.

Sephie took another step away and, dropping her train, hid her hands behind her back, as though she feared they might touch the pony without her permission.

Rokewode approached her, as he might a terrified wild animal, easing towards her, wary of startling her, "Sephie, she's a very placid creature, I promise you and so old that I doubt she can walk let alone trot. She's used to having small children on her back. Come, just step a little closer. There's no need to be frightened." He took her hand from where it was hiding and held it firmly in his. She looked at it as though it had in some way betrayed her and then tried to remove it from his grasp.

"Sephie, please," he said in coaxing tones. She looked up at him, her eyes wide, her pupils dilated. "I'll be with you all the way. Look, I'll hold your hand and we'll just take our time, all right?"

She looked back at their clasped hands and after a brief pause, she nodded. Anything, even horses, to keep his hand holding hers, she thought a trifle incoherently. She allowed him to lead her forward a few steps but as they drew nearer to the beast, she began to tug on his hand again. He stopped trying to move her and just waited, gently squeezing her fingers in his. After a moment he could feel she'd relaxed a bit and he took another step. Sephie seeing him moving away from her, followed.

God, thought Leander bitterly, she'd probably follow him over a damn cliff!

Rokewode could feel her hand trembling in his and wondered what the hell could have happened to make her so afraid. This unexpected reaction to a harmless old pony had given him pause for thought. He realised that whatever she'd endured in her short life had left hidden shadows lurking beneath her deceptively sunlit surface. She was deliberately hiding her past from them and also the traumatic repercussions of that past. Sephie's eyes were tightly closed. She couldn't even bear to look at the animal.

"Would you like to go back to the house?" he asked softly.

She opened her eyes and stared gravely at their linked hands and shook her head.

"Come then, another step. Trust me. I'll not leave you."

Her grey eyes flashed up to his and the expression in them made him come to a decision. He might indeed be making a serious mistake, but he didn't care; he'd inform Cobham that he wanted every detail about Sephie's past revealed and that he'd pay any amount of money to find the truth. He was determined to understand what this girl had suffered and make the perpetrators pay for what they had done.

The horse raised her head and made a soft sound through her nose. Leander stroked her head to calm her and thought she was probably picking up on Sephie's fear.

Rokewode felt her pull away again but held her firm, this time moving one hand to her back and drawing her into a half-embrace.

"You can do this, Sephie. For God's sake, you put out flames with your bare hands! This is nothing. Just a stupid old pony! Take a step with me," he whispered near her ear. She took a step. "Another." She took another. They were finally beside the animal and she could smell the sweet musty oil from its coat. "There now, open your eyes. I've got you."

She obeyed and found all she could see was his waistcoat, which was reassuring. He turned her in his arms, and she could see the side of the terrible beast. She pressed her lips together determined not to let Theo down. The warmth from his arms gave her strength but she clung onto his hand.

"Now, I want you to stretch out your hand with mine — *with mine!* All we're going to do is touch Bess on her neck. That's good."

Her hand, in *his*. That's what she concentrated upon. Then, beneath her fingers, warm and velvety, the solid, muscular side of the pony. Sephie's breathing was rapid and her heart was racing. She *remembered* horses. The sounds and the smells. The violence. The *pain*.

She pulled her hand away and buried her head into Rokewode's broad chest, his arms folded around her and held her. He cast a speaking glance over her head at his patient but concerned friend and Leander quietly led Bess away across the yard.

"Sephie, *Sephie!* God, I wish you could tell me what happened to you! Why this fear?" He felt her shake her head frantically. "Perhaps I can help you. Let me help. There's nothing to be afraid of. I won't allow anything to happen to you. You're safe here with us. Is it Henry Pippin?" He felt her body stiffen in his arms. He looked around and saw that Tony and Biddy had long since disappeared and Leander had removed Bess out of their sight. He gently lifted Sephie off the ground and walked with her to the nearby stone steps, perched her on them and sat down next to her. He kept hold of her hand and she leant into his side like a child might.

"Sephie, please would you write down what has made you feel like this? I think if you told someone you might begin to feel better."

She buried her face into his arm but made no other sign. He thought that he shouldn't push her anymore in case she became more upset but at the same time realised that whatever Cobham found out he would not be able to discover the personal details which had made her this frightened. Somehow, he had to coax the truth from her. For a while they just sat there, leaning, until Sephie stopped shaking. She would have happily stayed there forever.

The sound of Snowball returning fifteen minutes later, with a flushed and triumphant Biddy upon her back, made Sephie sit up and straighten her hair. She nervously peeped up at Rokewode and he pushed a stray curl back from her forehead. A gesture which made her heart thump against her ribs. Then, and he had no idea why, he planted the softest kiss on the end of her nose and immediately regretted it.

Sir Anthony lifted Biddy from her horse and set her down on the ground. She was bursting with excitement. She was good at riding! Anthony had praised her natural ability and said that it wouldn't be long before she was cantering along Rotten Row like a regular dasher! She saw Sephie and Lord Rokewode sitting together on the steps and realised with satisfaction that Sephie hadn't even managed to get on her pony! Everything was perfect, although, she would much rather have had Lord Rokewode teaching her and witnessing her achievement than the over-enthusiastic Sir Anthony Calver. She liked him but he was all too readily her dedicated admirer and somehow their relationship was lacking any spark, any heart-stopping thrills. She wanted to be carried away by love and not followed about by a doting puppy who did everything he was told without question. She also wanted a fine title and an Abbey. At least she need have no fear that Sephie would steal her coveted future away from her!

"Are you ready to return to the house?" asked Rokewode, looking down at the curve of her cheeks, now thankfully showing a little colour.

Sephie heaved a tremulous sigh and nodded.

"Come along then. I'll take you home."

Home, she thought. Home. Where *is* home?

Hell and damnation, thought Rokewode, I'm starting to read her mind! I know exactly what she thought then and I have no answer for her.

He led her back to the house and handed her over to his startled sister with a brief explanation and then quit Grosvenor Square for the evening, going directly to Great Russell Street, where he knew Mrs Sheraton would be waiting impatiently for him. He needed some unadulterated time with his mistress. He needed to find himself again; he was beginning to feel as though he'd been swallowed up by wholesomeness and he was feeling suffocated and constricted. He needed a few nights of guilt-free debauchery to cleanse his soul of any lingering feelings of encroaching worthiness. He shuddered as he entered Mrs Sheraton's salon and tried to banish all thoughts of dancing chaste cotillions and accident-prone virgins. Here, at least, he knew what he was getting, he knew exactly what she was, he had no illusions. There was no mystery and no need to worry about anything other than pleasure; pleasure without compunction, pleasure without engaging the head or the heart. And, perhaps, when he thought about it, he did feel a little guilt for using her but in the end, everyone gets what they deserve, and such a brass-faced deceiver deserved no better.

She was arranged upon the sofa, surrounded by her ghastly little group of acolytes and was surprised enough, when she looked up and saw him, to allow it to show. And it wasn't a good surprised. She quickly masked the emotion, but he wasn't in the least thrown by her reaction, knowing that she must have been expecting to be rejected after the Hyde Park affair. He looked around the room at the usual crowd of sycophantic faces and he didn't even acknowledge them, just held the door open in an emphatic fashion. Mr Selwyn Vauville exchanged a look with Mrs Sheraton but she waved her hand dismissively and they all reluctantly left the room without a word.

Rokewode shut the door behind them and found himself a seat near the fire. Mrs Sheraton watched him warily, although this time nothing showed upon her beautiful face apart from a kind of silent acquiescence. She knew she had ground to make up, that he'd still be seething about her appearance at his stupid picnic. It'd been weeks since the incident and she hadn't had a word from him. She'd heard the gossip, of course; she kept her spies close and paid them well. She'd had all the news about the wretched dance classes and riding fiascos and dislocated shoulders and didn't wonder he'd finally turned up to see her. He must be desperate to escape all the tedious schoolgirls and his demanding family at Grosvenor Square — what a dead bore it must be for him. She adjusted her position so that he could appreciate just how her dark green satin gown moulded to her curves, better than any milky miss straight from the nursery. That shapeless creature from the fair was no competition for her; he would soon tire of such a whey-faced nonentity and realise that he needed a woman who could satisfy his needs in ways Miss Pippin could never dream of.

Rokewode was thinking that the salon smelt like a brothel, heavy with overpowering perfume and the stink of wine and tobacco. He'd never really noticed it before but now it made him feel slightly queasy. The furnishings were opulent and rich in colour, dark reds and greens, the fabrics heavy velvets and satins. He raked his fingers through his hair and pondered his options. If he left now, he may never be able to complete the onerous task he'd set himself and if he stayed, he'd have to live with himself afterwards and the consequences of having failed. Would it be worth the stain on his soul? He decided in that moment that it would. We all get what we deserve, he reminded himself. Small consolation for what he must do, but when he took everything into consideration, he felt justified.

He stood and went to her, held out his hand and pulled her to her feet; she came willingly, her green gown slipping seductively from one curved, white shoulder. She drew his head down and kissed him, but was momentarily unnerved when he didn't immediately respond, so she redoubled her efforts and achieved the result she was looking for. She took his hand and led him away to her bedchamber. He followed her into that familiar dark and oppressive cave and shut the door on his conscience and a certain pair of laughing grey eyes.

* * *

How could she tell him! It was impossible. If she wrote it down, it would be permanent, put into dark inky words, so ugly on the page, for all to see, for all to witness her shame. No, she could never tell anyone. She must keep it locked away inside where nobody could find it. If it were allowed out into the light of day, her life wouldn't be worth living. She thought of the sound of horses, clattering and snorting and whinnying in fright and she clapped her hands over her ears but that didn't help because the noises were inside her head. Everyone carried a parcel of their own sadness and grief around with them and dealt with it in their own way; she chose to push hers away and bury it deep where it could hide in the shadows and she could forget about it — for now. She'd been excited at first when Henry Pippin had found her and taken her away, making her promises of a new and splendid life; she thought she'd been saved from a life of religious torment. But it turned out that she'd just stumbled from one hell into another. Different hells, different torture. There was no point trying to escape the second one in case she was returned to the first. And then, there was the problem of what to do about poor Biddy, who had also been trapped and with no way of escape from her own father. Once forced into the fairground life she had very little choice about her future and was dragged from place to place as a human exhibit, which in the end had only served to make her less than human from sheer necessity; how could one remain human in such circumstances and not die a little inside?

No, she never wanted him to know, even though she would be leaving after Christmas. After the Ball. She wanted to always carry with her the look on his face when he'd seen her after the accident and when he'd kissed her on her nose! That would keep her warm when she was far away from Grosvenor Square and all of the wonderful Rokewodes.

She was no fool though. She knew he'd disappeared the night after the failed riding lesson to be with Mrs Sheraton. She'd heard Kitty mutter to her mother that he should be more careful with his reputation and their family name. Since then, she'd tried to stay out of his way so that he wouldn't begin to feel she was any more of a burden than he must already think her.

She continued working on the plans for the Christmas Ball and diligently learning the dance steps, when Monsieur Hercule Tijou came each week for their lessons. She was not in the least surprised when Lord Rokewode made his excuses and his place was taken by a slightly unwilling Sir Ambrose, who had clearly been brow-beaten by his wife into joining the rehearsals. Kitty danced with her husband so that she could keep him in line and Biddy continued to dance with Anthony. Freddie was irate that he was still paired with Babyngton because he said he greatly treasured his toes and Sephie danced with Leander who, it turned out, was surprisingly light-footed. She liked being with him because he didn't ask her questions she was unable to answer, and he was extremely solicitous without ever making her feel in the least awkward. Despite everything, she found she enjoyed the relaxed atmosphere of their makeshift ballroom and the laughter — above all, the laughter. It helped assuage her wounds for a short while each time.

Rokewode was away from Grosvenor Square for almost ten days. They saw nothing of him at all. Heard nothing. His mother started to complain about his neglect and rail against That Awful Woman. She declared that women of her ilk should be chased out of town. Pilloried and horsewhipped. Kitty tried to calm her, but nothing seemed to work. Sephie sat with her and made herself useful, running about at her beck and call, fetching things and ordering tea and toast to cheer her up and showing her the latest fashion plates to distract her. Eventually Lady Rokewode patted her hand and smiled, "You're a very good girl, Sephie. I don't know what I'd do without you. Shall we go over the guest list again just to make sure we haven't forgotten anyone important?"

Sephie raced out of the room to collect the list from where she'd left it. She flew into the library and stopped dead. Sitting at the desk was Lord Rokewode, pen in hand, a pile of papers in front of him. He looked up at her but didn't smile. She thought he looked tired and gaunt.

She glanced at her papers on the window seat and pointed at them. He rose and picked them up, taking a casual look at them before crossing the room to hand them to her.

"The Christmas Ball preparations? They're going well?"

She nodded and then cocked her head on one side, an indication, he knew very well meant that she was asking him a question. This time he chose to ignore it, he wasn't in the mood. She lowered her gaze and with a tiny, insincere smile she left the room before he was able to change his mind and blurt out that his week had been absolutely dreadful in every aspect. He returned to the desk and the enormous pile of papers that Major Cobham had handed him at their second meeting yesterday and stared blankly at them for several minutes.

He had met Cobham at his offices again and knew immediately from the man's expression that he had found something. For some reason he hedged for a good five minutes before allowing the lawyer to begin his story. After being so certain that he wanted to know everything, he was suddenly assailed by doubts. Over a week with Margaret had filled him with self-loathing and a measure of regret that he had set this scheme in motion in the first place.

Cobham had shuffled papers for a while until he could be sure he had Lord Rokewode's undivided attention. He had often seen this, a client's sudden, last-minute realisation that the truth may not be what they want after all.

"My lord, I have done as you requested. It's all here in your folder but I would like to explain, if I may, in my own words, what I have discovered."

Rokewode was filled with a mixture of emotions, none of which did him any credit, but he gave the lawyer permission to speak.

There was no clearing of his throat, in polite preparation; he just stated facts baldly and left Rokewode reeling.

Thirteen

"Miss Fane, or as I will refer to her from now on, Persephone, is as you suspected, a foundling. She was taken to the famous foundling hospital in Bloomsbury by a woman. We don't know who that woman was yet, but I'm afraid she was turned away because Persephone was already over two years old and they have a strict age limit of a year. The woman was apparently approached by a local gang of men who are known to prey on desperate women with promises to find a place for their children in the hospital for a small payment. The child was reluctantly handed over to these men. A witness who worked at the hospital said that just like all the mothers, this woman wept on being parted from the child. But, regardless, let her go. The witness assures me that the lady was young and probably some kind of respectable servant, shabbily attired and much distressed. This is, I have to say, very typical of the poor women who are forced to leave their children in one of these places. The child was taken by one man in particular and the lady left sitting on the steps of the hospital, where our witness went to comfort her. It is said that the lady then showed her a silver key hanging around her own neck. This key was to unlock a small padlock necklace which the child wore, engraved with her name. The mothers often left keepsakes with the children so that they could recognise them at a later date if they should ever wish to reclaim them. I suspect that the necklace was later sold for beer money. The lady said there would never be a chance that she'd be able to reclaim the child and told the witness that the child was called Persephone and that hopefully she would get to spend at least half of her life in the sunlight." Cobham gave his client a knowing look, "Interesting, y'see? Knew her Greek myths. When asked what her name was the lady had wept and answered that she was called Meryall. The witness remembered particularly because it was such an ill-suited name for such a sad lady. Then, she left and that was the last she was ever seen at the hospital."

Rokewode could contain himself no longer, "What happened to the child after she was taken? Do you know that yet?"

Cobham templed his fingers under his chin and contemplated his agitated companion, "Yes, I do. Are you sure you want to know, my lord?"

"Just spit it out, man! What happened to Sephie?"

Cobham sighed, he never liked this bit, "I have managed to trace those men and two of them happily gave up the third for a few guineas. His name is Edwin Stokey."

Rokewode started to his feet, "Give me his direction at once I want to ask him some questions myself!"

"Sit, Lord Rokewode, please. I'm afraid you'd get no answer as he was executed five years ago."

"Executed? What was his crime?"

Cobham sat back, his short, fat fingers gripping the arms of his chair, "Ultimately, murder. But, for our purposes — torture and neglect."

Rokewode slumped forward, head in hands. "Sephie?"

"Yes, my lord. I'm afraid it isn't uncommon amongst those who use foundlings as slave labour. There have been many famous cases going to trial resulting in other executions. Things have begun to improve but back then, malpractice was rife. There were no safeguards, and many children were abandoned at the mercy of some truly unspeakable villains. We have to be grateful that she survived. Others didn't and that was why Stokey was hanged." He stood and went to the sideboard and poured out two brandies and put a glass on the desk in front of his client. Rokewode grabbed it and downed it in one.

"So, our story with Stokey ended on the gallows but I have included in the folder details of his and others' treatment of

Persephone and I'm afraid it's not a pretty tale. There is one rather unexpected discovery though."

"Tell me," said Rokewode hoarsely.

"Persephone was able to talk when she was first taken in by Stokey and his wife. Neighbours all attested to hearing her speak or make childlike noises when she first arrived in the house. She was apparently a cheerful little thing."

"God," groaned Rokewode, not sure how much more he could endure.

"I still have more investigations to do but I do know that she was rescued from the Stokey's house and taken to a hospital where — she was treated for — " he hesitated again, "injuries and after she'd had time to recover from the physical wounds, she was sent to a small charity school for orphans run by a well-meaning but strict parson and his spinster sister. There, I believe she found some respite from the horrors of her early life and was taught to read and write by the sister and supplied with books for her learning and although their regime was harsh, she received, by contrast, a little Christian compassion. And, just as we begin to believe that her story might end well, she is stolen away by Henry Pippin to become a different kind of slave. His intentions, according to his alehouse companions were less than honourable. As yet, I have no evidence of what went on in his establishment when Persephone was in his — care. Probably the only people who will know the truth about that are Miss Pippin and Persephone herself. But, my lord, I'm loath to tell you that I suspect the worst. You may never get the full story from Persephone — it may be too traumatic for her to relate."

"I wouldn't want her to have to relive it. How is she even able to carry on? How can she smile and dance and laugh? How does she still want to make others happy when she has lived so little and suffered so much?"

"I believe she's making up for lost time. And, her nature, as far as I can ascertain, is naturally kind and forgiving and her character strong; nothing would be able to change that unless perhaps she was betrayed by those she loved. She hasn't had much opportunity to love or be loved but I think with your family she's found an outlet for all that she has to give. You have a good deal to think about," said the lawyer trying to guess how his client was going to deal with this information. He could see that he'd been profoundly moved and was probably spoiling for a fight. He'd seen it before when injustices were revealed; frustration often made the victims resort to brief but satisfying violence. It was a natural reaction to finding that the criminal had managed to get away with the crime scot-free. He pitied the depraved Henry Pippin should Lord Rokewode ever come face-to-face with him. The Earl looked like a man who could easily turn violent if given cause and he was already simmering with a cold and deadly rage.

"I have yet to discover anything about this Meryall lady. An unusual name, thankfully, which might make the search somewhat easier, but I can find no trace of her. I still have some avenues I haven't investigated so am hopeful, but one never knows. She may have died long ago or left the country, or her disguise could be so convincing she may walk among us and we would have no clue to her identity. We have no way of knowing."

"I don't care how much it costs — "

"It's not a matter of money, my lord! I will do my damnedest to solve this case satisfactorily. And I still stand by my original offer about Persephone. My wife agrees wholeheartedly."

Rokewode rubbed both his hands over his face. He felt as though the ground under his feet was crumbling away and he wanted to murder someone. *Several* people. He was not used to losing control of any situation — he always had everything in hand. But this had floored him. He was floundering. He wanted revenge. He wanted the truth. He wanted someone to suffer. He wanted to escape this feeling of helplessness and guilt. Above everything he wanted Sephie to know she was safe. How was he to make sure that everything would turn out to their advantage when there were so many elements over which he held no sway. This business had to take precedence over his other dilemma, the one of Mrs Sheraton. That, he would have to deal with at a later date, which was tiresome as he'd wanted it over and done with; he wasn't sure if he was able to continue with the charade. An image of Sephie's upturned face as they halted the dance returned to him, followed by the look of surprise in her eyes when he'd kissed the tip of her nose.

Cobham took a sip of his brandy and then looking at what remained in the glass, tipped it all into his mouth, "She will be damaged, that goes without saying. She has known no security or love or been able to depend upon anyone. She must be a thoroughly lost soul. A lost soul looking for somewhere to perch. You must be careful about what you offer her and find a way to make her understand that her life with you isn't temporary because I fear that any setback or disappointment may spur her into doing something rash."

"Good God, Cobham! You don't think she'd try to — ?" ejaculated Rokewode.

"Again, we have no way of knowing what she may do. She'll need stability. Will you inform your mother and sister of what we've found?"

Rokewode scrubbed at his tired eyes again, unable to focus on what the lawyer was telling him. Who could he tell? Would his mother understand that what had happened had not been Sephie's fault? Lady Rokewode was intolerant at the best of times; how would she manage when she knew that Sephie, her willing little helpmate was a foundling, a bastard and who knows what else? How was *he* going to manage now he knew this about her? Would it change anything? Perhaps Kitty would be the one. She could be remarkably sensible at times. Or Leander. Leander had a pragmatic streak a mile wide and was undoubtedly fond of the girl.

"I suggest you sleep on it, my lord and look at it with fresh eyes in the morning."

Rokewode agreed and stood up, "I can't thank you enough for this, Cobham. Whatever else happens, I can, at least, make her safe now. Let me know if there's anything you need. I shall forever be in your debt. I look forward to hearing from you again soon."

"I am happy to trust you with her care. I think it's above all fortunate that she fell into your hands and not some other's. God was watching over her in that moment, even if He had taken his eye off her for a moment."

They shook hands and Rokewode left to return home to St James's Square where he paced his drawing room floor until gone midnight.

* * *

Miss Bell had taken Miss Pippin and Sephie to the Circulating Library. Miss Pippin was dragging her feet as they crossed the street to their nearest library. Miss Bell was expounding on the virtues of being able to take so many books to read for a very reasonable annual fee when a cheery shout assailed their ears and Biddy looked up and saw, with great relief, Sir Anthony and Tom Babyngton strolling towards them. Oh, thanks goodness, she thought happily, Anthony had got her message taken the day before to his house by the young housemaid, Mabel, who had a romantic heart and swift feet. She couldn't have born two hours in the circulating library just looking at books! What a dead bore! And here they came to her rescue, looking so handsome and debonair. Now she could enjoy the outing without offending anyone.

* * *

While everyone was out, Lord Rokewode told Kitty and Leander everything.

It was one of the hardest things he'd ever had to do but he felt strongly that they should know in order to be able to understand the problem and help where they could. He certainly couldn't confide in Tony and Freddie who had never managed to keep a secret in their lives. And Babyngton he knew would be utterly useless in every department. He had decided that his mother was probably better off not knowing because one never could guarantee which way she'd turn, and he'd rather not be dealing with an attack of the vapours just at the moment. She could remain in blissful ignorance and Sephie could continue to be at her beck and call if she wanted.

His sister and best friend were silent throughout the telling of the story and for several minutes after he had finished, they said nothing, their faces frozen into masks as they tried to assimilate what they'd been told.

Kitty sat staring at him blankly, unable to form words, and then began to cry silently, the tears sliding down her pale cheeks while Leander shook his head in disbelief.

"No, Theo! This is too much. I can't believe it. I *won't* believe it! That little thing? So much horror. This terrible man, Stokey? He's dead for sure?"

Theo nodded, "He is. Hung by the neck. I wish I could have got my hands on him first but there's still Mr Pippin to be dealt with. Major Cobham is on his trail and I have complete faith in my man. Mr Henry Pippin will be brought to justice. But I may just kill him first though."

"*Theo!*" exclaimed Kitty through the choking tears, "You must let the law take its course or you'll end up at Tyburn."

"They don't hang people at Tyburn anymore, Kit."

"Well, I don't care! That *poor* girl! What she's been through! How will she ever recover? Oh, to *think* — ! And she's so cheerful and smiles at everything and laughs at ostrich feathers!"

Rokewode raised his eyebrows, "She *does?*"

"Every time she's offered a feather to appreciate by a milliner, her eyes light up with laughter and she has to hide a smile. I don't know why! Perhaps feathers have some particular significance for her."

Theo smiled to himself, "I believe they have."

"So, what is the plan?" asked Leander gruffly.

"We keep Sephie safe and make sure that Biddy's also kept under close observation. It's a huge concern that Sephie could be knocked down like that in broad daylight and with so many witnesses. We must be alert at all times and not let them out of our sight."

"You think the accident was — ?"

"No accident. Cobham swears it was deliberate and I'd believe that man if he said the moon was the sun and the sun was the moon. I just can't fathom who or why yet. Although I suspect Henry Pippin is hoping to stop her talking," replied Rokewode, with a frown, "That's another thing I haven't mentioned — apparently Sephie was able to talk when she was a child. I called on Doctor Emerson this morning and he says it's possible to lose one's voice and become mute because of trauma. It's hardly surprising that there should be some outward sign of what she has been through."

"Oh, the poor darling!" cried Kitty, weeping again. She buried her face in her hands and gave herself up to unrestrained sobbing. Her brother patted her shoulder in a perfunctory manner.

"She must not find out that we know. I fear it would drive her away and further into danger. I think she'd be mortified. Also, I don't want this to spread any further in case it gives Henry Pippin warning and a chance to escape justice. So, we wait while Cobham continues his investigations, and we guard Sephie. I also think we should perhaps consider removing to Rokewode Abbey for a while before the Ball. It's going to be difficult to keep an eye on them while they're able to freely wander the streets of London as I fear that Sephie is inclined to be rather impetuous."

"Oh, that's a splendid idea! And we can go from the Abbey to Fairtree Manor quite easily," said Kitty, brightening up a little. "I suppose Sephie is only like this because she's been set free from constraints and is finally testing her wings. She may settle down eventually when she finds her feet."

"I doubt it," murmured Rokewode, "There's a telling glint in her eye which makes me think that the real, and, I have to say, slightly unnerving Sephie is the one slowly emerging right before our eyes. The problem, of course, will be keeping her from flying off at every opportunity but at the same time, I have no wish to clip her wings."

Leander was clearly mulling something over, stroking his chin thoughtfully, "Have to mention it, although, feel a bit as though I'm betraying her — "

"It stays between these walls. We've one goal in mind so anything you think might be pertinent — "

"It's just that, I've noticed Theo, that she'll do anything you say. Keen to please you. Like a duckling! Following the first thing it sees!"

Rokewode grimaced, "Afraid you're probably right, dear friend. Noticed it myself."

"It's almost as though she were reborn in the fire and when she woke up there you were, Theo! Mother Duck!" said his sister with a watery grin. "How odd that she should choose you of all people!"

"Thank you, Kit for your sisterly vote of confidence. Just in case you fear I might abuse her misplaced devotion, I can assure you that I have my hands full already and have no intention of giving her the wrong impression."

'Oh, I know, dear! She is not at all in your style!" laughed Kitty.

Leander cast his friend a sidelong glance and wondered about the particularly grim set to his mouth. It seemed to him that since Sephie and Biddy had arrived in Grosvenor Square there had been some subtle changes in Theo. His usually nonchalant attitude to life and people in general had been replaced by a decidedly more irritable but responsible air. Leander chuckled to himself thinking that it was almost as though he'd had to become a father figure overnight. A role he'd studiously avoided all his life. When his father, Hugh Rokewode, died, leaving the young Theodore in charge of the family and estates, it had taken a couple of years before he'd realised that he had to step up and halt the rot. Oh, he'd gone through the motions at first and made the right gestures in order to fob off any criticism, but it hadn't taken long for him to revert back to his blithe old self and abandon any responsibility he should have been shouldering. Funds had never been a problem so if there were ever any issues, he merely threw money at it to make it go away. To see him rehearsing a cotillion, organising a picnic or giving a riding lesson with all the patience of a saint had made Leander stop and think. Was that hard shell he hid behind starting to crack?

"So, do we tell anyone else? Certainly not Mama but what about Miss Edie?"

Rokewode gave a gentle shake of the head, "I can't see any benefit in telling her at the moment. She no doubt sees a good deal for herself, she is so very perspicacious. I think I shall wait until it is absolutely necessary. The fewer who know the better. I wouldn't like Sephie to find out and think we'd all been conspiring together. It would hurt her beyond measure."

There, thought Leander, with some satisfaction, that's it.

* * *

Biddy wandered around the book-laden tables with undisguised indifference. Miss Bell and Sephie were gathering books into piles as though they intended to start their own library! Babyngton was carrying a small tower of volumes in his arms and following them around the room like a genial lapdog. The room smelt musty and dusty and Biddy longed to escape into the fresh air. Sir Anthony was leaning against the edge of a table, hands thrust deep in his breeches' pockets, watching her with amusement.

"I suspect reading is not really to your liking, Miss Pippin," he said with a wry smile. "Prefer to be doing somethin' else?"

She looked at him from under her dark eyelashes, with, she hoped, just the right amount of coquetry, "La! I've never seen so many dull tomes all in one place!"

"Staggerin', ain't it? Who has the time to read all of these? Dull dogs. I certainly don't. Far too busy admiring true beauty! No time for anything else."

Biddy lowered her eyes and allowed herself a pleased smile. There could be no doubt that she had Sir Anthony corralled. She just wasn't sure that he was what she wanted. She was still yearning to have Lord Rokewode also fenced in with her troupe of admirers, but he was showing no sign at the moment of being interested in anyone other than his ancient but, admittedly, beautiful mistress. Mabel, Biddy's talkative lady's maid, had been extremely forthcoming about Mrs Sheraton; it seemed that the servants heard a good deal more than one thought! She'd learnt a lot about all kinds of things from Mabel, who had keen ears and was adept at listening at doors and happy to divulge any secrets she discovered.

"Sir Anthony! Really, you must not be so bold! It's not at all proper!" said Biddy archly.

Anthony had no qualms about flirting with Miss Pippin for she seemed to have a thoroughly good understanding of how to deport herself. There was a knowingness about her which he assumed was based on experience and although a small voice in the back of his head told him to beware, he ignored it. She was just so ridiculously pretty. He couldn't stop thinking about her.

"What say you, we drop into Gunter's on the way back to Grosvenor Square? Would you like that? An ice or some cheesecake? I'd give anything to pop a chocolate drop between those lips of yours! Not that they need sweetening!"

Miss Pippin, who despite everything, still had an enduring sense of propriety, a remnant from her early days with a mother who had cared about such things, coloured a rosy pink and turned her back on him. She was not prepared to compromise herself for a mere Baronet with a small park in Wiltshire. Unless, of course, the worst came to the worst and she had no other choice.

"Beg pardon, Miss Pippin! No intention of making you blush! Gone too far! Forgive me and my runaway tongue!" exclaimed Sir Anthony, sheepishly.

Miss Bell who had been listening to their conversation, with one ear and growing alarm, finally felt moved to intervene, "Miss Biddy! Have you seen this delightful guidebook on the lakes of Cumberland, Westmorland and Lancashire? It even has poems on the subject and description in the most exquisite detail that one could feel almost as though one had been there oneself! I'm sure you would enjoy reading this on a rainy afternoon when there is nothing else to do but sit by the fire and dream of exotic places!"

Exotic? Cumberland? As far as she knew only sheep lived in Cumberland! And old farmers. Biddy went to Miss Bell's side and feigned interest in the dreary book. She could feel Sir Anthony's eyes follow her across the crowded room and turned to smile playfully at him over her shoulder.

Sephie was near the bay window where there was a table displaying some of the latest novels. She was carefully examining one called "Adolphus, or The Unnatural Brother," and wondering what on earth it could be about, when a sudden movement outside the window caught her eye and she glanced up. Passers-by were peering in through the glass panes at the books on display and others were strolling along the pavement in the Autumn sunshine; nothing unusual at all. Then, another furtive movement. She watched as a dark figure slid between two carriages and disappeared. Her heart faltered. She tried to breathe evenly but couldn't seem to control the waves of panic washing over her. She turned to look back at Biddy who was smiling teasingly at Sir Anthony. Biddy caught her eye and seeing the expression on her face hurried to her immediately.

"Sephie? What is it? Are you feeling unwell?"

Sephie pointed out into the street. Biddy looked but saw nothing but perambulating Londoners enjoying the afternoon.

"Did you see something?"

Sephie nodded vehemently and poked a finger into Biddy's breastbone, her eyes dark with fear.

Biddy turned pale and grabbed her hand, "Sephie! Are you saying you saw my — *father?*"

More anxious nodding and Biddy pulled at her friend's hand, dragging her across the room to where Miss Bell was standing watching them with mounting concern.

"Miss Bell? We must return to Grosvenor Square at once! It's imperative!"

Miss Bell, as always, unflappable, directed a speaking glance at Sir Anthony who, although inclined to behave foolishly, was not a stupid fellow, and he instantly took the required books and novels, checked them out of the library and gathering his gaggle of ladies together, he and Babyngton escorted them out into the street.

A murmured aside from Biddy told him all he needed to know, and he hurried them along Mount Street and into South Audley Street and encouraged them towards Grosvenor Square, like Christmas geese on their way to market.

They arrived somewhat breathlessly at the house and he battered at the door with his ebony cane. Bishoptree answered it in his habitually ponderous manner and announced that the family were in the drawing room and then relieved them of their pile of books with a disapproving frown.

At this point, Rokewode appeared to demand what all the noise was about and seeing their faces, ushered them into the drawing room without further ado.

Miss Bell saw Sephie into a chair and fetched a glass of water from the jug on the sideboard, which she handed to her but noted that the girl's hands were shaking.

Sir Anthony went straight to Rokewood and gave a brief explanation. Rokewood glanced across at Sephie who was clearly distressed and exchanged a look with Kitty and Leander.

"So, he *is* alive and still in the area. I think I shall send for Constable Thursby and then we shall all pack our bags and retire to Gloucestershire as soon as possible. I cannot tolerate that man being able to get so close to the girls and able to frighten them like this — it just isn't acceptable. I'll send a messenger ahead to alert my staff and we'll leave the day after tomorrow for Rokewode Abbey. I had better go and warn my mother as soon as possible so that she has plenty of time to fly up into the boughs and then recover from the shock. Tony, Babyngton can you both stay awhile? I have a few things that will need attending to and some letters to write. I must give my lawyer my direction in case of emergency and inform the

Bow Street constables that Pippin has been spotted nearby — I believe they'll be very interested."

"Gladly, Theo! Only too happy to be of assistance. Must say, I thought that Sephie was about to faint, but she's made of sterner stuff."

Rokewode gave Sephie one last glance, "You have no idea!" he remarked grimly and left the room.

Fourteen

Mrs Sheraton crushed the letter in her fist and let it fall to the floor. Mr Selwyn Vauville, Sir Leonard Tiploft and Mrs Alice Yelverton watched her with varying amounts of concern, relish and anticipation. Only very little of the former and a significant amount of the latter.

"He'll regret this, I can assure you. Nobody, *nobody* treats me this way!" She eyed the faces in her salon and tried to collect herself; she had no desire for her inner circle to see just how much she minded being abandoned so that her lover could spend some time at his country seat. She was outraged that after a week spent exclusively in her company that he hadn't declared himself or at the very least showered her with expensive jewellery and promises of a shared future. She had given freely of her time and expertise and didn't think it was unreasonable to expect some return from her investment. He was toying with her and she wouldn't stand for it. She would make him pay for his cavalier treatment and she knew just how to go about it. She had refused other quite satisfactory offers while she'd been waiting around for him to make up his mind and she wasn't getting any younger! She had to move fast to bring him scurrying back to her side.

"It must be that damn Pippin girl! She's the one causing this change of heart. She must be removed from the picture before she becomes even more of a problem. I think it might be time to implement my next little scheme."

"While he's away in Gloucestershire? Good idea, he's bound to be gone a few weeks if he has estate business to deal with. That'll give us plenty of time to make sure that nothing goes awry. *Finally*, I get my reward!" declared Selwyn Vauville with oily satisfaction. "I've been so looking forward to getting my hands on her."

"You're a disgrace to mankind, Selwyn! You should be ashamed for lusting after such an innocent young maiden."

"I like to try new things. You can hardly blame me! So tantalising."

"Well, Rokewode won't want her back after we've finished with her that much is certain! She'll be out in the cold and you can play with her to your — heart's content."

"Not sure it's my heart that'll be content, my love!" laughed Selwyn Vauville.

* * *

Sephie and Ann were packing the trunk with gowns and fichus, petticoats, a new caraco jacket in harebell blue linen and a delicate pelerine of cream lace which Kitty had given her. There were hats and bonnets to go in their boxes and all manner of furbelows and fripperies to be remembered, wrapped and packed. Sephie hadn't realised that she'd already accumulated so much. It made her feel very guilty indeed. They seemed to be costing Theo a fortune and she felt she had to repay him somehow.

Kitty wandered into the bedchamber and sat on the bed to watch the proceedings, pointing out that above anything Sephie would need warm clothes as Rokewode Abbey was extremely draughty with cold stone floors and wainscoting so ancient the wind whistled through the gaps. And mice. There were many mice. It really was a nightmare of a house and she didn't know why Theo put up with it. Even if he filled it with a dozen children and dogs and an army of servants and gardeners, it would still be an echoing unwelcoming mausoleum where you could drop dead and nobody would come across your mouldering body for weeks!

Sephie laughed and mimed a ghostly apparition to Kitty.

"Oh, heavens, yes. Of *course!* There's the Weeping Grey Lady and the Fat Wailing Monk. You see, the house makes *everyone* miserable. Even the resident ghosts!"

Sephie grinned, her eyes dancing, and Kitty again admired how she could just live in the moment. She idly twirled a ringlet that trailed across her shoulder, "Naturally, my stupid brother loves the place. We grew up there and he knew one day it would all be his and used to taunt me that I'd be thrown out as soon as someone was idiotic enough to offer for me." As usual, as soon as she mentioned Theo, Sephie pretended she was hardly paying attention at all, but Kitty knew that she was hanging on her every word. When Leander had pointed out that Sephie was always eager to obey any order Theo issued, Kitty had taken a long hard look at their odd little houseguest and come to the conclusion that Sephie had, without the shadow of a doubt, fallen in love with her brother, which was likely to prove quite an inconvenience because, even if he left That Awful Woman, Theo was never going to be able to forget Sephie's turbulent history. There had been rogues and reprobates and rakes in the Rokewode family tree, going back centuries, many of them still not spoken about in polite circles, but never was there a bastard or someone who was so fatally tainted by their past. It didn't matter that she was such an engaging creature, Theo was, above everything, a proud man and would never allow his family name to be besmirched. The best he could do was to take Sephie as his new mistress and Kitty was fairly certain that would never happen — Sephie was just not in Theo's line at all. What a pity she was such an unremarkable looking girl, so very small and plain and then, of course, there was the problem of her being mute. So many obstacles! No, it would never work out.

Kitty suddenly jumped up from the bed and went to Sephie and hugged her fiercely, dropping a kiss onto her cheek.

Sephie wondered what she had done to deserve such an uncharacteristic show of affection. She'd never been spontaneously embraced by anyone other than Biddy and theirs was a relationship forged — not in fire exactly, but out of fear and hopelessness. Now, she'd had two kisses, Kitty's and the other one on the end of her nose, given out of affection.

There was a soft but insistent scratching at the door and Ann opened it to allow Amadeus to prance in, his excited little legs getting in a tangle so that he fell onto his face. Kitty swooped him up into her arms and kissed his dark wet nose. Sephie sighed, of course here even the dog was regularly kissed, so perhaps it meant nothing.

"There you are, naughty beast! Oh, you're going to love the Abbey grounds! So many things to chase after — squirrels and rabbits and sheep and even a herd of deer! Although, I think you might want to wait until you've grown a bit before you try that! Isn't he just darling?"

Sephie nodded absent-mindedly as she folded another chemise and handed it to Ann, who tucked it carefully into the trunk. She was thinking back to her life before and wondering where it might have ended had the booth not caught fire; had Sir Anthony not decided to take his friends to see the Singing Mermaid and found them and rescued them. It had changed beyond belief and she was frightened now that it would change back again, and this would all be just a distant dream. It wasn't just Theo, it was all of them, even dear Sir Ambrose and Lady Rokewode, they were all so kind. Still, she'd make the most of her time with them and not dwell on the darkness to come. She smiled up at Kitty and thought she and Amadeus weren't that dissimilar really, both lucky to have found such a good home.

It wasn't long before Biddy joined them trailing two gowns, one in a rich burnt orange and the other claret red, "Which one shall I take? I haven't room for both. This? Or this?" She held each one up to her face in turn, "Red? Or Orange?"

"Oh, the red one, without a doubt!" said Kitty as Sephie pointed to the orange gown.

Kitty laughed and Sephie grinned. Biddy stamped her foot, "Be serious! Which one? I can't fit both in!"

Sephie held out her hand for the orange one and carefully folded it up and placed it in her trunk.

"Well, that's solved that little dilemma!" said Kitty, as Biddy ran off to get more gowns to cram into Sephie's luggage.

"You know, Sephie, you really shouldn't allow her to walk all over you. You're too submissive when it comes to Biddy," she said softly, but was thinking that Sephie was inclined to be too submissive when it came to Theo as well — *and* their mother — in fact, now she thought about it, with anyone in a position of authority. She watched Sephie turn her face away to hide her expression and felt the beginnings of a white-hot rage take root inside her; rage against the men who had done this to her, destroying her confidence and stealing her childhood, her dreams, her future. Kitty had lived a life of privilege, had been cared for and cosseted and knew little about the lives of the disadvantaged. She was aware that Ambrose had given a good deal of alms away to the poor and needy and had been proud but nonchalant about his generosity, understanding that it was just something that the wealthy did and never really considering how easy it was to be generous when you had plenty. She realised that she'd been shielded from the ugliness of life in all its revolting glory and, if she was honest with herself, she knew that she'd turned her usually searching gaze away so that the suffering wouldn't taint her happiness. She had never known what it was like to live hand to mouth, to fight for one's very existence or to have nobody to turn to for support. She'd listened to Theo recounting Sephie's life story and had been forced to wake up from her self-indulgent daze and come face-to-face with a world that frightened her. She had an uncontrollable urge to save Sephie, to step outside her own rarefied world and make a difference. She knew though that she must leave it to her brother, who clearly had a plan, and she didn't envy anyone who might try to thwart him; he'd always had a quick and deadly temper when prised out of his habitual state of insouciance. Recently she'd seen in him something which gave her a glimmer of hope that things might one day change for the better; she hoped that That Awful Woman might be about to get her marching orders, but one could never be certain with Theo — he might just be toying with them all.

Sephie was holding one of her new hats and absent-mindedly pulling an ostrich feather through her fingers, her mouth curling up at one corner in a secret smile and then with a small sigh she popped it in one of the hatboxes and firmly closed the lid.

Kitty couldn't wait to get her away from the dangers of London and into the safe Gloucestershire countryside and behind the massively thick medieval walls of Rokewode Abbey. She wanted to pull up the drawbridge — it was just a pity they didn't actually have one.

Lady Rokewode had not taken the news well. She'd demanded in a querulous voice why she was being so heartlessly tormented and why a lady of her advanced years and delicate health should be forced to travel right across the country in what was bound to be inclement weather in order to freeze to death or be eaten alive by rodents in that hellish ruin. Why *should* she have to abandon her comfortable routine, leave all her friends and their regular card parties and soirées in order to be rusticated like some disobedient student from Oxford? It just wasn't fair. She had to resort to sniffing her vinaigrette and fanning herself furiously and remained in a state of some wretchedness until Sephie pulled a stool up bedside her chair and sat stroking her hand in a soothing manner. Lady Rokewode eventually stopped gasping for breath and clutching her chest and patted the little hands holding hers. Persephone certainly was a comfort to her; she seemed to understand that all she needed was someone to listen to her, to pay attention to how she felt and then she didn't feel so frustrated about getting old and frail and being ignored. It was funny how ageing, if you were female, brought only isolation and neglect. Once your looks had dimmed it was as though you gradually faded from sight and became part of the furniture; they might as well lock you away in a cupboard or the cellar, with the dusty old out-of-date treasures that nobody wanted anymore and forget about you. You were only of any use to them when you could bear children, manage the household accounts and make other men envious. After that you were easily discarded like a pair of old shoes.

Sephie squeezed Lady Rokewode's hand and looked up at her with great understanding and that much-put-upon lady gazed into those kind grey eyes and forgot why she'd been so upset in the first place. It was the oddest thing. Afterwards she was content to have her clothes prepared and packed and began to look forward to winter at the Abbey and a Christmas Ball at Fairtree Manor. The world may have become topsy-turvy, but she was going to kick up her heels again and remember her girlhood when her infuriated father had been forced to fight off her numerous admirers at the door where they queued, hoping to engage her affections.

Her children eyed her with astonishment and wondered what had so suddenly changed her mind but said nothing in case she remembered that she was meant to be piqued and reached for the smelling salts again.

Lord Rokewode spent the days fruitfully tying up some loose ends and arranging for business to carry on as usual in his absence. He paid another visit to Major Cobham and listened to what that wise gentleman had to say and then had a long and valuable chat with Constable Thursby before he was able to give his full attention to arranging the travel plans and making sure everything went smoothly with the Herculean task of moving some dozen or so people across country without too much discomfort and weeping. Two lumbering travelling coaches had been sent on ahead, weighed down with trunks and bandboxes and portmanteaus. They'd be following the next day in three private post-chaises, his smart new curricle and another travelling coach. The ladies would travel in the well-appointed carriages and the gentlemen would ride alongside or drive the curricle.

Kitty arranged the seating plan, a rather ticklish campaign when the post-chaises only comfortably seated two people, and nobody wished to travel with Lady Rokewode. Kitty paired herself with her husband because he never minded her falling asleep on his shoulder and was always ready to comfort her when she inevitably became fractious and Biddy was placed with poor Miss Edie because the nanny could cope with absolutely anything. She'd received a special request from her mother to have Sephie in her carriage and Kitty thought at least she would be able to enjoy her flow of complaints not being interrupted all the way from London to the Abbey! Sephie, when she'd been asked if that would be acceptable, had nodded eagerly and Kitty thought, yes, endless stories about Theo's misspent youth would keep Sephie entertained and give her something to daydream about. Kitty sighed and wished things were not quite so complicated.

Theo instructed all the outriders to keep away from the side Sephie would be sitting on, so the close proximity of horses didn't alarm her. Her terror still haunted him, and he was determined that she should, with his help, somehow conquer that fear but also that he would find out what on earth could have given her such an irrational but all-consuming aversion. It seemed so oddly out of place when she was, in every other aspect, truly stout-hearted. He was over-seeing the final arrangements, with the help of Leander who was fastidious and exceedingly efficient and after a fair amount of negotiating, was finally satisfied that everything was as it should be. He had an overwhelming sense of relief to be leaving the city behind him with all its ungovernable hazards; the sooner he could get this motley collection of souls to the relative safety of the Abbey, the happier he'd be. He saw Miss Edie tucked up in a warm fur rug with a hot brick at her feet and Biddy ensconced bedside her, then watched as Ambrose handed his wife into their carriage, that damned dog yapping irritably in her arms — and then wondered why, at the very last minute, Sephie suddenly raced past him and disappeared into the house. He popped his head into his mother's carriage, and she told him she'd left her reticule on the hall table. Sephie reappeared beside him, slightly out of breath and he held out his hand to her; there was the slightest hesitation and then she placed her hand in his and he helped her up the steps into the carriage. She gave Lady Rokewode her reticule, tucked a warm rug around

Lady Rokewode's knees, settled herself and only then looked up at Theo.

He smiled at her and mouthed, "Thank you!"

She shook her head and gave a small shrug. She didn't mind. She liked his mother. Compared with the people who had unfortunately been her constant companions since the day she'd been abandoned, Lady Rokewode was an absolute angel, and she was more than happy to spend time with her. And anyway, if it took even the slightest burden from Theo's shoulders, she would readily endure being locked in a cage with a lion at feeding time. Listening to Lady Rokewode she found to be no hardship at all, she was so looking forward to leaving London for the first time in her life and seeing some new sights into the bargain, that she would happily forego all comforts.

"Mama will probably sleep a good deal of the way," said Theo, "And so, you're on the best side for a clear view of the countryside. You must say if you need to stop at any time or if you need help. Just let down the glass and wave a handkerchief — there'll be someone close at hand at all times. Now, we're about to leave. Have you everything you need?"

She nodded, her eyes alive with excitement and her cheeks flushed pink.

For the hundredth time he wondered how anyone could have ill-treated someone who was so clearly harmless.

She cocked her head at him.

He cursed silently, having forgotten that she saw far too much. He'd allowed his anger to show on his face and now she was questioning him. He smiled reassuringly at her and closed the door before he got himself deeper into trouble. She had already turned away to his mother.

The servants, including Paston, Ann, Mabel and Tony's sullen valet, James Mullens, were in the travelling coach and Leander was driving Theo's curricle, a job he would not have trusted to any of the others as Tony was notoriously reckless and Babyngton had no sense of direction. Leander was, in fact, an extremely fine whip, remaining composed whatever happened and never endangering the lives and limbs of passers-by. Theo was able to entrust his new vehicle to him without a qualm but knowing that the state of the country roads would mean that Leander would have plenty to complain about when they stopped for the night.

The postillions mounted up, wearing their distinctive white hats with curly brims and green coats with gold braid. Theo had decided against guards as there would be four gentlemen riding alongside the coaches and he felt there was safety in numbers and therefore did not expect to be attacked by highwaymen. They were all armed and everyone bar Babyngton was handy with a weapon. Freddie, astonishingly, being a particularly fine swordsman but Babyngton, was inclined to accidentally shoot anything that caught his overexcited eye.

After a quick appraisal of the cavalcade's readiness, Lord Rokewode gave the word and they were off, circling Grosvenor Square and heading out to the turnpike. The travelling coach bringing up the rear, Lady Rokewode out in front so that she didn't have to suffer travelling in a dust cloud, or having her chaise pelted with stones and mud, kicked up from the other coaches' wheels.

Sephie had her nose pressed against the glass as they made their slow way across London, passing Tyburn and then on towards Uxbridge and the Chilterns. The weather was fine for November and the roads, being mostly turnpike roads and suitably surfaced, were passable with a little care and as long as the rain held off they should manage to reach Stokenchurch, where they would spend the night at the George and Dragon, that day; however on a journey of forty miles with a stop for changing horses nearly every ten miles and over a dozen people involved, there were bound to be delays.

Theo was determined not to hurry them along at breakneck speed just because he was keen to get some miles between them and anyone who might threaten his family. *Family,* he mused, glancing around at the various participants of this new adventure — how interesting that I should call them that.

Babyngton reined in beside him, their mounts brushing flanks, "Hallo there, Theo! This is a bit of a lark, ain't it! Brilliant idea to get out of the city! Dashed if I'm not a trifle fatigued with the same old people and the same old places and all the terrifying matchmaking Mamas eyeing one up and asking how many acres one has. This will be a tonic to us all I think."

"Indeed, dear Babyngton, indeed," said Theo.

A while later, as the lead coaches toiled up a steep hill ahead of them, he was able have a word with Leander in the newly purchased curricle, "How's she handling, Lee?" he asked.

"Like a dream! Excellent all round. Fast and responsive, infinitely more biddable than mine."

Rokewode laughed, "Sounds like you're describing your perfect woman!"

Leander grinned, "My perfect woman is a little closer than she was yesterday. God, Theo! What if this don't work? What if she just laughs in my face?"

"Then she doesn't deserve you. You're quite a catch, y'know. I don't mean your vulgar and excessive wealth. I mean you are, beneath all the pedantic nonsense, a remarkably fine young man."

Leander rolled his eyes, "You make me sound like some dull country parson! Not exactly an enticing prospect when in pursuit of fair maidens."

Theo's horse bridled at a low hanging branch and he took a moment to calm him and get him back in line beside the curricle.

"Well, Sephie firmly believes Matilda's heart is already won but that you refused at the first jump. I don't think Sephie is very impressed with your tenacity!"

"I know. She poked me in the chest accusingly. It was quite salutary. That girl can be a little too perspicacious for my liking, Theo! By the way, heard anything else on the matter from your man?"

Theo's dark brows lowered, "He still has people looking for the woman, Meryall, who left her with Stokey but with no success as yet and he and Constable Thursby are hot on the trail of our dear Mr Henry Pippin. I feel with us out of the way they'll have a clearer line of sight and be able to make some progress. I'm confident that Cobham will ruthlessly hunt him down. He rather took to Sephie and he and his wife wish to adopt her should she need a home."

"I'm not in the least surprised, sweet little thing. Damnation, but she deserves a happy ending, Theo! Surely she has a home at Grosvenor Square! I can't bear to think about it. Keeps me up at night. I shall very soon take to drink at this rate."

"Hmmm," murmured Theo, "A bit late to start laying the blame at Sephie's door."

Leander snapped the tip of his whip over the horses' heads and glowered at his friend, "Think you're mistaking me for that drunken oaf, Tony! Never touch the stuff."

Theo gave a shout of laughter and urged his horse on up the hill after the carriages and curricle.

They stopped a few times to change horses with fresh ones he kept at the inns, and for other various reasons, all of them trifling but nevertheless made good time to Stokenchurch, reaching the George and Dragon just as it was getting dark.

Before the process of transferring everyone from carriage to inn became too chaotic, Theo and Leander made sure that Lady Rokewode was taken straight to her room, with Sephie following carrying all of Lady Rokewode's paraphernalia, books and reticules, shawls, fan and her trusty vinaigrette, while Tony and Freddie were in charge of making sure no stray horses crossed her path.

Fifteen

The inn was impressively large and rather grander than the usual run of coaching establishments. Theo had made sure that everything was booked in advance and the quietly enthusiastic owner was at the door to greet them, wearing his best blue coat with brass buttons and carefully tied neckcloth. He was welcoming without being obsequious and very much in charge of matters. Paston was busy tipping the ostlers and Theo thanked his own very loyal postillions before they turned in for supper and a well-deserved night's sleep and then he helped guide Miss Bell to her room and made sure that everyone in the party was attended to. The inn was teeming with servants and guests, and full of noise and strong cooking smells. The parlours were crowded but the landlord said they would have the dining room to themselves when they'd had time to wash and settle in. He informed Theo that the very best dinner that his inn could provide would be ready as soon as he wished.

Sephie and Biddy were sharing a bedchamber as the Rokewodes were taking up a large proportion of the available rooms. Sephie was glad to be able to lie on her bed for a moment and consider the day's events while Biddy dressed for dinner. It had been exhausting but entertaining and she'd enjoyed every minute of being in the company of Lady Rokewode who, it turned out, was really rather entertaining. Sephie thought that she'd become so demanding and unfortunately inclined to carp and complain because nobody took the time to listen to her. Lady Rokewode had regaled her with all kinds of stories from her past and it'd been fascinating to hear about her life with her husband, Lord Hugh Rokewode, and to learn about how difficult it was for a female to establish herself in society and not allow herself to become lost in the marriage, becoming no more than another member of her husband's staff with no worth of her own. It had taken her a while to find her feet and make sure that everyone understood that she wasn't just an insignificant part of his enormous entourage. She had opinions and ideas and she wasn't prepared to sit in the corner being a docile wife. So, she'd run the Earl ragged, which is probably why he'd earned a well-deserved reputation for being so unforgiving and cantankerous. Sadly, his son took after him. It'd been eye-opening for Sephie, who had no family of her own and no history, other than a nightmarish life spent with the Stokeys or the strict parson. Even though Lady Rokewode had clearly had quite a trying start to her marriage Sephie was envious of the tales she had to tell. They sounded much like the fairy tales she'd read in one of the books the parson's sister had given her, which she'd adored and read into tattered shreds, until the parson had discovered it and confiscated it, saying that such godless nonsense would do nothing for her lack of piety. She had mourned the loss of that book deeply and recited the stories to herself at night for comfort because she knew them nearly off-by-heart.

Biddy sent her to find Mabel, who had somehow gone missing since they arrived, and Biddy needed help with her hair.

Sephie dashed off down one of the long corridors which linked the rooms but got a little turned around and had to retrace her steps, and just as she was racing around the corner towards what she hoped would be the staircase, she saw Theo coming towards her. She pressed herself against the wall so that he could pass by, but he stopped and smiled down at her.

"I've just been hearing what a glorious travelling companion you are, and I wanted to thank you for whatever you managed to convey to my mother to make her so — amenable. We've never had such an uneventful journey. Normally, she complains from the moment we leave London to the moment we return. You have a very special gift, Sephie, for making others happy."

She peered up at him through the gloom and wished she could find some way to make *him* happy. She could sense the tension in him and wondered what was making him so stressed. It was probably just the onerous task of removing his entire family across the country to Gloucestershire. She felt guilty as she realised that it was partly her fault. If she hadn't come into his life bringing Henry Pippin with her, Theo would be happily continuing his normal existence without a care. She lowered her gaze and stared at the floor not wishing him to read her thoughts.

"Sephie?" he murmured and lifted her chin with one long finger. "Don't do that. This wasn't your fault. Henry Pippin is a very nasty character and I promise that he won't be able to hurt you anymore."

Her eyes flashed at him in the gathering shadows, as they searched his face. He returned her gaze and they just stood in suspended silence. It was only broken when two slightly inebriated gentlemen thoughtlessly barged past them, shoving them together against the wall. Theo put out his arms to protect her from the impact and her hands pressed against his chest to steady herself.

"Are you all right?" he asked, as he stepped away, but the words died in his throat as he saw the look in her eyes. "Good God! What is it? Sephie?"

She was visibly shaking, her eyes wide with fear.

"They were just boorish oafs, nothing to be worried about! Unless — unless it was *me?* Did I frighten you? Did I hurt you?"

She buried her face in her hands so that he couldn't see her shame. In the darkness the sudden violence had reminded her of times when she'd been at the mercy of others and their base desires. She'd felt panicked and afraid and, worst of all, helpless.

She felt him move a little closer and tried to calm her breathing.

"It's all right," he said softly, "Nobody can hurt you. I will not allow it." Then he gently put his arms around her and drew her to him and held her. Just held her until the shaking stopped and she removed her hands from her face and rested her pale cheek against his waistcoat. Two housemaids bustled along the corridor with piles of laundry in their arms and giggled as they passed the couple standing together in the shadows.

Eventually Sephie sighed. She knew this heaven couldn't last.

Theo knew he should let her go but had known a moment's peace holding her in his arms and couldn't help but wish it could continue so that he didn't have to think about anything else but, concerned that someone else might come along and see them, he reluctantly withdrew his arms and stepped away.

Sephie had felt terrified and now she felt bereft; she very nearly laughed at her own stupidity.

Theo had an inkling that her fear was a memory of some other dark place and the unspeakable brutality that she'd endured during her short life. He was at a loss to know how to cope with what Cobham had revealed to him but also how to protect Sephie without scaring her away. He feared she'd probably bolt if she knew how much they'd discovered.

"Everything will be all right once we get to the Abbey. You'll feel safe there."

She nodded and smiled at him a little wanly. She had felt safe just then, with his arms circling her and her head leaning on his chest. It felt as though she had found her home.

"Are you all right now?"

She nodded again and pointed towards the stairs.

"Would you like me to come with you?"

She shook her head although inside she was whispering, "Yes!"

He flicked her chin with a careless finger and she quickly turned away and went to find Mabel.

Theo watched her go with several regrets uppermost in his mind; he regretted the whole damn business, going to the fair and taking the girls to his mother's house and he regretted having just allowed himself to sample the effect Sephie seemed to have on people. With his arms about her he'd felt a strange kind of contentment enveloping him and he'd been tempted to stay there and give himself up to its thrall. He also regretted perhaps making Sephie's life even more complicated by showing her a measure of affection he could never share with her on a permanent basis. As Kitty had so succinctly put it, Sephie was not in his style at all.

Biddy looked wonderful in a gown of dusky pink with a white lace pelerine and her hair teased into clouds on either side of her exquisite face. She twirled in front of the mirror and finally declared herself ready. Sephie had changed into a rather unadorned grey gown without much enthusiasm and they walked downstairs together and into the dining room. Everyone was already there, and they all were aware that Biddy had arrived last so that she could make an entrance. Sephie slid away from her side, so that she could enjoy their admiration and she found her seat beside Lady Rokewode and kept her eyes on her plate in front of her. She didn't allow her gaze to wander down the long table to where Theo was sitting.

"Ho there! Sephie!" said Freddie, who was on her left side, "Ain't this an absolute wheeze? Here we all are in Stokenchurch when just this morning we were in London! And tomorrow we'll be at Rokewode Abbey. Imagine what our grandparents would have said! Modern times, eh?"

Lady Rokewode on hearing this unintentionally careless comment, Sephie having no relations of her own, reached under the table and squeezed Sephie's hand. Sephie looked up in some surprise. Lady Rokewode leant forward and whispered, "Freddie never could hold his drink, dear. Runs in his family, I'm afraid. His father was a shocking drunk as is his brother. Sad affair, his father left them never to return and his mother went into a decline. Of course, Freddie is the sweetest drunk imaginable, very affectionate and silly. But don't mind anything he says when he's in his cups! Doesn't mean it."

Sephie smiled. She didn't mind really, she knew Freddie was harmless and just said whatever came into his head, it didn't matter to her at all, one couldn't constantly be on one's guard about what one said, it just wasn't possible. What she did mind was that Theo was studiously not looking in her direction and she knew why. He was regretting that spontaneous moment in the corridor. She longed to reassure him that it didn't signify, that she would be leaving after Christmas and that his life would return to normal. She wanted to explain that she understood. She knew what she was and harboured no illusions about her future. She would always remember how she and Biddy had been rescued and sheltered and treated as though they were valued and that she would always carry with her, close to her heart. The food tasted like ashes in her mouth and she drank rather too much wine without thinking. She looked up and saw Biddy frowning at her and pushed her glass away.

That night she lay and stared at the canopy above her bed and made plans and tried not to think of the overwhelming fear she'd felt in the corridor or the reason she'd been able to overcome it. From now on she was determined to enjoy the last month and a half she had left with the Rokewodes and she would do her best to make sure everyone was happy, and that Leander and Matilda found each other again. She sighed because after her plans for the Rokewodes and their friends, her schemes became a little hazier and she couldn't quite envisage what might happen to her and she was also starting to worry that Biddy might not want to leave with her, she seemed quite content where she was and although they'd sworn to each other, when things were at their worst, that they'd always support each other, Sephie was now having serious doubts about Biddy's intentions.

* * *

They woke to a fine drizzle and lowering cloud but after a substantial breakfast, everyone was glad to be on the move again.

They eagerly clambered into the carriages and settled themselves. Just as Sephie was about to climb up the steps she spotted the empty dickey seat at the back of the post-chaise. She looked around at Theo, her eyes wide with mischief.

He narrowed his eyes, "No," he said unequivocally.

Her face fell and she quickly turned away to climb the steps into the carriage.

He let out a frustrated puff of breath and reaching out stopped her with a tap on her shoulder, "God, Sephie! It's drizzling! Are you sure?"

She nodded so enthusiastically that he was forced to laugh. "All right, but if you catch a chill, you cannot blame me! This is all your doing. Come, I'll help you up. But, only for a couple of miles or until you start to feel ill." He handed her up into the precarious-looking seat perched at the back of the cab, fetched a blanket and tucked it around her knees.

"I think you'll be better off without that adorable bonnet. Pull the hood of your cloak up to keep the drizzle at bay. And Sephie? If you want to stop, you must wave. I'll be riding just behind your carriage."

She handed him her bonnet and grinned at him, her rosy cheeks dimpling, and he shook his head in amused despair.

Kitty, who was just being helped into her carriage by Sir Ambrose, stopped to look disapprovingly at her brother.

"Theo! You're surely not going to allow her to sit there! It's far too dangerous! And a little unseemly!"

Theo shrugged, "I'm afraid she's made up her mind, Kit, and will not be deterred with talk of flying gravel, mud or even highwaymen! Small but unbelievably stubborn."

"I'm beginning to realise that whilst attempting to keep her safe, we shall have our work cut out for us! Well, keep an eye on her for heaven's sake! I shall know whom to blame if anything happens! All *right*, Ambrose, I'm *coming!*"

Theo had a word with the postillions, warning them to keep the pace as steady as they could. He then had a rather surprising lecture from his mother, "Darling, I really don't mind at all! It is a trifle odd but Sephie deserves some indulgence. As long as she doesn't get hurt. I shall take a little nap, I think." Theo wondered what had happened to the mother he had become used to.

The cavalcade set off again and Theo stayed resolutely just behind his mother's carriage to watch over Sephie. He couldn't help but laugh silently at her obvious excitement at being out in the open air and moving fast through the autumnal countryside. A couple of times he had to sternly reprimand her as she bounced up onto her feet to get a better view of a farmhouse, or river or flock of sheep. It was as though she had no fear of the unknown, only links to her past seemed to daunt her; and he began to think of her as a newborn, fascinated by everything she saw but as yet unaware of the dangers they may conceal. She'd never had the opportunity to consider how easy it would be to tumble headlong from a high dickey seat and get crushed by the following coach — she'd been otherwise occupied. But he wasn't going to think about that now. She turned in the seat and looked back over her shoulder at him. He'd never seen her look so happy or alive; her eyes were dancing as her loosened hair whipped across her laughing face. She was already damp from the persistent drizzle and clearly didn't care. Her behaviour might be considered hoydenish by those who had no clue to her history but, worryingly, he was beginning to see the world through her sparkling eyes.

"Game little thing, ain't she!" said Anthony, as he brought his horse alongside, "Never seen anything quite like it. Shame all females aren't more like her."

Theo smiled wryly, "It'd be damned exhausting if they were! She's such a curious mix of peaceful and wild. Never know what you're going to get."

"Today is wild, without a doubt!" laughed Anthony.

They rode on like that for some miles, Anthony mostly lingering outside Miss Bell's carriage and grinning in through the rain-spattered window at Biddy, who was heartily sick of being jostled about by the inconsiderate carriage and just wanted the journey to be over. She could see ahead to the lead coach and was able to observe her friend perched in the dickey seat. She'd be having words with her later! Of all the things to do! Not at all the behaviour of a refined female and Biddy feared she might be tarnished by association. There was a great deal at stake, and she didn't want Sephie's inappropriate conduct to spoil her own chances at an advantageous match. Being trapped in a carriage with Miss Bell was beginning to fray her nerves and she wondered how many more historical and geographical points of interest she could hear without screaming. She now knew the history of every church they'd passed and every manor house; she knew where Charles II had stayed, and which monasteries had been suppressed and where there were ancient Roman ruins and Saxon burial sites. It was a dead bore. It was like being lectured by a human encyclopaedia which barely drew breath.

Miss Bell, on the other hand, was having the time of her life. A long journey would have daunted most ladies of her age, but she revelled in travel of any kind. Not having had the opportunity to become accustomed to it, it was still a thrill; a nanny's life being, on the whole, fairly static and tedious by nature. She was in good company and well cared for and travelling in the finest style, in the most expensive and well-sprung carriage money could buy. She was hugely enjoying sharing her wide-ranging knowledge of the English countryside with Biddy, who was barely able to stifle her comical yawns; Miss Bell found the girl's unwillingness to learn about anything other than the latest fashions vastly amusing and her perversely mischievous side delighted in tormenting the poor creature.

At the next coaching inn, Theo handed Sephie down from the dickey seat so that she could seek some welcome warmth and comfort in the parlour, while the horses were changed, and everyone stretched their legs. The drizzle had finally given up and the sky was clearing. He found his mother fast asleep and snoring, so left her undisturbed in the carriage. Leander had an absolutely splendid grumble about the weather and the poor quality of the beef at the inn and the lumpy mattress at the George and Dragon and Theo let him have his head. He knew his friend would be getting anxious about seeing his grandmother and all the social activity looming on the horizon. Leander wasn't one to revel in anything that called upon him to be gregarious — he retreated into his shell and put up barricades. Theo was already becoming slightly concerned about how they were going to bring this whole scheme of Sephie's to a satisfactory conclusion. There were so many elements which could not be controlled with any degree of certainty; humans being notoriously hard to influence especially if they were as obstinate and peculiar as his friend Leander.

After a quick rest and some refreshment, the party resumed their places, apart from Sephie who reluctantly agreed to leave her dickey seat and return to Lady Rokewode's side.

"I'm sorry, Sephie, but the lanes on the next leg of the journey can be a little hazardous — the hills are steep, and the tracks narrow and rutted," he told her, callously ignoring her pleading eyes. "You'll be safer inside the carriage and my mother would be glad of your company." He felt it unsporting to use an inducement he knew she'd not be able to refuse but felt he'd no other choice. She'd given in immediately and returned to her unpaid duties of companion and nursemaid. He tried to catch her eye to convey his gratitude, but she resolutely avoided his gaze.

As they left Oxfordshire and entered his home county of Gloucestershire, he began to feel the usual excitement about seeing the Abbey again. They negotiated the steep hills around Burford and crested the hill beyond without too much difficulty as the roads had not yet turned to winter quagmires. As they crossed the high treeless expanse above the Rissingtons he was able to breathe more easily. Nearly home.

They passed Church Westcote and Nether Westcote and there the woods became dense and lush and the hills gentler, the climbs less precipitous, and finally the long drive down to the village of Church Iccomb, gently nestled in its combe and surrounded by orchards and pasture.

Natural springs and a small meandering river fed the village with good clean water and the farms on his land provided meat, fish, wool, milk and butter, bread, mead and ale and most of what he and his tenants needed to survive. As they made their weary way along the final mile or so, he saw neighbours he recognised and they waved or doffed their caps in greeting; he raised his whip in acknowledgement, pulling up his horse a few times to exchange words with a closer acquaintance. Sephie had lowered the glass in her carriage and was hanging out of the window to watch the Abbey come into view.

"There it is!" shouted Sir Anthony, catching sight of a glimpse of golden stone walls in the distance. He was happily looking forward to downing a long tankard of ale and his horse, sensing his excitement, became a little skittish, dancing sideways and snorting alongside Lady Rokewode's carriage. Sephie quickly ducked back into the coach and returned to her seat. Theo firmly rapped Tony's knuckles for being so careless and then went to reassure Sephie that the danger had gone. She cautiously reappeared in time to see Rokewode Abbey emerge gloriously from the sheltering swathes of trees which were cloaked in autumnal russets and golds.

The first thing that caught her eye was the beautiful rolling parkland and the woods stretching as far as the eye could see across the valley. In between there was the odd farm or small cottage, cobalt blue smoke curling from its chimney, with animals in their yards and workers in the fields. Then, the trees parted, and she could see the roof, towers and tall twisted chimneys of a very substantial building come into view. Surrounded by a high wall and a partial dry moat, it was well-defended against intruders. They passed a broad and picturesque lake, with a small island in the middle and as they drew closer to the Abbey, she saw an intimidating gatehouse in the encircling wall, a formidable barrier which looked deliberately unwelcoming. As they approached it the lead postillion blew his post-horn to alert the gatekeeper and she watched, entranced, as the gates opened, and their long procession of mud-spattered carriages passed through the astonishing archway and into an inner courtyard bordered by cloisters.

The carriages swung around the central area of grass and came to a halt in front of another gateway which led into the Abbey itself.

There was a moment's stillness and then pandemonium as the postillions jumped down and ran to the horse's heads, footmen appeared and began opening carriage doors; a butler and housekeeper took over organising the assimilation of a dozen guests into their household without so much as a raised eyebrow.

Lord Rokewode gave his mother his arm and escorted her into their family seat and his critical eye noted that all was as it should be. His staff were well-paid and highly trained, but he'd inherited his father's uncompromising nature and expected everything to be run efficiently with the least fuss. His butler, housekeeper and estate manager ran the place for him, and he'd never known them put a foot wrong, he had complete confidence in their abilities. They'd served his father for many years and knew the workings of the house and estate as well, if not better, than Theo did himself.

They entered the Great Hall and Sephie's intake of breath was audible.

Sixteen

Theo couldn't help himself, he looked at Sephie over his shoulder; he wanted to see her reaction.

Her head was tilted back, mouth open, grey eyes wide as she took in the vastness of the Hall, with its hammer beamed roof and the carved heads of Green Men, Dragons and Angels. It was like something out of a fairy-tale book.

He smiled. Her eyes found his and for an all too brief moment he delighted in her evident wonder. A part of him prayed she'd never lose that refreshingly innocent view on the world. He realised that he'd grown weary of the studied indifference of the jaded and indulged individuals he usually rubbed shoulders with. To him this Hall, this magnificent example of swaggering medieval architecture, had almost become commonplace because he'd grown up there, but he loved it and he'd come to understand his duty to it, to the building and its environs, to the many people who depended upon it and upon him. It was a great burden to bear but he was finally coming to terms with what was expected of him as the Lord of the Manor.

And there were those roguish dimples! He almost laughed out loud. She was so transparent; he could see exactly what she was thinking. Her speaking eyes told him that she thought it astoundingly beautiful but ridiculous; ridiculous that one small family would have need of such a cathedral-like chamber. Wait until she saw the rest of the Abbey! He found he wanted to be the one to give her the inevitable guided tour. He found that he needed to see her response to his beloved home. He caught himself thinking that and wondered why it should matter. Perhaps it was because she'd obviously been so deprived and neglected and he had a desire to be the one to make her smile, to bring new experiences to her door and expand her previously limited horizons. He turned quickly back to his mother who was greeting the housekeeper, Mrs Atherton and Chilton, the butler. Out of the corner of his eye, he saw Kitty lead Sephie away through the throng, past the draught-excluding screens at the end of the Hall, towards the main staircase and knew she'd be showing her to her bedchamber. Miss Bell, who knew her way around, was, with the help of a footman carrying her belongings, encouraging an exasperated-looking Biddy across the chequered floor to the stairs as well. Everything in hand, he thought, not without a flash of irritation that his sister would be the one to show Sephie the Long Gallery. He then studiously applied himself to his senior members of staff who were giving him news of the estate and his tenants. He knew he'd have to closet himself with his estate steward before long to catch up on all the overdue business which manifested itself when one was sole owner of an enterprise like Rokewode Abbey. It came with endless advantages but could also be a millstone, if one didn't stay involved and vigilant.

* * *

Sephie sat on the edge of her bed, her toes not able to touch the floor and her heart thumping in her chest as though she'd been running. She was tired and slightly damp still from the drizzle and had been reminded by Kitty to change her clothes for dinner. Ann was scurrying about the room unpacking and hanging gowns up so that the creases would drop out; she was chatting away about what she'd seen on her journey and marvelling over the Abbey.

"Oh, Miss Persephone! It's like a dream! I never seen the like. But it's so big I fear I'll get lost! My bedchamber has a window over the garden and is quite the best room I've ever had! But how I'll find my way back to you I've no idea! It's like a maze. And with so many staircases I just know I'll get into a muddle. Oh, and the paintings and treasures at every turn!

Did you see that suit of armour in the gallery? I thought it might just walk off as though it still had someone in it! I hope I don't hear clanking metal in the night! They say there are ghosts that roam the cloisters and the ruins! Oh, Miss, it's really quite frightening!"

Sephie agreed whilst thinking that for some reason she was not in the least daunted by anything she'd seen or hadn't yet seen! The thought of ghosts delighted her, and she rather hoped she might see one.

"Which gown will you wear for dinner, Miss?"

She glanced at the jumble of clothes and pointed to her favourite pink gown and watched as Ann gave it a good shaking and fluffed up the lace cuffs and collar.

Sephie still had the sensation that the countryside was flying past her and she was feeling a little dazed and tired. Ann gave her a knowing look, "Why don't you have a little rest before dinner, Miss? I'll come and wake you in an hour or so."

Sephie wanted to protest but her eyelids were heavy, and her limbs felt sluggish, so she agreed and allowed Ann to remove her shoes and tuck her up on the bed, covering her with the beautifully embroidered quilt. The moment her head touched the pillow, she was asleep. Ann quietly finished what she was doing and then tiptoed out of the room. Just as she was about to pull the door closed after her she saw Lord Rokewode coming along the corridor and dropped a curtsy.

"Everything all right, Ann? Do you have all you need?" he asked.

"Oh, heavens, yes! It's all so perfect! Thank you, my lord."

"And Miss Persephone? Is she well after the journey?"

"Yes, indeed, my lord, she's as good as she ever is. Never frowns, never grumbles. She's fallen asleep and I'm going to wake her before dinner. She was quite tired."

Theo took a step towards the door and glanced into the bedchamber to see Sephie curled up on the enormous four-poster bed. Her hand tucked under her flushed cheek, mousey curls falling across her forehead and her breathing steady.

"That's excellent. Too much fresh air and excitement for one day," he said softly.

Ann nodded, "She's a bit wayward sometimes but good as gold on the whole."

"Indeed," murmured Theo, "I want you to take very good care of Miss Persephone please, Ann. She may one day have need of your loyalty and friendship. And, just in case anything should happen, I want you to promise me that you'll stay by her side, come what may." He took one last look into the chamber, "I think I can trust you to keep watch over her?"

"Yes, my lord! I swear I'll never leave her, whatever happens!"

"Good girl," said Theo and he strode off to find his sister.

* * *

Kitty was sitting in a chair beside the fire in her bedchamber and was wriggling her stockinged toes before the flames. She looked up as Theo knocked and entered the room.

"My feet are damp! I shall probably get a chill on my lungs."

"No, you won't," said her brother unsympathetically, throwing himself into the opposite chair. "You're as tough as old boots, never ill in your life! Where's poor Ambrose?"

She wrinkled her nose, "Don't call him *poor* Ambrose! He's taken Amadeus out for a walk before dinner. I told him Paston could do it, but he was insistent that he needed to exercise his legs, he gets aches if he sits for too long. The injuries from the carriage accident. His shoulder pains him in cold, wet weather."

"And after sixty miles of non-stop talking he needs some peace and quiet."

"If I weren't so exhausted, I'd throw a shoe at you! Is everyone settling in? Mama is fine and having a rest before dinner."

"All seems to be well. Biddy has escaped Miss Edie and has bolted herself in her room! Tony, Leander, Tom and Freddie are sharing a pitcher of ale in the parlour and Sephie is fast asleep."

Kitty laughed, "I'm not surprised! She must wear herself out with all her passion!"

Theo looked thoughtfully at her, "Ann says she'll stay by Sephie whatever happens."

"God, Theo! Are you worried that something might?"

He shrugged his broad shoulders, "I'm fairly certain that there are those who wish her harm but I'm also confident that she'll be safer here than in London. The Abbey is like the mighty Basing House, well-fortified and more readily defended than Grosvenor Square."

"If my memory serves, Basing House fell to the Roundheads despite its famed defences! I hope you're right Theo! I couldn't bear anything — " began Kitty, frowning.

"I swear Kit, I'll not let anything happen to her."

She glowered at him, "I'm glad to hear you say that. There's something so defenceless about her, and yet she's as brave as anything I've ever seen." She idly smoothed the creases in her skirts, "Are you still thinking that Sephie and Biddy should be found positions?"

There was a long silence while he stared into the leaping flames, "No, I — feel sure that some unsuspecting fool will come up to scratch and Biddy will run rings around him and he'll probably end up on the River Tick, pockets entirely to let."

"And Sephie? She has less chance of making a good marriage."

He cast her a dark glance, "You think so?" He sighed, "I suppose you're right. Major Cobham and his wife wish to give her a home should she leave our care."

"Leave our care? Theo! Why would she do that?" cried Kitty much dismayed.

"I've no idea but — Cobham believes she may — even be driven to hurt herself should anything untoward happen."

"Good God! Theo, you can't be serious! She wouldn't — "

"I can't believe it either. But there's a possibility she may feel compelled to run away if she's cornered or in danger. Ann has promised to stay with her if she does. She seems a sensible and kind girl and I trust her to do her best for Sephie."

They sat in silence for a few minutes. The only sound the crackling of the fire.

"Theo?"

"Yes, Kit?"

"You won't break her heart, will you?"

Silence.

"I don't plan to," said Lord Rokewode eventually, feeling older and more fatigued than he'd ever done in his entire thirty-two years.

* * *

When she awoke, Sephie stretched and opened her eyes and looked around her. There was Ann smiling down at her and in front of the fire was a hip bath full of steaming water and she sat up keenly, eager to wash away the dust and grit from the journey. She'd caught a glimpse of her hair after her dickey seat adventure and she looked a terrible sight. She slid out of bed and Ann helped her undress, down to her chemise as always and step into the shallow bath. A while later, after a luxurious wash, Sephie was dry and being helped into the rose-pink gown. Ann dressed her hair simply with just a plain white riband threaded through her curls.

Biddy arrived wearing a deep blue gown and a fetching turban of striped satin with strings of beads draped elegantly around it.

"Oh, you look nice, Seph! Pink is most becoming on you. It gives your pale cheeks some colour. I think we'll go well together. Are you ready?"

Ann watched her young mistress and wondered why on earth she put up with Miss Pippin. Ann thought if she were her friend, she'd probably be tempted to give her a good slap.

Biddy wittered on and twirled in front of the looking glass, "Do you like my turban? It's all the rage apparently. Mabel fashioned it out of some material left over from my new round gown. I think it's rather becoming. You don't think it makes me look matronly, do you?"

Sephie loyally shook her head.

They made their way down to the Hall where they were to dine and Biddy exclaimed in delight as they skirted the screens at the end of the huge room; the table, lit by dozens of candles and beautifully laid out with silver, crystal, linen and flowers and bowls of fruit, looked very different. The enormous fire was stacked with large logs and the smoke was rushing up the chimney, carrying golden sparks up into the night sky. The gentlemen stood up as they entered, and Lord Rokewode and Sir Ambrose came to greet them and draw them to the table. Sephie had never felt quite so special or regal. Footmen were carrying dishes in from the kitchens and the aromas were already making her mouth water; she suddenly realised that she was extremely hungry.

Theo led her to her place, and she was delighted to find she was sitting next to Leander, who pulled out her chair for her, admired her gown and said she was looking much rested after her adventurous journey.

Theo made a short speech welcoming everyone to the Abbey and hoping they'd have a splendid time over the Christmas season and then he seated himself at the head of the table on Sephie's right. Miss Bell was making a fuss over Lady Rokewode who was at the other end of the long refractory table and Biddy was happily chatting to Sir Anthony who was opposite Sephie, his head of long golden curls close to Biddy's white-blonde ringlets; they looked perfect together, like a pair of seraphim.

Sephie's eyes were drawn up to the ceiling again, with its carved beams and sculpted heads; it was like nothing she'd ever seen before and the height made her feel very small and insignificant, but she was filled with admiration for the beauty of it. She tried to imagine its creation, the architects, builders, carpenters and stonemasons beginning the project with nothing but an idea in their heads, perhaps a few drawings and an unwavering belief that if they worked hard enough, they could make this beautiful building together.

"You'll get a crick in your neck, Sephie," remarked Theo, smiling. She lowered her chin and grinned at him.

"It's rather overwhelming at first, is it not? You'll eventually become more used to it until you barely notice it."

She shook her head in disbelief, she'd never get used to such a glorious work of art; she'd always be in danger of bumping into furniture as she gazed upwards to the heavens. She spied a particularly fierce-looking dragon winding its way around one of the main beams and looked to Theo for an explanation.

"My ancestor was apparently an imaginative soul," he said, interpreting her expression correctly, "With a peculiar penchant for the fantastical. You'll find these carved beasts hidden all over the Abbey — Unicorns, Dragons, Angels and Demons and all things ancient and mythological. I like to think they're watching over us and keeping evil spirits at bay, benevolent guardians, I suppose. He must have been quite a character."

The welcome home dinner was elaborate and delicious and Sephie tucked in as though she feared she might never get another meal. She wasn't entirely sure about the White Soup with cream and almonds but everything else was a treat she'd never forget. Boiled Ham with Pickled Cherries, Chicken Pie, Veal Cutlets, Venison and Trout, Lemon Pudding, Saffron Cake and Orange Jelly were mostly foods she'd never tasted before and each one was an adventure for her inexperienced tastebuds. She ate with undisguised appreciation, all the while listening to the conversations going on around her, nodding and smiling or shrugging and frowning, when asked her opinion on any subject. When asked by Babyngton if she would be hunting with them, she quickly shook her head, eyes firmly fixed upon her plate. Leander, seeing her discomfort, deftly changed the subject and suddenly everyone was discussing the merits of erecting a Grecian Temple on the island in the lake. Sephie took a breath and looked up to see that a footman was placing a cut-glass dish in front of her. She picked up the same type of spoon that she'd seen Kitty choose and took a mouthful. It was smooth and creamy and sweet and tasted of something she couldn't describe.

She cast a sideways glance up at Theo, who was sitting back in his chair watching her, "Chocolate Cream," he said.

Chocolate, she thought, I've heard of it but never had the opportunity to try it before. *Chocolate.* It was — indescribably good. She relished every luscious mouthful, scraping the last of the mixture out of the glass dish with studied dedication and laid down her spoon with some reluctance. Then, out of the corner of her eye she saw another dish of Chocolate Cream being pushed towards her.

Theo raised an eyebrow, "Please, eat mine. I'm entirely satisfied after a surfeit of Lemon Pudding."

She shook her head, resolute. He pushed it closer with a sly grin. She frowned at it as though it were a temptation she should be able to resist. The long fingers gave it another push and with a weak little sigh she picked up her spoon again and gave in.

"I think I should add Chocolate Cream to the list of useful bribes," murmured Theo.

She dimpled at him and continued to spoon the pudding into her happy mouth.

He sat back and observed her with a crooked smile.

Miss Bell, pausing halfway through a sentence to Tom Babyngton about whether the apple pie contained nutmeg or cinnamon, saw Theodore's interesting reaction and enjoyed another thrilling wave of goosebumps. She did so love it when she was proved right.

After a lengthy dinner, the ladies retired to the drawing room while the covers were removed, and the gentlemen enjoyed their port and a discussion about estate management and the ideal material for constructing a temple. They eventually tired of such dull conversation and joined the ladies.

Leander, Tom, Tony and Freddie set up a card table for a rowdy rubber of whist. Ambrose was deep in a book and Biddy, sitting with Kitty and Miss Bell on one of the sofas, was trying forlornly to catch Anthony's eye. Sephie was helping Lady Rokewode wind yarn into balls and listening to her recount fascinating tales about the Abbey's chequered past. About the wealthy nobleman building it for the Cistercian monks in the twelfth century and how in subsequent years it was destroyed and then rebuilt over time by various rulers, until nobody could afford the costs anymore and it was allowed, shamefully, to fall into ruins by one of their less than admirable ancestors. All that was left was the hotchpotch of additions and remnants, the south aisle, one wall of the nave and the cloisters, around which was built an early Tudor mansion with a nonsensical corner tower, ornate archways, twisted chimneys and later Gothick augmentations, all sheltering within the defunct moat and surrounding high walls that had been partly reconstructed from the stone of the main transepts, the quire and the chapter house.

Theo was bone-weary. He stretched out in a high-backed armchair, crossed his booted legs at the ankles and thrust his hands deep into his pockets. It was quite a tiring journey from London when he was just by himself but transporting so many people safely across country took a good deal of planning and thought and he'd the added burden of a possible outside threat to some of the party, which meant that relaxation was impossible. At least, now that they were at the Abbey things might be a little more manageable. He closed his eyes for a moment thinking of the coming Christmas Ball and what it would take to make sure that Leander didn't abscond out of sheer terror. He opened them again and found Miss Edie's eyes upon him. He raised an eyebrow at her and she smiled, and he knew she was aware that there was something afoot. She was the most perspicacious of females with a lively imagination and wicked sense of humour. He had always felt an undercurrent of guilt that she'd had no other choice, as a dependent spinster with no relations, but to remain with the family and had just transferred her undisputed skills to minding his mother, but she'd always taken an amused slant on her odd life at Grosvenor Square and was keen to confirm, whenever questioned, that she was extremely content with her position. They couldn't do without her so he chose to believe her, quashing any misgivings he might have.

Miss Bell was busy thinking, turning things over in her mind and trying to find answers. She wished that her darling Theodore could tell her what was going on but realised that whatever the dilemma was, it was clearly too early to share it with her. She felt certain that both Kitty and Leander were in on it; she'd seen the secretive but eloquent looks they'd exchanged, and she was fairly sure that it concerned the two girls. That much was obvious to her, but she couldn't yet see where the danger would come from. And she was confident that there *was* danger otherwise why would Theodore have bundled the whole family into a fleet of carriages and brought them to this veritable fortress just as winter approached? She would remain alert and be ready to help whenever she was needed.

A great shout came from Anthony at the card-table as he jumped to his feet and threw his cards down in disgust.

"Babyngton, you utter scoundrel! Are you *cheating?*" he exclaimed.

Babyngton looked astounded, "I most certainly am *not!*" he expostulated.

Freddie rolled his eyes, "Tony, sit down! Babyngton ain't clever enough to cheat, you dolt!"

This seemed to make complete sense to Sir Anthony, so he took his seat again and continued to play as though nothing untoward had happened.

It wasn't long before Miss Bell retired to her bedchamber and Kitty and Ambrose followed a short while later. Biddy was yawning fit to crack her jaw because nobody was taking any notice of her and the men were still focused on their cards. It looked as though Lord Rokewode had drifted off to sleep and Lady Rokewode was talking Sephie to death. Eventually, she'd had enough and bidding everyone a curt goodnight, she left the room. The door closed behind her and Theo opened his eyes.

Sephie was wide-eyed at his mother's tale of how the Abbey had been used to hide various refugees and dissidents over the centuries and how many had come to grief within the walls of their home. She told her how, during the persecution of Catholics, one unfortunate monk had been carefully hidden in the priest-hole but everyone else in his religious community had either been driven out or killed and he had been left to die in the hidey-hole and his bones were only discovered years later when the house was being altered.

Theo was watching Sephie from across the room, his eyes half-closed and sleepy. Her cheeks were flushed with a mixture of fear and excitement, her lips eagerly parted, her hands clasped tightly in her lap, the balls of yarn quite forgotten. His mother excelled at spinning a ghost story, having a dramatic turn of mind and a natural desire to be centre stage. In Sephie, she had found her perfect audience. Lady Rokewode finished the story with a ghastly flourish and Sephie drew her breath in with delighted terror.

Theo chuckled, "Mama? How is it that the ghost of the monk is so very fat, when he was nought but a pile of bones when he was finally found?"

"Oh, Theo, you should know never to spoil a good story with the truth!" said his mother happily.

Sephie looked at him and frowned, she didn't want the tale ruined either. She then made a questioning motion and he laughed out loud.

"You wish to know where the priest hole is?"

She nodded eagerly.

He shook his head in mock despair, "I'll show you tomorrow."

She jumped up and approached him, holding out her hand.

"God, Sephie, *really?*" he groaned and reluctantly got to his feet and took her hand. He led her out of the drawing room and into the Great Hall, to the enormous fireplace which was a later addition to the room. He picked up a branch of candles from the table and held it for her so that she could see into the dark recesses beside the now smouldering embers in the grate.

"See if you can find the latch," he said teasingly.

She stepped into the wide hearth and began to fearlessly feel around the walls for the trigger to the secret room. He could hear her rapid breathing and laughed. She glanced over her shoulder, her eyes sparkling, and, to his dismay, he felt an odd sensation in his chest, a kind of strange ache which he found completely baffling. His heart thumped a little uncomfortably in his throat and he wondered if he were having a heart attack like his father.

There was a sudden sharp clicking noise from within the shadows and Sephie turned and grinned at him in triumph. She was too slight to move the door herself, so he joined her and helped push the secret stone panel open. It moved slowly with a dry grating sound and he lifted the candles so that they could see inside the tunnel.

"It leads to a narrow room within the inner wall. Please tell me you have seen enough!"

Those damn irrepressible dimples! They spoke volumes.

He sighed and led the way into the gloomy space. She caught hold of his sleeve and held it as they edged along the tunnel. After about ten feet they came to a tiny room, which contained nothing but a stone seat. He held the candles up so that Sephie could appreciate the full glory of the terrible little room. He glanced at her and found she was staring at the bench, the candles making the unshed tears in her eyes glimmer.

"Sephie, you cannot be crying for the Fat Wailing Monk? You're far too soft-hearted. Nobody mourns the Abbey's ghosts."

She looked up at him, her sad little face lit by the steady candle flame and for some unfathomable reason he reached out and gently wiped a lone tear away from her cheek with his thumb. She put a hand up as though to stop him and then quickly turned away and disappeared along the dark tunnel.

He stood for moment and wondered what the hell had come over him. He swore under his breath and followed her out.

She was standing a little way from the fireplace, her back to him.

"Sephie? I'm so sorry. I just — meant to — " He didn't know what he'd meant to do. He found that he was completely mystified by his own actions. He suddenly felt as though he were losing his grip on his emotions and he found it both infuriating and somehow stirring. He took a step closer to her, but she suddenly spun around, giving him the benefit of her brightest smile, which he immediately saw didn't reach her eyes. She made a little curtsy, the colour in her cheeks high and then fairly flew from the Hall.

Lady Rokewode was just coming out of the drawing room, so Sephie took all her paraphernalia from her and accompanied her up to her bedchamber, glad of the distraction. After she had handed Lady Rokewode over to her lady's maid, Sephie ran to her own room and shut the door firmly upon the memory of Theo's conscience-stricken face. It didn't stop him haunting her dreams though and she spent a sleepless night trapped in dark confined spaces trying desperately to find a way out.

Seventeen

Following a morning spent closeted in the library with his estate steward, Mr Roland Ashby, catching up on all the Abbey business, Theo insisted that Leander should accompany him out for a quick ride around the nearest parts of the property to see how everything had been progressing in his absence.

After the third time Theo had either ignored his comment or given a brusque response to a question, Leander reined in his horse and stopped to consider the stiff back of his friend as he rode along the edge of a wood ahead of him. Theo realising he was alone, wheeled his horse around to see what had become of his companion.

"What ails you?" he asked.

Leander contemplated him for a long moment, "Theo, have I done something to offend you?"

"Never!" responded Theo instantly. "Why on earth would you think that?"

"You're being particularly taciturn and although I'm used to the vagaries of your moods, I cannot fathom what may have caused this morning's peculiar behaviour."

Theo grimaced and leant forward to pat his impatient mount on its neck. "A long journey and a late night. That's all."

Leander gave him a look of amused disbelief, "Doing it too brown, my dear friend. You're a seasoned traveller and often stay up to the early hours in your club or at parties. No, it's not that. I'd hazard a guess that it's the added worry of protecting Sephie and Biddy, but I know you have that in hand."

"Mountains out of molehills, Lee. I assure you there's nothing amiss."

Leander eyed Theo with suspicion, "There's something you're not telling me. No, don't deny it! I've known you since we were schoolboys and I know when I'm being fobbed off with a cock and bull story."

"Let it go," said Theo abruptly.

"God, Theo! You know you can tell me anything! My lips are sealed! I'm a closed vault! Have I ever betrayed you?"

"Of course not. I know I can trust you but this — I don't even know what *this* is!" Theo slumped a little in the saddle, "To be perfectly frank, Leander, I'm in something of a quandary."

"Well, I can't advise you or sympathise until you tell me what it's about."

Theo stared out across the ploughed fields towards Bledington and said nothing for a minute. Leander waited patiently.

"I think I may have unintentionally given someone the wrong idea about my sentiments."

"Ah, I see. You mean, you've misled some poor female into believing that you might care for them more than you do?"

A frowning silence.

Leander watched a covey of partridge fly low across the field and settle beside a hedge. "This female? You cannot just tell her the truth?"

"No."

"And you're absolutely sure that you've no feelings for her; feelings which you might perhaps be suppressing because of the unsuitability of her station?"

Theo gave his friend a sharp glance, "Leander?"

"You must think me very unobservant! You mean Sephie, of course. What have you said to her to mislead her?"

Startled by a jackdaw swooping out of the wood, Theo's horse danced a few steps into the field and while he regained control, he wondered how much he should divulge. He was rather taken aback to find Leander already had an inkling of the problem; he'd been certain that nobody would have a clue.

"I don't think I've *said* anything untoward, but I may have overstepped by making an inappropriate gesture — " He took a deep breath, "I know she was affected by the moment — or something."

"Do you know why you may have been prompted to make this false move?"

"I have no damned idea at all!"

Leander fixed him with a slightly disapproving frown, "I think you do, Theo! But I think your damned pride is, as usual, an enormous stumbling block and you're not prepared to admit to yourself that Sephie has somehow got under your skin. I think you'll find everyone here has somehow been altered by her presence. It's almost as though the appalling life she's endured has given her an insight into everyone's true nature. She seems to be able to see what people need, even when they hardly know themselves. Or maybe she always had that gift, that ability to make people happier. Maybe she's managed to cling onto it despite having been confined in a hell we can only imagine." He tried to assess how his words were affecting his companion, but met with a blank mask, "I think my dear friend, that you see something in her, not just to pity or rescue, like a stray wounded animal, but something which has, astonishingly, finally broken down the barricades around your well-defended heart."

"Damn it, Leander! You don't know what you're saying. It's not true. I haven't any feelings for her other than — the natural concern any human being would have for such another unfortunate human being. She merely brings out my charitable side. Nothing more."

Leander raised his eyebrows, "You're lying to yourself. Ask yourself how you felt when you saw her lying in the street after the carriage hit her. Or when Cobham told you all she'd been through. Were you indifferent? I think not. I think you care about her — you just refuse to admit it because it'll complicate your well-ordered life and mean that your world will have to change. It doesn't fit in with your plans. She doesn't really fit into anyone's plans. She's thrown us all out of our habitual stupor — almost as though we've all been asleep, and she's shaken us awake. You feel it, and so do I. Your mother! Have you not noticed how she's become less truculent and is very much more amenable? She smiles when she sees Sephie and will sit talking to her for an age and it's not just because Sephie listens. Even Kitty loves her, and we all know that your sister is notoriously hard to please! You know what I think it is? I think Sephie holds up a mirror, so we see ourselves through her eyes. And because she's quiet and unassuming we barely notice the effect she has upon us and gradually we learn a little about ourselves and we aren't even aware of the influence she's having upon us. You, my friend, have had your portcullis removed without your knowledge! It could be viewed as a miracle. I thought you were a lost cause."

A muscle clenched in Theo's jaw, "I think you've run mad, Leander. She's just — a temporary disturbance. She and Biddy will eventually leave, and we shall return to our normal routines."

Leander made a scoffing sound, "You can deny it all you like, Theo but make sure that you don't leave it too late to admit the truth to yourself."

Theo kicked his horse into action with a little too much repressed anger and Leander, realising the discussion had now been summarily closed, followed him.

* * *

At breakfast Sephie was looking puffy-eyed and subdued and Kitty wondered what had happened to upset her. She then saw that Theo was in one of his familiar brusque moods, eating in silence and speaking in gruff monosyllables. After finishing his meal, he pushed his chair back with unnecessary force, declaring he'd be busy all day with estate matters. Sephie didn't even raise her eyes from her plate and it was ridiculously obvious that they'd had some sort of falling-out. Kitty sighed, because she had no doubt her stupid brother had done or said something thoughtless, and now she'd be forced into the role of peacemaker. A little while later she had the opportunity, while showing Biddy and Sephie the Abbey ruins, with Tony and Miss Bell, to have a quiet word with her.

"Sephie, my love? You seem a bit down in the mouth. Are you all right?"

Sephie nodded and smiled. The smile was so false that Kitty was hard-pressed not to laugh out loud.

"I suspect that my darling brother has been his usual thoughtless self and said something unforgivable?"

No response.

"You know, I have no illusions about him, so will not mind at all if you wish to share it with me. You could write it down?"

A tiny shake of the head.

"Well, I shall just suppose that he's at fault because he usually is. Did he scold you? No? Mama says you went off to find the priest-hole together last night — did he scare you with tales of ghosts? So, perhaps then he said or did something inappropriate and alarmed you?"

Sephie's eyes swiftly met hers and she saw the answer in them although Sephie was vehemently shaking her head. So, Sephie had retreated into her shell because of something Theo had said or done and, taking into account the girl's harrowing childhood, one could hardly blame her. Also, it was obvious to anyone with an iota of sense that Sephie had fallen in love with Theo but probably had a clear idea in her own mind that she wasn't ever going to be suitable, even if Theo could be made to admit his feelings to her. What a horrible muddle, thought Kitty crossly. She didn't know what to do for the best. It seemed to her that there was no perfect solution. Someone was bound to be hurt and she was fairly certain that it'd be Sephie. Theo was thirty-two, he had experience and Sephie was a mere eighteen years old and although she'd already suffered more than most people in an entire lifetime, she was such an innocent in many ways and, not being able to readily express her feelings and thoughts, must be very limiting and frustrating for her. Guessing how she felt wasn't really satisfactory.

Kitty thought the situation couldn't possibly become any more complicated.

"I want you to know that I'm on your side, Sephie! If there's anything I can do to help, I want you to please let me know. I know how Theo can be and I am often driven to despair, but I will *not* have you being bullied or hurt!"

Sephie put her hand on Kitty's arm and gave her a pleading look.

"No, don't worry, I won't say anything! But I shall not allow him to ride roughshod over you. Oh, I'm sorry, I can see I'm upsetting you! Come, let us go and admire the cloisters and the moat. There is so much for you to see!" and linking her arm through Sephie's they marched off after an enthused Miss Bell who was providing Tony and Biddy with a fascinating and detailed historical commentary, which neither was listening to.

* * *

The days passed and they all found there was plenty to do. There were long rambling walks when the weather was fine, and the gentlemen went hunting and shooting. The ladies played Quadrille or Whist, read their novels, embroidered or just chatted whilst nibbling on sweetmeats and sipping sweet wine or hot chocolate, which Sephie thought was heaven in a cup.

Sephie knew she had retreated a little into the shadows again and was at a loss to explain, even to herself, exactly why. Theo's unexpected show of warmth in the priest hole had shocked her out of her state of starry-eyed bliss. It had suddenly occurred to her, in that terrible dark tunnel, that whatever happened she'd never be able to have what she so desperately craved. She'd been damaged beyond redemption and repair and no man, especially the stiff-necked Theo, would ever be able to overlook that and she would always be alone. That surprising show of tenderness had made her realise that she was in more danger of revealing her feelings than she'd imagined. She had to remember that after the Ball she'd be leaving and would never see him again. She had to remember that if he knew everything he'd be repulsed and could never be light-hearted with her again, would never be able to have her in his house or near his family. It was only lies and subterfuge keeping her at the Abbey. If the truth came out and they discovered she was so unforgivably contaminated, she wouldn't be allowed to stay in case she defiled the family. At least if they never discovered her shame, she'd be able to think of them without too much pain and regret after she'd left them.

One afternoon, the sun came out with a weak promise of some winter warmth and made a valiant attempt to coax the Rokewodes and their guests out into the open air. Sir Anthony suggested that they should row out to the island in the lake to see if a temple might be at all feasible, so Theo, Tony and Freddie, with school-boyish enthusiasm, pulled the rowing boats out of the boathouse and with them in one vessel and Babyngton and Ambrose in another, they raced off to the little wooded island, their voices carrying clearly across the water to those still on the shore.

"God, look at Tony! Silly fool. Sit down before you capsize the damn boat!" called Leander, exasperated. It seemed Anthony was intent on changing places with Freddie in the prow and was in danger of tipping headlong into the water. After a ticking off from Theo, Tony sat down again and they safely reached the island, beached the boats and they all jumped out and disappeared into the trees, their exclamations perfectly audible.

The rest of the party wandered along the edge of the small river which fed the lake and then as the afternoon wore on and the sun sank down behind the clouds, it grew suddenly very cold and they returned to the house for hot drinks and some cakes beside the roaring fire. The intrepid explorers finally returned, looking pleased with themselves and Freddie found a large book on Grecian temples in the library and they pored over it for a while discussing the various types of columns and whether it should be a square or round building and which side it should face, and which goddess should grace its perfectly proportioned spaces.

Sephie sat with Lady Rokewode listening to her idle chatter about household matters and the fashionable art of cutting *shades* or *profiles*. Then, enthused by her subject, Lady Rokewode suggested they should try making some themselves. She instructed Miss Bell to find the black cards and scissors and set about creating a profile of Kitty, who patiently posed in front of her, in profile, while Lady Rokewode struggled to get a likeness. There was much laughter when the portrait was examined and found to be somewhat wanting. Kitty said she was insulted by the unflattering length of her nose and took up the scissors herself to attempt to copy her husband's rather unprepossessing profile. It then became a battle to find who was most skilled at wielding the scissors. It seemed that the gentlemen were keen to recreate Biddy's exquisite profile and she sat for Tony first, followed by Tom and then Freddie. None of them managed to replicate her matchless profile and she was clearly disappointed when shown the results. Sephie sat quietly beside Lady Rokewode watching their antics; she cleared up the mess they were all making, gathering the bits of black card and putting them on the fire and handing out new cards to those who were still keen to compete.

Leander, never one to join in any kind of shared activities if he could possibly help it, went to stand behind Theo's chair, where he leant for a few minutes watching Ambrose make a very creditable attempt at Kitty's likeness.

"Nobody has asked Sephie to sit yet," he murmured helpfully.

Theo, who had been observing the mayhem from a jaundiced eye, had already noted this inescapable fact. He had chosen to ignore it. Leander's words were now making him feel a pang of guilt as he caught sight of Sephie's face. She, of course, was showing no sign of being aware that she'd been left out of the silly beauty contest; she was smiling as she watched Freddie carefully cutting Lady Rokewode's once arresting profile out of the black card and appeared to be enjoying the entertainment going on around her.

Theo ground his teeth. He cast a scowling glance at Leander who was somehow managing to look innocent of any devious scheming. With an exasperated sigh, he rose and approached Sephie. He took up some card and a pair of scissors and pulled up a chair next to her. She looked up in some surprise and her cheeks flushed. With a flick of his finger, he turned her profile towards him and told her to sit still. She did as she was told. Amadeus, sensing that Sephie needed some comfort, capered across the carpet to her and scrabbled at her skirts with his tiny paws. Without moving her head too much, she reached down and lifted him up into her arms where he energetically jumped up trying to lick her face. She grinned at him and kissed his nose and then he happily settled down on her lap to have his ears rubbed.

"That dog is without loyalty or shame," said Kitty.

After about ten minutes of intense concentration, Theo had finished and held up his *shade* for inspection.

Kitty took it and showed everyone, "It's beautiful, Theo! You always were rather gifted artistically." She showed Sephie, who, if she'd been pink before, now flamed scarlet.

The portrait was exquisitely rendered, and a superb likeness although, as everyone would agree later, in private, it had somehow made Sephie look a beauty.

Sephie stared at it in wonderment but shook her head.

"It looks just like you, even if I say so myself," said Theo softly.

"Your profile is definitely your best angle," said Biddy, pleased to see her friend so happy about such a trifling thing and wondering what on earth Lord Rokewode had been looking at as he snipped away the paper. It barely looked like Sephie at all!

Leander, looking at the surprising result, dared to hope and Miss Bell surreptitiously smoothed down the goosebumps on her arms.

Theo observed everyone's faces as they admired his handiwork and wondered why they all seemed so astonished. As far as he was concerned, he'd made an accurate portrait of Sephie. He gave her the *shade* and she tucked it carefully between the pages of the book she'd been reading.

Later that night, as she lay in her bed, unable to sleep, she took it out and looked at it again. No, she thought sadly, it looked nothing like her at all, but Theo had made it with his own hands, and she'd take it with her when she left as a reminder. When she left.

* * *

The plans for the Christmas Ball were still being altered daily and as it drew nearer the excitement was building in everyone but Leander who was filled with a sense of creeping dread. He had written to his grandmother from London explaining what he and his friends were proposing and had received a very swift and terse response which had not eased his disquiet. With three weeks to go before the ball he decided it was time to visit his own house, which was some fifteen miles from Church Iccomb, beyond Kingham and just into Oxfordshire.

"Theo, I'm going across to see my grandmother tomorrow. I was wondering if you'd care to come and give me some moral support?"

"With pleasure, my dear cowardly friend," replied Theo, "Although, I'm not at all sure how I'll be able to assist."

"She likes you so that might help."

"Are you sure? I wasn't aware that she liked *anyone!*"

"Oh, she thinks you very charming and handsome and has frequently said that if I ever wish to find a female willing to put up with my peculiarities, I shouldn't make a habit of keeping you company because I'll never shine in comparison! She's nothing if not brutally honest!"

"She's a damned Gorgon! You should pay no attention to her. Anyway, what about Matilda? She never gave me a second look!"

"Matilda is one in a million."

"She must be, if she thinks you to be such a paragon."

Leander wandered off across the Great Hall, "Oh, by the bye," he remarked casually over his shoulder, "I've asked Kitty and Sephie to come with us. Biddy wasn't at all keen to get back into a carriage again and the others will all be out hunting, apart from Miss Bell and your mother. I'm hoping some female support might help soften the dear Baroness up a little."

"That is highly unlikely, I fear. And did Sephie agree to accompany us?"

"She did! As soon as I'd told her that I couldn't do without her support, she immediately clasped my hand and nodded happily."

"She didn't object to my presence?"

"Not at all. Were you expecting her too?"

"I have no idea, Lee. I thought — "

"When I told her that Kitty would be happy to chaperone, she seemed perfectly content. We can ride and they can travel post-chaise. It's not far. I think she has a yearning to see as much of the countryside as she can, having never been out of London before and obviously having had such a restricted life."

"I fully understand that and I've no objections."

"Good, because I wouldn't have listened to them anyway!"

Theo laughed, "I think you've also been bewitched by our little Persephone."

Leander gave him a calculating look, "Bewitched? I think you might be right, Theo."

Eighteen

Fairtree Manor was a fine example of all things Tudor. It was perfect in form and balance and every part of it had been carefully thought out and with money no object it'd been constructed from the very finest materials and by the best craftsmen. Everything was in its place; everything was beyond compare.

Sephie gazed up at its unmistakeable perfection and couldn't help but compare it unfavourably to the Abbey, where beauty had not been taken into account, where a fortress had been required and had been erected from the rubble left from many other ruined versions of the original building; where no architects and draughtsmen had put their clever heads together and come up with a coherent plan so divinely flawless that people gasped in awe when they first saw it.

Sephie would have taken the Abbey over Fairtree Manor any day. She looked at the Manor's matched windows and chimneys and its immaculate gardens and she admired but could not love. She caught Theo's eye and despite everything that had happened, she couldn't hide her feelings.

He smiled at her, "I heartily agree. Sometimes perfection is not the answer."

Baroness Gage was formidable. She commanded the room and cowed Leander. Even Kitty was unnaturally subdued in her presence and only Theo seemed able to hold a conversation with her without relapsing into silence after a few words.

Sephie sat very still with her hands folded neatly in her lap and listened.

Baroness Gage was used to winning arguments by battering people into submission. She had driven two husbands into early graves and firmly believed that they'd died because of a weakness in their character but in fact they'd died from terror and exhaustion. Leander seldom returned home to Fairtree in case he followed suit and when he was there, he said little that might draw attention to him and tried not to look her directly in the eye in case she turned him into stone.

His grandmother seemed to be consumed by some nameless simmering rage, every word which escaped her grim little mouth was razor sharp and barbed, every glance she shot at her quaking grandson was critical and it was relentless. Eventually even Theo ran out of commonplace remarks and he looked to Leander with a quizzical expression.

Leander cleared his throat, "So, Grandmama, we have come to talk about — the Ball. We shall have to begin work on the ballroom and talk to the staff, if you're comfortable with that?"

His grandmother fixed him with a basilisk stare, "Comfortable! *Now,* you think to ask if I am to be comfortable with such chaos and disruption in my own home. I am old, Leander! I do not need such turmoil at my great age. I cannot think why you should want to make a fool of yourself with this ridiculous Ball! You will be a laughingstock. How will I be able to hold my head up when my neighbours are making mocking comments behind my back? I really do not understand you at all. I fear you take after your mother. She was feather-brained and weak. No gumption at all. I never could see what your father saw in her."

Kindness, thought Leander, bleakly. And a gentle spirit which was a balm to his father's much bullied soul.

Sephie kept her eyes on Baroness Gage and thought what a lonely and bitter lady she was, and she felt deep pity for her. She had everything money could buy but, in the end, had nothing because her privileged life had rendered her unsympathetic and consequently unloveable. So instead of asking for love and support she pushed everyone away so that they wouldn't see her frailty and desperation. She'd rather be alone than allow Leander to feel obliged to dance attendance upon her. Pride, thought Sephie sadly — it had a good deal to answer for.

Baroness Gage became suddenly aware that she was being contemplated in a somewhat disconcerting fashion from a pair of steady grey eyes. She looked at the small still figure sitting in silence beside Lady Kitty. She considered her for a moment and dismissed her as a plain nonentity. *But* this nonentity held her gaze, looking right back at her, directly, without flinching. What impudence! What temerity!

"Who is this — person, Leander?" she demanded.

Leander sighed, "As I've already explained, Grandmama, this is Miss Fane. Persephone. She's a friend of Lady Rokewode's and is the one who has done most of the organising for the Ball."

The Baroness eyed Sephie with disapproval, "Has she indeed! And what have you to say for yourself, Miss Fane?"

"Miss Fane is unable to speak, my lady," interposed Theo blandly.

"Mute, eh? Does she understand what is said?"

"Very much so," he replied with a dry chuckle.

"Well, isn't that novel! And where did you find her?"

A wry smile, "I think you could say that she found us, my lady."

The Baroness fixed Sephie with a frosty stare. "Is that so!" she uttered but was disconcerted to find that Miss Fane's gaze did not waver. "And her family?"

"We are her family," said Kitty.

Baroness Gage saw the faint blush steal up over Miss Fane's pale cheeks and thought there was more to this story than met the eye. Her interest was piqued, and she determined to find out more about this strange creature.

"I mean are her family respectable?"

Leander choked.

The Baroness looked directly at Sephie.

Sephie smiled slightly and deliberately shook her head.

Baroness Gage let out a guffaw of delighted laughter.

* * *

"Well, I'll be damned," said Leander, as they inspected the ballroom with his housekeeper and butler. "Who'd have thought! She actually laughed! Don't remember ever hearing that before in my whole life. Quite unnerved me, I must say. Poor Sephie, being commanded to stay for a solo performance! I do feel we should have rescued her."

"She seemed very relaxed about it," said Kitty admiringly.

"She'll be just fine," remarked Theo.

* * *

Sephie was being bombarded with questions which she barely had time to respond to before more were thrown at her. She felt a little like the walls of a besieged city being peppered with cannonballs.

"Family disgraced, eh? Below the salt? Not fit for society? Ha! Is that so? This is getting more and more interesting! I'll have you know that despite appearances, I come from a long line of degenerates and I must admit to being extremely proud of every one of them! I loathe mealy-mouthed sycophants. I am sick of toadeaters. I want to boot them up their fawning backsides!"

Sephie bit her lip but her eyes twinkled, and Baroness Gage laughed again, "I think we shall deal famously together! What a pity that you and Leander — " She saw Sephie's eyes lower for the first time and leant forward to forcefully pat the girl's knee. "Someone else, eh? Ha! Let me guess! No mystery there though! The devilishly handsome Theodore? Of course! What girl could resist? If I myself were a little younger — ! So, this is most intriguing! You have formed an attachment and — he is naturally unaware. What a mutton-headed fool. Spoiled, of course. Nobody could be that good-looking and not have been ruined by it. His father was rather dashing too, you know! But extremely disagreeable for the most part. Poor Theodore, he had a great deal of nonsense to put up with. Now, how shall we contrive to bring this about?" She saw Sephie's alarm and chuckled. "Oh, have no fear! I will be discreet. But I have a desire to see that Rokewode family loosen their stays a little! They are all far too buttoned-up. A bit of bad blood will do them the world of good and I could do with some entertainment. I cannot thank you enough for organising this damned Ball. I think it will be rather enjoyable!"

An astounded Leander bid his grandmother farewell and was told in no uncertain terms that he should bring that odd little creature back again because she had much enjoyed her company.

"Damn me!" he muttered to Theo as they mounted up again and followed the post-chaise along the drive. "Never seen the like, Theo! The Baroness was entirely won over and said she's going to order a new ballgown for herself. Although she still found time to inform me that I was sadly lacking in the brain department and that you were more of a ninny than she had first thought!"

"So, in fact you and I haven't come out of this very well in the end but Sephie, it appears, has been raised to the position of idolised goddess. Without ever saying a word. It puts us to shame."

Kitty, relieved that the visit was over, allowed the laughter to bubble up and impulsively kissed Sephie on her hot cheek. "You're a dark horse, my dear! I never know what's going to happen next! You keep us all on our toes. God in heaven! The sound of the Baroness laughing I shall take to my grave!"

As they arrived back at the Abbey Sephie breathed a sigh of relief — it felt like home. She jumped down from the carriage without waiting to be handed down and looked up at the golden walls in front of her, built for strength and safety and felt nothing but love for the history in the ancient mortar and the people who lived so securely within them.

At dinner everyone was regaled with the story of their triumphant visit to Fairtree Manor and they were astonished and delighted by its unexpected success, congratulating Sephie on soothing the savage beast. Sephie, who had done nothing apart from be truthful when dissembling had been expected, waved away their misplaced praise in embarrassment.

*   *   *

A few days later, Sephie had a sudden urge to explore the grounds, which stretched beyond the walls and the lake and were sorely tempting to a girl who had spent most of her life trapped in dismal inside spaces. She rose early, dressed herself without the help of Ann and pulled on her warmest cloak and her walking boots; singularly inadequate footwear for the terrain but all a true lady was ever expected to need, and she set forth with a lively step.

The sky was damselfly blue and there was no wind; it was perfect walking weather. She left the grounds by way of a small side gate and struck out across the fields beside the Abbey, heading towards the rather tempting beechwood which bordered the lake and the river. She had never had the good fortune to encounter a wood before and was slightly daunted by the size of the trees at close quarters; they towered over her like silent giants, their drooping branches reaching for her as she passed. She laughed at herself as she wound in and out of their smooth trunks, her feet crunching on the beechmast concealed amongst the dried leaves and twigs on the floor of the wood. It was exhilarating to be out by herself and in charge of the direction she took next. She skipped a few steps in sheer delight. She tramped further into the depths of the wood for a while and then thought she'd better head back towards the fields before she got completely lost so worked her way back until she could see more light filtering through the gloom. She could see the sparkle of the lake in the distance and knew she was on the right track. She was just clambering over a fallen tree in her path when she spied a strange little building partly hidden amongst the trees. She marched over to it to inspect it. It could have been a home especially made for one of the fairground dwarves, it was so small. There were turfed banks on either side of the entrance and a short path led to a solid-looking door. The roof was domed like a tiny Italian *duomo* and there were no windows. It was intriguing and she wondered why anyone would build such a structure so far from the house. She approached the door and saw that it wasn't bolted. With a slight thrill, she lifted the latch and with some difficulty pushed the door open to reveal a short tunnel and another door. She entered the building and studied the next door, it looked very substantial but had no lock. She opened it and to her surprise found a darkly cavernous space built neatly of brick, the walls curving away into deep shadows. It was disappointingly empty. She pulled the door closed again and turned to leave. There was a grating sound by the entrance, a bang and suddenly she was plunged into compete darkness. She ran along the tunnel and crashed into the door. She beat on it with her fists. There was nothing but the sound of her own panicked breathing.

* * *

Kitty and Ambrose found their chairs and sat down to breakfast. Babyngton and Freddie wandered in, arm in arm, arguing about whether the dinners at a chophouse were superior to those of a coffee-house. Still undecided, they arranged themselves at the table and greeted everyone with loud good cheer. Anthony was already there and horrifying Biddy with gory tales of their last hunt. Miss Bell and Lady Rokewode were discussing the merits of the book they had just read, The Supposed Daughter or Innocent Imposter. Leander, idly listening to their chatter, was glad Sephie was not in the room as he knew she'd have found the subject matter uncomfortable. Theo entered the Hall and after dropping a kiss on his mother's cheek, he seated himself and asked Leander if he'd slept well.

"Like a log and no longer haunted by dreams of my grandmother chasing me around the Manor with a broadsword."

Theo laughed, "Well, at least some good has come from this trip. Even if the Ball falls flat!"

"It wouldn't dare after all the effort gone into its planning. Have you seen the pile of papers that Sephie has accumulated? The interminable lists! She's even done little drawings of the decorations for the ballroom. She's leaving nothing to chance."

"It's as though she wished to repay us," remarked Kitty, thoughtfully. "Where is she anyway? Is she still in bed, Biddy?"

"I haven't seen her this morning," replied Biddy carelessly.

"Perhaps she has the headache and has stayed in bed?" suggested Miss Bell, "Although," she added, "She never seems to get headaches."

"I expect she'll be down in a minute," said Kitty.

* * *

An hour later as they rose from the table, Ann appeared from behind the screens and scurried up to Kitty, she dropped a hasty curtsy and whispered something to her. Kitty frowned and caught Theo's eye.

"What is it?" he asked, joining them.

"It seems that Ann cannot find Sephie. She wasn't in her room early this morning when Ann went to stoke the fire and lay out her gown."

"What time was this?" said Theo, addressing the maid.

"I always go in at seven, my lord."

"And she'd already gone by then? Her clothes? Cloak? Shoes?"

"Her walking shoes are gone and her thick winter cloak."

Theo looked at his sister, who was now a little pale. "And she said nothing about going out? A note?"

"No, my lord. Nothing."

"Leander!"

* * *

"She would *not* just leave without a note or a sign!" cried Kitty. "I know she wouldn't!"

"No, you're right," said Leander, "I don't believe she would either. Did she give any clue to you, Theo?"

Theo stared at him, "She made no indication — "

"She may have made some sign, but you didn't recognise her intention?"

"There was *nothing*," snapped Theo.

"We need to search for her," said Freddie, taking off his wig and throwing it onto the table amongst the remains of breakfast, "An organised search party. Each of us to take part of the grounds and search it thoroughly. She may not have gone far."

* * *

They threw on coats and hats and with careful instructions about where to search, they disappeared off into the grounds.

* * *

After an hour they returned, empty handed and dispirited. The servants had joined in and combed the house, the gardens and the outhouses.

They were gathered in the Great Hall awaiting further orders. Kitty suddenly looked down at Amadeus who was impatiently scrabbling at her skirt and picked him up distractedly. She glanced at him irritably as he yapped noisily.

"Theo! *Amadeus!*" she exclaimed in a shrill voice.

Theo frowned at the ridiculous little lap-dog, "Well, just put him in the damned parlour — ! Good God, Kit! Of *course!* Give him to me, at once!" He snatched the unfortunate beast from his mistress's arms. "Ann, run and fetch me something belonging to Miss Sephie! Anything, a scarf or gloves! Quickly!"

* * *

Theo put Amadeus down on the grass and let him sniff the pelerine. The dog bounced off across the grass and then stopped a few feet away, sniffed the air and scampered back to Theo.

"Amadeus," he said in a voice of authority, "Find!" He proffered the pelerine again. The tiny beast ran in excited circles delighted with the attention he was getting and then flopped down, panting.

"He can't do it! He's not trained," said Kitty desperately.

Theo wasn't giving up that easily and pushed the dog's nose into the lace cape.

Amadeus, sensing that something was required of him, jumped up and sniffed the ground intently. Then, just as Kitty was bemoaning the fact that she hadn't chosen some kind of useful hunting dog, Amadeus set off briskly across the lawn to the side door in the wall.

With a shout of "View halloo!" Sir Anthony raced after the stumpy-legged creature and opened the door to allow the dog a clear path.

They all followed as the excited beast bounced through the longer grass alongside the river, every so often disappearing from sight and then reappearing slightly further on, his tail wagging furiously.

They reached the edge of the wood and he stopped to sniff the air, then the ground and then with an ear-splitting yip, he dashed off through the trees. They trailed after him, wondering if he was leading them on a wild-goose chase but just as Kitty was saying she'd have to sit down or pass out, Amadeus began to bark in earnest.

"Dash it! The *icehouse!*" shouted Anthony, sprinting away through the trees.

Theo and Anthony ran down the path to the door and both saw that the door was bolted but not padlocked, just impossible to open from the inside. Amadeus was dancing around their feet and getting in their way, so Kitty dived in and grabbed him, carrying him to safety.

Theo slid the bolt and opened the door.

Curled up in a heap in the corner of the tunnel was Sephie. For a moment he thought she was dead. For a second his heart faltered, and his legs didn't seem to want to work and then he was lifting her up and carrying her out into the daylight. She weighed nothing at all in his arms as he carried her back to the Abbey.

Nineteen

"The doctor will be here within the hour," said Ambrose to Kitty in the corridor outside Sephie's bedchamber.

"I'll tell Theo and Miss Bell at once. She still hasn't come round."

Kitty returned to Sephie's bedside and informed her brother that the doctor was on his way.

"Is there any sign of her waking?"

Theo shook his head, his eyes on the tiny figure in the bed. Her face was ashen and although Ann had changed her into a dry warm nightshift and stoked the fire until it roared, and placed a hot brick wrapped in wool in the bed with her, Sephie was still cold to the touch. She hadn't moved since she'd been found.

In the back of Theo's mind was the memory of the bolted door. Bolted from the outside. This had been a deliberately malicious act. Someone had set out to hurt Sephie. Someone had succeeded.

Kitty perched on the edge of the bed and held Sephie's frozen hand in hers.

"Sephie, please wake up! We're all here and you're safe," she whispered but there was no response. Kitty began to cry, "What if she never — ?"

"God, Kit! She'll be all right. She has to be! She's stronger than any of us."

"Theodore is right, Kitty — Persephone just needs to know that it's safe for her to come home," said Miss Bell.

They sat in silence and watched Sephie not move. She seemed to barely be breathing and Kitty found she was holding her own breath as she waited for Sephie's next breath.

Then suddenly her eyes opened, and she was fighting Kitty and struggling to breathe, and Kitty tried to calm her, but the panic just increased, her movements becoming more violent. Kitty leapt up from the bed, "Theo! *Do something!* She listens to you!"

Theo moved quickly to the bed and sitting beside her, stopped her arms from flailing around as though she were struggling to escape something in the darkness.

"Sephie," he said softly but firmly, "You're safe now. You can stop fighting." He moved closer and put his arms around her shaking body, sliding his hands under her back and holding her tightly. He could feel the fear in her and the rigidity of her body told him that she was still trapped in that tunnel. He pulled her up and against his chest and held her, his mouth against her hair. "Sephie, stop it! I've got you! Nothing can hurt you. Miss Edie and Kitty are here. We'll protect you. I'll protect you. Sephie, *Sephie!*"

Gradually, as he murmured to her, she became calmer, the terror slowly lessened, and she stopped trying to escape. He gently rocked her as he would a baby. God only knew what memories the incident would be bringing back to her. He looked up at Miss Edie and knew he'd have to tell her. With imminent and undeniable danger right at their door, everyone should be alerted to the fact so that they could keep an eye out and prevent anything like this happening again.

There was a moment when the shaking had almost stopped, and a kind of stillness returned, and she turned her head and rested her cheek against his shoulder with a small sigh. Theo's eyes met Kitty's over Sephie's head and Kitty burst into a fresh bout of tears.

* * *

After examining his patient, Doctor Martin Brook, who'd served the family for many years, was pleased to inform Lord Rokewode that she would undoubtedly recover from her ordeal.

"I am concerned though, my lord," he said quietly, in the privacy of the parlour, "Can you tell me anything about her history?"

Theo shrugged casually, "There's not much to know, Martin. We believe that she was meant to go to a foundling hospital in London but was instead taken by a — man called Edwin Stokey who was eventually hung for his appalling crimes and then, after being rescued from his abode, she went to lodge with a parson and his sister for some years and then was abducted by Henry Pippin, who forced Sephie and his daughter, Biddy, to work at a fair."

The doctor stroked his beard and studied Lord Rokewode from narrowed eyes, "Do you know how Sephie was treated in these places?"

Theo, unable to trust his voice, nodded.

Doctor Brook took a turn about the parlour. "Well, Lord Rokewode, you stand as her guardian, so I am bound to inform you of what I have discovered."

"Go on."

The doctor came to a halt in front of him and looked searchingly into his face, "She has been much ill-treated, I'm afraid. It's like nothing I've ever seen before. Except perhaps on some criminal in the stocks or on the gallows."

"What do you mean?" demanded Theo.

"There is evidence — clear evidence of years of violent abuse, my lord. Her back is criss-crossed with scars and burns, as are other parts of her body. I doubt she'd have allowed me to see this if she hadn't been half out of her mind with fear after being shut in the icehouse. And there's a part of me that wishes I hadn't seen it. This will haunt me to my grave."

Theo felt numb. He sat down and put his head in his hands, unable to take in the doctor's words.

"My attorney said the hospital suggested she must have been in an accident." he said hoarsely.

"No, my lord, that cannot be, these scars have been inflicted by the hand of a human, with evil intent, although I use the word human loosely. This child has been tortured and defiled in ways I cannot even begin to describe. I'm astonished that she's able to function normally. I've seen seasoned soldiers broken by such treatment, never to recover. The very fact that she's been able to withstand such appalling treatment makes me think that this latest incident is but a minor hiccup to her and once she realises that she's safe, she'll return to her usual demeanour, whatever that may be."

"She has no voice, Martin. Our doctor in London suggested it might have been lost because of some trauma she suffered, and I now see that he was too close to the terrible truth."

"I've seen it before in patients damaged by the horror of war or by anguish too great to endure. I suppose it's only to be expected. How does she manage to communicate?"

"She manages remarkably well. She is perfectly eloquent just using her hands and her — lively eyes."

The doctor smiled and shook his head, "I thank the good Lord that she found you and your family."

Theo got to his feet and was surprised to find his legs a little unsteady. "Thank you for coming and sharing this with me. It will help me understand and — I shall, of course, vigorously seek the perpetrators and bring them to justice. They will not escape my revenge."

"My lord, be careful, I fear these are ruthless men."

"I think they will find they're up against some equally ruthless adversaries," said Lord Rokewode in chilling tones.

* * *

Kitty wouldn't stop weeping until Miss Bell told her firmly that if she didn't cease the terrible wailing that she would be forced to slap her to bring her to her senses.

Of course, Miss Edie took the news with her usual *sang-froid*, explaining that she'd already known something was not quite right. Theo decided it would be best for everyone if they knew something of the truth and had told Tony, Freddie and Tom a little of what Sephie had suffered and the danger she, and possibly Biddy, was in but had left out the worst details. Kitty told her husband and he listened in complete dismay and rather surprisingly, for such a mild-mannered man, promised a grisly end to anyone who had hurt Sephie.

Theo then relentlessly questioned a sobbing and apparently remorseful Biddy who explained that she'd known all along about the scars but said Sephie didn't want anyone to know about them. She admitted that her father had been one of the many who'd ill-treated Sephie but quickly defended her own lack of action by explaining Henry Pippin was not a man who could easily be persuaded to stop. Biddy had been terrified of receiving a beating herself, or even worse. She held onto Kitty's hand and watched Lord Rokewode's face darken so alarmingly she was suddenly very grateful he hadn't joined her band of followers after all.

Everyone was in a state of shock and disbelief. Anthony was knocking back brandy at a startling rate even for him and Freddie was poking the fire with such violence that Babyngton felt obliged to remove the fire iron from his hand before he did some serious damage. Theo allowed them a short while to try to come to terms with what they'd heard and then he impressed upon them, in no uncertain terms, that they'd have to hide their newfound knowledge from Sephie. She must not discover that her secret was out. They must also be on their guard at all times in order to make sure that nothing like the icehouse incident happened again.

"Should we not cancel the Ball?" asked Leander, rather hopefully.

"No, we should not! At the moment it's what Sephie is living for. She's so hopeful of a happy ending for you that it's giving her a reason to not take flight," said Theo grimly. "We'll see this through to the end and I'm determined that we shall find a way to eradicate the danger once and for all."

*   *   *

Kitty and Miss Bell, with the loyal help of Ann, took it in turns to sit with Sephie until she regained her senses. It seemed that the extreme cold had taken its toll and she suffered a raised temperature and a chesty cold for a few days but other than that, she made a steady recovery. She enjoyed a cheering stream of visitors to her bedside bringing her books and flowers and little gifts. Theo came bearing a glass dish of Chocolate Cream, which made her smile and she tucked into it with her usual delight and Theo thought with some relief that they might be over the worst of it.

She licked the spoon clean and handed back the empty dish, a faint pink staining her cheeks.

"I believe Chocolate Cream might just be your only weakness!" said Theo. She shook her head, her dimples much in evidence. "Oh, and, of course, Pineapple Ice Cream," he added, laughing.

Sephie thought that she mustn't get carried away with all the attention she was getting; it was only because she'd been silly enough to get stuck in the icehouse.

After two days in bed, she was allowed up and Kitty let her sit by the fire in the parlour and read her books. Sephie noted that she was never left alone for more than a few minutes at a time and thought everyone was being a bit over-protective. Kitty had relinquished Amadeus almost entirely into Sephie's care as it was plain to everyone that the horrible little dog much preferred her company. Kitty didn't mind once she saw that Sephie was able to reap some comfort from having the dog nearby.

Leander had to have a quiet word with Freddie who couldn't help but look at Sephie with big sad puppy eyes, sympathy oozing out of every pore. "If you carry on like this Frederick, she'll guess that you know. For God's sake pull yourself together!"

Theo paced and raged and wrote letters to Major Cobham and Constable Thursby, demanding immediate results from their enquiries. He tried to busy himself so that he couldn't find time to imagine how Sephie had come by the scars. If he allowed himself to think about it, he became overwhelmed with the desire to commit murder on an industrial scale.

He instructed Roland Ashby to hire some more men to patrol the grounds, warning him to be on the lookout for strangers or anything out of the ordinary. He did everything in his power to make the Abbey into the fortress it was meant to be, but still he couldn't rest. Something was nagging at him, something he couldn't quite catch hold of and pin down. He felt the inexplicable need to check regularly on Sephie's whereabouts and if she couldn't immediately be found, he felt obliged to search the house until he came across her and then was forced to make weak excuses for repeatedly appearing for no apparent reason.

He deliberately kept himself busy from morning until night so that he could keep from dwelling upon the sight of Sephie lying motionless in the cold mossy darkness. He awoke in a sweat from dreams where he arrived at the icehouse too late to find her still alive, her body hanging lifeless in his arms.

Kitty told him on several occasions that he was being unnecessarily terse with everyone and asked him if he'd found out anything more about the icehouse incident, but he was unable to provide any more information to help soothe her frayed nerves. No letters had yet arrived from London, so he was still floundering in uncertainty.

If Sephie noticed the distinct sea change in the mood of the party, she made no sign. Biddy was trying desperately to make up for her evident lack of compassion but found that even Anthony's once reliably stormy passion had cooled somewhat since they'd found out that she hadn't made any effort to save Sephie from her father's unwanted attentions. She felt hard-done-by and misunderstood but realised that if she wanted to attend the Ball, she'd have to show that she could change. She eventually concluded that there was one sure way to curry favour and show herself in a good light.

Biddy knocked on the library door and was invited in. Lord Rokewode was at his desk and didn't look too happy to see her. Her heart quailed a little, but she stepped forward, her prettiest smile upon her face.

"My lord, I was wondering if I might have a word with you?"

He put down his pen with a faint sigh, "Come and sit, Biddy. What troubles you?"

She swallowed nervously, "I've something I feel I should show you — perhaps I should've done it earlier — but — I'd no way of knowing then that my silence might in any way bring harm to — anyone."

Theo watched her from guarded eyes, "You mean Sephie?"

"Yes, I do. I knew my father had — I *knew* — but, as I said, I had not the strength to prevent it. And I was protecting myself, which I realise was selfish. When I heard he was dead, I was so glad I could've danced on his grave! I was relieved he couldn't hurt us anymore but then, he *lived,* and I knew he wouldn't rest until he'd made us suffer. When you announced that we were all coming here I was glad to be leaving London so that he couldn't find us."

"You believe it was your father who tried to hurt Sephie?"

"I'd better show you, my lord, because it'll be easier. Here," she said and handed him a small packet of letters. "I answered them because, at first, I will admit that I was flattered, but then I realised they were in deadly earnest and I became frightened, so I didn't reply again, and I didn't meet them as they requested and then we came here, and I thought we were safe — " She fished out a handkerchief and wiped her eyes affectingly.

Theo, ignoring her theatrics, opened one of the letters and read the contents. He glanced up at Biddy, "You *agreed* to this?"

She nodded not daring to say anything because he looked as though he might shout at her.

There were three letters and when Theo had finished reading them, he threw them onto his desk as though he feared contamination. He was silent for a few moments and then rose abruptly, moving around the desk to tower over Biddy, "You'll say nothing of this to anyone. Do you understand? If you divulge the contents of these letters, I will not be responsible for my actions. You should have told me as soon as you received them, it could have prevented Sephie being hurt. You're a very foolish girl but I understand that your life hasn't been an easy one. I also think that if Sephie can see something in you worth saving, I must be willing to believe that you can change. I trust Sephie."

Biddy opened her mouth to say something, then closed it again, thinking perhaps it wasn't the thing to blurt out when she was now expected to be a better person. It rankled though that she was being accused of so much and Sephie was found to be innocent at every turn. It just wasn't fair.

Theo watched the door close behind her and tried to recall how his life was before he had so stupidly allowed Anthony to inveigle him into going to Bartholomew Fair. He seemed to remember that it'd been rather unremarkable and reassuringly sedate. This new life he'd been propelled into was not at all to his liking. To think he'd been used to seeking excitement and thrills at boxing matches and horse races in order to convince himself that he was alive! He had no need of that now. He had real and imminent danger to contend with. And Sephie, — he had Sephie to watch over. It was turning out to be a full-time occupation.

Twenty

Selwyn Vauville was looking distinctly uncomfortable. His brow was beaded with sweat and his fingers twitched convulsively in the safety of his breeches pockets. His heart was thumping a little erratically in his throat, but he still managed to keep his voice gratifyingly steady. He had learnt over the years to not show alarm or weakness. It did one no favours. When faced with a ravening wild animal one was always advised not to look it directly in the eye for fear of antagonising it even more.

He was examining the polished toe of his Hessian boot as though merely mildly interested in the quality of the shine, but his palms were slippery, and he was having to concentrate hard so as not to fidget openly.

Mrs Sheraton's rage was cold and life-threatening. She'd been thwarted just when she believed she was about to gain the upper hand and it had made her as deadly as a rattled cobra. Inevitably she was going to make someone pay for these mistakes, but Selwyn Vauville had no plans to become another of her hapless victims; he'd seen too many fall by the wayside never to recover and he meant to survive this latest trial by fire — not only survive but emerge triumphant. He sensed Leonard Tiploft, out of the corner of his eye, trying to blend with the floral Chinese wallpaper, which wouldn't be beyond a possibility considering the garish nature of the coat he'd chosen to wear that morning. And Alice Yelverton was slowly sinking back into the cushions on the sofa hoping to find shelter there.

"So, they're all safely ensconced at Rokewode Abbey and this is the best you can do?" Mrs Sheraton asked mildly.

Nobody said anything for fear of attracting her attention.

"I was under the impression that this was all in hand, Selwyn. I am absolutely certain that you said you were in control and that I would be delighted with the result. No?"

Selwyn Vauville dug his fingernails into his greasy palms and said a silent prayer, "Margaret, *mi amore*, it's but a slight aberration, we shall rectify it in a trice. You have my word."

Mrs Sheraton smiled, "Your word seems to mean little these days, Selwyn. There was a time when I was able to rely upon you, but it appears that not even your twisted inclinations are enough to ensure you remain loyal. I think you should remember what happened to our dear Bertram! He was stupid enough to forget where his allegiance lay. I wouldn't wish you to end up like him. That would be a great shame."

Selwyn swallowed nervously and hoped his high neckcloth hid that telltale sign of terror. "I'd never betray you, Margaret," he said truthfully, knowing that she kept all his darkest secrets and wouldn't hesitate to use them against him if he failed her. "We will prevail, but it may take more time to organise. There will be no mistake this time, I swear."

Mrs Sheraton observed him for a moment, her fingers idly stroking an ivory paper knife, "If you want your reward, you'd better make sure that there are no more oversights. Is our spy still *in situ*?"

"Yes, and extremely willing to comply."

"Anything for a few guineas, eh? So, it's true then, Theo is taking an interest in the mute? He must be losing his grip! Make sure you don't lose *your* grip this time, Selwyn or there will be a heavy price to pay."

"It came as quite a surprise to all of us and you'll admit that even you had the wrong impression," murmured Selwyn daringly.

"Beware, Selwyn! You're on very thin ice."

* * *

"She's here to see *you*, Sephie," said Kitty, "Doctor Brook will explain."

Doctor Brook ushered a plump, fresh-faced young girl into the parlour and addressed Sephie, who had been sitting beside the fire reading. "This is Grace Glover, she's twenty-three and lives over in Moreton."

Sephie greeted her with a warm smile; she'd no idea what this was about but she liked the doctor and trusted him.

"Miss Fane, Grace has been deaf from birth, as are two of her sisters and her mother. Smallpox, y'see? What's interesting, in their case, is that they've taught themselves how to use their hands to speak to each other. It's a kind of finger spelling and she's here to help you learn the language, if you'd care to try? I know you're not deaf, like Grace, but I thought if you knew even a few of the signs it may help you communicate more efficiently. Of course, it goes without saying that everyone else would have to try to learn the language as well. What do you think?"

Sephie looked from the doctor to Grace to Kitty and then nodded fiercely.

"I believe Lady Roysten already mentioned to you the Frenchman's book about sign language for the deaf? Well, I feel this would be even more appropriate as Grace is English and you'll be able to see the hand movements precisely for yourself. It'll obviously take a while for you to learn it from scratch and for it to sink in and become second nature but at least we can make a start."

Sephie smiled at Grace, who, lifting her hand, made a small waving gesture. Sephie looked at the doctor.

"She said *Hallo!*" he explained, "Some of the signs are obvious, even to me!" he laughed.

Sephie turned back to Grace and waved her hand shyly at the girl. Grace then made another shape by linking both her hands and pointed to herself and then at Sephie. Sephie knew immediately what she was saying and burst into silent tears.

* * *

"And you're absolutely sure that this is a good idea, Martin?"

"My lord, it can do no harm. The sisters and their mother have developed their own language and talk to each other at speed and with great fluency, it's quite a sight to behold, I can assure you! I'm not saying it'll solve all her problems, but it cannot hinder her. If everyone learns just a few of the most important signs, Miss Fane will be able to make herself understood more readily and surely that must be beneficial?"

"Indeed, as long as she's happy to try then I'm certain everyone at the Abbey will be more than willing to help. She's already helped us more than I can even begin to explain. She deserves a little in return."

"May I enquire if you've had any luck with your quest to find those who have treated her so badly?"

"As yet I've had little success in relation to this latest incident but still await a response from Major Cobham about his investigation. Constable Thursby has informed me that Mr Henry Pippin seems to have disappeared from his usual haunts and none of his cronies have seen him for some while. It would appear that he's moved elsewhere. Perhaps back to his Hampshire home of Whitchurch."

"Or perhaps to Gloucestershire where he can make a nuisance of himself if he so wishes?" suggested the doctor.

Lord Rokewode's mouth thinned to a grim line, "You're right, of course. He must have had ample opportunity to travel with the fair and develop connections around the country with fairground people who would give him shelter and assistance."

"I noticed that you've armed men in the grounds. This must surely be an effective disincentive? And the Abbey seems to be brimming with athletic young men willing to put up a fight!"

Theo laughed, "Very much so. I'm having a struggle to keep them from casually shooting at anything that moves in the grounds. They're rather over-excitable. Roland Ashby has hired some reliable ex-soldiers to patrol the estate and apart from having to attend the damn Ball at Fairtree Manor, we're not planning any excursions this side of Christmas. I shall attempt to keep everyone where I can see them. I hope you and your wife will be going to the Ball?"

"My lord, if I caused my darling Sarah to miss the Ball of the decade, I fear I'd be turned out of the house without hope of return! We shall *certainly* be there, as will half the district if what my patients say is true!"

"Excellent. I look forward to having more news to tell you before then."

They returned to the parlour and found a lively scene with Sephie running around from item to item demanding to know the sign for everything. Kitty had collapsed into a chair and was watching in exhausted amusement whilst trying valiantly to learn the hand movements herself.

"This is *impossible*, Theo! I'm far too old to learn new things! Sephie is just going to end up having to talk to herself!" she complained.

Sephie looked up and saw Theo and, dancing over to him, made a shape with both her hands and pointed to him.

"Friends," said Kitty helpfully, her bottom lip trembling dangerously.

Theo smiled down at Sephie and carefully made the same sign in response. Sephie clapped her hands with joy.

Theo met the doctor's eyes, "I see I must thank you Martin. It's clearly already a resounding success. I can see that we're all to be run ragged by the added excitement. Will you be able to bring Grace to the Abbey again? If not, she could stay with us awhile — until Sephie feels she's learned enough."

"Of course! I'll happily drive her across. She's to stay with us from now on as our new kitchen maid, so we can spare her whenever she's needed here — she is extremely keen to help."

"Truly, I cannot thank you enough — "

"Please don't! Happy to be able to help Sephie, my lord. She's an absolute joy."

Lord Rokewode flicked his eyes to the absolute joy who was gleefully mimicking Grace's hand movements, her eyes sparkling, her cheeks dimpled, and he felt a strange sensation in his chest again, like a fist squeezing his heart.

* * *

There followed several days of energetic gesticulating and much laughter before things settled down again and Sephie realised just how much she was able to convey with this newfound way of communicating. She wasn't able to explain complicated concepts but found she could, at least, join in some conversations and have her voice heard for the first time. She even found, to her delight, that it worked on Amadeus, a flat hand thrust at the small dog stopped him in his tracks and he'd sit in shocked surprise. Anthony seemed unable to remember the signs so made up his own which added a deal of confusion to any conversation and Freddie unexpectedly proved to be rather gifted at expressing himself with excellent recall of all the hand movements. Leander, unsurprisingly, was quietly efficient and diligent in learning the precise sign for everything so that he could understand what Sephie was trying to say and soon became the most fluent, along with Sephie herself, who somehow magically soaked up the information and retained it. As the date for the Ball approached, Leander became increasingly more morose as he imagined becoming an object of ridicule for the entire county. He moaned that he'd have to return to London to hide from all the mockery. He imagined Miss Matilda Fleete attending with her betrothed and laughing behind her hand at his pathetic attempts to win her back. He imagined her dancing with the dreadful Mr Adam Gibbs, who would, of course, turn out to be a graceful dancer, and a gifted storyteller, able to hold an audience in the palm of his hand with ease and leave them laughing and remarking what an outstandingly talented and entertaining fellow he was.

"I can't go," stated Leander with absolute finality.

Theo laughed, "You're being remarkably absurd, even for you, Lee! It's your Ball. You have no choice."

"Well, I'm sorry but I'd rather be locked in the cellar with nobody but the Baroness for company," he declared miserably. "And rats."

"If you don't appear the whole thing will have been for naught and all Sephie's work will go to waste. Just look at those eyes! How can you deny them?"

Sephie was kneeling on the drawing room floor, playing with Amadeus and listening to their conversation. She knew that Leander had to overcome the accumulating sense of dread and panic, but he seemed particularly resolute today, solidly determined that his suffering should end.

She was fully aware that he couldn't resist any female pleading with him directly and had been devious enough to keep him from bolting by using this tactic whenever his terror became too much for him to bear. He was a martyr to his shattered nerves and was proving harder to convince as each day passed.

Sephie removed Amadeus from beneath her petticoat, where he was trying to find the ball of yarn he'd been chewing, got to her feet and went straight to Leander and put her arms around his waist and hugged him.

He caught Theo's eye over her head and raised his eyebrows.

Theo laughed, "She has no shame whatsoever and will do anything to make sure you and Matilda find your happy ending," and he turned away to ferociously kick a log back into the grate.

Leander observed his rigid back with interest.

* * *

Then one day Theo suggested to Sephie that it was time to try riding again. She glowered at him and signed an unequivocal refusal. But he was gently insistent and said that one couldn't manage in the country without being able to ride. He ignored her mutinous expression and taking her hand led her out to the stables where Leander was walking a stocky pony around the yard. She pulled back on his hand in an effort to keep distance between her and the animal. She could hear the other horses in their stalls, snorting and blowing and whinnying and the pony's hooves clattering on the cobbles, sounding sharp and menacing.

"This pony, Locket, is as old as the hills, Kitty learned to ride on her. She doesn't have a mean bone in her body. I'm not even sure she'll be able to walk with you on her back despite the fact that you're as light as a feather! Come, will you at least try for me, Sephie?"

Leander frowned at his friend and thought he was being a little unsporting to use such persuasion, Theo knew very well that Sephie would do anything for him, even if he wouldn't admit it to himself.

Sephie nodded but held onto his hand tightly.

They approached Locket and managed to get right up to her before Sephie's feet seemed to get stuck. Theo squeezed her hand and said some encouraging words and she took another step.

He slowly placed their joined hands on the pony's neck and allowed Sephie to get used to just touching the animal. Her eyes were closed, and her body tensed ready for flight.

They stood like that until he felt her slowly relax and then he moved their hands to Locket's head. That went better than expected and Sephie remained calm.

Encouraged by her unexpected composure Theo asked if she was ready to try sitting in the saddle.

"Are you sure, Theo? Maybe another day!" murmured Leander anxiously.

They were both taken aback when Sephie nodded although she kept her eyes resolutely closed.

Theo explained that he would lift her up into the saddle and all she had to do was sit. Sephie agreed.

Theo put his hands on her waist and lifted her the short distance to the pony's back. He heard her scared intake of breath and then she was perched side-saddle. He could hear her panicked breathing and taking her hand in his, placed it on the pommel and then hooked her right knee over the pommel horn and carefully slid her left foot into the slipper stirrup. She allowed him to manoeuvre her like a doll. She kept her eyes closed.

Leander held Locket steady while Theo settled Sephie and arranged her skirts.

After a few minutes for her to become accustomed to being in the saddle, Leander urged the pony forward and it took a few steps. Theo was holding Sephie with one hand on her waist and the other holding her hand on the pommel.

"I won't let you fall," he told her.

They managed to do a circuit of the yard.

"Sephie, can you open your eyes?"

No response.

"I think that's probably enough now," said Leander gruffly and pulled the pony to a gentle halt. He was looking at Sephie's grim little face and the tears sliding unnoticed from beneath her closed eyelids. "God, Theo! Get her down at once!"

Theo lifted her down from Locket's back and let her slide down until her feet were safely on the ground and began to remove his arms, but her legs buckled under her and he had to hold her up. Leander, cursing under this breath, led the little pony away to her stall.

"You were very brave," said Theo, "I'm immensely proud of you."

She finally opened her eyes and looked up at him.

His breath caught in his throat.

"Sephie?"

Her face was tear-stained, and her eyes reddened. But it wasn't this which arrested him, it was the expression of abject misery in her eyes. He felt as though the simple act of forcing her to ride had released some of the pent-up emotions she'd managed, up until that moment, to keep under lock and key. He didn't know if he should be worried or glad. He didn't know if it'd be beneficial or detrimental. He only knew that she was suffering.

He lifted her up into his arms and carried her to the nearby granary. He kicked open the door and set her down upon a hay bale. He then paced the floor of the ancient barn as though trying to find a way to express his feelings. Sephie watched him from anxious eyes.

He finally came to a standstill in front of her. "Damn it! Don't look at me like that! I'm not going to hurt you. I know I shouldn't have pushed you to ride the damn pony. I just thought — " He rubbed his eyes with an impatient hand, "I'm not Leander! He seems able to comfort you. I only seem to make everything worse." He took another turn about the barn and then stood in silence staring up at the beamed ceiling.

"Why are you so scared of horses, Sephie? This fear you have is not reasonable. It's almost like a kind of madness. What happened to make you so afraid?"

Sephie continued to watch him warily, her heart in her mouth.

"It seems to be the sound of them more than anything. The sound of their hooves. Were you near stables? Did something happen to you there?"

The grey eyes told him everything he needed to know. They gave away far too much.

"God in heaven. Did someone — ?"

Still she made no movement, barely even blinking as she watched in fascinated terror as he relentlessly unravelled her secrets.

"The sound of frantic horses — it reminds you — "

The tears spilled over.

He sat down beside her and pulled her roughly into his arms. She resisted at first, her slight body stiff and unyielding and then she went limp, leaning against him in sheer exhaustion, the effort of keeping secrets had taken a heavy toll.

"Is that where — the scars on your back — ?"

She flinched and tried to pull out of his embrace, but he held her firmly, stroking her hair.

"Doctor Brook saw them when he examined you and as I'm your legal guardian, of sorts, he felt duty-bound to tell me.

He meant only to help you. I suspect it started when you were with Edwin Stokey, when you were no more than a child. I understand from my attorney, Major Cobham, that it's common practice for children to be ill-treated once they leave the foundling home. I wish to God — "

He buried his face in her hair and they remained there, locked together, until both their heart rates returned to normal and Sephie stopped shaking.

She made a little movement within his arms and he released her. She didn't look at him but made the sign for *Sorry*. He took her hands in his, holding them still, and shook his head, "Don't apologise! This isn't your fault. None of it. You were just a child and are entirely blameless. Do you hear me?" He looked down into her blotchy, tear-streaked face and had an inexplicable urge to comfort her. He put his fingers under her chin and tipped it up a little and then gently pressed his lips against her surprised ones, which opened in a little gasp of shock and he slid his other hand into the small of her back and pulled her closer, deepening his kiss as she responded, her mouth softening under his as she willingly kissed him back.

"What in damnation — ?" exclaimed Leander furiously, as he entered the barn.

Twenty-One

Have you lost your damned mind!" shouted Leander, "What the hell were you thinking? You've taken advantage of her when she's at her most vulnerable! You should be ashamed!" He wanted to punch him on the nose but as Theo was considerably taller than him, a keen fencer and therefore rather muscular, he had to be content with shouting. "Sephie only got on that damned stupid pony because you asked her! She wouldn't have done it for anyone else! God, but you're a crass blockheaded fool! After all she's been through! Of all the moments to choose to — " he stopped and eyed a subdued Theo, with sudden suspicion, "What did you *say* to her?"

"I just kissed her, Leander. I wanted to comfort her."

"Then you should have given her some damned Chocolate Cream! Not molested her! D'you not think she's suffered enough?"

"I wasn't thinking clearly."

"Well, that much is obvious! What if I hadn't arrived — ?"

"Don't be ridiculous. It was just a kiss."

Leander made an explosive sound of derision, "You idiot! That child *loves* you! I would hazard a guess that you're the *only* person she's ever loved in all her horrifying eighteen years. And what a lamentable choice! You stand as her guardian! Can't you see that during her short life she's only been misused and knows only how to appease men? She's accustomed to men wanting something from her and has learned that whatever she does, they'll take it anyway. She wasn't given much in the first place but has become little more than a vessel for their basest desires and terrifying rages. How will you explain to her that it was *just a kiss?* That it meant nothing! That you're just like those other men, those *monsters* in the darkest corners of her life. You *rescued* her, Theo! She naturally feels love and gratitude and *you* — you've shown her that you also want something from her. Not marriage, of course, nothing so pure or permanent. How would the *beau monde* react to that, I wonder? Lord Theodore Rokewode marrying a nameless foundling from a fairground! Would she be invited to dine, do you think? Would she be accepted into their drawing rooms? Of course not! She'd be spurned and so would you and she'd end up blaming herself! Why can you not see this? My God, Theo, what have you done?"

Leander, having somehow allowed himself to hope that Sephie and Theo could somehow find happiness together, had realised, too late, that such dreams were an impossibility. Society would not be understanding or forgiving and would shun Sephie, who despite her innate courage, wouldn't be able to withstand the slights and slurs she'd inevitably receive and worse than that, he knew that once she saw how Theo would undoubtedly be rejected by his own kind, she'd never be happy, knowing she'd brought disgrace upon him and his family. He was now absolutely certain that Theo felt something for Sephie but knew his stiff-necked friend would be unable to forget his duty to his family name; they were a proud lot these Rokewodes and although he always declared blithely that he came from a long line of libertines, there was no room on the family tree for any by-blows however delightful they may be. Leander was also sure that if Sephie was offered the position of Theo's mistress, she'd gladly take it, without considering the consequences. And *that*, Leander could not countenance. It was the most appalling muddle, and he could see no satisfactory solution. He'd told Sephie about Major Cobham and his wife wishing to adopt her and hoped she might consider that as an option if the worst came to the worst. It would mean, at least, she wouldn't have to crawl back to the fair and Henry Pippin, or indeed, be forced to become a housemaid or work in a flower shop. No, he thought, she'd be well cared for and maybe even find some kind of love and would eventually be able to forget all about Theo and his family and make an honest, happy life for herself. That would be the answer. He had to believe it.

Theo was staring down into the fire and waiting for Leander to resume his tirade. He knew that he was in the wrong. He knew these feelings he'd been having were not real, they were a mere lapse in his usual good judgement He was beginning to think that Sephie might possess magical powers as she seemed to be able to make everyone love her. He kicked the wrought iron fender with his booted foot and turned to face Leander.

"You're right, of course. I'm entirely at fault. I shall, as soon as I know the danger is over and dealt with satisfactorily and the Ball is over and done with, make sure that both girls are given a chance of new homes and families. I shall not force my attentions upon her again."

"There's the rub though, Theo. She doesn't see it like that. Your attentions are welcome. Poor child. The problem in my mind is that I'm not sure she's able to separate her past from the present. Known nothing else for her entire life. Been trained to accept the treatment meted out to her and to suppress everything that makes her Sephie. Only now is she beginning to come to life. We should allow her to grow up. To become more than just the abused child."

Theo shook his head slightly, "I'd no idea you were so observant Leander. It seems you see more than I ever could. Kitty always said I was hide-bound just like my father."

"She's right. Always seen the similarities. But you've changed. Sephie's changed you. Changed all of us. As I said before, she's a mirror, for us to see ourselves. It's hard to face the truth and realise you may not be as perfect as you once thought. Made me face my fears. Not entirely comfortable with it yet but at least I can see what needs to be done." He paused as he heard a commotion outside, voices raised and Amadeus yapping and then fixed Theo with a direct gaze, "Promise me you won't break her heart Theo."

Theo ground his teeth, "Why does everyone think I'm going to break her heart? I wouldn't hurt her for the world."

"I suppose because in the end her heart being broken has nothing to do with you, or anyone else and everything to do with her," said Leander obliquely, going to see who on earth was causing such a rumpus in the Hall.

* * *

Sephie sat in front of the looking-glass and contemplated her face. She'd always been honest with herself about the way she looked and if she forgot for a moment just how unprepossessing she really was, Biddy was always there to remind her. She didn't mind. She'd been a witness to the kind of attention Biddy received and hadn't craved that kind of false admiration and uncontrolled lust in the least. They'd both been fully aware, in the end, that only one thing was required of them and unless they wanted to be beaten into submission, they had no choice but to comply. Sephie had tried running away from Edwin Stokey several times but had been caught each time and returned to him and her life was always even worse afterwards.

Now she'd ruined things here too. Leander was so angry with her he couldn't even meet her eyes and had sent her back to the house with such suppressed rage that she'd fled and hidden herself away in her bedchamber to weep alone. She kept repeating to herself that once the Ball was over, she'd be leaving and then the Rokewodes could forget all about her and all the trouble she'd brought to their door.

Leaning forward, she peered at her reflection. At her mouth. It wasn't remotely memorable, not in colour or shape. But Theo had kissed it. She had no idea why he had done so. She stroked a wondering finger across her lips and tried to recall the touch of his mouth on hers. She felt a surge of shame as she remembered how eagerly she'd kissed him back and thought that he was sure to be shocked by such indecent behaviour. She'd shown that she wasn't fit to be in their company.

She looked critically at her eyes, which were so very ordinary, an unexciting grey like watered-down storm clouds; not at all like Biddy's sky-blue ones, their cerulean brilliance unforgettable. Her eyebrows were too straight and too dark and her nose utterly unremarkable. To top it all, her hair was an uninteresting shade of brown, the only positive note being that it at least curled naturally. No, she'd nothing to recommend her, nothing to make anyone paint her portrait or write poetry to her, or even just remember having seen her, so entirely forgettable was she. She wasn't despondent about it — she'd never thought anything else — but after being kissed so wonderfully, she thought it might show upon her face but was disappointed to find that she looked exactly the same as before apart from her puffy red eyes.

As she'd scurried from the granary, propelled by shame and guilt and the awful sight of Leander's shocked countenance, she'd glanced back at Theo over her shoulder and he'd raised one hand and made the sign for *Sorry*.

She knew that she loved Theo, with a passion so strong that she would have blindly done anything for him, even if it cost her everything but she was not insensible to the fact that to feel such an all-consuming ardour for someone was perhaps not ideal or acceptable. When he held her, she felt as though, for the first time in her life that she'd finally found a place of safety, somewhere she could shelter from all the terrors she so yearned to escape. She'd had no idea such a place even existed and to discover it so unexpectedly was shocking to her. She had occasionally met with some kindness in her eighteen years; the parson's sister, although hatchet-faced and bigoted and decidedly unchristian at times, had after a while relented just enough to teach an inspired Sephie to read and write and allowed her to have books, as long as she approved the subjects. Sephie had been a fast learner and ploughed through the books at speed. In the end she had to be grateful to the woman, as she'd opened up a new world for her, despite her otherwise thoughtless and sometimes cold-hearted treatment. It had shown her that there might be a better life for her somewhere if she could only find a way to escape and search for it. Astonishingly, it had managed to find her.

Theo was an unashamed libertine. Sephie had heard the comments, not meant for her ears. The very fact that he so openly kept a mistress was proof of this. Everyone seemed ready to accept Mrs Sheraton with a transparency which made Sephie think that being a mistress to a high-ranking nobleman was entirely permissible. Although Leander had been disparaging, he was generally inclined to be disparaging about most things — it was his way. She loved Leander, but only in a way, she supposed, that she would have loved a brother, had she been fortunate enough to have one. He'd been her stalwart supporter since the beginning and whatever happened she knew that he always had her best interests at heart. She was alarmed about what he might have said to Theo but was fairly sure that he wouldn't do anything too drastic being reticent by nature and not given to violent outbursts. She wouldn't want him to ruin Theo's beautiful face.

She put her chin in her hands and closing her eyes, tried to conjure up that beautiful face. She knew she must keep out of his way as much as possible until the Ball, which, as they lived in the same house, would not be easy, but she had no wish to see regret and disappointment in those beautiful hazel eyes. She must focus on Leander and Matilda.

She needed Biddy's support. She wasn't sure if she would be brave enough to leave without encouragement.

* * *

Biddy was astonished. She wasn't at all sure that she'd understood. The signs Sephie was using were mostly still a mystery to her. She really had better things to do than learn silly hand movements, it made her feel foolish. She had tried, for Sephie's sake but found it difficult to retain the meanings of the shapes. Still, she was fairly certain that Sephie was indicating that she wanted to leave Rokewode Abbey after the Ball. Even though Biddy hadn't been having the best of times, she at least felt safe from the threat of danger from her father, who must surely be planning his revenge. She felt secure within the intimidating high walls of the Abbey and with so many fiery young men there to defend her.

"If you think that I'm going to run away with you, you must be mad, Seph! I'm not leaving. I like it here. I'm sorry," she said.

Sephie smiled. She liked it too.

"You don't understand," said Biddy, "I might have a chance of a very respectable marriage and a life of comfort. Why would I wish to throw that away? Perhaps my talent will be being a good and dutiful wife to a baronet."

Sephie was careful not to show her thoughts on this imaginative conjecture. She shrugged slightly and pretended that she had accepted Biddy's change of heart; she couldn't blame her friend for wanting to remain at the Abbey where she might find her happiness at last. Biddy had suffered dreadfully and Sephie thought that she deserved a chance of a loving family of her own.

She would just have to leave on her own.

* * *

"I am thoroughly convinced that everything is ready, Sephie," said Kitty with her usual confidence. "We only have to decide which gowns to wear now. The masks will be here tomorrow."

Sephie was ticking off things on her list, the tip of her tongue sticking out between her teeth as she concentrated hard on the final preparations for the Ball.

Kitty had been going over the fine details all morning with Sephie and Miss Edie, who was a dab hand at seeing what needed to be done and suggesting more efficient ways to accomplish them. The door opened and Theo entered the drawing room, his eyes immediately, Kitty noted, going to Sephie as she pored over her papers at the desk in the window, chewing on the end of her dip pen and unaware of his presence.

Theo smiled, "That's a bad habit Sephie and will ruin your teeth," he said, "And the pen."

Sephie jumped nervously and turned to face him, her cheeks flushed, and her eyes startled. She laid down the pen guiltily and Theo cursed himself for having spoiled their former affable relationship by behaving without any consideration for her feelings. He wished to God that she could talk to him and explain what had happened to her. He was becoming consumed with a need to know her entire history and this need to understand her puzzled him greatly, as he was generally a man who had little desire to delve into other people's business. He was finding that however hard he tried he was unable to eradicate the punishing thoughts which haunted both his waking and sleeping moments. Nothing in his previous thirty-two years had prepared him for such an onslaught of emotions, such terrible confusion and disruption to his usually well-ordered thoughts.

"Have you come to help or hinder?" asked his sister with some asperity. "We've been closeted in here all morning and are weary from trying to make sure everything is arranged just so. Sephie is a hard taskmaster and won't let us rest until we've combed over every detail countless times."

Theo glanced back to the tyrant at the desk, "Well, if you and Miss Edie would like to take a well-earned rest, I am extremely happy to take your places for a while and make my contribution to the arrangements. I feel it only fair that I should do my part as Leander is my dearest friend."

Kitty got to her feet at once, "That's a splendid idea Theo! Miss Edie and I will go and sit with Mama, whom I fear will think she's being sorely neglected!" And with a few words of encouragement for Sephie, the two ladies left the room.

There followed an uncomfortable silence before Theo crossed the space between them and sat down beside Sephie at the desk.

She eyed him warily from under her dark frowning brows.

"Sephie, I wanted to talk with you."

She shrank away a little, her cheeks losing their colour. Was he going to ask her to leave? Or accuse her of deplorable behaviour? Had he discovered something about her?

He observed the reaction and reached out a hand to reassure her, but she withdrew even further, and he let his hand fall. He sighed, "Please don't be afraid! I am not come to distress you. I wanted to — apologise. I should never have made you ride. It was utterly insensitive and had I known — the truth, I would never have forced it upon you. I shouldn't have — kissed you either, Sephie, it wasn't right, when you were so upset. I've always been too high-handed, as Kitty will no doubt tell you. You were so very brave, and I was bullying and boorish. Is there any way that I might be able to convince you to forgive me?"

Sephie was looking up at him in astonishment, unable to believe what she was hearing. She'd been so certain that he'd come to ask her to remove herself from his ancestral home and instead he was asking her forgiveness. She wanted to tell him that, in her eyes, there was nothing to forgive. He had never been anything but kind to her and she loved him with all her heart because he'd rescued her from that Hell and treated her as though she were as good as anyone else. She cocked her head and contemplated him with a sudden impish glint.

His eyes narrowed, "*By the pricking of my thumbs....*" he murmured.

She grinned and made the sign for *Thank you* and then handed him a sheet of paper.

He glanced at it, "This looks ominously like a speech to me."

She bit her lip and nodded.

"I see. My punishment is that I am to give a speech at the Ball? Should that not be Leander's job as it's his family home?"

Sephie rolled her eyes.

"No, of course, you're right. He'd run off and hide in the cellar until the whole thing was over. Poor Leander, he was never comfortable with crowds." Theo frowned and regarded her thoughtfully, "You know — he's extremely angry with me. And rightly so. He thinks the world of you and believes I've behaved dishonourably. Again, I'm embarrassed to admit that he's right. We've never quarrelled before. He hates any kind of confrontation and yet for the last few days he's been berating me at every opportunity. I am determined to make it up to both of you somehow."

A small paper booklet was thrust into his hand. He glanced through it with dawning alarm, "Good God! Please tell me this is not my dance card! I thought only the ladies were given these?" He looked at her with amusement, "So, this is to be my atonement? According to this I shall be dancing with every ineligible female in the county."

Sephie dimpled at him.

Theo shook his head, "It seems that I have been suitably admonished and must accept my punishment. Which I shall try to do, with good grace," he said solemnly. "I hope one day that you'll be able to trust me again."

She regarded him gravely and then made the sign for *Friends*.

He smiled, "Indeed. Friends. Always."

Twenty-Two

If you are to wear the white, Seph, I think I shall wear the red. What a contrast that shall make!"

Yes, thought Ann, as she took out yet another gown from the linen press, a contrast where *you* will outshine Miss Sephie with ease. How very thoughtful of you! She pursed her lips and draped a pale blue taffeta gown across the bed. Really, Miss Pippin was unbearable sometimes; Ann had no idea how Miss Sephie put up with her. She cast her eyes over her young mistress, who was gazing in raptures at her friend twirling before the mirror with the red gown held up against her perfect face. Ann sighed, knowing that Miss Sephie would obviously put up with anything. She turned back to the press and tried to blot out the horrific glimpse she'd had of Sephie's back, when the chemise, she always insisted on wearing, had slipped, to reveal the awful reason for her modesty. From that moment Ann had decided that she would stand guard over this tiny but ferociously brave girl. Even before Lord Rokewode had asked her to, she'd taken on the role of protector. She had even managed to pick up a few of the signs they used to speak to each other, and Miss Sephie had been delighted.

Biddy collapsed into a nearby chair in a cloud of cherry-red satin. "So, I'm to dance attendance upon Sir Leander! That will be very peculiar, I must say. He takes no notice of me at all as a rule. I am to make Miss Fleete jealous?" she laughed gaily. "It sounds like one of those plays at the fair! I wonder what she looks like. Has he described her to you? Is she a country mouse? Bound to be if she's a parson's daughter. And, of course, they'll only have a local seamstress to make their clothes. Nothing as rich and elegant as this."

Ann, firmly buttoning her lip, took the gown from Biddy and hung it up so the creases would drop out before the night of the Ball was upon them.

Kitty arrived carrying a box.

"Masks!" she declared and handed the appropriate ones to Sephie and Biddy.

Biddy held her black and gold mask up with something of a pout, "It's lovely but it'll disguise most of my face!"

Kitty met Ann's eyes across the room and gave her head a slight shake, Ann looked ready to do battle.

"I think you'll find that your hair colouring, un-powdered naturally, will be enough to draw all eyes to you Biddy. And with that quite *shocking* scarlet — you will be the *belle* of the Ball, without a doubt. And, of course, this is *exactly* what we need. You are to be the centre of attention! Without you the Ball would be an abject failure. We are all entirely dependent upon your outstanding beauty to win the day!"

Biddy preened a little and tried to imagine the scene. All eyes upon her and everyone green with envy. She simply couldn't wait. "Oh, Seph, let me see your mask!" she cried, suddenly remembering to be more considerate.

Sephie raised the silver and crystal mask to her face and they all made admiring comments and Sephie quickly laid it down on the bed beside her. She was unable to think of the Ball without her stomach writhing into painful knots. It was only a few days away now and each day sped past as though determined that she should have as little time with Theo and the Rokewodes as possible. She treasured every stolen moment. She squirrelled them away for the years ahead. Every time Babyngton trod on her foot in dance practice and apologised so earnestly until everyone was shouting at him in despair; every time Lady Rokewode patted her hand and called her a "Dear little thing"; every time Kitty embraced her like a sister or Sir Ambrose exchanged a conspiratorial long-suffering glance with her; or Miss Edie twinkled at her over some preposterous comment Anthony had made; or the sight of Freddie and Leander arguing about who was supposed to take the role of the gentleman in the dance — Or, those few quiet moments she had alone with Theo, when everyone else was occupied with their own thoughts and business. When he just came and perched on the edge of the large desk in the library while she crossed more things off her lists and added even more. Or when she was sitting with his mother in the drawing room and he would appear and settle into his favourite chair by the fire, booted legs stretched out in front of him, his fists thrust deep into his breeches pockets. She'd think he'd fallen asleep to begin with but then he'd quietly chuckle at some amusing passage Lady Rokewode would read out of the latest novel and show that he was still awake. These moments were like gold-dust and she carefully swept them up into her memory.

For his part, Theo couldn't seem to stop himself from seeking Sephie out. He told himself it was because he was keeping a watchful eye upon her, like any diligent guardian would, but it was actually because he found some sort of peace when in her company and it wasn't because she couldn't talk; she was as lively, if not livelier than even Kitty! No, it was that he found himself craving the feelings he had discovered when he was with her, a strange kind of contentment that he'd never experienced before. When he was out seeing to estate business with Roland Ashby, he found his mind wandering. He would often, much to his steward's obvious annoyance, cut short the meeting and wander back to the Abbey, telling himself that he had sound reasons to stroll from room to room until he came across Sephie racing around the library tugging a ball of yarn behind her and Amadeus chasing after it, yapping loudly. Or he would turn up just in time to assist her with arranging the Christmas holly and ivy along the highest part of the main staircase, which she was struggling to reach. He held the chair steady for her and when she wobbled slightly, he put a hand on her waist to stop her tipping over. (Sephie wished she was the kind of female who could pretend to fall again so that he would save her. But, sadly, she wasn't.) And Theo just told himself that he was being properly concerned for her welfare and not giving in to an irresistible urge to be near her.

If Kitty or Miss Edie noticed the unusual frequency of his appearances with only the very flimsiest of excuses, they said nothing, merely exchanging quiet glances. Leander, however, who was still smarting over his friend's behaviour, was not nearly so restrained.

"Theo, is not Roland waiting for you in the cloisters? If you're not careful he'll find a more attentive employer and then where will you be? This place would collapse into ruins within a few months without his hand on the reins."

Theo, understanding that he was still on probation, meekly did as he was instructed.

* * *

Two days before the Ball, Ann was getting Sephie ready for bed when her toe hit something tucked away out of sight under the bed. She pulled it out, suspecting Sephie, who was as untidy as a small child, had accidentally kicked something under the bed. It was a cloth drawstring bag, which when opened, she discovered, was stuffed with clothes and shoes. She turned and held it up to her mistress, eyebrows raised.

Sephie blushed to the roots of her hair and was unable to look Ann in the eye.

"Miss Sephie?"

Sephie looked at her with pleading eyes.

"What *is* this?" demanded the maid peremptorily.

Sephie made no move. She sat very still. She had no idea how to explain.

"It looks very much to me as though you're planning to run away," Ann glared at her young mistress in disapproval. "Why would you want to do that? You're happy here! You're safe here from whatever it is that you're escaping. Lord Rokewode would never allow anything to happen to you."

Sephie's eyes filled with tears and she buried her face in her hands. Ann, immediately sorry for her aggressive tone, put her arms around her and held her so until she'd stopped sobbing.

"So, you're determined to leave. You must have very good reasons indeed. I have to tell you Miss Sephie that I've seen your scars and know that you've been much mistreated but even so, I cannot understand why you'd wish to leave the Abbey for you cannot want to return to the people who did this to you."

Sephie shook her head vehemently.

"And, if you don't mind my saying so, I've seen the way you look at Lord Rokewode. Why would you want to leave him?"

The silent sobbing increased and Sephie leant against Ann's shoulder, her small body shaking.

Ann stroked her back soothingly and wondered what to do for the best. "All right, all right! It's all going to be just fine. We will somehow manage to get through this. Were you thinking of leaving after the Ball? Yes? Then, I shall go with you. No, I *shall!* You cannot go alone. And, besides, Lord Rokewode has told me to stay by you whatever happens!"

Sephie raised her head and stared at Ann in amazement. He *had?* Why should he do such a thing? She impatiently wiped the tears away from her cheeks and tried to pull herself together. Had he suspected that she might flee? Had Biddy said something? Sephie couldn't fathom how he might have guessed her plans. But he'd told Ann to look after her. It was a comforting thought that he cared enough to do that. She was at a loss but the mere idea of having the kind and sensible Ann for company was a boon to her rapidly flagging spirits. Although she had no desire, let alone right, to drag Ann away from her home nor, in truth, would she want Ann to find out her secrets. She squeezed the maid's hand and gave her a watery smile. She would have to slip away without Ann noticing and somehow, she would manage to survive without the Rokewodes. Without Theo.

Ann wondered whether to tell Lord Rokewode about Sephie's plans. She decided to wait until the day of the Ball and to hope that her mistress changed her mind before it was too late. Lord Rokewode had said nothing about warning him;

he'd just instructed her to stay with Miss Sephie, come-what-may. That she would certainly do. Nobody was going to hurt Miss Sephie while she was around to protect her; she hadn't survived growing up with six hateful older brothers without learning a thing or two!

* * *

Christmas Eve, just one day before the Ball, was fraught. Sephie was frantic, worried that something might go wrong, and she would be blamed. The Abbey looked beautiful cloaked in full Christmas splendour and Sephie was loathe to leave it for Fairtree Manor because she knew she'd never see it again. She would always picture it like this, lush with fragrant greenery and sparkling with candlelight, a magical kingdom like in the book of fairy tales. Kitty was in a whirl, racing hither and thither for no apparent reason. Sephie had to tuck Amadeus permanently under her arm in order to stop him randomly biting passing ankles, he had become so over-excited, sensing a disturbance in the air. Sir Anthony was driving his valet, James Mullens, to become a secret drinker — (he swiped the odd bottle of wine from the Abbey's large and well-stocked cellar) — in order to cope with the ever-increasing piles of discarded neckcloths forming snowy drifts in Anthony's bedchamber.

And Leander was a seething mass of disparate emotions; one minute hope, the next flat despair. They tried to calm him, but it only seemed to make things worse so mostly everyone steered clear of him; seeing him coming towards them down a corridor, they'd spin on their heels and rush away in the opposite direction before he could waylay them. He had a permanently feverish flush across his usually pale cheeks and his eyes were glazed as though he were sickening for something. At dinner he would stare disconsolately at his plate, pushing the food around and not eating a morsel of it. Nobody would meet his eye if he happened to look up, not wishing to engage him in conversation which would be bound to end badly. He was certain that the whole thing would be a fiasco of such massive proportions that he'd have to leave the country and live abroad for the rest of his life and that Matilda would laugh in his face and tell everyone that she'd always despised him.

Sephie, watching him suffer, eventually could stand it no longer and wrote him a note, as she was unable to convey how she felt with hand shapes.

He took it from her and frowned, "What's this? Yet more lists?"

She waited patiently while he unfolded it and read the contents.

My Most Dear Leander,

Firstly, thank you for everything and I love you so very much.
But I have to tell you that you're being extremely silly and childish, and you really must stop before you lose all your friends or have a serious heart attack.
If Matilda is as wonderful as you say she is, she would never laugh in your face. I think she's only doing this in the first place because of your own stupidity.
Please, try to be brave and I promise you that we shall triumph!

Your very devoted friend,

Sephie
P.S. And please forgive Theo — he can't help being the way he is.

Leander looked up from the letter to her expectant face, she was so obviously nervous about how he might react that he laughed out loud.

"God, Sephie! Am I really being such a fool? I'm so sorry. I never meant to be such trial to you. It's just that I get so agitated at the thought of it and the part I have to play. I'm not at all sure that I shall be able to carry it off, but I promise you that I shall try my damnedest!"

Sephie flew at him and hugged him and that's how Theo found them when he entered the drawing room a moment later. He stopped in his tracks and stared. On hearing the door open, Sephie pulled back with a guilty start and Leander, turning and seeing his friend's stupefied face, held out the letter to him, "You had better read this, Theo as it is a little to do with you. I have been read the Riot Act and am now resolved to face up to whatever the Ball may bring with the same courage our Sephie has. Also, by the bye, I forgive you but only because I'm rather afraid of Sephie and what she might do to me if I don't!"

Theo scanned the letter, "Straight to the point as usual! Although I'm not at all sure what she means by the last part! Can't help being the way I am? Should I be insulted?"

They both regarded Sephie, who just smiled.

* * *

Lord Rokewode, having snapped at both his sister and then his mother with unaccustomed bad humour, had taken himself off to bed and slammed his bedchamber door with unnecessary force. He'd then dismissed his valet with a curt word, which made that fellow remark to Mr Chilton, the long-serving butler, that something was very much amiss with his master and he expected to see fireworks before very long, if not an actual murder.

* * *

The day of the Christmas Ball arrived at last, and the Abbey had fallen oddly silent as though there had been a death in the family.

"The lull before the storm," remarked Sir Ambrose, gloomily.

Kitty pushed away her breakfast, declaring that she couldn't possibly eat another mouthful because she was so fatigued after not sleeping a wink all night.

Sir Anthony gobbled up his food with his usual gusto, saying that if he was expected to dance all night without collapsing from exhaustion then he needed to consume a hearty breakfast.

Leander, looking like a man about to go to the gallows, was trying heroically not to allow his terror to boil over and spoil the day for everyone else. He had, for Sephie's sake, decided to put on a brave face but it was only a wafer-thin mask.

Lady Rokewode was in a high state of excitement, having decided that she was going to throw off all restraints and have a little fun before she was forced to take to her bed and wither away in lonely misery. She was delighted with her new gown of lilac silk with its quantities of lace and ribbons. She decided to wear her hair powdered and bedecked with dyed plumes and pearls.

Freddie and Babyngton were doing some last-minute dance practice in the Great Hall, which kept everyone amused. Babyngton was certain that he would forget which part he was dancing and end up confusing the whole ballroom when he accidentally danced the lady's part.

Kitty noted that Sephie was rather subdued and pointed it out to Leander who was sitting next to her as always.

"Are you all right, Sephie?" he asked her under his breath.

She looked up at him, smiled and nodded but he noticed that she wasn't joining in the conversations with her new-found signs and seemed to be listening to everything that was said with serious intent as though committing it all to memory.

"Looking forward to your first Ball?"

An emphatically signed *Yes!*

* * *

Two travelling coaches carrying their luggage for the overnight stay and some of the servants who were required to go with them, set off early for Fairtree Manor.

After breakfast everyone gathered in the drawing room which had been richly arrayed with greenery, so that the Rokewodes could hand out some gifts to their friends.

Little packets of sweetmeats tied with scarlet ribands, snuff boxes and brooches, books for Miss Edie and a pretty new reticule for Biddy.

When Theo handed Sephie a long narrow box, she was embarrassed and didn't know where to look.

"Go on, open it!" ordered Kitty, "What can it be?"

Sephie flipped the box open and gasped.

Nestling in the tissue paper was the most beautiful ostrich feather fan. She took it out with trembling fingers and allowed it to fan out in her hands. The sticks and the guard were made of mother of pearl and the leaves of white feathers.

She bit her lip and tried valiantly not to cry but failed. She had never seen anything so exquisite and couldn't quite believe it was meant for her. After a moment, she looked up, the tears glistening on her pink cheeks. Her shining eyes met Theo's and his expression was inscrutable.

"Do you like it?" he murmured for her ears only.

She had no way of responding which conveyed her feelings well enough. She looked back at the shining mother of pearl and the pretty feathers quivering in her hands and her mouth curled at the corners and her dimples appeared.

"I'll take that as a yes, then?" he said softly.

She nodded so slightly he barely saw it. This time, he thought, he had done well. His heart thumped a little erratically in his chest and he dragged himself away and back into the room full of chattering people.

Kitty caught Miss Edie's eye and raised her eyebrows. Miss Edie was pleased with Theodore and concluded that he might yet be saved.

Leander gave Sephie a tiny posy of velvet and silk snowdrops to pin to her gown and Kitty gave her a delicate silver bracelet studded with glittering diamonds. She was so overwhelmed by all the attention and generosity that it rendered her entirely wide-eyed and unable to communicate. She went to sit with Biddy who was thrilled with her unexpected gifts of a gold and ruby clip for her hair and a pair of black kid gloves.

From under her lashes, Sephie watched Theo act the perfect host and she stroked the feathers in her hand and wondered if she would ever be able to let go of the fan. She thought probably not.

Eventually the time came for everyone to retire to their bedchambers to either rest or begin the lengthy preparations for the Ball.

* * *

Ann was waiting for Sephie with everything ready for her. The hip bath was in front of the fire and a housemaid was just finishing filling it with scented water. Once they were alone, Ann helped her out of her clothes, even her chemise and was careful not to stare at the weals and scars, some old, some more recent on her back. Ann washed her mistress as gently as she could, anxious not to hurt or upset her. Her bag was packed and sitting alongside Sephie's in the coach and she was ready to leave, if she had to.

Once dried and clad in her underclothes, Ann slipped the warm off-white satin gown, with its spangled petticoat, over her head and began to tweak it into place. She tied the silver sash and pinned the snowdrops onto her shoulder. Kitty had suggested that her hair remained un-powdered like Biddy's and Ann was able to encourage her natural curls into a soft style which suited her face, simply adorned with a narrow white riband and diamond clip belonging to Kitty. She only wore the silver and diamond bracelet and carried the precious fan, its tasselled cord firmly around her wrist.

Ann stood back to admire her handiwork, "Miss Sephie, you do look so pretty! The white makes you glow like an angel!"

Biddy entering the bedchamber stopped, aghast. "Oh," she said, taken aback. "That gown — well, it's very *becoming!* I've never seen you so in looks, Sephie!" She held out the skirts of her gown, "What do you think of mine?"

Sephie thought Biddy looked like the Queen of the Faeries, the scarlet silk against her pale skin and hair was utterly bewitching. She hugged her and Biddy scolded her for creasing her gown.

Ann hoped she tripped over the hem on the way downstairs.

* * *

Conversation just petered out in the Great Hall when Biddy sailed in, shyly followed by Sephie.

"Good God!" muttered Sir Anthony, dumbfounded.

"Oh, my!" cried Kitty, "I'm not sure I want to go now, I shall look like an old dowager, in comparison!" Her husband gave her a look which told her she could never seem dowdy to his eyes and she fluttered her eyelashes at him coquettishly and he went rather pink. She giggled, her confidence fully restored.

Theo, turning away from his conversation with Roland Ashby, came to a halt mid-sentence. He didn't see anything but the girl who looked as though she was made of early morning mist, frosted cobwebs and winter sunlight sparkling on freshly fallen snow.

It took him several moments to recover the powers of speech.

Sir Anthony was the first to break the silence, dashing to Biddy's side, bowing and kissing her hand in the grand manner, "Miss Pippin, you are an absolute vision! Tonight, you will take the county by storm!" and he led her across the Hall to the waiting group of soon-to-be-revellers.

Theo, somehow managing to stir himself out of his stunned state, approached Sephie and taking her trembling hand in his, turned it upwards and pressed a cool kiss into its palm. Her eyes flew to his, startled. His eyes were shadowed and dark, no golden glints showing.

"Sephie, you look — enchanting. I am at your feet."

Sephie peeped up at him, not believing what she was hearing. Biddy had said the gown did wonders for her but when she'd looked at herself critically in the glass, she had just seen her familiar lacklustre self looking back, the eyes rather more haunted than usual. Theo still held her hand in his, her fingers curled around his and even as the others greeted her and enthusiastically expressed their admiration, he kept his gentle hold on her.

They were enjoying a final glass of Christmas Punch before setting off and Kitty was bossily reminding them of the plans, making sure that everyone knew what they were to do.

Leander gravitated to Sephie's side and bent to fondly kiss her cheek, "I just wanted to thank you for everything before we are swallowed up by the hordes of ravening beasts at the Manor. We may not get a chance to speak once the play has begun and we are all lurching towards certain doom. I know how much love and effort you've put into this and I can't even begin to express how grateful I am for all your hard work. Oh, that sounds a bit stiff and formal but Sephie — you are the little sister I never had and always wanted, and I love you very much."

Sephie was starting to believe that she was still asleep and dreaming. She wanted to pinch herself to see if she was really awake. She placed a hand over her heart and then pointed to him. She loved him. She felt Theo's grip tighten slightly on her hand. She returned the pressure not daring to look at him.

"Whatever the outcome tonight," continued Leander, "I will never forget."

Anthony bounced over to them, barely able to contain his excitement, "I must say, this is all looking exceedingly promising! Sephie, you look like a snow angel! Come, you must be cold standing there so far from the fire!" and he pulled her away from Theo and Leander and pressed a glass of punch into the hand which had seconds before been so safely tucked into Theo's.

She looked down at the dark red punch swirling in the glass and thought she'd better not drink any in case it befuddled her; she had to keep a clear head for all she had to accomplish tonight. Everyone was depending upon her and she mustn't let them down.

Twenty-Three

Happily, the weather held fine, no rain clouds gathered on the horizon; a clear inky blue sky arched above their heads, pierced by stars and the facade of Fairtree Manor was perfectly lit by a bright shining moon and the many lanterns and torches blazing along the driveway and all around the house. It was quite breath-taking. Ranks of liveried footmen lined the garden paths and the grand sweep of steps leading up to the front doors. They were the first to arrive as Leander was required to greet the guests with his grandmother. They were ushered into the cavernous Great Hall, which was set out with long refectory tables, decorated with traditional greenery, the massive fire roaring and crackling and hundreds of candles ablaze. Footmen took their cloaks, and they were shown to their allotted bedchambers so they could tidy themselves after the journey.

Ann was already waiting for Sephie and had a bowl of warm water for her to wash in and a refreshing glass of lemonade to revive her. Their bags were on the ottoman, ready for later but Sephie studiously avoided looking at them, reluctant to acknowledge how the evening was going to end. Ann attended to her hair, smoothing and primping it back to its best, chatting all the while about the wonders of such an elegant and well-appointed house.

"Miss Sephie, my brother, Simon will be here at three o'clock, in the gig. He has promised not to tell anyone. Are you still determined to leave?"

Sephie was still for a moment and then she nodded just once.

Ann pursed her lips; if it really came to it, she would alert Lord Rokewode and he would stop Miss Sephie from running away. She couldn't see the sense in it, to exchange this life of luxury for the unknown seemed rash in the extreme but Sephie was unable or unwilling to explain her reasons for flight. She suspected it had to do with her feelings for Lord Rokewode. Ann was a young woman with an indomitable spirit and a deep sense of loyalty and once she'd given her word, that was it as far as she was concerned. There would be no going back. She had only been forced to involve her brother once she'd realised that Sephie's escape plan was disastrously flawed; with no mode of transport organised to take them from the Manor to their place of safety, they would have been forced to walk in the dark and cold for miles until they came to the first available in which might have a connection to the stagecoach. The other flaw was that Sephie had no money of her own. Fortunately, Ann was someone who had scrimped and saved all her life and had managed to gather enough for them to at least get out of the county.

There was a knock on the door and a housemaid entered and announced, rather apologetically, that Baroness Gage wished to see Sephie in her bedchamber, immediately. She and Ann exchanged glances and Sephie made a face. Ann laughed, "You'll be fine! I've heard that she likes you. Can't think why!" she added with a knowing wink.

The housemaid led Sephie along the regimented corridors until they came to the main wing of the house. She opened the imposing door and Sephie stepped timidly into an impressively over-furnished bedchamber. She stood on the threshold until she heard the Baroness bark an order at her, "Come in then! Stop dawdling there like a scared little rabbit!"

Sephie crossed the huge room to stand near the chair where the Baroness was comfortably ensconced. She curtsied very prettily and folded her hands in front of her.

The Baroness raised her eyeglass and peered at her. "Well, you certainly have scrubbed up nicely! Not so plain now, are you! Any reaction from our handsome hero? Ah, I see there was! Splendid! He'd be a fool not to notice. I understand that tonight is for the benefit of my silly grandson? No, don't frown at me, he is *extremely* silly, always has been. I love him despite his ridiculous foibles. It was his mother's fault. She doted on him, being the only child and ruined him with her anxieties for his safety; lived in fear of him hurting himself or succumbing to a deadly fever. It was no way for the poor child to live. Became too frightened to even breathe! Theo helped though, took him away and made sure that Leander had some kind of a life, but one cannot completely alter what is learned in childhood, at your mother's knee. Ah, of course, *you* had no mother to speak of, did you! Well, I must say you've done very well without her, whoever she may have been. It's a damn shame though that you can't speak. Be entertaining to know what was going on inside that busy little head of yours. Right! Now, I want you to take me downstairs in a minute. Go and collect your things and that other creature, Miss Pippin and we shall be off. What do you think to my attire? I can still claim to turn heads, wouldn't you say?"

Sephie took in the astounding puce taffeta gown with its old-fashioned panniers, her rouged cheeks and the copious patches and enormous teetering wig perched upon her head, which was slipping slightly over one eyebrow, and agreed politely but with a decided twinkle.

"That's my girl!" laughed the Baroness, delighted. "I look a start, do I not? It's my privilege to look any way I want now. Nobody dare tell me otherwise — apart from you, of course! Actually, it's probably just as well you *can't* speak! God knows what you might say! Go! Be back here in ten minutes."

Sephie grinned and scurried away to find Biddy and put her beautiful silver mask on.

* * *

As they descended the grand staircase, they were gently applauded by the awaiting group at the bottom of the stairs. The Baroness, clinging onto Sephie for dear life, waved a regal hand and inclined her head. Sephie put up a quick hand to steady the wig which seemed to have a mind of its own with a marked inclination to slide whenever Baroness Gage moved her head too far in any direction.

They reached the bottom without incident and were guided into the Great Hall where they were to greet the guests. They could hear the first carriages arriving and Sephie took a shaky breath as the doors opened.

A rush of cold air was followed by a clutch of be-cloaked and masked and somewhat awestruck local dignitaries. The cloaks were removed to reveal an array of newly acquired finery, glittering jewels and floating fabrics in every possible colour. Sephie thought they looked like exotic butterflies and observed them keenly but really, she was waiting for just one person to arrive. Miss Matilda Fleete. She kept an eye on Leander because she knew his face would tell her when the mysterious star of their show arrived.

Baroness Gage seated herself next to Lady Rokewode, in a richly carved throne-like chair and they immediately put their heads together to exchange pleasantries and some idle gossip. They were not in the least alike but were united by their titles and wealth and the centuries of ancestral history which still surrounded and supported them.

Biddy was standing against a background of holly and ivy and made a striking picture, the splash of cherry red, the alabaster white of her perfect skin, the moonlight-bright ringlets and the black and scarlet mask, made nearly every guest catch their breath as they entered the Hall. Next to her, as planned, stood a surprisingly cool looking Leander, elegant in a dark blue cutaway coat, cream waistcoat, blue knee breeches and white stockings and shining buckled shoes. His short-cropped hair artfully arranged into careless curls and his snow-white cravat tied to an inch. He wore, like all the gentlemen, just a plain black Domino mask. He and Biddy looked like a painting and every eye couldn't help but be drawn to them, as they stood practically shoulder to shoulder, as though joined. The message could not have been any clearer. Biddy, as instructed, was casting him flirtatious glances from under her sooty eyelashes and every so often her fluttering fingers would stray to settle for a second on his arm and he would lightly touch them with his.

"So far so good," murmured a most beloved voice beside her.

She beamed up at his masked face.

For a moment he looked deep into her eyes and she made herself hold his gaze. "I'd like to speak with you after the Ball, Sephie, if that would be all right?"

She cocked her head to one side.

"Nothing to worry about, so don't be alarmed," he reassured her.

Freddie and Babyngton came to tell Sephie how marvellous she looked and to compliment her on all the plans for the Ball. Then, Theo was taken away by Kitty to greet more guests as they poured through the doors in a never-ending stream. Eventually she couldn't see across the room anymore. Then, there was a little frisson of excitement and a small group of people arrived, were divested of their cloaks and immediately warmly welcomed by Kitty and Theo. Sephie stole a glance at Leander and knew that this was what they'd been waiting for.

Miss Matilda Fleete, in a gown of moss green silk and a mask made of golden leaves, her shiny copper curls caressing freckled shoulders, cast remarkably green eyes around the Hall, with what she hoped was casual interest. Her eyes flickered as they passed Sir Leander Gage, who was bending his dear head to hear what his companion was saying to him.

Miss Fleete's gaze paused for the briefest moment upon that companion and her heart thumped a little wildly in her irked bosom. She had never seen a creature so lovely in all her life and was exasperated to find her only true love quite clearly flirting with such a beauty. She tossed her head and addressed herself to the business of wishing her neighbours and friends a Merry Christmas.

That one look had been enough for Sephie. She knew without the shadow of a doubt that Matilda Fleete still loved Leander. She nodded very firmly at Sir Anthony and watched with fascination as he approached their quarry to set the plan in motion.

Anthony bowed nicely to Reverend Fleete, kissed Matilda and briefly acknowledged Mr Adam Gibbs, who was hovering in the background, looking distinctly uncomfortable.

After a short chat, Sir Anthony and Kitty led the Fleetes through the growing throng to where Baroness Gage sat in state, receiving the more important guests and making them feel special to be singled out for her notice. Leander and Biddy were standing just to one side and as they approached, Anthony saw Leander visibly flinch like a skittish deer and hoped he wouldn't give the game away too early by bolting. He sent him a quelling look and Leander redoubled his efforts with Biddy, who had entered the spirit of the charade with a good deal of exuberance. She flashed her eyes at Leander, openly sending him come-hither looks and whispering conspiratorially in his ear.

Kitty rolled her eyes at Theo, "She should surely be on the stage!" she muttered. "She's born to this."

"She certainly is. But do look at the effect she's having on poor Matilda."

Kitty took a quick peek at Miss Fleete. That poor girl was clinging onto her rather tall and ruggedly handsome betrothed with the impression of someone who was coming up for air for the last time. Mr Adam Gibbs, who was nodding at something the Baroness was saying to him, patted Miss Fleete's hopeful hand on his arm and gently removed it, smoothing out the creases in his sleeve with a slightly aggrieved frown.

Baroness Gage, having had enough of the tedious fellow, waved Leander over.

Leander deliberately took Biddy's hand in his and drew her towards his grandmother and his childhood sweetheart. Mr Adam Gibbs briskly introduced himself and they exchanged overly polite words. Then, Leander turned to face Miss Fleete and smiled his rather devastating smile at her, a mixture of gentle good humour with a light sprinkling of sadness.

Miss Fleete blushed a rosy pink and then had to suffer being introduced to Miss Pippin, who taking her role very seriously indeed, lowered her voice to a throaty murmur and told Miss Fleete that she'd heard a great deal about her from Leander.

"Why, he is *forever* talking of your exploits, Miss Fleete! If I were less sure of him, I'm sure I'd be a martyr to raging jealousy! You certainly were an intrepid child! Tree-climbing and birdwatching! So, very different to my childhood. La! I was never even allowed *near* the garden in case I got muddy or hurt myself!"

Miss Matilda Fleete, watching Miss Pippin reach out and touch Leander's arm yet again, thought that it was no wonder he was besotted with her, she was absolutely mesmerising. She tried desperately to be magnanimous but found she was unable to think of anything other than how stupid she'd been to accept Adam's hasty proposal when she still had such strong feelings for Leander. She had allowed her disappointment and anger to force her hand. Then she excused her behaviour on the grounds that it had, after all, been Leander who ceased corresponding, not her. She was entirely blameless. And with that comforting thought she widened her smile and applied herself to chatting animatedly with Biddy as though she'd not a care in the world.

Sephie and Kitty were standing watching this little tableau with bated breath.

"Oh, Lord, I do believe that Matilda's just decided to see it through!" said Kitty, irritably. "Her chin went up just then and now she's looking horribly determined. What are we to do now? What if she thinks that Biddy is too much competition and gives up? Perhaps she doesn't have the spirit to fight for him. Perhaps it's too late already."

Sephie shook her head. She had seen that initial look and knew it wasn't too late. The dancing would help things along and then the final arrow to the heart — if Biddy could somehow contrive to bring that about, all would be well and Sephie's dream of a happy Leander would come true. She liked the look of Matilda; not at all what she'd expected, not at all a great beauty, but animated and unusual with her unfashionably red hair and freckles. Sephie could just imagine her running wild with Leander in the woods and chasing butterflies in the meadows. Her liveliness was the perfect foil for Leander's rather dour and cautious nature.

The Hall was now packed, elbow to elbow with some four hundred people, the heat was stifling, and the noise had reached almost unbearable levels. Wine and champagne flowed, and faces were glowing warmly. Music drifted down from the minstrel's gallery as though from heaven and a little troupe of masked actors wound their way through the crowd making people laugh with their comedic antics. Several of the guests were already a little worse for wear after liberal amounts of alcohol. One portly fellow staggered past Sephie, knocking into her accidentally; she cringed away from him and when he began to apologise loudly for the mistake, she was unable to say anything to stop him or his roving hands. Suddenly, Theo was by her side and fending off the drunk with a few well-chosen words and the man hiccupped wildly and then wandered away wondering why the funny little girl had been so aloof.

She signed *Thank you* and Theo took her firmly by the hand and led her over to Kitty and Sir Ambrose and he left Sephie in their tender care, "Don't go back into the crowd by yourself — you'll be crushed or accosted," he told her sternly. Then he'd smiled which set Sephie's heart aflutter.

The imperious butler eventually announced that the dancing was about to begin in the ballroom and the guests started to disperse. The older members of the assembly stayed in the Hall where they could finally hear one another, while the more vigorous amongst them made their way to the immense ballroom at the back of the house, where they found another orchestra and a perfectly polished dance floor. The high ceiling was hung with numerous candelabras and chandeliers and the light was dazzling. There were colonnades and arched alcoves along the walls and elegant sofas arranged along the edges of the room for the weary dancers. On the first floor there was a balcony which went all around the room, so the dancing could be observed from above and another minstrel's gallery for the musicians. The room was decorated with swags of dark green velvet and garlands of greenery tied with scarlet ribands. There was a Master of Ceremonies with an exceedingly loud voice and he called for everyone in the first dance, a minuet, to take their places and within minutes there was dancing.

Kitty and Ambrose escorted Sephie into the ballroom and they were followed by Leander and Biddy and then Anthony, Freddie and Babyngton. It wasn't long before the ballroom was full to the brim and everyone was able to show off their skills at the cotillion and quadrille. Sephie watched in amusement as Theo dutifully asked all the ladies on his dance card if they would stand up with him and even knowing that it had been her idea in the first place, she couldn't help feeling somewhat envious. She sat on one of the sofas with Sir Ambrose and surveyed the dancers choosing their partners and taking their places for a second cotillion. She saw Leander bowing over Biddy's hand and a little further down the row, a flushed Miss Fleete studiously not taking any notice of them at all. Mr Adam Gibbs's temper had clearly not improved as he appeared to be exchanging rather heated words with his betrothed. Then the dance began, and they were separated by the movements. Half an hour later as that dance came to a close and all the participants scattered to find a cool drink and somewhere to sit, another dance was called, a quadrille and the dancers began to gather.

"Would you care to stand up with me?" asked Lord Rokewode, holding out his hand to Sephie, "I seem to have a rather convenient gap in my dance card!"

She didn't hesitate, smiling in delight. She'd had three glasses of champagne and was beginning to feel very slightly giddy. She beamed up at him as he led her out onto the dance floor.

Kitty leant against her husband's side as they watched Sephie's and Theo's progress through the dance.

"She looks beautiful when she's with him, doesn't she? They look as though they belong together. And she loves him so much. I wish — " she sighed.

Ambrose took her hand and gave it a reassuring squeeze, "You know, I'm a firm believer in trusting to Fate. If it is ordained, then so it shall be. When I fell so hopelessly in love with you, my darling, I decided that I would be patient and wear you down with my persistence but in the end, Fate took a hand and here we are!"

Kitty looked up at him and wondered how she could ever have not recognised what a wonderful man he was. She leant closer and kissed him, "I adore you, you old fool," she told him.

Sephie put her hand into Theo's as they circled each other in the dance.

"Is the evening coming up to your expectations?" he asked her, over the din of the music and chatter.

She nodded happily. It was so much better than she'd ever hoped.

"It's all thanks to you, Sephie. Everything."

They were separated by the dance again and he could see her frowning, her dark brows drawn down in a fierce line. She never liked being thanked. Kitty had suggested that Sephie wanted to repay them in some way and he had to agree. She was glowering as though he'd trodden on the hem of her gown, not praised her for her efforts.

As they joined hands again, he laughed softly, "Sephie! I take it back. I didn't mean to thank you or compliment you. It was a slip of the tongue. Please forgive me."

She twinkled up at him through the sparkly silver mask. They moved apart but this time she was smiling.

Twenty-Four

Theo, watching Sephie dancing, her face alight with the joy of just being allowed to be an eighteen-year-old girl at her first Ball, wondered how on earth he had ever considered her plain. It seemed quite remarkable that at first, he had barely noticed her. And he tried to remember when it was that she had first begun to trespass upon his thoughts. She passed him in the movement of the dance and cast him a look of complete rapture. He decided that he always wanted her to look like that. He frowned as the outside world impinged upon his musing; the reality was that society would have something to say about such an alliance and the idea of taking her as his mistress was abhorrent to him. Thoughts of his present mistress crowded in upon him and he had to shake them off so that he didn't spoil Sephie's moment. She was always so uncannily aware of any change in mood that one had to school one's thoughts carefully so as not to give too much away and even then, she seemed to see into one's soul. She floated passed him again and on impulse, he reached out and trailed his fingers down her arm, it startled her, and she looked at him in puzzlement as she circled the next dancer. Damn it! What was he thinking? Sephie had been hurt and he knew that whatever he did would just compound that and she wouldn't complain. Both Kitty and Leander had warned him to take care and he thought he had but was beginning to realise that there was no easy way out of his predicament. He had to make a choice.

Leander had begun to enjoy himself despite everything and because he knew Matilda so very well, was fully aware that she was gently fuming. Kitty informed him that this was a good thing as indifference would be fatal to their carefully laid plans.

It was hard though, not being able to talk with her and just being forced to watch her from a distance as she danced with the vile Mr Gibbs. It was coming up to midnight when they had planned the denouement and he was on edge as he fretted about the outcome. There was nothing he could do about it now.

The moment she'd seen Freddie remove Mr Adam Gibbs to another part of the room ostensibly to talk with an acquaintance, Kitty had moved in stealthily to talk to Matilda.

"Matilda! How lovely you look! That gown is quite delicious with your colouring. How are you enjoying the evening?"

Miss Fleete, who was not enjoying herself at all, smiled insincerely, "I am having a truly wonderful night. We don't get the chance for such jollity as a rule. Country life can be a little too sedate at times. It's quite delightful to see so many friends."

"Oh, I'm sure I know exactly what you mean! And I don't suppose that Leander is inclined to entertain at Fairtree very much, being such a terrible stick-in-the-mud!"

"He's *not* — !" began Miss Fleete passionately.

Kitty patted her hand, "No, of *course* he's not! He's merely a trifle shy and reticent. Who can blame him? After living with the Baroness, one cannot help being surprised that he's as lovely as he is! He is so very — eccentric. We are all hoping that Miss Pippin will be the saving of him." She glanced at her companion and saw that the colour had fled from her cheeks and feeling rather mean, she continued, "They are so perfectly matched are they not? Are you all right, Matilda?"

Miss Fleete made a small choking sound, "I — *I* had hoped to be the saving of him," she whispered in tremulous accents, "But it seems that it is too late." She took out a handkerchief and dabbed at her brimming eyes, "I have been such a fool!"

Kitty, believing that the moment had come, took her hand and said in a concerned undertone, "Come! We shall go and find somewhere to freshen ourselves! We cannot have you crying in public," and she gave a swift signal to Babyngton who was loitering nearby and escorted the sniffling Miss Fleete from the Hall.

* * *

"They're on their way!" panted Babyngton, racing down the hallway and skidding into the anteroom at the end of it.

Sir Anthony and Biddy looked at each other a little doubtfully through the gloom. The sound of the orchestra and the heavy scent of the over-perfumed masses filled the house.

"Can I just say, Biddy, that I think you're pluck to the backbone for agreeing to this! What a performance!"

"Thank you, Sir Anthony but I am merely doing what I have always done. Pretending. I am exceedingly good at it. One has to be good at something, I suppose."

"You are marvellous! I think I can hear them coming. Are you ready?"

"Yes, indeed I am!"

"Here's to success in the Second Act and triumph in the Third!"

* * *

"Just along here, Matilda. They have a room for ladies to tidy and wash themselves. So very thoughtful, d'you not think? Although they might have lit a few more candles! It's very dark."

Kitty swept Miss Fleete along the corridor without compunction, even though she was rather nervous about the outcome, she was keen to see the results of their labours.

They turned the corner and were immediately almost upon the couple concealed in the shadows, their arms about each other and their lips firmly locked in a passionate embrace.

Miss Fleete saw the unmistakable scarlet gown. Oh, dear God, she thought, now I must see Leander kissing that girl! How cruel! She paused, wondering whether to turn back and then saw the man's profile and long golden curls and knew that it was not her beloved Leander.

She put a shaking hand to her mouth to try to stop the words which welled up, but to no avail. "*Miss Pippin!* Oh, how *dare* you!" she cried, utterly distraught, "You — you *harlot!* You wicked woman! To treat such a wonderful man so shabbily! It breaks my heart! Oh, he will be *devastated!*" And before anyone could say anything at all she had run back along the corridor towards the ballroom and would have hurtled sobbing into the dancers, had not a pair of arms stopped her and held her.

"*Matilda!* What on earth — ?" said Leander, pretending to be taken aback.

Miss Fleete, blinded by burning tears, stared into his kind eyes and tried to pull away but he held fast.

"Oh, Leander! *Please!* Let me go! I cannot bear — ! I am so sorry! If only I could prevent — ! It is too much! Oh, *Leander!*" She babbled incoherently and then collapsed upon his chest and sobbed uncontrollably.

Sir Leander Gage, with surprising presence of mind, gently pulled her back into the safety of the corridor and allowed himself to hold her tenderly in his aching arms. He kissed the top of her head and then her cheek and then with a whispered apology, kissed her mouth with all the pent-up passion he had been holding at bay for far too long. She, thankfully, completely forgot herself and all the bitterness and sorrow and kissed him back, her arms about his neck, she gave herself up to a much longed-for moment of unbridled ardour.

After a few moments she rested her head on his shoulder and heard him give a little chuckle.

"*Leander?*"

He held her away from him and smiled at her with such love that she forgot what she was going to say.

"Matilda Fleete, I must declare now, before someone steals you from me again, that I love you, have always loved you, will always love you and must own to being a stupid dolt for not telling you this years ago. Please forgive me!"

"Oh, *oh! Leander!*" sighed Miss Fleete, in ecstasy. "Do you *really?* What about Miss Pippin?"

Another chuckle, "I have *never* loved anyone else, Mattie! And one day, when things are a little less fraught, I shall tell you all about Miss Pippin and how very helpful she has been in returning you to me. But I am very much afraid that it will once again make you take against me and I will lose you."

Miss Fleete smiled at him, "Nothing could ever do that, I promise. I love you so very dearly and if it hadn't been for my pride and foolishness, we could've been together all this time."

"We're together now, come what may."

A terrible thought occurred to Miss Fleete, "Oh, no, Leander! We shall have to tell Adam! He will be so horribly angry!"

"Have no fear, my love, I shall punch him on the nose. I've been longing to all evening!"

"Leander! Don't you dare! He's much taller than you and will knock you down!"

"I really don't care, my darling. Now, could I please kiss you again?"

"Oh, yes *please!* And in the future? You have no need to ask my permission!" and he laughed and, much to her delight, took her at her word.

* * *

Along the corridor, Kitty, Miss Biddy Pippin and Sir Anthony were waiting with Babyngton for an opportunity to return to the Ball but were, for a few more moments, forced to lurk in the darkness until the kissing had stopped. They were all feeling rather pleased with themselves and greatly pleased with the obvious success of their machinations.

* * *

Sephie had been watching from the Ballroom and knew that the devious plan had worked. Theo was just behind her, splendidly handsome all in black and silver, a snow-white cravat at his neck and leaning nonchalantly against the dark panelled wall. His eyes were on her, not the last act of the evening's entertainment. He was, however, hugely relieved that the end result was what Sephie had longed for and was happy to see Leander finally find his true love.

The dancers still danced, even though their feet were hurting, and they were flushed from the heat and far too much champagne. Some were at the tables in the Hall where a delicious looking repast had been set out and were tucking into all kinds of pies and meats and comfits. Some were slumped on the sofas, hoping for a second wind before the next round of dancing and others gathered into gossiping knots.

Theo gave a signal to a waiting footman who quickly disappeared to the kitchens.

"Sephie?"

She turned to him, her face still lit with reflected joy.

"Are you happy?"

She nodded.

"Good. I'm glad. You've made Leander a happy man. I will never forget that. You've given the Rokewodes a great deal, y'know. Is there anything I can do for *you*?"

Yes, she thought. You could love me like I love you.

She shook her head.

The footman appeared at Theo's side and handed him a small cut-glass dish.

Theo handed it to Sephie.

She peered at it, dimpled at him and took up the spoon.

Pineapple ice cream.

"I swear, it's not a bribe! Just a small, much-deserved reward." And he guided her to a nearby unoccupied sofa, and they sat down together. He watched in fascination as she enjoyed the ice cream and thought he would never tire of watching her experience new things.

They sat like that for some time, until the others all came bustling out of the corridor full of tales of their exploits and Leander and Matilda appeared looking flushed and joyful. Leander introduced Miss Fleete to Sephie.

"Sephie is an absolute wonder! She arranged all of this," said Leander and dropped a kiss onto Sephie's cheek. "We are all sensible of the fact that none of this would have happened without her. I, for one, shall aways be in her debt."

Sephie shook her head in embarrassment.

In order to prevent further awkwardness, Sir Anthony suggested that they should all take to the dance floor again as a country dance was just about to begin.

It was heartily agreed upon and they all dispersed to find their places and the Master of Ceremonies was forced to allow them to participate as they looked as though they wouldn't listen to him if he denied them a place.

"Would you like to dance again?" asked Theo.

She shook her head. She just wanted to stay here with him like this, listening to the music and watching their friends caper about the room with such child-like abandon. She caught sight of poor Mr Adam Gibbs and wondered how he would take the news and who would break it to him. She saw Paston and James Mullens go by bearing large trays of glasses and she waved to them; Paston smiled at her.

Lady Rokewode tottered into the ballroom and seeing her son, gestured to him imperiously. He rose to his feet, "I won't be a moment Sephie. I expect she just needs escorting to her bedchamber. It's very late for her, nearly one o'clock."

Sephie's colour drained out of her face and he frowned down at her, "What is it? Are you feeling quite well?"

She nodded rather faintly, thinking that there was not much time.

"I'll be back in a few minutes. Stay there!"

She smiled at him and he strode off to take his exhausted mother upstairs.

Sephie waited for a while but her heart was racing so fast that she could barely breathe, and her thoughts were plaguing her. She couldn't stop thinking that in less than two hours she would be leaving and would never see him again. She stared at the dancers but didn't see them.

Then, suddenly, she made up her mind and leapt up from the sofa and raced across the ballroom and into the Great Hall. She darted up the stairs and into the corridor, but once she reached it, she stopped and asked herself crossly what on earth she thought she was doing. You're a fool, Persephone! She stood swaying for a moment, unsure, so tempted and then sighing, turned and began to make her way back towards the staircase.

"Sephie?" he said softly, from the other end of the corridor.

She stopped. Considered. Re-considered. And recklessly discarded all sensible and rational argument.

She turned and flew along the dimly lit passage, straight into his arms. He lifted her off her feet and she threw her arms around his neck and kissed him with all the love in her heart. There was no hesitation, he kissed her back, with a hunger which surprised even him. He fell back against the nearest door although she weighed nothing at all and felt for the latch, his legs not quite as steady as he'd have liked. They tumbled through into the unoccupied and dark bedchamber, and he closed the door on everything which might dare to make him come to his senses. He wrapped his arms tightly about her and buried his head in her neck, breathing in her sweet scent and just revelling in her closeness. He took the few steps to the bed and sat down with her on his lap, and reaching up, undid the ribbons which held her mask in place. He threw it to the floor.

"Sephie, Sephie! What are you doing? I promised Leander that I wouldn't — ! You don't know what you're doing!" he whispered hoarsely.

Sephie took his face in her hands and pressed her lips to his, trying to convey to him that she knew exactly what she was doing. She had no doubt at all in her mind. She wanted to block out all the other times, all the days and nights when it hadn't been her decision, when she'd had no choice and she had not been considered as even human. This would cleanse her soul. She just knew it.

The moonlight coming through the window was bright and lit the room with silvery blues, making diamond patterns on the floor.

Theo knew that he should put her away from him and leave the room, but she was gazing at him from wide grey eyes, her lips parted and her breath coming in excited little gasps. He groaned deep in his throat and she smiled triumphantly.

"God, I want you so very much!" he murmured.

She pushed her hands against his chest, and he fell back onto the bed and watched impatiently as she tugged up her petticoats and struggled to get out of her gown. He laughed softly and helped her drag it up over her head, causing her hair to tumble down over her shoulders. She was just wearing a short corset over her chemise. He reached around her, which brought them closer and he found her eager mouth again and continued kissing her whilst expertly unlacing the corset at the back.

"Stop *wriggling!* You're making it extremely difficult!"

He finally got it undone and it followed her other clothes onto the growing pile on the floor.

"Just that damn chemise now," he said huskily. She raised herself onto her knees so that he could release it and watched it sail over her head into the shadows.

She took a deep steadying breath and leant forward again, and his hands slowly slid around her waist to her back. She tried not to stiffen as his fingers touched for the first time the awful patchwork of ridges. She felt him catch his breath and she put a silencing finger to his lips. His fingers trailed from her shoulders and down to the small of her back and then even further down, exploring every inch of her skin. She shuddered as they reached her upper thighs, knowing that he would find scars there too, but she steeled herself for his searching touch. None of the marks mattered to her anymore. In this much longed-for moment, she felt as though she were being reborn, as though his hands were healing her as they roamed over her body. She was able to believe that he was the first to touch her so intimately and any feeling of shame was banished by his tenderness. His hands moved around to her stomach and slid up over her ribs to her breasts; she sighed shakily and catching his hands in hers, pressed them against her body.

Beneath her she felt the stirrings of his interest and pushing his hands away began to undo his breeches while he shrugged himself out of his coat and waistcoat.

He raised his hips and the breeches soon joined her clothes beside the bed. She placed her hands on his chest under his shirt and felt his heart thumping beneath her palms and smiled shyly at him. Then suddenly she was underneath him and he was sliding his hands up the inside curve of her thighs and spreading her legs apart and his fingers were seeking her hidden places and making her sigh with wanton pleasure. She pressed his hand hard against her and arched her back, aching with desire for him.

"Sephie, God, *Sephie!* I want — "

She urgently pulled him closer with all her strength.

He shifted his weight and gently pushed into her, making her gasp. Her legs wrapped around him and held him against her. He would never be close enough.

* * *

She wept silently. Nothing would ever be the same again. She lay very still feeling the weight of him, one muscular arm pinning her, his hip resting across hers. For the first time ever she felt no fear, only love. She knew he was asleep; his breathing was steady. She listened for a few minutes, enjoying the sound. She gave him a gentle push, he sighed and rolled back just enough so that she could manage to slide out from beneath him. As she quietly moved to the edge of the bed, the bracket clock on the mantel struck three o'clock.

* * *

Ann was waiting anxiously in her bedchamber. "Oh, Miss Sephie, where have you been? I've been so worried! I thought maybe you'd changed your mind!"

Sephie shook her head and allowed Ann to help her out of her finery and into an old grey gown and then into her warmest cloak and sensible outdoor boots. She laid Kitty's diamond hair clip on the gown which was draped on the bed and then carefully packed her fan back into its box and with the silver bracelet safely in a velvet pouch, she put them into her bag. She pinned the snowdrop brooch onto her gown. She wouldn't take anything else, but these things had been given to her, so she felt they were truly hers.

She thought that they must be quick, she had to leave before Theo awoke and found her gone and she was frightened that Simon would drive away without them, thinking that they weren't coming.

"Miss Sephie, are you sure about this? You could stay with the Rokewodes at the Abbey! We don't have to run away."

Sephie pulled her hood up and went to the door. Ann sighed, "All right then. But I wish — " said Ann, but found she was speaking to thin air.

* * *

They tiptoed down the back stairs and through the scullery, into the buttery and then out of the back door into the yard. The moon lit their way. They had just gone through the gate in the wall at the side of the house and were edging their way along the wall to where Simon said he'd be waiting when they heard the gravel scrunch behind them.

"Simon?" whispered Ann.

Sephie turned towards the noise but felt a hand grab her and another clamp itself roughly over her mouth. She saw Ann struggling and heard her try to scream but she too was overpowered by another dark figure.

Twenty-Five

Theo awoke with a smile on his face. He sighed and rolled over, reaching out. But there was nothing but cold emptiness. He sat up.

He was alone. Sephie had gone. Her clothes and shoes. The scent of her lingered on him but was faint.

He swung his feet to the floor.

She'd left him. To return to the Ball? To her own bedchamber, in case they were discovered? Probably. He smiled, remembering and felt his stomach lurch with excitement. He laughed out loud. He'd never felt like this before. So all-consumed by longing. He began to drag his clothes back on. He would go and find her and try to explain to her how he felt. His limbs were sluggish, and his mind kept wandering to those precious moments spent with her. His could still feel the scars beneath his fingers; the network of wheals telling a story so horrific that he couldn't even begin to understand; he'd discovered that they weren't just on her back but in places that should have been sacrosanct. She had knowledge which had been learnt in violence that he'd rather not have to fully consider but she'd somehow managed to give herself to him as though he were the very first. Despite her obvious desire to be with him in that moment, he'd sensed her uncertainty, her hope that he wouldn't think of the ugliness of her past and believe her to be stained by it. He understood that she'd wanted him to take away the pain and he'd tried with every fibre of his being to transport her out of that anguished hell. He wanted to keep her in the light, in the warmth, with him.

Lord Rokewode entered the Ballroom, his eyes searching for a particular face, but not immediately finding it, he sought out his sister who was languishing on a sofa, leaning sleepily against her husband, who, in turn, was stretched out as though slumbering.

"Kit? Have you seen Sephie?"

She opened one eye and peered blearily at him. "Not since she ran after you," she murmured, one eyebrow raised. "Did she find you, I wonder?"

Theo had the grace to look a trifle discomfited, "She did. But now I can't find her."

"Perhaps she's gone to her bed. She must be exhausted after all the planning and preparations and then dancing and — "

"Yes, of course," he quickly interrupted, not meeting her eyes.

"Ann will know where she is," said Kitty through a yawn.

"Of course," said Theo.

"Have you come to a decision? About Sephie?"

Her brother regarded her for a moment, frowning, "I know that I want to make her happy. Is that enough?"

Kitty shrugged, "For Sephie, yes. But then *anything* would be enough for her — she is used to having nothing. To be given even the smallest sign of being cherished by you would be like heaven to her. She has nothing to compare it with. When you think of what she has been through — " She stopped when she saw the look which crossed his face. "Theo?"

He rubbed his eyes fretfully, "She — I cannot even explain — I have a better understanding — but God, I would have killed Stokey, Kit! Without remorse. And if we find Pippin — he'd better hope he's taken by the constables before I get my hands on him! Where the hell can she be? I'm going to find Ann. By the bye, has someone told Mr Gibbs that there is to be a slight change in his plans?"

Kitty's sleepy eyes roamed around the Ballroom where the crowds were slowly thinning, some having fallen by the wayside, some having already left for their homes and some still valiantly dancing despite their pinching shoes, blistered toes and aching heads.

"He's over there in the corner — with Biddy doing her best to comfort him. Perhaps they'd do well together? What a thought! And there are Leander and Matilda holding hands and staring into each other's eyes — deeply touching. And dear Miss Edie took the Baroness upstairs a while ago because she was beginning to snap at the staff. Oh, for heaven's sake, go, Theo! Go and find her."

Theo strode away towards the kitchens.

"Ambrose, darling? Are you awake? Did you hear? I wish I was more shocked, but I seem to have become inured to immoral behaviour! I must admit that I find it rather liberating."

"I'm delighted to hear it," said Ambrose without opening his eyes. "That bodes very well for me!"

* * *

"Ann isn't here, my lord. She went to tend Miss Fane a couple of hours ago. She hasn't come back yet," said the housekeeper.

Theo thanked her and marched off upstairs to knock gently upon Sephie's door.

There was no answer. He knocked again and then, getting no response, opened the door.

The bedchamber was in darkness. He knew immediately that it was empty. He quickly lit a candle and looked around. His gaze fell on the silvery gown laid out so carefully on the bed, the borrowed diamond clip resting in its shining folds.

And he knew.

* * *

Kitty saw him coming and, suddenly alert, she leapt to her feet, rousing Ambrose from his slumber.

'What is it? Is she — ?"

Theo's face told her everything. "She's gone. Ann too."

Kitty felt a little faint and had to sit down again. "Gone? What do you mean? Gone where? Why would she run away? Theo! I don't understand."

Theo said nothing. He raised a hand and caught Leander's attention. Leander seeing his friend's ashen face grabbed Matilda and hastened across the Ballroom. Sir Anthony, Freddie and Babyngton were swift to follow suit.

He briefly explained the situation to them and organised a search of the house and grounds. They threw warm capes and coats on and went out to comb the estate. Kitty, Ambrose and Matilda, with the help of some footmen searched the house from top to bottom.

Over an hour later, after all the guests had gone and there was still no sign of Sephie or Ann, Freddie came hurrying to find Theo.

He held out his hand, "This was found on the ground beyond the west gate, Theo."

Theo looked down at the brooch made of velvet snowdrops and died a little inside.

"So, she *has* left me," he said softly.

* * *

Sephie opened her eyes. Her head was aching and the shoulder she'd dislocated was throbbing painfully. She felt rather sick. Taking a deep breath, she realised that her mouth was bound with a piece of cloth and her wrists were tied behind her back. She was in a coach of some kind, which seemed to be moving at reckless speed along a bumpy road. She could hear the driver shouting at the horses. Next to her was Ann, in the same condition, bound and gagged. Sephie slid closer to her and nudged her. After a moment Ann started awake and her eyes widened in alarm. She saw Sephie peering at her through the gloom and sighed in relief. She'd no idea what was going on but if Miss Sephie was all right then things might not be so bad and at least she'd kept her promise to Lord Rokewode.

Now, she thought, how do we get out of these damned bindings?

* * *

"Is there anything you're keeping from us Biddy?" asked Kitty, as considerately as she could. "You must tell us if Sephie mentioned to you what she was planning."

Biddy looked outraged, "I keep *telling* you! She told me *nothing*. I'll admit that early on we had made plans to leave together but when she realised that I'd changed my mind, I thought she'd given up on the whole thing. Honestly, I'd tell you if I knew anything at all. Ann is with her, so she'll be all right, won't she?"

Kitty patted her arm, seeing that she was becoming agitated, "Yes, I expect that something happened to alarm her, and she's just panicked," and cast a quick accusing glance at Theo, who was deep in thought, "But, no doubt she'll come to her senses and return before long. We can but hope." She cast her mind back for any indications of something being amiss, or clues to her state of mind.

"Biddy, when we were at the picnic, something happened, and you became suddenly distraught. Sephie calmed you down. It was about you singing." He saw the telltale colour rise in the girl's cheeks and then just as swiftly, fade away leaving her pale. "I need to know what that was about. Nobody will be angry with you. We must know everything now, before it's too late."

Biddy looked around at all the faces turned toward her and for once wasn't happy to be the centre of attention. "I can't," she whispered.

Kitty took her hands in hers, "Biddy dear, you want to be sure that Sephie is safe surely? She saved you from the fire, did she not?"

Biddy nodded, "Yes. She was always braver than me. Even when — there was no hope. But, if I tell you, you'll never forgive me and will think badly of Sephie!"

"That's not true," said Kitty, "We know something of what you've suffered and realise that in such circumstances people do things that may seem unforgivable but are just a means to staying alive. Don't be afraid. We're on your side."

Biddy took a deep breath and honest tears began to slide down her colourless cheeks, "Please don't be angry. You see, it was my father — when he first saw Sephie, with the parson, she was in the garden — and she was singing — like — like an angel. So, he took her."

There was complete silence.

Biddy looked around anxiously, "She couldn't speak but she could sing — not words — but this beautiful sound. I've never heard her speak. That's why she was treated so badly — they used to get angry with her because she refused to show any emotion. They thought because she could sing, she was just being stubborn, and they tried to make her talk. I could hear them. I used to cover my ears. I did help her afterwards, I *promise*, I dressed her wounds. I flirted with the men hoping they'd take me instead sometimes, but she angered them so much that it became an obsession with them. They didn't beat me or do — what they did to Sephie. They threatened me with violence but didn't dare ruin — my looks because that's how they made their money. Sephie had none to ruin so they took out their frustration on her. And my father — I can't tell you — I'm so sorry! I wish he were dead."

Kitty gathered her into her arms, "It's not your fault, Biddy. You did the best you could. None of us know how we would react in such a terrible situation. It should never have happened. Cruelty like that — "

"So," said Theo, "You posed as the mermaid and Sephie sang. It's beginning to make more sense. Do you have any idea where Sephie might run to? Did she know anyone who might take her in and hide her?"

"No," came the muffled reply, "We weren't allowed to know anyone in case we begged for help. Occasionally the fairground people would try to talk to us, but they got scared off by the doorkeepers who kept us under lock and key. They were very violent. We thought that's how it would always be until the fire. And then you and Anthony came. And everything changed."

'But why would she run away?" asked Leander, "It doesn't make sense. She was happy here. I know she was," he frowned up at Theo, "Unless you quarrelled with her!"

Theo shook his head, "We didn't quarrel."

"She loves you Theo!" snapped Leander, "She'd do anything for you — she wouldn't leave you — unless — she felt that by staying she might bring disgrace to your family. What did you say to her?"

Theo looked his best friend straight in the eye for a long moment but said nothing.

Leander turned away.

"I'm not sure I understand what is happening," said Miss Fleete despairingly.

"I think we're all having something of a problem with it, Matilda," said Kitty, "It's not easy for any of us. But there is one thing which we do know and that's Sephie. She seems to have decided that flight is the only answer. If only she'd been able to speak to us — we could have told her everything would be all right. I think she's trying to protect us. Silly girl. You see, she feels that her past means she's beyond redemption and she'd do anything to prevent those she loves being disgraced, as she sees it. There is no reasoning why she should have fallen so deeply in love with my stupid brother. That was just unfortunate."

"Thank you," said Theo blandly.

"She awoke from that terrible nightmare of her life as it was, and he was the first person she saw and that was that. There's no rational explanation. She just fell so deeply in love with him and he became her whole life. Theo, of all people! Then she just decided that you and Leander must be together, and I believe she was waiting for the proper outcome, always knowing that she would be leaving as soon as Leander was happy."

Leander made a suffocated sound and Matilda linked arms with him and rested her bright head against his shoulder.

"So, what are we to do, Theo?" asked Sir Ambrose.

"I shall return to London as soon as I can and consult with Major Cobham and Bow Street. There must be some way of discovering her direction. I have faith in her maid, Ann, who is a steady character and not without a deal of common sense; she appears to be devoted to Sephie. While she's with her, I have confidence that Sephie is in good hands. Tomorrow, you will all return to the Abbey and I shall organise a wider search just to make sure they haven't been seen as they made their escape." He paused as he noticed Paston edging towards them, "Paston? Have you discovered anything?"

"Not exactly, my lord, but someone wishes to speak with you," said Paston.

"Bring them to me here, please."

Paston hurried away but in just a couple of minutes returned accompanied by a small, wiry fellow in a dark coat, his broad brimmed hat clutched nervously in his hands.

Theo eyed him suspiciously, "I'm Rokewode — you wanted to see me?"

The man nodded, "Aye, my lord. I been waitin' for almost two hours now an' I'd like to get the horses back to their stable. It be cold out there and still no sign of my sister."

Theo frowned, "You're going to have to give me a little more information because I've no idea what you're talking about. Who are you and who is your sister?"

The man shuffled uneasily, "I'm Simon Coggshall and my sister, Ann, works as a lady's maid at the Abbey."

"Go on," said Theo grimly.

"Ann told me to be here at three o'clock, an' I was, in plenty of time, I might add. I was supposed to take them to the nearest stagecoach inn, and I been waitin' ever since then but they never came. I didn't want to leave without makin' sure they don't need me no more, see?"

"I think I'm beginning to," said Theo. "Do you have any idea where they were going?"

"Ann said London, my lord, but she told me not to tell anyone what I was doin'."

"No surprise there. Did you see anything suspicious while you were waiting?"

"Hard to tell, there bein' so many coaches and such out there, footmen all over the place," shrugged Simon Coggshall.

"Of course. Paston, take Mr Coggshall to the kitchens, make sure he has some refreshment before he sets off and a guinea for his troubles. Thank you, for coming to me, you've been very helpful. If you hear anything, please let me know as soon as possible."

"Aye, m'lord."

Paston escorted Coggshall away and Theo turned back to his enthralled audience.

"What the hell is going on, Theo? Do you have any idea at all?" demanded Anthony tiring of the endless obfuscation.

"I am starting to, I think, " said Theo, his expression unreadable. "I'm fairly certain that Sephie and Ann were planning to run away with the help of the very patient Mr Coggshall but were intercepted by persons unknown. In short, they have been abducted."

There was an explosion of exclamations and some pithy swearing as the group of exhausted friends tried to come to terms with this new slant on an already turbulent evening.

Biddy burst into noisy tears. Kitty buried her head into her husband's solid shoulder and tried not to think. Matilda was thinking that this was, without doubt, the most eventful and confusing Ball she'd ever attended.

"Abducted? By whom?" asked Leander, through clenched teeth.

"That is, as yet, still open to debate but the smoke is clearing a little and I'm beginning to see that this is rather more complicated than we first imagined." He surveyed his friends and family with a keen eye, "But, at dawn, I shall leave for London."

"I'm going with you," said Leander, in a voice which brooked no argument.

"Me too," added Sir Anthony.

Theo nodded, "I won't argue with that. Happy to have some company. Tom, Freddie, I'd like you to stay here for the moment and make sure that the Abbey is guarded, and the family are safe. But I may have need of you in London before very long, so be ready. Ambrose, I'm leaving the ladies in your capable hands, Mama, Kit, Biddy and Miss Edie — for which I can only apologise."

"Good Lord, Theo, delighted to do my share. Anything for that taking little thing — she's an absolute Trojan. Do anything for her."

As this started Kitty weeping, Ambrose told them that he would take his wife to her bed as she was tired and becoming flustered. Theo then suggested that everyone should try to sleep and assured them that everything would soon be in hand and not to worry.

Leander reluctantly saw Matilda into her carriage with her father and a monosyllabic Mr Adam Gibbs and watched them leave whilst suffering a mixture of emotions. The others dispersed to their bedchambers and Leander and Anthony went to gather together their things for the journey. Theo advised them to snatch a few hours' sleep, saying that they'd leave at six.

* * *

Theo was still in the Great Hall talking with the staff and thanking the musicians when Anthony dashed back downstairs in just his shirtsleeves.

"What now, Tony? Mislaid your favourite neckcloth?"

"Worse than that Theo! Seem to have mislaid my damned valet!"

"Have you indeed! Now, that is exceedingly interesting. What's the fellow's name?"

"James Mullens. Surly beggar but good with my clothes and a dab hand at keeping my cravats in order."

Theo considered this for a moment, "He was in the Hall earlier, with Paston, Sephie — Sephie waved to them! Paston! Come here please!"

Paston fearing he'd made some terrible mistake, approached his employer with trepidation.

"Paston. What do you know about James Mullens?"

Paston looked astonished, "Mullens, my lord? Why, he's a shifty sort of cove, if Sir Anthony don't mind me sayin'. Never liked him much. Got an eye for the ladies and don't mind helping himself to the brandy when nobody's looking. Bone idle, too."

Theo exchanged a glance with Anthony, "Have you, by any chance, noticed if he has more money than usual recently?"

"Aye, my lord! He was flashing it about a bit back at the Abbey, sayin' his aunt had died and left him a pretty penny. Shamming it."

"Anything else?"

"Always going for long walks by himself and popping up in odd parts of the house with no good reason. I think he liked listening at doors, my lord."

"Thank you, Paston, you've been remarkably helpful, and I won't forget it." He watched the footman leave and turned back to Anthony. "So, my dear boy! It seems that you've been harbouring a criminal all this time! I must say it makes everything a deal more easy to understand. Once I can talk with Cobham and one or two others, I shall know where we stand and be able to think more rationally. I'm hoping we've a few days leeway. I don't think Sephie and Ann will be in real danger until they reach London, and their abductors won't know yet that we're on their heels already. Mullens will have given inside information of course and will possibly have had an insight into what Sephie was planning."

"Will admit to never really liking the fellow, Theo, but had no dashed idea that he might be involved in anything nefarious or I'd have sent him packing! This must be hard for you. It's as plain as a pikestaff that you care for her," said Anthony blithely.

"Is it?" enquired Theo dubiously, dark eyebrows raised.

"Well, if *I* can see it, when I'm not really famed for my intellect, it must be! What will you do when you find the culprits?"

"Strangle them with my bare hands," responded Theo with all seriousness.

Twenty-Six

By getting Sephie to turn away, Ann gently removed the gag from Sephie's mouth and then, sitting back-to-back Sephie managed to untie her hands. The coach was struggling up a steep hill and was travelling slowly enough for Ann to brace herself while she untied Sephie's bindings; it was quite a struggle but using their teeth and a lot of determination, they finally succeeded in working their way free.

The coach soon began to speed up again as it reached the level road at the top of the hill.

"We must somehow get out of the carriage the next time they stop, Miss Sephie! You must be ready. We can't jump while it's moving, they're going at such a lick, the fall would probably kill us! But we must get away before it's too late. I'm thinking that if they've gone to all this trouble to take us like this, they're not planning to take us somewhere nice for a cup of hot chocolate!"

Dawn was breaking and they were able to look out of the windows but as neither of them knew the route, they'd no idea where they were heading.

"I think as they have to change horses every ten miles or so, we haven't got long to make up our minds. Do we try to escape before we get to our destination or wait until we're sure of where we are?"

There was no answer while Sephie considered their choices, then she made a sign for running.

Ann nodded, "All right. We run. D'you know who might be behind this? D'you think it's Henry Pippin. I've heard Biddy talking about him. He sounds like a horrid piece. A regular loose screw. Sounds like he would want to have his revenge for losing his only money-spinner. Can't think why he'd want to abduct *me* though!" She gave Sephie an odd look, "*Unless*, of course, they were expecting Miss Biddy to be the one escaping with you. That would make more sense. Well, he's going to be *very* disappointed! I'm hardly a great beauty like Miss Biddy! And there's no way I'm wearing a damn mermaid's tail!" and she started to laugh a little wildly.

Sephie held her hand and patted it but could not contradict her as she'd already had the same thought. They had wanted Biddy not Ann. Ann was about the same height and had been heavily cloaked. It had been a natural mistake. Sephie had to be a tiny bit grateful that she wasn't trapped in the carriage hurtling through the countryside with only a hysterical Biddy for company but was, at the same time, sorry for Ann who didn't deserve such a fate as this.

Eventually the coach, having reached the top of the long hill and travelled another mile or so, was forced to stop to change horses. The girls were ready, and as soon as the ostlers were making themselves busy, Ann quickly opened the door of the coach and jumped down, Sephie threw down their bags and jumped after her.

They found themselves outside a shabby inn, which seemed barely awake at that time in the morning and Ann grabbed Sephie by the hand and they ran around the side of the building hoping to find somewhere to hide. They stopped in the grey shadows alongside an adjoining barn and waited, trying to still their panicked breathing and listening to the shouts from the ostlers and then an enraged bellow from the driver and his henchman as they found their captives had somehow escaped. Ann pulled on Sephie's hand and they edged away from the yard. Then suddenly there was the sound of boots on cobbles, and angry swearing and they were upon them and it was too late.

* * *

Theo, Leander and Anthony, riding hard, made good time and relentlessly driven on by Theo, who would not stop for anything but changing the horses, they reached the outskirts of London by early evening that same day. Theo parted company with his companions, who were sent home to rest for a while and await further instructions, while he rode straight to Major Cobham's place of business.

Major Walter Cobham was mildly surprised to see Lord Rokewode stride into his rooms.

"My lord? I wasn't expecting you quite so soon."

Theo raised his eyebrows as he threw himself gratefully into the chair opposite his attorney, "You were expecting me?"

"Naturally. After I'd replied to your letters, I thought that you might be impatient to return to London."

Theo frowned, "I must have crossed with your correspondence. I have not received your response. We were forced to return earlier than expected due to some grievous circumstances. You've discovered something?"

"Indeed, my lord. I have found Mr Henry Pippin."

Theo leant forward, suddenly more alert, "Where is he?"

"I have a man watching him. He's taken refuge in the rookeries, near Covent Garden. A filthy establishment run by a repellent monster of a bawd. He must feel very much at home there. He seldom leaves the place to do anything other than frequent taverns."

"You're certain?"

"Absolutely. He seems to have given up on all thoughts of fairs and being a showman and fallen into a sordid life of alcohol, laudanum and debauchery. I am hardly surprised, given his previous history. But what has brought you back to London, Lord Rokewode?"

"I hardly dare tell you," said Theo, "Sephie and her maid have been abducted."

"Good God! Do you know by whom?"

"I am on their trail. We discovered their direction by asking in the coaching inns for any sign of travellers in a suspicious hurry. We had several sightings so I'm fairly certain they're here in the city."

"If there's anything I can do — "

"I'm exceedingly grateful for all you've done already, Cobham. I will get Sephie back or die trying," stated Theo in harsh tones.

The Major cast him an interested glance, "Have there been any more developments? If you'll pardon my presumption, I sense something of a change in you."

"I think you could safely say that things have altered. I will gladly admit to being a much-changed man."

Cobham smiled, "I'm pleased to hear it, my lord. Am I right to suppose it is Miss Sephie's doing?"

Theo bent and put his head in his hands, exhaustion suddenly overtaking him in waves, "She — she has changed us all in one way or another. I tried so hard to resist but she was inexorable. Someone so small, so silent and yet, so utterly irresistible. I feel as though I've been bewitched. There was another attempt on her life at Rokewode Abbey, even more successful than the last and I realised then — but I fear I've been a damned fool, callous and selfish, and the result is that she was attempting to run away when she was abducted. Having had sixty miles of hard riding to ponder my mistakes at great length, I see that she — she came to me just before she left, after the Ball, to say goodbye. I see it now. I see that she loves me although I truly have no idea why — family and friends kept telling me so — and I — I find — too late — that I cannot live without her."

"Despite her past?"

Theo looked up, his eyes shadowed, face gaunt with fatigue, "Her past is *nothing* to me. I just want to erase it from her mind. I now know her physical scars, but my only desire is to consign to oblivion the scars which are making her run from me. The scars I can't see. I will admit to having been intolerant of human frailty in the past, to having very little sympathy with those who show weakness, and it has taken this girl — this valiant little creature, to show me that it is *I* who am weak and frail. She's a tower of strength and fortitude and brimming with so much love — God, I *must* find her! She is everything to me," his voice was choked with emotion and for a moment he seemed as though he might be overcome by the pent-up anguish and suffering.

Major Cobham sat silently observing him, thinking that here was a man who had finally been snapped out of his state of self-imposed inertia and back into a brutal world of passion and pain; a good distance away from his previous numbness which had been a constant companion probably since his father had died. He was watching a man emerging from a deep sleep to find that true love was found in giving, not taking, and that one had to experience the depths of wretchedness in order to be able to truly appreciate the rare moments of real happiness. He felt strangely proud that Lord Rokewode had managed to discover this despite all the obstacles. Now all he had to do was find Miss Sephie.

"What now, my lord?" he asked.

Lord Rokewode got to his feet with renewed determination, "I have some people to see. Old friends and acquaintances and one or two new enemies. And there are scores to settle. I'm very much looking forward to getting some long-awaited satisfaction."

Cobham rose and came around his desk to put a firmly encouraging hand on Theo's shoulder, "I wish you all the luck in the world and hope you'll keep me informed of the outcome."

"Naturally, my good fellow! You'll be one of the first to know."

They said their goodbyes and after the door had shut behind Lord Rokewode, Major Cobham sat down with a large glass of brandy and an even larger smile.

* * *

There was an odd taste in her mouth. Bitter and sickly-sweet. It made her feel queasy. Her stomach churned and she tried to sit up but found one hand was bound with a length of soft cord to the post of the four-poster bed. She moved to the edge of the mattress and dangled her feet to the floor. Her head swam and she had to close her eyes and take a deep breath to steady herself. The room swam around her.

The bedchamber she found herself in was dimly lit by a stumpy candle on the mantelpiece, although cold blue daylight was trying to insinuate itself between the shutters, falling feebly into the shadowed and unfamiliar room.

Sephie sat very still for a moment and contemplated her situation. There was no sign of Ann. She was alone and wearing only her chemise. Barefoot. Her hair was hanging down over her shoulders and she had no idea how long she'd been there. She was fairly sure she wasn't in a tavern. The room smelt strongly of musky perfume and other less pleasant odours, used bedlinen and unwashed bodies. She could smell cheap tobacco and stale alcohol; smells she knew well from her past. She shuddered, hoping against hope that this wasn't what she feared. She pulled at the knot at her wrist, but with only one hand and her teeth, found it to be tied too tightly to loosen. She recognised that cord had been used so that her wrist wouldn't be marked. Ironic, she thought, considering the other marks elsewhere on her body.

She couldn't help her wayward thoughts straying to Theo's long fingers trailing gently over her skin, following each one of those raised and ugly scars and kissing every one as though they were beautiful; she could still feel the warm touch of his mouth travelling across her hip and down between her thighs and heard again his soft greedy moan as he explored her intimately and she closed her eyes and smiled to herself.

Then, giving herself an impatient shake, she applied her mind to her present predicament. Where was she and how was she to escape? She could hear noises outside her room, doors banging and muffled laughter, voices raised and the sounds of a busy house.

As her eyes became accustomed to the lack of light in the room, she was able to see that she was in some kind of boudoir; the furnishings were opulent, the wallpaper vivid and in rather poor taste, the velvet bed-hangings and curtains, a rich dark pink and the rug overly patterned. It was a woman's bedchamber, of that she was certain, but it had an air about it which she didn't quite understand; it felt impersonal and shabby, as though much used but little cared for. She couldn't hear any sounds from the street, no carriages or cries of vendors selling their wares, nothing to give any clue to where she might be. Nothing to give her any hope.

She noticed a glass of water on the table beside the bed and wondered if she dared drink it. She was so thirsty. The peculiar taste in her mouth she knew had been some kind of sleeping draught, she'd been forced many times to take some by Henry Pippin, when she'd become too difficult to handle, they'd drugged her. In a way she hadn't minded being insensible, it had meant that time passed, and she had no memory of it, like forgetting a nightmare in that moment between sleep and awaking. She knew that something unspeakable had happened, but it could be quickly left behind, unopened, unread. She had found ways of coping with the life they created for her, concentrating on surviving each day and always hoping for something better. She had recited the fairy tales to herself when she was in her darkest moments and tried to make sure that Biddy didn't despair.

That first wonderful day of freedom, when she'd opened her eyes and looked up to see Theo bending over her, she'd thought she'd died and gone to heaven. He was like every image she'd conjured of the heroes in the forbidden fairy tale book. So handsome and aloof and yet so concerned for her welfare. It hadn't taken her very long to foolishly fall in love with him. But even though he'd reluctantly accepted her final farewell gesture, she knew that she was below the salt, as Biddy liked to put it, and that he was bound by loyalty and duty to his noble family name. She had never entertained expectations, happy just to be near him for as long as possible; she had no illusions about what she was and until she'd put on the magical white ball gown she'd never even been noticed. It had been quite unnerving to have everyone suddenly see her. She was so used to the shadows they'd become a part of her.

She listened to the strange sounds outside the room and tried to fathom what kind of people made such an unruly din and wondered when someone would come and explain what was to become of her. And she worried about what had happened to Ann.

* * *

Henry Pippin had been enjoying the evening in his local alehouse and was staggering back to the brothel where he presently resided. It was the perfect solution, he did a little maintenance around the bawdy house, acted as doorkeeper and disciplined the whores when they stepped out of line. He was allowed to sample the wares as long as he did no damage to the goods. It was working out very well. He was able to relieve some of the punters of their money and possessions once they were helplessly inebriated and was making a pretty decent living from it. One day he planned to find his daughter and that other troublesome little whore again and make them pay for running away leaving him without an income. He'd tested the waters to see if he could get close enough to them, but they were being too closely guarded and he'd had to give up until he could find a sure way of making them suffer. He laughed to himself thinking that they were probably living in terror expecting him to appear again at any moment.

He made his way unsteadily along the street, weaving between the other drunks and the prostitutes who loitered on the street corners. He had no need to contemplate these disgusting old hags, bloated and desperate and raddled with disease, because he had plenty of fresh meat to choose from back at the brothel. He stopped to relieve himself against an alley wall and the smell of his beer-laden piss was the last thing he ever experienced in this life, apart from the sudden jolt of fear he felt when a cold steel blade slid smoothly into his jugular, his eyes goggled and he made a panicked gurgling sound, coughing blood and vomit as he sank down into the stinking puddle of still-warm urine.

His assailant looked down at the crumpled lifeless body, wiped his dagger on the victim's coat and then with the slightest shrug, strolled nonchalantly away down the dark alley and disappeared.

* * *

James Mullens was toying with the golden guineas in his pocket, running them through his fingers and listening to the entrancing music they made. He had enough now to ensure that he wouldn't have to work for at least a year. He'd been paid well for his endeavours even though it meant having to give up his comfortable position with that imbecile, Sir Anthony Calver. He'd had enough of damned neckcloths and polishing boots, of watching his employer swan off to enjoy himself all night while he was forced to wait up for his return. He wasn't cut out to be a valet, it was beneath his dignity.

He rather thought he'd like to buy himself a smart new coat and some boots, cut a bit of a dash; find a friendly card game and try his luck at the table, as fortune seemed to be favouring him at the moment. He felt sure that he could double his earnings in one night and be able to afford some well-deserved luxuries. He'd like to turn heads, have the ladies staring after him longingly and make the gentlemen green with envy. He swaggered along the street and didn't hear the sound of the carriage drawing up alongside him, so lost was he in his fantasy, nor did he hear the two men approach him from behind. The next thing he knew he was being bundled onto the floor of the vehicle and being held down rather too firmly by someone's knee on the back of his neck.

* * *

Mr Mullens blinked blearily as the hood was removed from his head, his eyes full of grit and dust. He realised with a start of fear that he was tightly bound to a chair. The room was dark, and he couldn't make out much apart from some sinister shadowy figures against the dim light of a lantern. He swallowed hard and found he was a little short of saliva.

"Mr Mullens, I believe?" said a silky voice he didn't much like the sound of.

He tried to look around him to see if there was any escape route.

"You're not going anywhere just yet, I'm afraid," said the same voice, not sounding at all apologetic.

He coughed and tried to find some words, "Where — am I?"

"Well, that hardly matters, does it? It'll be the last place you ever see."

He gulped, the blood rushing in his head, "But — I don't understand — who are you? Why am I here?"

"So many questions. Perhaps it might have been prudent to ask some before you decided to so recklessly take your life in your hands."

"My life? What — d'you mean?"

"I mean, that had you stopped for a moment and thought things through before accepting such an ill-advised assignment — you might have been spared a good deal of pain and suffering."

"Pain — s-suffering — ?" stammered Mullens.

"There — *now* you're beginning to understand. You're a little slow, if you don't mind me saying. I'll admit to being rather disappointed. I thought that someone who'd been so carefully selected to act as a spy and murderer's accomplice, would be a bit more, well — quick-witted. It's a wonder that you managed to be as successful as you were. You seem to be sadly lacking in intelligence. I think you should have taken time to weigh up the rewards against the inevitable retribution. Whatever you were paid, my friend, it wasn't nearly enough."

Mr Mullens, feeling rather weak and shaky, was beginning to understand the enormity of his miscalculation. The voice had an unpleasant edge to its elegant and temperate tones, and he was thinking that the guineas nestling in his pocket would be worth little to him if he were dead.

"I'm sorry — I didn't think it through — they were so persuasive — " he faltered.

"They?"

"I never saw them. There was always a go-between. Just a servant. With instructions and money. It was too good to ignore."

"Pity. I think you're about to discover that you should have been a little more judicious in your decisions. However, in order to give you a fair chance at saving your pathetic skin, you have a few moments to try to remember any important details you may have forgotten to share with us."

James Mullens thought frantically while the panic began to mount, "I — I — can't remember because — there wasn't anything. Each time it was just the same servant — and some guineas in a purse. He handed it over and told me what to do. He said if I succeeded then there would be more. He also suggested that if I failed, I would be punished. I was given no choice," he whined.

"Oh, I believe you were. In fact, had you had the sense to tell your employer about the plan right at the beginning, there would have been an even greater reward for you. A fortune, in fact. And, more importantly, we would have let you live."

Mullens cried out, "No! *Please!* I didn't mean to harm anyone! I just told them what was being said behind closed doors! I passed on information, that's all."

"And delivered a perfectly innocent child into their hands to be murdered in cold blood," said the voice coldly.

"*No!* They said — she would be safe — it was only to repay a grievance — a wrong!"

"A grievance? Is that so? You are finally beginning to interest me."

Sensing that he might still be able to wriggle out of danger Mullens thought rapidly, "The servant, he was tall and wigged and I think probably foreign. French, maybe? And he said it was no more than revenge for a perceived slight. So, I thought it couldn't be that serious. I swear, I had no idea they might kill the girl!"

He heard his captor move a little closer and flinched away.

"I can assure you that if any harm comes to her — any harm at all — if one hair on her head is harmed, I will take great pleasure in making sure that your death is long and painful," and the voice held such suppressed violence that Mullens thought he was going to choke him there and then and was relieved when after a minute or two he found he was still alive.

"All right, take him, and no need to be gentle."

James Mullens had the hood replaced and found himself and the chair, bodily lifted and carried from the room.

His captor picked up the lantern and followed them, his mind carefully considering the information he'd been given, a cold and deadly light in his fine hazel eyes.

Twenty-Seven

Constable Thursby contemplated the peculiar sight in front of the Bow Street magistrate's court with a mixture of confusion and satisfaction. Someone, it appeared, was keen to do his work for him. The note pinned to the quivering wreck before him stated quite clearly that he was responsible for a gruesome murder in Covent Garden, the night before last. They'd already brought the blood-soaked body of Mr Henry Pippin in and had been impressed by the ruthlessly efficient method of dispatch. They'd asked questions in the area and not surprisingly found nobody willing to speak to them. Nobody had seen anything. Yes, they knew of Mr Pippin and were all ready to admit to disliking him and could name at least half a dozen others who held grudges against him and would be glad to see him lying in a pool of his own blood. A few of the prostitutes from the bawdyhouse went even further and blurted out that they wished they'd been there to see him breathe his last. Constable Thursby, having heard some of his brutal exploits and after interviewing a few of his unfortunate victims, was unable to prevent that feeling of satisfaction increasing and decided that he was not at all unhappy that someone was dealing out punishment. That *someone* had taken the law into his own hands, but it was clear that he'd just one particular goal in mind and the constable was content, for the moment, to allow him free rein, knowing that once justice had been satisfactorily meted out, he would cease his activities. He also knew that the unknown assailant had good reasons for his actions, because he had chosen to share them with him. Exceedingly good reasons.

He looked down at the sobbing valet and grinned, "Well, you've certainly been done to a turn! Looks like you're going to be dangling from the end of a rope before very long, Mr Mullens and can't say I'm at all sorry. The world will be a better place without you in it. You won't be missed."

* * *

Anthony and Leander were partaking of a hearty breakfast of ham, beef and eggs washed down with ale and listening avidly to Theo.

"We just await Tom and Freddie's arrival and then we shall be ready. They will have set off at dawn and should be here late this afternoon barring Tom getting them lost on the way."

"Freddie will keep him under control. He'll be as keen as mustard, sensing a scrap in the offing and will be eager to get here as soon as possible! You have no fears for those at the Abbey now?"

"None at all. I've kept the extra patrols and now that Pippin and Mullens are out of the game, the danger is all here in London and Sephie and Ann are at the centre of it. By the bye we shall be attending a rather select party later tonight, uninvited, of course."

"I can't wait," said Anthony with his mouth full of some unusually tender beef, "This is some of the finest beef I've had in a long while, Theo! Where did you find it?"

"I'm so delighted you're enjoying it, Tony," said Theo wryly. "I have no idea where it came from. Perhaps you'd like me to go down to the kitchens and ask the housekeeper?"

"Yes, that would be — oh, I see, you're funning! Well, it's not a laughing matter — a really good bit of beef is hard to come by!"

Leander rolled his eyes, "Hardly of import just at the moment, you utter dolt! We've bigger things to consider than your stomach. Honestly Theo, we'd have been better off bringing Ambrose! At least he wouldn't be distracted by his damn breakfast!"

"Tony will prove useful, I have no doubt. He's surprisingly good when his back's against the wall. Fine pair of fists, as you know."

A footman appeared at the door with a letter for Theo. He read it and turned to his friends, "Well, it seems that Cobham has come up trumps again. He says the woman, Meryall, who left Sephie with Edwin Stokey, has been found at last. Managed to trace her through a letter she wrote to the Foundling Hospital, a few years after the event, when she was hoping to find out if they knew who had taken the child. Of course, they could only tell her that he was part of a notorious gang of men who preyed upon desperate women like her. He's found her full name and direction."

"Who is she, Theo?" asked Leander eagerly.

"Miss Meryall Chase. Nursemaid to the children of a country squire from Horsham in Sussex."

There was a thoughtful silence in the room, Anthony pausing between mouthfuls, "Miss? A nursemaid? Sephie's mother?"

"It looks that way."

"And the father?"

"Unknown, but because the midwife forced the information out of her at the birth, he's thought to be the farrier's son and it seems she was raped which explains the rush to be rid of the damning evidence."

Leander was watching his friend's face with interest, "Theo? This means Sephie is — "

"I know what it damn well means, Leander!" snapped Lord Rokewode impatiently. "It means Sephie has a living relation. Miss Persephone Chase has a family, of sorts."

"Her mother wishes to see her?"

"Apparently, she does. Although how she'll come to terms with what has happened to Sephie since she abandoned her, I have no clue. It will be unbearably hard for both of them, I fear."

"And, what about you? How will you come to terms with this news?"

Theo eyed Leander blankly, "Until I have her safely back with us, I'm not thinking of anything else."

* * *

Sephie heard the metallic scrape of bolts being drawn and she braced herself.

Someone entered the room holding a branch of candles, followed by another person bearing a tray.

The woman put the candles down on the table and approached the bed.

"Food and some brandy which I'd advise you to drink. You'll be needing it later."

Sephie noted that the woman wasn't a servant but rather obviously well-bred and dressed in expensive finery and was even more baffled. Nothing seemed to make sense to her, and she was unable to ask. The other woman put down the tray on the bed and left the room.

"So, you can't speak. That'll be an added attraction. Bound to cause a stir with our more discerning clients. You'll be a sensation looking so young and being mute into the bargain. And as long as you behave, things will work out well for all of us. Now, eat your supper and knock back that brandy. You'll need all your strength for what's in store."

Sephie shook her head.

The woman frowned at her, "It's for your own good. Your first is a regular and not given to being thwarted. Do you understand?"

Sephie looked mutinously at her.

"Look, you'll make it worse if you fight. Take my advice and just give him what he wants. I'm warning you! Nobody will come to your rescue. Nobody knows where you are. It's not like you're a virgin anyway."

The woman pushed the tray towards Sephie and, saying that she'd leave the candles so that she could eat, she left the room, bolting the door behind her.

So, thought Sephie, I'm in some kind of whorehouse, run by a rather refined sort of lady, which seemed unusual. Perhaps the kind of house where influential men could find high class courtesans for their pleasure. The boudoir certainly seemed to be vastly superior to anything she'd imagined.

She regarded the food on the tray with suspicion and then thought that her captors would not want her unconscious so decided that it was probably safe to eat and anyway, she was famished. She picked at the rather dry bread and old cheese and ate the pickled egg. She felt a little better afterwards and risked taking a sip of the brandy. It was watered down so was easier to drink and she downed the whole beaker in one go.

* * *

Lord Rokewode, Sir Leander Gage, Sir Anthony Calver, Lord Frederick Knoyll and Mr Tom Babyngton regarded the footman guarding the door with indolent good humour.

"I believe you would be sensible to allow us in before things get out of hand," said Lord Rokewode, smiling in what the footman thought was a rather menacing fashion.

"It's more than me job's worth, my lord!" he said nervously. He didn't like the way Lord Knoyll was fondling the sword at his hip.

"Is it more than your life's worth?" asked Rokewode pleasantly.

The footman gulped and coming to a sudden decision, stepped back allowing the five men to enter the hallway.

They made their way up to the first floor and along to the withdrawing room at the end of the elegantly wide corridor. The tall footman on duty at that door, saw nothing amiss with the group of guests approaching him and let them in without demur.

Sir Anthony cast him an interested glance as he passed, "*Bonsoir, mon amie*," he said cheerily.

"*Bonsoir, M'sieur*," responded the footman, unwisely.

Sir Anthony Calver smiled.

They entered the large, crowded room and stood for a moment in the doorway to calmly survey the company.

The conversation dwindled, faces turned towards them, eyes widened, and expressions froze.

Mrs Margaret Sheraton rose from the sofa and held out her hand in greeting to Lord Rokewode, but it was ignored, and she let it fall, "Theo, darling! How unexpected. And you've brought your playfellows too. Isn't that just sweet! Come on in and make yourself at home. We were just saying we were a little short on gentlemen this evening."

Lord Rokewode regarded her companions with disdain, "I can see that, Margaret. I see no gentlemen present at all."

Babyngton let out a snort of laughter.

"Amusing, my lord," said Mrs Sheraton stiffly. "May I ask when you got back from the Abbey? I thought you were to be away much longer."

"We had a sudden change of plans, my dear, which could not be ignored. I discovered that I had mislaid something exceedingly precious and found it necessary to return to London with all haste to retrieve it."

Mrs Sheraton snapped open her fan with one sharp flick of her wrist and fanned her warm cheeks, "Is that so? May I enquire what you have lost? I might be able to help you recover it," she smiled her beautiful smile, but it went nowhere near her eyes.

"I wondered if you might," murmured Lord Rokewode.

"I have to ask though, if it was so precious how came you to lose it in the first place?"

"Ah, you see, to begin with I had no idea just how much I treasured it but when I found it was under threat, I began to realise that it was indeed *priceless*."

"Well, it seems as though you've been extremely careless with it and therefore deserve to lose it. Wouldn't you say so, Selwyn?"

Mr Selwyn Vauville had been observing this entertaining performance and hoping nobody would draw attention to him. He had an important appointment later with their latest addition, which could not wait, and even though it was not quite the reward he'd been anticipating, it was still something he was looking forward to. He would have to admit to having been hugely disappointed to begin with, but once Margaret had explained how the mistake had been made, he was more than happy to be a little more flexible and patient. There would surely be ample opportunities in the future to taste Miss Pippin's delicious wares. Now, facing these five rather robust and cold-blooded looking individuals, he was beginning to doubt that the outcome was going to be quite as gratifying as he'd hoped.

"*Mi amore,*" he said, in a voice which was rather shakier than he'd have liked, "I heartily agree. One should take the greatest care of one's valuable possessions."

Lord Rokewode laughed mirthlessly, "Oh, it's not a *possession*. I think you may have misunderstood. Although, it *is* something which I am planning to keep very safe in the future. I will not be parted from it again."

Mrs Sheraton's exquisite cheeks lost some of their high colour, "You cannot be serious!" she blurted out and then seeing the look upon his face, immediately regretted the outburst.

"I can assure you that I am deadly serious. I have no idea why you might doubt my word," said Lord Rokewode at his most urbane.

'I — I — was only surprised my lord because you have always been so strongly opposed to inferior — "

"I would be exceedingly careful if I were you, Margaret," he interrupted icily.

"I find it amusing Theo, to see that you have so lowered your usually high standards. Only the best was ever good enough for you. Your mother must find it vastly entertaining. I wish I could have seen her face when you told her — "

Theo made a sudden instinctive move towards her, Mr Selwyn Vauville reached for his small-sword and several of the men in the salon flinched and brought forth an array of small but deadly-looking weapons.

Lord Rokewode smiled, "There is another thing I would like to discuss with you my dear. I feel sure that you must wonder why I never — er — came up to scratch."

Mrs Sheraton flashed her dark eyes at him, "I have not the slightest interest — "

"Ah, but I think I shall tell you anyway. You see, I once had a rather splendid and loyal friend. We were inseparable at school and at Oxford, were we not, Leander?"

Sir Leander Gage nodded, "The very best of friends. Always the three of us."

Lord Rokewode's hand strayed idly to the handle of his sword, "He was perhaps a little — eccentric. And occasionally made poor decisions which sadly made him vulnerable to those of a more devious nature. He was also rather inclined to fall in with the wrong types and then one day he found himself caught like a fly in a cobweb and — well, I think you know the rest."

Mrs Sheraton took a step backwards and practically fell onto the sofa as though her legs had collapsed under her. She put a trembling hand to her mouth.

"Precisely, dear Margaret, *precisely*. There, I can see that you are beginning to see the light. Bertram Littleby. A flawed young man but nevertheless possessed of a good and kind heart. And you — you drove him to his death with all the indifference of someone dispatching an annoying insect. I don't suppose you have given him much thought over the last two years — but I have. And I have been waiting patiently for the day when I would make you pay for your cruelty and treachery. Today is the day. Today your comfortable existence comes to an abrupt end and I will no longer have to endure being in your repellent presence, which, I must tell you, has been a thorn in my flesh. I can also now inform you that I know about every single one of your colossal debts and have bought up all your outstanding bills and now am the proud owner of — oh, let me see — *everything*. You own nothing, not even the clothes you stand up in."

Mr Selwyn Vauville, with a rush of enraged blood to the head, drew his sword in one swift movement and lunged at Lord Rokewode but hardly appeared to have moved at all before Lord Frederick Knoyll's sword was at his throat, slicing a painful incision just above his bobbing Adam's apple.

"I wouldn't move another inch, if I were you Selwyn. Freddie is notoriously twitchy when under pressure. His hand just goes into convulsions and he cannot be blamed for the consequences."

Mrs Sheraton was slumped on the sofa unable to catch her breath. Her head was spinning, and she felt sick. Lord Rokewode was watching her from narrowed eyes, a slight twist to the corner of his mouth.

She saw Mrs Alice Yelverton appear at a side door, in the corner of the drawing room and gave her a warning look, Mrs Yelverton silently backed out of the room again before anyone spotted her.

"Oh, and there is the other small matter of attempted murder which Constable Thursby seems rather keen on pursuing." Lord Rokewode glanced at the clock on the mantlepiece, "The constables will be here shortly to talk with you."

Mrs Sheraton, seeing her life disintegrating around her gave a hollow laugh, "So, Theo, you've finished me. I hope you're satisfied because you'll never find happiness with — with that ugly little *whore!* Even Selwyn's had her now! She's just a filthy cast-off and you'll never be able to forget — "

She didn't get any further than that because her lovely long neck was being throttled and she was gasping for air, her hands flailing ineffectually at Lord Rokewode's chest as though she could flap him away, but the fingers just tightened their grip, biting into her flesh.

"Best not actually kill her," said Sir Leander Gage thoughtfully. "Might be a trifle difficult to explain."

Lord Rokewode gave a short laugh and released her, and she fell backwards onto the sofa again, clutching at her bruised neck and choking violently.

"No, you're right. It would be too easy anyway. This way she'll suffer for a very long time. So much more satisfying." He turned away from her, "Come, Tom and Leander, we shall search the house. Every damn room until we find them."

Sir Anthony Calver and Lord Frederick Knoyll kept an eye on the stunned guests in the drawing room while the others made a thorough search of the house.

They found nothing.

Twenty-Eight

The Bow Street constables and their enthusiastic men arrived (keen to show the gentry who was in charge) and took over the house, sending home those who had no connection with the criminal activity they were investigating and separating out the suspects from the fairly innocent bystanders.

Theo was looking ashen and Leander was trying his best to calm him, "We'll find them, Theo. This place is crawling with officials now. It won't be long."

"I was so certain they'd be here — "

Anthony, who was sitting on the stairs watching the French footman try to sidle around the dark edges of the hall without being noticed, suddenly rose to his feet, strode across to him and demonstrated his astonishingly efficient right hook. The Frenchman clutched his nose and tried to stem the blood which was dribbling down his chin. An observant constable grabbed the footman by the arm and dragged him outside to the awaiting coaches promising him more of the same if he didn't behave.

Anthony rubbed his knuckles, "Didn't like the look of him one little bit," he declared.

"Has anyone checked the courtyard at the back?" asked Freddie.

Leander headed for the rear door, "Come on, Theo, while they're tidying up here — "

* * *

Sephie sat on the edge of the bed and wished the woman had left some sharp cutlery that she could have sawed her bindings with. She'd been expected to eat with her fingers and the beaker looked unbreakable.

She looked around the room for anything she might use to free herself. Her eye fell on the flickering candles.

She stood up and stretched the restraint as far as it would go and then, not for the first time, wished she was a good deal taller. She reached out her arm, ignoring the pain in her shoulder, wriggling her fingers as though it might lengthen them, and finally, after much straining, managed to touch the base of the candelabra. With infinite patience she plucked at the metal base, bit by bit edging it towards her until it was just within reach. She made a desperate lunge, hoping she wouldn't knock the whole thing to the floor. It toppled but she managed to grasp it as it fell and swooped it out of the air, holding it firmly as she reeled backwards, landing sprawled half on the bed. She let out a frightened puff of air and sat for a moment to steady herself. When she had calmed down, she placed the candelabra on the floor beside her and held the cord binding over a flame. After a short while it began to blacken and finally to smoulder.

Then she imagined she heard voices in the distance. Was she too late? She could hear the sound of men talking. She cocked her head and listened intently. They sounded very far away.

Her heart skipped a beat. She thought she heard a voice she knew. The blood began to pound loudly in her head. She was breathing fast as though she'd been running.

She could hear them talking outside the window. There must be a courtyard behind the house making the voices reverberate.

That voice, that voice! Oh, God, she knew it so well! She pulled towards the window but could get nowhere near. If only she could beat on it with her fists and make him hear!

She tore at the burnt cord, but it wouldn't give way. She picked up the beaker and hurled it, but it just hit the wall and fell to the ground barely making a sound. The wooden tray followed it, to no avail.

The voices were getting fainter.
They didn't know she was there.
They were leaving.
She was panicking, unable to breathe, tears pouring down her face, choking her.
She couldn't hear them anymore.

She opened her mouth and screamed.
"*Theo!*"

Theo and Leander returning to the house on the other side of the courtyard stopped in their tracks.
Theo span and sprinted back out into the yard.
No light came from any of the facing windows. He could see nothing.
"*Sephie!*"

Sephie's legs buckled, and she collapsed onto the floor, "Theo, I'm here." she whispered.

Theo and Leander raced across the courtyard and into the house at the rear of the block. It took them a few minutes to search the rooms on the ground floor, bursting in on torrid scenes stolen from a Hogarth etching; buxom wenches astride elderly naked gentlemen; drunken rakes and masked females wielding whips. Ignoring the outraged shouts, they quickly made their way up to the second floor and, after a fruitless search of the main bedchambers, mostly unoccupied, to a room at the far end of a dark corridor. It was bolted on the outside.
Theo slid the bolts and opening the door, saw her at last.
"Sephie!" he cried hoarsely, and he was beside her, reaching out his arms and gathering her to him, pulling her close, stoking her hair and saying her name over and over.
She collapsed against him and sobbed into his waistcoat, convulsed with trembling.

Leander turned away, unable to watch, his throat so tight and painful that he couldn't swallow.

Theo held her and rocked her gently until the muffled whimpering lessened and her panicked breathing had steadied.

"You said my name, Sephie! You *spoke!*"

He put a finger under her chin and lifted her tear-stained face up to his, he looked into her eyes, puffy and red from crying and exhaustion and his breath caught, choking him. Never in his life had he ever seen anything as beautiful as this girl in his arms.

He bent his head and tenderly kissed her.

"Theo," she murmured huskily, as his mouth continued to search hers.

"God, say it again! I never thought — to hear you — I thought I'd lost you. We had no idea about this house. If you hadn't called out — ! Leander is here — and the others. Are you all right? Did they hurt you?"

She shook her head, "I'm — all right now. They were going to — " she whispered, her voice barely audible.

"Don't speak of it now. Why did you run away from me? When I found you'd left me, I was at my wit's end. And then, when we realised you'd been abducted — Sephie, I — will you please — marry me so that I can keep you safe?"

She pulled away from him, knitting her dark brows.

"I'm sorry! I shouldn't have asked you here! God, what a fool I am. I'm just so relieved to have found you, I'm not thinking straight."

He seemed to shake himself out of his overwrought state and quickly began to undo her charred restraints while she watched him lovingly, wondering what on earth she had done to deserve such ridiculous happiness.

Once freed from the bindings, he helped her to her feet but realising she had no strength left, he swept her up in his arms and holding her tightly against him, her head buried in his neck, he carried her downstairs, through the courtyard and into the hallway of Mrs Sheraton's house.

The others were waiting patiently in the hallway, smiling with relief.

Sitting in a chair beside them, wrapped in a blanket, was Ann. She cried out when she saw Theo with Sephie in his arms and flew to them and insisted upon holding Sephie's hand all the way to Grosvenor Square in the carriage. Theo and Leander travelled with them and Sephie remained happily wrapped in Theo's embrace. She nestled against him, covered by his coat, and feeling the warmth emanating from his body. His arm circled her waist, one hand resting on her hip.

Once at his mother's house, he took her straight up to her room and reluctantly set her down upon her bed. Ann immediately threw her arms about Sephie and they hugged, crying. Theo watched them for a moment and met Sephie's eyes over Ann's shoulder. He just looked at her as though not quite believing she was within reach. He couldn't tear his eyes away.

She smiled at him, her mouth curling up at the corners and handed back his coat, he sighed and left the room.

* * *

Leander was waiting for him in the drawing room, the others having gone to their own homes and beds in the hopes of catching up on a few hours' sleep before what promised to be yet another hectic day.

"How is she, Theo? Unharmed? Ann seems to have managed well. They'd locked her in one of the attics, but she was thankfully unmolested. She just wanted to know if Sephie was all right."

"We were in time. They hadn't — she'd tried to burn the bindings with a candle to escape. She's the most — astounding woman I've ever met. She called my name, Leander! She spoke! I've never heard a sweeter sound in my life! I've asked her to marry me."

Leander looked momentarily astonished and then grinned and clapped his friend on the back, "Well, dash it, Theo! May I be the first to offer my congratulations! I couldn't be happier for you."

"She hasn't agreed yet. I should have waited until she'd recovered — but I know she loves me — she couldn't have been so — at Fairtree — there was no doubting it — so I must just be patient — "

Leander nodded and agreed with him but privately thought it a little odd that Sephie hadn't immediately accepted his offer.

* * *

Ann tucked Sephie into her bed in clean nightclothes and sat with her for a while until she'd drifted off to sleep. She'd listened to Sephie's plans and although her voice wasn't strong, the merest whisper, Ann said that she'd do anything for her, even if she didn't agree with it. She tried to dissuade her, she reasoned and pleaded but Sephie was adamant so eventually she'd given in, thinking that it would be better, after suffering such an ordeal, to allow her to sleep on it. After a night's rest she would feel differently and be able to see that she was making a terrible mistake. She was just too tired to think clearly at the moment and was rushing into a decision made out of panic. Ann went to her own bed gladly, but some niggling reservations kept her awake for a while and then, finding no ready solution, decided that she would do whatever Miss Sephie wanted and pray that everything would work out for the best. She had faith in true love.

* * *

The next day Theo rose early after a restless night and was busy tying up loose ends. He wrote to Major Cobham to thank him again, inform him of the outcome of their efforts and to tell him of their plans. He received a visit from Constable Thursby, who was clearly delighted be able to tell him about his night's work, taking particular pleasure in a detailed description of Mr Selwyn Vauville in floods of tears and the pitiful sight of Mrs Sheraton begging her good friends for help and being summarily rejected as they fled her house. They found a Mrs Alice Yelverton, the bawdyhouse owner, hiding in a linen cupboard and Sir Leonard Tiploft in the unused bread oven in the kitchen, his cerise satin coat covered in soot which seemed to affect him very deeply. All in all, a very satisfying evening. However, he did feel obliged to warn Lord Rokewode to keep out of trouble in the future but was smiling as he did so.

Given all his own carriages were already in Gloucestershire, Theo was forced to hire a couple of post-chaise to carry them back to Rokewode Abbey, where he thought Sephie would be happiest.

Sephie, he thought, *Sephie*. And he had to control an urge to run upstairs to see her. No, let her sleep! She must be exhausted. He thought back to when he'd first seen her, a soot-blackened little tigress, hammering his chest with her fists. *And though she be but little, she is fierce.* He smiled and though she would probably run him ragged in years to come, he didn't care; he would happily forsake his well-ordered old life for a chaotic and passionate one with Sephie. He would never again know a moment's peace and laughed out loud, the sound of his own happiness startling him.

The others turned up in time for a late breakfast and to catch up on the news. They were all keen to return to the Abbey to let everyone there know that Sephie and Ann were safe, and Leander was impatient to see Matilda and make sure she hadn't changed her mind about him while he was away.

When Theo told them that he and Leander had found Sephie when she'd called out his name, they were dumbfounded, but then Theo explained what the doctor had said about her losing her voice because of the trauma she'd suffered and how she'd been able to speak as a child before the horror of her early years with Edwin Stokey had rendered her speechless. He thought that the shock of thinking he might not find her imprisoned in the high-class brothel that Mrs Sheraton and her friends had been running in plain sight for aristocratic clients, had thankfully allowed her voice to come back.

He then told them that he'd offered his hand and they were ecstatic. They were all just congratulating him when the door opened and Bishoptree appeared, looking even more down in the mouth than usual.

"My lord, I apologise for interrupting but there's a small matter I think you should know about."

"No need to apologise, what is it?"

Bishoptree cleared his throat, "I'm sorry to inform you that Miss Persephone and Ann have left."

"Left? What do you mean?" demanded Theo, curtly.

"They seem to have packed their bags and left the house, my lord."

* * *

Once he had seen the evidence for himself and the truth had finally sunk in, Theo turned to Leander in absolute despair, "Why in God's name does she keep running away from me?"

Leander, sensing a monumental explosion, trod warily, "I have no idea — females are a complete mystery to me, always have been. Is it possible that you may have inadvertently said something to her and caused this precipitous flight?"

"I offered her marriage! Why would that cause her to flee — *again*? It makes no damn sense at all!"

"Theo, you asked her to marry you whilst she was tied up in a brothel."

"That was obviously not my intention! I wanted her to know that I would keep her safe!" said Theo, raking his hands through his hair.

Leander began to see light, "You told her you wanted to marry her to keep her *safe*?"

"Well, naturally! It was paramount at the time!"

Leander sighed, "I should have said that it was paramount to tell her that you love her."

"Well, of course!"

"And therefore, you told her, unequivocally, that you love her?"

"I — I — may not have actually said it then, but she knows that I do! Why else would I offer her marriage?"

"Apparently, to keep her out of danger," said Leander blandly.

Theo froze, his face drained of all colour, "You think —?"

"I *think* that you're a blockheaded fool," announced Leander furiously, "I suppose I've always suspected it, but this damn well proves it. Sephie has lived a life without love, without kindness, without family to turn to and advise her. She has somehow survived a nightmarish existence where she suffered more than any of us can ever imagine and still managed to come out of it able to put others first, to love others first and willing to sacrifice her happiness for the one she loves. *You.* She will never marry you because she thinks she'd bring shame and ignominy upon your pompous, worthless family name. She probably believes you're offering for her because you feel guilty about — about compromising her. Or that you can think of no other way of effectively dealing with her. Dear God, Theo! If you weren't so damn tall and broad-shouldered, I'd get Tony to draw your damn cork! You don't deserve her! She's better off without you."

Theo stood in stunned silence, staring at his friend's enraged face.

"Hear, hear!" said Freddie, slowly clapping his hands in accord.

"Couldn't have said it better myself!" said Anthony approvingly.

"Fellow's a regular slow-top," remarked Babyngton.

Theo held up his hands in surrender, "I agree. You're right. I see it now. I must find her. Where in damnation would she go?"

Leander stroked his chin thoughtfully, "I don't think she'll stay in London — she was never truly happy here. I doubt she'd return to Whitchurch. What about Major Cobham? She knows about him wanting to adopt her, no? She may seek shelter with him. Theo, you and I will go to his place and check. Freddie and Babyngton, you get to the nearest stagecoach office and see if anyone answering to their description has bought tickets this morning. Tony, you're in charge of what I think will be an inevitable journey back to the Abbey as soon as we have made absolutely sure that she's not still here in London. At least we know that Ann is with her, which is reassuring."

They all dispersed to tackle their various tasks and as they left the house, Leander put his hand on Theo's arm, "You know, despite the fact that I seem to spend most of my time castigating you these days, I know that you love Sephie and, if we can find her again, will make her happy. I also know that you can't be entirely blamed for your stupidity. Sephie would beg me to forgive you, so, I do. Now, let us go and bring that damn runaway home for the last time!"

Twenty-Nine

Sephie slept with her head on Ann's shoulder, which was wet with tears. Ann had taken control of the journey as Sephie was in no fit state to do anything other than tell Ann where she wanted to go and then sit like a broken doll, unable to think of anything apart from how much she loved Theo. Ann tried to get her to talk, to use her voice but she could only speak a few words before it became faint and faded away. What voice she had was husky and soft and Ann had to bend her head closer to catch the words. If she tried too hard to speak it disappeared altogether leaving her frustrated and confused so Ann allowed her to speak only when she truly felt the need. It made for a rather stressful journey, what with all the crying as well.

By the time they reached Burford, Sephie had fallen completely silent which Ann found even more disconcerting. They left the stagecoach and Ann hired a gig to take them to their destination. It meant a long drive in the cold rain which had been falling since mid-afternoon and by the time the driver of the gig helped them down and bid them farewell, they were both soaked to the skin.

The butler, recognising them, let them into the Great Hall and bid them stay there until he had sent a maid up to see if his mistress was still awake.

A few minutes later the maid appeared and said Miss Persephone was to go right up.

Sephie took off her cloak, forlornly tried to straighten her hair, hugged Ann and followed the maid up the stairs.

The huge bedchamber was still vastly over-furnished and rather dark, the four-poster being the only spot lit by a candelabra.

"Well, come over here, you silly child and allow me to hazard a guess as to what you've done now!" commanded Baroness Gage.

Sephie approached the enormous bed and looked nervously at the ferocious lady propped up against the pillows, her face mostly swamped by an overlarge frilly nightcap.

"Come, draw up that chair and let us see if we can work out why you have suddenly appeared at Fairtree in the middle of the night. You look utterly fagged, my dear. Am I to suppose that this has something to do with my stupid grandson's handsome friend?"

Sephie chewed her lip and nodded and pulled the chair closer to the bed, slumping down into it gratefully, her legs shaking with tiredness.

"That doesn't surprise me in the slightest. I had no illusions about the path to true love running smoothly but will admit to having had high hopes that you two might be able to come to some suitable arrangement which would answer. Of course, as he's a friend of Leander's, bound to be a bit of a numbskull. Oh, you can shake your head all you like but you can't deny that the boy is a hide-bound, stiff-necked fool! And you can't pull the wool over my eyes! I saw how you were with each other at the Ball — I may be ancient but I'm not blind! And my maid was very forthcoming about the comings and goings during the night! Oh, you may well blush and cast down your eyes! Not the behaviour of a *lady*," she declared and then observing Sephie's stricken expression, relented and let out a bark of laughter, "In my day, I would have done the exact same thing! I was never one to play by the rules. Rules are made to be broken in my book. So, having been imprudently wanton you thought you'd better run away? And then, I hear, you were abducted. You certainly know how to keep everyone on their toes! So, off hares our handsome hero to rescue you and he obviously finds you and then something happens to throw you into confusion once more. And off you run again. It's becoming an exceedingly tiresome habit, m'dear! What can have happened I wonder to make flight the only option this time?"

"He asked me to marry him," breathed Sephie.

The Baroness's face was a picture, "Ah, now, this is quite the development! You can speak! As I understand it, from my stupid grandson, you were able to talk as a child but lost the ability due to your appalling upbringing? Is that right? So, tell me, you clearly love Theodore, and he seems determined to make you his bride, which I am assuming is because he loves you too — "

"No. He wants only to keep me safe and — make an honest woman of me," whispered Sephie, gruffly.

"Ridiculous!"

"It's my fault for throwing myself at him. I knew we could never be together because of my background and all that has happened to me. I'm so far beneath him and tainted beyond measure but I just wanted to say goodbye and have something to remember — to erase the others — "

The Baroness held up an imperious hand, "Enough! There is no need, my dear child, I am fully aware and really it matters not what your past may have been — what matters is your future. Oh, this is all vastly entertaining! If my guess is anything to go by, I suspect those nincompoops will already be on their way to the Abbey so by tomorrow afternoon I believe I shall be feeling extremely unwell, probably hovering at death's door. No, no, don't look so concerned! I shall only be shamming! I shall have a note sent to Leander begging him to come at once. What fun! I have been longing to play the part of dying grandmother just to find if anyone cares about me. This will be the perfect opportunity. It will be most revealing. You and I shall have a splendid time, but you must go to bed at once or you'll look even more of a sight in the morning. However, I must insist that you do not mindlessly worship Theodore — he is deeply flawed and needs someone to stand up to him. You are *not* his inferior and there's no need for you to escape one prison just to become someone else's captive because you feel unworthy. To be perfectly frank Sephie, I find

I am quite encouraged, when I look at you, to believe that this truly is a love match out of a fairy tale!"

Sephie gave her a tremulous smile, knowing precisely what she was alluding to.

"Now, kiss my withered old cheek and go off to your bed! Naughty girl! Keeping an old lady up all night, it's bound to make me poorly," and the Baroness let out a hearty laugh and shooed Sephie away.

* * *

Kitty stared at the exhausted faces before her with tears in her eyes, "They're safe? Rescued! But you've already lost them again? Is that what you're telling us? How can you have been so careless? Where are they? Oh, Theo! They're not here. Why haven't they come to us?"

Theo was, by this time, too tired to speak and sat contemplating the pattern on the rug as though it greatly interested him. He saw nothing. He'd been so sure that Sephie would return to the Abbey to be with Kitty and Biddy and Miss Edie that he hadn't even thought of the possibility of them not being there. It had come as a shock to discover that he was no nearer finding her.

Miss Bell had, the moment she'd seen the five weary mud-spattered travellers, made sure that food and drink was immediately provided although none of them had done more than down a glass of ale or wine and Anthony was staring broodingly into a glass of brandy, but hadn't touched it yet. The drawing room seemed very crowded and the mood was low. She had never seen Theodore in such a state of flat despair and although she was relieved to see that he was capable of such unbridled emotion, she was also alarmed by the sight of his drawn face and overwhelming air of desolation. Having been given a brief description of their moment of sweet revenge upon the cause of all their woes and their rescuing exploits and Theodore's shatter-brained proposal in the brothel, Miss Bell was hardly able to blame Sephie for disappearing again.

"Am I to understand Theodore, that you have offered marriage to that quiet little creature?" demanded Lady Rokewode querulously, unable to follow the whole conversation but having managed to grasp this one astounding fact.

"Yes, Mama. I mean to marry her, if she'll have me and will not hear one word said against her so you had better take care," snapped Theo.

Lady Rokewode glared at him, "Well, isn't that just *like* you, Theodore! Always assuming the worst. I couldn't be happier for you. I like the odd little — "

"*Sephie!*" growled her son.

" — I *like* Sephie, she's most unusual and I must say she made me feel very much calmer when she was with me. So soothing."

"As though she were some kind of balm one applies — " muttered Kitty, bitterly.

"I'm just saying that I thoroughly *approve* of your choice Theodore, although it may be a trifle unexpected."

"Thank you, Mama. But it makes no odds to me who approves — I will have her whatever anyone thinks," said Theo wearily.

"So, what do we do next," asked Leander.

"We will have to question the stagecoach drivers. We know they set off from London and headed this way. We didn't think to ask beyond Oxford as we were sure by then of their direction. I will hire more men to search and I shall write to Cobham to see if he can come up with anything — "

The door opened to reveal Chilton, the butler, holding a letter. Theo jumped up and eagerly took it from him, but on reading the direction on the front, his face fell, and he handed it on to Leander, who, looking slightly startled, opened it and read the contents.

"Dash it! It's from my housekeeper. She says that the Baroness is gravely ill and calling for me! I must go at once Theo!"

"Of course, I shall come with you."

* * *

And so, a rather larger than expected cavalcade of carriages and riders arrived at Fairtree Manor where they were all shown into the withdrawing room, by the admirably unruffled butler, while Leander dashed upstairs two-by-two to see his ailing grandmother.

He found her lying like a corpse in her bed, the familiar family physician, Doctor Brook, in attendance. He looked up at Leander and quietly shook his head, his mouth a grim line. He was holding Baroness Gage by her limp wrist and after a moment laid her hand back on the counterpane, with a despairing sigh.

Leander started forward, "She's not — !"

"No, Sir Leander, she's hanging on by a mere thread. I thought she'd be gone already but she's stubborn and I believe she's just been waiting for you to come before — before she allows God to take her to His bosom."

At this there was a small choking sound from the bed and Doctor Brook was forced to turn away from the terrible scene to hide his shaking shoulders, he made his rather muffled excuses and left the room unable to contain his mirth any longer.

"Grandmama!" cried Leander throwing himself onto his knees bedside the bed, "I'm here! Please don't give up! I can't manage without you — you're all the family I have left." He took her hand in his and was slightly taken aback by how warm it was, "Is there anything I can do for you? Just say the word."

Baroness Gage opened her eyes a fraction and made a feeble effort to speak, Leander moved closer to catch her precious words.

"You must marry — Matilda — as soon as decently possible. Don't allow her — to get away again. Now, fetch — Theodore. I must — speak with him — " she managed, with every sign of being about to breathe her last.

"*Theo?* Really? Oh, of course, whatever you wish! I shall get him at once!"

* * *

Looking somewhat puzzled, Theo approached the bed.

"Baroness? You called for me?"

She let out a long sigh, "You've — come. Thank God — almost too late."

"Too late?"

Baroness Gage closed her eyes, determined to enjoy every last minute of her finest performance; she lay very still, barely breathing.

"Baroness?"

"*Grandmama?*"

She came to with an impressive fit of wheezing and then managed to say with great difficulty, her voice faint and trembling, "I don't have long — I just ask one more thing of you Theodore — do you — love Sephie?"

Theo paled and stared in confusion at the old lady.

She opened her gleaming eyes wide, "Well, *do* you?"

"I love her more than you can possibly imagine. I would do anything for her. She is my life."

"Nicely said," declared Baroness Gage, sitting up in a decidedly perky fashion and straightening her nightcap.

Leander made a strangled sound and Theo took an involuntary step backwards.

"And you think her beautiful?"

Theo nodded, remembering a pair of gentle grey eyes, "I think she's the most beautiful woman I have ever seen."

"That is absolutely *fascinating,*" said the Baroness, thinking of Sephie's undoubtedly plain little face. "Would you be good enough to fetch me a glass of brandy, Theo? I find I am in dire need of a restorative. The best sort, from the decanter in the Great Hall. Leander do stop goggling at me! It's very disconcerting. Why are you still standing there and not racing at full tilt to Matilda? I don't know what the world is coming to! Gentlemen are just not what they used to be — no gumption, no guts! Now, in my day — !"

* * *

A frowning Theo skirted the ornately carved wooden screens and strode into the Great Hall. He had no idea what had just happened but knew that Baroness Gage was not to be denied.

Brandy, in the decanter on the sideboard.

He came to a standstill.

There was someone seated in a large Jacobean chair by the blazing fire.

He felt a familiar pain in his chest and wondered again if he was about to have a heart attack.

"Hallo, Theo," said Sephie softly.

The beautiful sound of her husky voice made the hair on the back of his neck stand on end. Her lovely grey eyes were looking at him quite serenely, her hands were folded primly in her lap. He took a step towards her, but she held up a commanding hand and he faltered.

"*Sephie!* Where the hell have you been? We looked everywhere for you!"

"I've been here."

"Here? But why?"

"Because I cannot marry you," she said quietly.

"Yes, you can! You have to! I will make you."

She smiled wisely, "You cannot force me, Theo."

Theo ground his teeth, "I don't understand! I want to marry you more than anything! I know I should never have proposed to you in that terrible place. It was stupid and thoughtless. But you *can't* keep running away from me. It just won't do! People will start to think that you don't love me, and I know that you do."

"Yes, I do," said Sephie calmly, "God knows why though. You're arrogant and far too used to getting your own way and spoiled and demanding and far too tall."

"Too *tall?*"

"Yes, we'd look ridiculous together."

"Sephie, be serious!"

"I am. Very serious."

Theo rubbed an impatient hand over his tired eyes, "All right. What do you want me to do to prove that we belong together? I'll do anything."

She cocked her head, "A quest? What a splendid idea! But there are no dragons to fight anymore — you've disposed of them all and I'm no longer imprisoned in a tower. You freed me — and I can now speak for myself, so the evil spell has been broken. What happens next in the fairy tale book?"

Theo's eyes darkened, "I believe the Prince kisses the fair maiden."

Sephie's dimples appeared and her eyes sparkled. Theo's heart lurched.

"And then what?" asked the fair maiden.

"And then they live happily ever after."

"That seems a trifle unlikely. They never quarrel?"

"Oh, yes they do, fiercely but they always make up afterwards."

"Oh? *How?*"

"I think you know, Sephie."

She grinned up at him, "Yes, I do. And I'm trying desperately to think of something that we can quarrel about!"

"*Sephie!* Don't be so provocative!"

She laughed, a throaty little chuckle and Theo advanced across the space between them. This time she didn't stop him. He stood in front of her and held out his hand. She put her small hand in his and watched in fascination as he got down on one knee.

"Persephone, will you please marry me? I can't damn well live without you. I love you. As, I am fairly sure, you already know! And I'll have you know that I think I loved you right from the moment you first punched me in the chest with your tiny fists. It just took a while for me to realise it."

"I love you too, so very much and yes, I will marry you but only if you take me home right now — well, after I've talked to everyone, but then I want you to take me home because I want — I want you to — do what you did before!"

Theo reached up and pulled her down onto his knee, "With pleasure!" and his eager mouth found hers and she threw her arms around his neck and gave herself up to a rather rough and passionate kiss.

* * *

The drawing room door opened and Sephie practically skipped into the room, followed by a proud and beaming Theo.

"Oh, my God! Sephie!" shrieked Kitty and threw herself at her, Amadeus barking frantically as he frolicked around their feet. Sephie kissed and hugged everyone there and explained that she had indeed got her voice back. Eventually, she was able to make her way across the room to Lady Rokewode. She knelt in front of her and looked up at her pleadingly, "I know I'm perhaps not what you'd imagined as a future daughter-in-law, but *please* may I marry your wonderful son?"

Lady Rokewode, much touched, took Sephie's hands in hers, "You may, although I feel I must warn you that he was always a great trial to us." She dropped a kiss onto Sephie's forehead and becoming rather tearful said, "I think you'll be good for him."

"Oh, I shall!" declared Sephie. "I am going to *rescue* him!"

Theo's mother laughed and patted her hand, "I wish you luck, my dear!"

Biddy approached her rather timidly and after kissing her, told her that Mr Adam Gibbs had invited her to take tea with his mother and sisters and she would need advice about what to wear. Miss Bell gave her an enormous hug said her goose-bumps were never wrong and quietly warned Sephie that Theodore, although, on the whole, an adorable boy, was rather headstrong and intent upon getting his own way. She told her not to allow him to ride roughshod over her. Sephie assured her that she wouldn't. She was embraced enthusiastically by Anthony, Freddie and a misty-eyed Babyngton.

And then, a tearful Sephie hugged Leander fiercely and cried into his neck a little, until Theo, becoming a trifle jealous, gently hauled her away.

"You have to come with *me* now," he said in a high-handed fashion.

She laughed up at him, her eyes dancing, "All right, I'm coming!" She turned back to the others in the room, "He's taking me home now," she told them happily.

Epilogue

Theo handed Sephie into the post-chaise, jumped in after her and closed the door. The coachman cracked the whip and the carriage jolted forwards.

Sephie sat looking at him for a moment, chewing her lip.

He opened his arms, and she flew into them and by the time they reached the Abbey, Sephie's lips were rather bruised and her hair ruffled. She had to order Theo to help her rearrange her disordered gown so that she didn't look as though she'd been ravished.

* * *

Chilton opened the door to his master, who was, to his astonishment, carrying a pink-cheeked and giggling Miss Persephone in his arms. The butler opened his mouth to say something.

"Not now Chilton, not now! Can't you see I'm busy!" and Theo strode up the staircase bearing his euphoric bride-to-be, leaving the butler staring after him, a wide grin on his face.

Theo reached his bedchamber and Sephie stretched down and, as she lifted the latch, he kicked the door open and then stood a little uncertainly in the middle of the room.

"Bed," said Sephie firmly.

He gently lowered her onto it and took a step back.

"Are you sure?" he asked her, a little shakily.

"Oh, without a doubt!" said Sephie, "As long as *you're* sure?"

"I've never been more sure of anything in my life," he knelt down in front of her and slid his arms about her hips. "I'm going to say this so that you know and never have any doubts.

Your scars, Sephie — I love them because they're a part of you — they were acquired in battle, a battle which you won. I hate how they happened, but I want you to know that every single part of you is precious to me and that those who hurt you can never do so again."

"What has happened to them?"

"Pippin is dead and Mullens soon to be."

"By your hand?"

"Yes."

"Good. And — Mrs Sheraton?"

"Ruined and imprisoned. I will tell you everything later. *Much* later."

Sephie nodded.

"But I was saying that I want to help heal your other scars, the ones I can't see but I know that they're still there in the shadows."

Sephie leant forward, put her arms about his neck and pressed her smiling lips to his, "Oh Theo, my love! Don't you *know*? You took the shadows away, the night of the Ball. When you kissed my scars and loved me like you did, as though I were beautiful, as though I were good enough!"

"Damn it, you *are* beautiful! And I'm going to spend a lifetime telling you so. And you're far *too* good! I just hope that I can be good enough for you. You rescued me, Sephie, when I had given up all hope. I was dead inside and you found me and gave me a reason to live. God, I *love* it when you say my name."

"Theo. *Theo!*" she whispered in his ear.

He groaned low in his throat and pushed her back onto the bed, rather roughly lifting her gown out of the way and finding her with his urgent hands, pulling her by the hips until she was closer to him and then keeping his eyes locked on hers, he lowered his head and sought her hidden areas, opening them for his touch. She was panting and begging him and when he drove her to the edge and then stopped, she let out a husky scream of frustration and he laughed in sheer delight and swiftly loosening his breeches, he pulled her down onto his welcoming lap, sliding into her as though they were parts of a puzzle fitting together perfectly and she moaned into his neck, clinging and biting his shoulder with her sharp little teeth. He tilted her head up and kissed her deeply, her mouth softening under his — loving his little tigress with all his heart. And when he brought her to that moment of shuddering bliss, he was looking into her eyes as she cried with happiness. He stood up, lifting her in his arms, and still joined, they fell back onto the bed, bound together.

A long while later, after they'd both slept, he'd held her tightly against him and had told her about her mother, Meryall, and Sephie had fallen silent for too long and he'd begun to worry but he told her that if she wanted to see her mother, he'd be by her side the whole time. She finally agreed that she would meet her but on hearing her whole history, she asked him if he minded that her past was so sordid and he reminded her that his life hadn't exactly been that of a saint and she'd chuckled rather hoarsely, as her voice was tired, and asked him if he could please move a little closer to her as she didn't like it when he was too far away.

"How close? This close?"

"Closer."

"Is *this* close enough, my darling?"

She shook her head, dimpling.

He grinned and made the sign for *I love you* and finally found the closeness she was looking for. She let out a contented sigh and whispered his name.

The End

This story is influenced by a real case which occurred in 1767. Elizabeth Brownrigg, a respected midwife, was given custody of several female children from the Foundling Hospital to use as servants but one, Mary Clifford, was so badly treated she died before she could be saved.

Neighbours finally reported the midwife, and the other girls were rescued. Brownrigg was eventually executed for her crimes and the laws were changed to provide more safety for the foundlings

Historical Romance
by Caroline Elkington

Set in the years shown

A Very Civil War (1645)
Dark Lantern (1755)
The House on the Hill (1765)
Three Sisters (1772)
The Widow (1782)
Out of the Shadows (1792)

A VERY CIVIL WAR 1645

Con's life in the small Cotswold village, where she spent an idyllic childhood, is nothing out of the ordinary, which is good because she likes ordinary. She likes safe.

Her three boisterous nephews have come to stay for the summer holidays, and she's determined to show them that life in the countryside can be fun — she has no idea just how exciting it's about to get.

Whilst out exploring with them in the fields near the village, they find themselves face to face with a Roundhead colonel from the English Civil Wars and, due to some glitching twenty-first century technology, Con is transported back to 1645 and into a world she only recognises from books and historical dramas on television and finds hard to understand. She reluctantly falls for the gruff officer, who is recovering from injuries sustained in recent hostilities with Royalists but must battle archaic attitudes and unexpected violence in order to survive.

With no way of getting back to her family and her nice secure real life and unable to reveal who she really is, for fear of being thought a witch, she struggles to acclimatise to her new life and must fight her growing feelings for Colonel Sir Lucas Deverell and deal with the daily problems of life in the seventeenth century and the encroaching war. When she intervenes to save a dying man, suspicions are raised and she begins to fear for her life, with enemies on all sides.

Constance Harcourt discovers a love that crosses centuries and all barriers, but which could potentially end in heartbreak. Can the power of True Love overcome the power of the Universe?

This is a time-slip story filled with passionate romance, the very real threat of persecution and war, the charm of the Cotswolds and touches of Beauty and the Beast.

Dark Lantern
1755

An unexpected funeral, a new life with unwelcoming relations and a mysterious stranger who is destined to change her life forever. Martha Pentreath has been thrust into a bewildering and perilous adventure.

Set in 1755, on the wild coast between Cornwall and Devon, this swashbuckling tale of high society and secretive seafarers follows Martha as she valiantly juggles her conflicting roles, one moment hard at work in the kitchens of Polgrey Hall and the next elbow to elbow with the local gentry.

Then as dragoons scour the coast for smugglers, she finds herself beholden to the captain of a lugger tellingly built for speed. Unsure whom to trust, Martha soon realises that everything she thought she knew was a lie and people are not what they seem.

With undercurrents of The Scarlet Pimpernel, Cinderella and Jamaica Inn, this is a story of windswept cliffs, wreckers, betrayal, secrets, murder and passionate romance.

Martha fights back against those who would relish her downfall and discovers the shocking truth about her own family. But she will find loyalty and friendship and a love that will surprise her but also bring her heartache.

THE HOUSE on the HILL
1765

After falling on hard times due to a family scandal, Henrietta Swift lives with her grandfather in a dilapidated farmhouse and is quite content to live without luxury or even basic comforts.

However, she's being watched.

Someone has plans for her and despite suffering misgivings she has no real choice but to accept their surprising proposition in order to give her beloved grandfather a better life.

It leads her to Galdre Knap, a darkly mysterious house, where her enigmatic employer, Torquhil Guivre, requires a companion for his seriously ill sister, Eirwen, who is being brought home to convalesce.

With her habitual optimism, Henrietta believes all will be well — until the other-worldly Eirwen arrives in a snowstorm. The house then begins to reveal its long-buried secrets and Henrietta must battle to save those she loves from the sinister forces that threaten their safety and her happiness.

In the process, she unexpectedly finds true love and discovers that the world is filled with real magic and that she is capable of far more than she ever thought possible.

Here be Dragons and Enchantment and Happy Ever Afters.

THREE SISTERS
1772

The prim and proper Augusta Pennington has taken over the management of a failing Ladies' Seminary with her two sisters, grumpy Flora and wild Pandora. Their elderly aunts, Ida and Euphemia Beauchamp, can no longer run the school and have been forced to hand over the reins. They are losing pupils, as they lag the fashions in female education, and are struggling financially.

Their scandalous and irascible neighbour, Sir Marcus Denby, is reluctantly drawn into their ventures by the younger sister, Pandora, who tumbles from one scrape into another, without any concern for her safety or her family's reputation.

With the help of Quince, a delinquent hound, Pandora befriends Sir Marcus's estranged daughter, Imogen, who has been much neglected by her beautiful but venomous mother.

Augusta, initially repelled by Sir Marcus's notoriety, tries desperately to resist the growing attraction between them. It takes a series of mishaps and the arrival of some unwanted guests to finally make Augusta understand that not everything is as it seems and love really can conquer all.

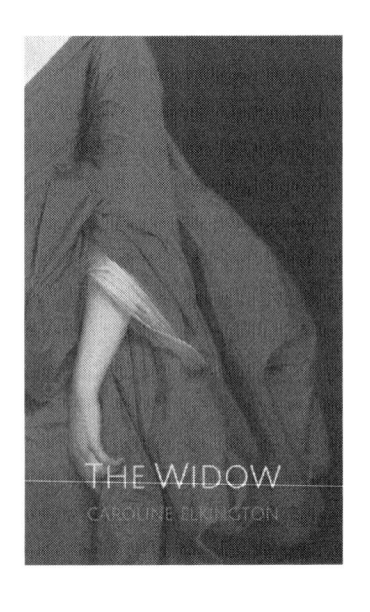

THE WIDOW
1782

Nathaniel Heywood arrived at Winterborne Place with no intention of remaining there for longer than it took to conclude a business proposition on behalf of his impulsive friend Emery Talmarch.

Impecunious, cynical and world-weary, he is reluctant to shoulder any kind of responsibility. Nathaniel was just looking for an easy way to make some money to save Emery from debtor's prison and possibly worse. He had no idea that he would be offered such an outrageous proposal by his host, Lord Winterborne, and find himself swiftly drawn into a web of intrigue and danger. He wants nothing more than to escape and be trouble-free again.

Above anything else he wanted his freedom.

And then he meets Grace.

OUT of the SHADOWS
1792

In this deeply romantic thriller, an inebriated and perhaps foolhardy visit to London's Bartholomew Fair begins with an eye to some lighthearted entertainment and ends with a tragic accident.

Theo Rokewode and his close friends find themselves unexpectedly encumbered with two young girls in desperate need of rescue. As a result, their usually ordered lives are turned upside down as danger stalks the girls into the hallowed halls of refined Georgian London and beyond to Rokewode Abbey in Gloucestershire.

Sephie and Biddy are hugely relieved to be rescued from the brutal life they had been forced to endure but know that they are still not truly safe. Only they know what could be coming and as Sephie loses her heart to Theo, she dreads the truth about her past being revealed and determines to somehow repay her new-found friends for their gallantry and unquestioning hospitality, but vows to leave before the man she loves so desperately sees her for what she really is.

Her carefully laid plans bring both delight and disaster as her past finally catches up with her and mayhem ensues, as Theo, his eccentric friends and family valiantly attempt to put the lid back on the Pandora's Box they'd unwittingly opened that fateful night at the fair.

About Caroline Elkington

When not writing novels, Caroline's reading them - every few days a knock on the door brings more. She has always preferred the feel — and smell — of a real book.

She began reading out of boredom as she was tucked up in bed by her mother, herself an avid reader, at a ridiculously early hour.

In the winter months she read by moving her book sideways back and forth to catch a slither of light that shone through the crack between the hinges of her bedroom door.

Fast forward sixty years and she's someone who knows what she wants from a book: to be immersed in history (preferably Georgian), to be captivated by a romantic hero, to be thrilled by the story, and to feel uplifted at the end.

After a long career that began with fashion design and morphed into painting ornately costumed portraits and teaching art, she has a strong eye for the kind of detail that draws the reader into a scene.

Review This Novel and See More by Caroline

Point your phone's camera at the code.
A banner will appear on your screen.
Tap it to see Caroline's novels on Amazon.